A SMALL COLONIAL WAR

Book One: Ark Royal
Book Two: The Nelson Touch
Book Three: The Trafalgar Gambit
Book Four: Warspite
Book Five: A Savage War of Peace
Book Six: A Small Colonial War

A SMALL COLONIAL WAR

CHRISTOPHER G NUTTALL

The characters and events portrayed in this book are fictitious. Any similarity to real persons, living or dead, is coincidental and not intended by the author.

ISBN-13: 9781517147068
ISBN-10: 1517147069

http://www.chrishanger.net
http://chrishanger.wordpress.com/
http://www.facebook.com/ChristopherGNuttall

Cover by Justin Adams
http://www.variastudios.com/

All Comments Welcome!

DEDICATION

To the men and women of the British Armed Forces.

"If you desire peace, prepare for war."

PROLOGUE I

Published In British Space Review, 2208

Sir.

With the benefit of hindsight, it is alarmingly clear that the Indians manipulated events on Vesy from the start.

They could not, of course, have *known* that HMS *Warspite* (and a handful of Russian deserters) would stumble across a planet of primitive aliens. Despite the presence of tramlines within the system that lead to Indian-controlled systems, they were certainly unaware of Vesy, if only because they could have laid claim to the system themselves long before *Warspite* arrived. However, the speed of their reaction - and their capture of Pegasus—suggests they had a plan drawn up for military operations long before the start of the crisis, which was hastily updated when Vesy was discovered. Vesy, therefore, merely provided an excuse.

I have to admit that they played their role masterfully. While we - and the other Great Powers - attempted to deal carefully with the Vesy, the Indians met them as equals, dealt with them openly and offered unlimited supplies of weapons and ammunition. Furthermore, it is now clear that the Indians *also* encouraged their Vesy allies to wage war on *our* Vesy allies. The combination of weapons, technical advice, protection from orbital bombardment and the promise of much - much - more was decisive. Our base on Vesy, Fort Knight, was effectively smashed and our position destroyed. Captain Naiser's decision to withdraw from the system cannot be faulted, at least on a tactical level. However, it left the Indians in possession of the system and in a position to rapidly expand their grip on the sector.

Politically, their objective appears to be two-fold. One: to secure acknowledgement of themselves as a Great Power, with all the rights and responsibilities claimed by the Big Five. Two: to secure control over Vesy, Pegasus and Cromwell, thus allowing them to claim ownership of both their tramlines and the star systems beyond. If left unchecked, the Indians will be in a position to dictate settlement of twelve known Earth-like worlds and untold numbers of stars and planets beyond. Their grip on the chokepoints represented by the tramlines will be unshakable.

It goes without saying that we cannot allow this land grab on an interstellar scale to succeed, regardless of the cost. The various treaties governing interstellar settlement are at risk. *We* claimed Pegasus, in line with the treaties; we *cannot* allow the Indians to invade and occupy the system permanently, if only to prevent other powers from trying to lay claim to Britannia, Nova Scotia and our other settled worlds. This precedent, if allowed to stand, will undermine the basis of interstellar settlement for hundreds of years to come.

Furthermore, the Indians have committed acts of war. They have killed - directly or indirectly - dozens of British personnel and civilians, as well as personnel from several different nations. We cannot allow them to get away with their crimes. It will make us look weak, unwilling to stand up for our interests - and, if we learned nothing else from the Age of Unrest, it was that weakness invites attack. Indeed, the Indians would not have dared pick a fight with us before the First Interstellar War gravely weakened the Royal Navy. With several other interstellar powers - if second-rank powers - girding their loins to overthrow the pre-war order, we cannot let this challenge go unanswered.

There is no room for a diplomatic solution. This is not a dispute over just which party discovered a new system first, nor is it a skirmish over mining rights between a pair of asteroid miners. The Indian occupation of Pegasus and *de facto* claim to Vesy is a naked act of aggression, cloaked in a tissue-thin set of justifications that have no mileage outside India itself. Anything short of the recovery of Pegasus and the reopening of Vesy would be indistinguishable from allowing the Indians to get away with their actions.

A SMALL COLONIAL WAR

Book One: Ark Royal
Book Two: The Nelson Touch
Book Three: The Trafalgar Gambit
Book Four: Warspite
Book Five: A Savage War of Peace
Book Six: A Small Colonial War

A SMALL COLONIAL WAR

CHRISTOPHER G NUTTALL

The characters and events portrayed in this book are fictitious. Any similarity to real persons, living or dead, is coincidental and not intended by the author.

Printed in the United States of America.

ISBN-13: 9781517147068
ISBN-10: 1517147069

http://www.chrishanger.net
http://chrishanger.wordpress.com/
http://www.facebook.com/ChristopherGNuttall

Cover by Justin Adams
http://www.variastudios.com/

All Comments Welcome!

DEDICATION

To the men and women of the British Armed Forces.

"If you desire peace, prepare for war."

PROLOGUE I

Published In British Space Review, 2208

Sir.

With the benefit of hindsight, it is alarmingly clear that the Indians manipulated events on Vesy from the start.

They could not, of course, have *known* that HMS *Warspite* (and a handful of Russian deserters) would stumble across a planet of primitive aliens. Despite the presence of tramlines within the system that lead to Indian-controlled systems, they were certainly unaware of Vesy, if only because they could have laid claim to the system themselves long before *Warspite* arrived. However, the speed of their reaction - and their capture of Pegasus—suggests they had a plan drawn up for military operations long before the start of the crisis, which was hastily updated when Vesy was discovered. Vesy, therefore, merely provided an excuse.

I have to admit that they played their role masterfully. While we - and the other Great Powers - attempted to deal carefully with the Vesy, the Indians met them as equals, dealt with them openly and offered unlimited supplies of weapons and ammunition. Furthermore, it is now clear that the Indians *also* encouraged their Vesy allies to wage war on *our* Vesy allies. The combination of weapons, technical advice, protection from orbital bombardment and the promise of much - much - more was decisive. Our base on Vesy, Fort Knight, was effectively smashed and our position destroyed. Captain Naiser's decision to withdraw from the system cannot be faulted, at least on a tactical level. However, it left the Indians in possession of the system and in a position to rapidly expand their grip on the sector.

Politically, their objective appears to be two-fold. One: to secure acknowledgement of themselves as a Great Power, with all the rights and responsibilities claimed by the Big Five. Two: to secure control over Vesy, Pegasus and Cromwell, thus allowing them to claim ownership of both their tramlines and the star systems beyond. If left unchecked, the Indians will be in a position to dictate settlement of twelve known Earth-like worlds and untold numbers of stars and planets beyond. Their grip on the chokepoints represented by the tramlines will be unshakable.

It goes without saying that we cannot allow this land grab on an interstellar scale to succeed, regardless of the cost. The various treaties governing interstellar settlement are at risk. *We* claimed Pegasus, in line with the treaties; we *cannot* allow the Indians to invade and occupy the system permanently, if only to prevent other powers from trying to lay claim to Britannia, Nova Scotia and our other settled worlds. This precedent, if allowed to stand, will undermine the basis of interstellar settlement for hundreds of years to come.

Furthermore, the Indians have committed acts of war. They have killed - directly or indirectly - dozens of British personnel and civilians, as well as personnel from several different nations. We cannot allow them to get away with their crimes. It will make us look weak, unwilling to stand up for our interests - and, if we learned nothing else from the Age of Unrest, it was that weakness invites attack. Indeed, the Indians would not have dared pick a fight with us before the First Interstellar War gravely weakened the Royal Navy. With several other interstellar powers - if second-rank powers - girding their loins to overthrow the pre-war order, we cannot let this challenge go unanswered.

There is no room for a diplomatic solution. This is not a dispute over just which party discovered a new system first, nor is it a skirmish over mining rights between a pair of asteroid miners. The Indian occupation of Pegasus and *de facto* claim to Vesy is a naked act of aggression, cloaked in a tissue-thin set of justifications that have no mileage outside India itself. Anything short of the recovery of Pegasus and the reopening of Vesy would be indistinguishable from allowing the Indians to get away with their actions.

The future of Britain as an independent spacefaring power is in doubt. I look to the men and women of the Royal Navy to take the offensive and show the galaxy, once again, the fighting spirit that saved Britain from collapse and took our nation to heights undreamt of by our ancestors.

Yours

Admiral Sir Joseph Porter (Ret.)

PROLOGUE II

Government Bunker, New Delhi, India

"You do realise this is a gamble?"

Prime Minister Mohandas Singh nodded, not bothering to turn away from the starchart to acknowledge the presence of Chaudhuri Bose, his Foreign Minister. Bose had been a mistake in his opinion, a man forced on him by political realities. He simply lacked the nerve to do what had to be done, while Mohandas - in his own opinion - knew all too well that there were times when one *needed* to gamble. The future of India as an independent spacefaring power hung in the balance.

"I have sent the ultimatum to the British," Bose said, when Mohandas made no response. "It will not be long before they respond."

He paused, significantly. "Do you expect them to surrender without a fight?"

"They will be alone," Mohandas said. "The Americans are having their election, the French are too concerned about their internal politics to care about either Vesy or Clarke and the other Great Powers are neutral. They will have to face us on their own."

"They have more ships than us," Bose pointed out.

"We have more *modern* ships," Mohandas countered. He swung round to scowl at the Foreign Minister. Bose had simply never impressed him. Like all diplomats, he was far too prepared to compromise with his fellows, making concessions just to get them to sign on the dotted line. Hell, he even *wore* a western suit and shaved his beard. "And they cannot afford to weaken themselves any further."

He smiled at the thought. It wasn't *pleasant* to admit that India owed her present position - a fair match for a Great Power for the first time in a century - to the first human-alien war, but it was true. The Tadpoles had weakened *all* of the Great Powers, leaving them unable - and perhaps unwilling - to fight to maintain their supremacy. If the British swallowed their pride and conceded the Indian demands, they would be weakened... but if they fought, they would weaken themselves still further. A victorious war would cost them badly at a time when neither they nor any of the other Great Powers could afford to be weakened.

"They may feel they will be challenged again, if they concede our demands," Bose offered.

That, Mohandas had to admit, was true. If there was one lesson Britain - and the other Great Powers - had drawn from the Age of Unrest, it was that showing weakness was fatal. They'd put that lesson to good use too, taking control of space and hammering any rogue state that showed itself inclined to cause trouble beyond its own borders. Until the Tadpoles had shown themselves, the British military had been primarily involved in punitive strikes.

And we wouldn't have risked taking the offensive before the war, he thought, privately. *We would have lost the shooting match.*

It was a galling thought. India had worked itself into a position of power after the British had withdrawn from India, only to lose it during the Age of Unrest. The social unrest, the riots, the final war with Pakistan... they had all cost India dearly. They'd been slow to take advantage of new developments in drive technology and slower also to establish extra-solar colonies. By the time India could reasonably call itself an interstellar power, the Great Powers were way ahead of it. They'd flatly refused to grant India the honour of considering it another Great Power.

And it was something Mohandas wanted for India, wanted very much.

"We have a window of opportunity," he said, flatly. "Five years, perhaps ten...the window will be closed. Or we may have a second war with the Tadpoles. We have to move now."

He looked up at the starchart, thinking hard. The original plan had been to take control of Clarke - before the British could turn it into a major colony - and demand Great Power status in recognition of the fact they could not be dislodged without a major war. Mohandas would have happily returned Clarke to the British in exchange for that single concession, for the acknowledgement that India was completely independent of the rest of the human race. But Vesy...the discovery of Vesy had been a stroke of luck. Now, India would not only control access to two whole sectors, but an entire alien race. And who knew what the Vesy would become, given time?

But it also meant that British personnel were killed when we moved to secure Vesy, he thought, grimly. *They may find it harder to back down.*

Bose cleared his throat. "And if they do go to war?"

"Then they will have to rely on their navy against ours," Mohandas said. He studied the starchart for a long moment, silently calculating vectors. It would take the British several months to put together a task force, if nothing else. His men would have time to dig in...if, of course, the British didn't concede defeat without a fight. "And *we* will have more modern ships and the advantage of the interior defence."

"I hope you're right," Bose said. He made no attempt to hide the doubt in his voice. "This could cost us everything."

Mohandas nodded, curtly. Bose was right. It *could* cost India everything, although the Solar Treaty would ensure that losses were limited. India would be humiliated, her extra-solar interests would be claimed by the British and her navy would be crippled. They'd be the laughing stock of the planet. Even the Tadpoles would be sniggering...

But the prospect of victory was worth the risk.

"Keep talking to the other powers," he ordered. He rather doubted it would make much difference - the British were a Great Power, after all - but it was worth trying. "Convince them, if you can, to put pressure on the British."

And stay out of military affairs, he added, silently. *This is no place for milksops.*

Bose bowed. "Of course, Prime Minister," he said. "I shall pray for us all."

CHAPTER ONE

Clarke III, Pegasus System

"The tin-cans are retreating, Governor."

"Understood," Governor Harry Brown said. "Did they inflict any damage?"

"I don't believe so," Lillian Turner said. She'd never expected to be manning a tactical console, but she was the closest thing to a tactical officer on the colony. "They merely exchanged long-range fire with the Indian ships and then bugged out."

She sucked in her breath, feeling fear pulsing through her chest. She'd grown used to the thought of spending the rest of her days on Clarke; it might not be Earth, or even Luna City, but the rapidly-growing colony *did* have a sort of charm. The colonists had eyed her doubtfully for a few months, then decided her obvious willingness to work - and make up for the sins of the past - was a point in her favour. She'd even made a handful of friends. But now...

I may be sent back to Earth, she thought, morbidly. *And who knows what will happen to me there*?

"Keep monitoring them," Brown ordered. The Governor hadn't been one of her biggest supporters at first, but he'd given her a fair chance. "Let me know if they attempt to communicate with us."

"Yes, sir," Lillian said.

She caught a glimpse of her reflection in the viewscreen and sighed. Her dark eyes looked tired and worn and her dark hair was hanging down around her face; her pale skin looked too pale after months on Clarke, where the sun barely shone. She hadn't had much sleep since the first warning message from Vesy...and none, since the Indian ships had jumped into the system and commenced a leisurely flight towards Clarke. They could have been at Clarke within hours, if they'd pushed their drives hard. Instead, they'd taken over a day to make a slow stately progress to the gas giant's moon.

Probably wanted to make us sweat, she thought, darkly. *They know damn well no one's coming to help us.*

Her eyes sharpened as new icons appeared on the display. "Governor," she said. "They're launching assault shuttles."

The Governor rose to his feet and paced over to stand behind her. "ETA?"

"Thirty minutes," Lillian said. He didn't ask where they were going, but then there was no real need. There wasn't anywhere else on Clarke III worth visiting, save for the colony and its two thousand colonists. "They're not even trying to hide their presence."

"They may be a little bit nervous about flying through the snowstorms," the Governor said, curtly. "*We're* nervous and we've been on this planet for a year."

Lillian rather doubted it - the Royal Marines she'd met had been gung ho about diving into hurricanes and she had a feeling the Indian marines were very similar - but she kept that thought to herself. Instead, she tracked the Indian shuttles as they entered the atmosphere, monitoring them through the handful of stealthed satellites in orbit. The Indians would find them eventually and shut them down, she was sure, if they bothered to make the effort. Both sides knew the colony couldn't hold out for long.

"My best guess is that they're going to come down near Davis Mountain," she said, as the shuttles dove further into the planet's atmosphere. "That would put them within easy walking distance of the colony."

"Looks like it," the Governor agreed.

He stepped back and keyed his wristcom, then started to mutter orders to the scratch defence force. A handful of soldiers - mainly reservists - and a couple of colonial policemen...it wasn't enough to do more than slow the Indians down for a few minutes. Lillian and the other colonists had been digging trenches and improvising traps ever since they'd gotten the word, but they simply didn't have the men to hold for long.

And if the Indians get tired of our defiance, they can simply drop rocks on us from high overhead, Lillian thought, grimly. *They can smash us flat if they don't mind losing the colony.*

It was a chilling thought. There had been an agreement - ever since the human race had started expanding through the tramlines - that colonies weren't to be bombarded indiscriminately. Whatever the cause of the disagreement - or war - it didn't excuse destroying the only thing keeping humans alive in the unforgiving vastness of interstellar space. But if the Indians had been prepared to allow countless people to die on Vesy, they might well be prepared to bombard Clarke into submission from orbit. They wouldn't be able to use the colony for themselves...

They'll want the colony, she told herself, hoping desperately that she was right. *It would take them too long to duplicate our work.*

Her console beeped, once. "Sir," she said. "The Indians have landed."

"Try and get a drone over there," the Governor ordered. "I'll have the defenders stand ready."

Lillian nodded, clicking through the options on her screen until she located the drones and launched one into the air. She'd flown drones before, on Earth, but it was nowhere near so easy to fly them on Clarke. The snowstorms would happily knock a drone out of the air if she made a single mistake, leaving the colony without any eyes in the sky. Indeed, the Governor had banned flying drones in anything other than the direst emergencies. The beancounters on Earth would complain - loudly - if Clarke expended them all within the first month.

We should have practiced flying them anyway, she thought, as the drone made its way towards Davis Mountain. Davis had been a colonist who'd gone climbing in a protective suit, only to be caught in an avalanche and buried somewhere below the half-frozen ocean. *We might have been able to improve the drone guidance systems before now.*

She gritted her teeth as a particularly nasty gust of wind slapped the drone, sending it cart-wheeling across the sky before she managed to regain control. The RPV had a computer core that was meant to handle the basics of flying, but it hadn't developed its own understanding of the environment yet. In theory, a drone that crashed could have the core salvaged and loaded into another drone - thus allowing the second drone to learn from the mistakes of the first - but in practice they simply hadn't wanted to waste the tiny vehicles. That, she suspected, might have been a mistake.

"Contact," she said. "Three shuttles; seventy armoured men."

The Governor bent over her shoulder - so close she could smell the odour of tobacco on his breath - as the Indians came into view. The assault shuttles didn't look that different from British designs - the war had forced the various Great Powers to standardise as much as they could - but the armoured combat suits looked more primitive than the suits she'd seen on *Warspite*. Their wearers were already starting the short march towards the colony. Behind them, a handful of light tanks rolled off the shuttles, one of them rotating a gun to point towards the drone. Moments later, the screen went blank.

"Contact lost," she said, formally. "They're on their way, Governor."

"Noted," the Governor said.

The minutes ticked by with agonising slowness. Lillian knew, without a shadow of a doubt, that the defenders couldn't hope to win, yet she also knew the Governor couldn't simply order a surrender. Whatever happened afterwards, the colony could not be said to have surrendered without a fight. But as the monitors started to pick up the advancing forces, she found herself wishing the Governor would change his mind. She *knew* some of the men out there, girding themselves for a brief struggle. Some of them had disliked her - the policemen had kept a sharp eye on her for the first two months - but none of them deserved to die for nothing.

She winced as the radio buzzed. "I have nine armoured men in my sights," Sergeant Harkin said. He was actually a retired soldier, someone who'd been demobbed two years after the war and secured a posting to Clarke for reasons that he'd never really shared with anyone else. Lillian liked him more than she cared to admit. "They're advancing towards the first trench."

"Engage at will," the Governor ordered.

Lillian closed her eyes for a long moment as the first set of combat reports came in. The defenders fired a handful of shots, then fell back to the next line of defences, forcing the Indians to waste time clearing trenches that were already abandoned. A handful of Indian soldiers were caught in improvised traps - she felt a moment of vindictive glee as it became clear that a handful of intruders would never see India again - but it wasn't enough to do more than annoy the advancing soldiers. They knew as well as she did that they had all the time in the world to clear the trenches.

"Nine intruders down," Sergeant Harkin reported. "I..."

His message cut off. Lillian glanced at the sensors and cursed under her breath as she realised the enemy had hit his position with a missile. The remaining defenders were pulling back, but they were rapidly running out of space. It wouldn't be long before the Indians were in a position to either storm the colony doors or merely blast their way through the prefabricated walls. Either way, the colony couldn't hold out any longer.

The Governor evidently agreed. "Contact the Indians," he ordered. "Now."

Lillian swallowed as she tapped commands into her console. The Indians hadn't even *tried* to open communications. She couldn't help wondering if that meant the Indians had *no* interest in demanding and accepting surrender. The remaining defenders were still trying, but their position had been hopeless from the start...

"I have a link," she reported. The screen blinked to life, showing a dark-skinned man with a neatly-trimmed beard. "Governor?"

The Governor cleared his throat. "I am Governor Harry Brown, Governor of the Pegasus System."

"I am General Anjeet Patel," the Indian said. He didn't seem inclined to beat around the bush. "Your position is hopeless."

"I understand," the Governor said. His voice was tightly-controlled, but Lillian could hear the hint of anger underlying his words. "I wish to open talks..."

"My terms are quite simple," Patel said, cutting him off. "You will order your remaining defenders to surrender and open the doors, allowing my men to occupy the colony. You will make no attempt to destroy your computers, your life support infrastructure or anything else that may be required. You may destroy classified files, but not anything relating to the colony and its personnel."

He paused for a long moment. "For the duration of the present emergency, Clarke III will be governed under Indian military law. Your people - military and civilian - will have nothing to fear as long as they obey orders. Prisoners will be treated in line with the standard Luna Conventions."

Lillian nodded to herself, unable to keep herself from feeling relieved. The Great Powers showed no mercy to insurgents, revolutionaries and terrorists, but the Luna Conventions applied to national troops who hadn't been caught breaking the laws of war. It would have been insane for the Indians to act otherwise, yet the mere act of starting a war was insane when it would only weaken humanity. Who knew *what* the Tadpoles would do?

"I understand," the Governor said, stiffly. "However, I am quite unable to acknowledge the permanent surrender of either the colony or the system itself."

"That is understood," Patel said. "My men will advance to secure the colony."

His image vanished from the display. Lillian heard the Governor mutter a curse under his breath before keying his wristcom and issuing the surrender order. She felt an unpleasant knot in her stomach as she watched through the cameras as the Indians closed in on the defenders, who had dropped their weapons and were standing with their hands in the air. The Indians seemed to be trying to be reasonably civilised, but they were still careful to escort the prisoners - at gunpoint - into a tracked vehicle before opening the doors and entering the colony.

"Purge the classified files," the Governor ordered, quietly.

He sounded defeated. Lillian felt a chill running down her spine as she keyed the command into the system, starting off a process that would wipe, reformat and finally destroy the classified datacore. The Governor hadn't had many secrets, she was sure, but destroying his codes and ciphers was a tacit admission that all was lost. She nodded to herself as the destruction was confirmed, then verified; she glanced at the Governor, who was watching as the Indians slowly advanced though his colony. Civilians who stumbled into their path were told to return to their quarters and wait for orders.

"At least they're not brutalising the civilians," the Governor mused. He sounded as though he were speaking to himself, rather than to her. "But they'll need them, won't they?"

Lillian nodded. Clarke wasn't a habitable world. It had taken two months of intensive effort to build up a life support infrastructure, let alone establish a geothermal power source and start mining for raw materials. The Indians would need to secure the colony, but they'd also need the men and women who made the colony work, at least until they brought in their own people and learned the ropes. They'd have to be insane to mistreat the civilians.

But the sick feeling in her chest wouldn't go away. It felt like hours before the Indians finally stepped into the control centre and looked around, holding their weapons at the ready. Lillian hadn't been so scared since the day she'd been arrested on *Warspite*. The Indian soldiers looked tough, determined and utterly ruthless. She'd been taught the basics of shooting - several ships had been boarded during the war - but she knew she was no match for them.

"Step away from the console," one of the Indians ordered. "Now."

Lillian obeyed, careful to keep her hands visible at all times. She *had* only been a lowly engineering officer, but she'd had the same training program as every other junior officer; she knew, all too well, that the first hours of an invasion and occupation were always the worst. The invaders would be jumpy, unsure of their ground, while the locals would be unwilling to tamely accept occupation. Accidents happened...and it was unlikely that anyone would care if the Indians shot her. The years when lawyers paralysed trigger fingers were long over.

Another Indian strode into the control centre, wearing a dress uniform. Lillian had to admit he looked handsome, but there was a coldness in his eyes she didn't like. The men following him took the consoles and went to work, pulling up the operating subroutines and examining them quickly, looking for backdoors, viruses and other hidden surprises. Lillian knew they wouldn't find anything more significant than a handful of porn caches the Governor wasn't supposed to know about. Clarke's system just wasn't large enough to hide much more.

And we didn't exactly expect occupation, she thought, sourly. *We would have rigged the system thoroughly if we had.*

"Governor," the Indian said. "I am Colonel Vasanta Darzi, Governor of Clarke."

Lillian saw the Governor tense, but he kept his voice under tight control. "Harry Brown," he said, shortly. "Governor of Clarke."

The Indian shrugged. "My men have occupied the colony," he said. "From this moment onwards, Clarke will be governed under my law. I expect your people to assist in maintaining the colony for the foreseeable future, until the current...*unpleasantness* is cleared up. Under the circumstances, this may cause some awkwardness with your government; in the event of your people being threatened with charges of treason or collaboration, we will be happy to testify that you were forced to work under duress."

And the Government might not buy it, Lillian thought. There was a fine line between working under duress - real or implied - and outright collaboration. And the people on the spot might not be able to see that line. They would be judged harshly by outsiders who had never been within a hundred light years of Clarke. *If they feel otherwise, we may wind up going home to our deaths.*

"My personnel should not be forced to work on defences or military-related projects," the Governor said. "I believe my government would understand the need to keep working on life support."

"That is understood," Darzi said. "In the long term, your personnel will be free to relocate themselves to British territory or apply for Indian citizenship. If they choose the former, the Indian Government has already agreed to pay for their relocation and compensate them for their efforts on Clarke.

"However" - he held up a hand warningly - "I am also obliged to warn you that any resistance, active or passive, will be treated as a hostile act. Any attacks on my personnel or attempts to sabotage the defences will be severely punished, in line with the Luna Conventions. Insurgents and those who support them will face the death penalty. I advise you to make that *very* clear to your personnel."

"I understand," the Governor said, tartly.

Lillian cringed, inwardly. British territory hadn't been occupied since the Second World War, unless one counted the social unrest of the Troubles. No one knew how to behave under enemy occupation...

"I do not, however, believe that my government will simply concede Clarke to you without a fight," the Governor added. "In that case, I expect you to do everything you can to protect the civilian population."

"In that case, we will certainly try," Darzi said. Oddly, Lillian had the feeling he meant every word. India wouldn't look very good if innocent civilians were caught in the crossfire. "But by the time your military can respond, if your government is intent on a fight, we will be ready."

CHAPTER TWO

10 Downing Street, London, Earth

"There's a line of protesters outside, sir," the driver said.

"Stay clear of them," Vice Admiral Sir James Montrose Fitzwilliam ordered. It had been years since the violent protests that had shaken London to the core, but memories ran deep among the elite. "Get us past the gates and into Downing Street as fast as you can."

"Aye, sir," the driver said.

James sucked in his breath as the car passed the protesters, half of whom seemed to be carrying banners condemning the Indians. The other half seemed to be a mixed group, ranging from pacifists to Britain First; the latter, idiotically, demanding that money and resources be lavished on rebuilding Britain rather than expanding the navy and securing the peace. A long line of policemen stood between the two groups, while a handful of armoured soldiers waited at the gates to Downing Street. Protests were fine - they were a way to blow off steam - but outright violence would be squashed with terrifying speed. London could not risk a return to anarchy.

And we came close to that during the war, James thought. He'd been on *Ark Royal* at the time, raiding enemy space and blissfully unaware that the enemy was returning the favour by attacking Earth. They'd never had the slightest awareness that Earth was threatened until they returned home to discover that the planet had been attacked. *A second round of chaos will destroy us.*

He pulled a small mirror out of his pocket and inspected himself quickly. At forty-five, with jet-black hair and shaven face, he still looked reasonably handsome, although he was grimly aware that he was no longer as spry as he used to be. The war - and the long battle to rebuild the Royal Navy afterwards - had taken its toll. He closed the mirror, picked up his briefcase and braced himself as the car rolled to a stop. Moments later, the driver opened the door and saluted as James climbed out. The policemen standing outside Ten Downing Street waved him through the door without hesitation. They'd have checked his Navy ID as the car passed through the gates.

"Admiral Fitzwilliam," a young woman said. She was probably in her early twenties, he decided, with long brown hair tied into a bun. The suit she wore made her look rather like a penguin, he decided, but he knew better than to underestimate her. She wouldn't have reached her position so young unless she was highly competent. "They're waiting for you in the COBRA Room."

"Thank you," James said.

He clutched his suitcase tightly as the girl led him down a long flight of stairs into the bunker complex below Ten Downing Street. It might *look* like a row of houses, but in reality it was a facade; the houses had long since been woven together into a single huge complex, the tip of the iceberg. Below them, there was a network of bunkers, administrative centres and barracks for troops. The *real* work was done far from the prying eyes of the public and the media. They passed two security checkpoints before finally coming to a halt in front of a set of sealed doors. Someone's child had drawn a painting of a cobra and left it there, marking the room. James couldn't help smiling at the image as the doors were opened, allowing him to step into the room.

"James," Uncle Winchester said. "Please, take a seat."

James nodded, curtly. Uncle Winchester - Henry Winchester, Secretary of State for Defence - had been trying to shape his life for years. In hindsight, James had to admit he might have had a point, but it didn't please him to be a pawn in his uncle's games. Or, for that matter, to be forced to choose between loyalty to his superior officer - a man he had come to respect - and loyalty to his family. He accepted a cup of tea from the steward and glanced at the clock on the wall as a handful of other attendees stepped into the room. There was no sign of the Prime Minister.

"The latest news isn't good," Uncle Winchester muttered. "I've heard..."

He broke off as the doors opened, admitting Prime Minister Steven Goodwill. James rose to his feet, along with everyone else, as the Prime Minister made his way to the head of the table and sat down, his gaze sweeping from face to face. The doors closed firmly as the rest of the attendees sat down, the stewards returning to their seats beside the drinks machine. They'd be cleared for everything, James knew, but it still felt like a security nightmare to him. And yet, he had the feeling that most people in the room would be horrified at the thought of getting their own tea.

"Gentlemen," the Prime Minister said. His voice was very cold. "It is no exaggeration, I feel, to say that today's meeting may decide the fate of the British Commonwealth."

He paused. James watched him carefully, wondering just which way the Prime Minister would jump. The man had guided Britain through five years of recovery, a task that had turned his hair grey, but did he have the nerve to resist the Indians? To commit Britain to an interstellar war against a human enemy? Or would he look for an excuse to pull back and concede defeat?

The Prime Minister nodded to the young woman. "Sandra?"

Sandra cleared her throat as she tapped a switch. A holographic starchart appeared above the table, glowing with tactical icons. James silently parsed out the tramlines that led to Pegasus, Cromwell and Vesy, noting with disgust that all three of them were shaded in red. *He*, at least, had no doubts about what should be done. The Indians could not be allowed to get away with such blatant acts of aggression.

"Thank you, Prime Minister," Sandra said. She'd be one of the Prime Minister's personal intelligence officers, James decided. "The situation is as follows.

"The Indians have definitely occupied both Vesy and Pegasus - specifically, Clarke III," she said. "We believe they have occupied Cromwell too, but the only evidence we have for that is a flash message relayed down the chain of communications beacons before the Indians took the beacons offline. In any case, our tactical staff believes that the Indians would have good reason to occupy Cromwell. They would find it easier to block our advance through that system.

"Despite their advance, losses have been minimal. There was a brief exchange of fire at Clarke III before the destroyers retreated; the Indians did not pursue. They have returned almost all of the prisoners they took on Vesy, who testify to their good treatment. In some cases, the Indians even ransomed the prisoners from the aliens who took them captive. The only exceptions, as far as we can determine, are a handful of men who are critically wounded and are currently undergoing treatment."

"How nice of the Indians," Uncle Winchester muttered.

Sandra ignored him. "The Indians have been reported in Boston, but so far they have not made any hostile moves against the planet. We believe the Indians have no intention of trying to occupy the system as that will add the Americans to their list of enemies. However..."

The Prime Minister held up a hand. "That will do, for the moment," he said. He cleared his throat. "I received the ultimatum from the Indians personally."

James sucked in his breath. It was rare, very rare, for Heads of Government to handle diplomatic discussions personally. There was just too great a risk of a personality clash that would lead to diplomatic rows, or even all-out war. It was generally better to allow the diplomatic offices to handle such matters at first, knowing that they could be disowned if necessary. A diplomat could be declared *persona non grata* and sent home. It was a great deal harder to ignore a Head of Government.

"It's a strange piece of work," the Prime Minister continued. "For an ultimatum, it has some oddly conciliatory phrases."

"The Indians may themselves be divided," Neville Murchison said. The Foreign Secretary leaned forward. "They may not be as determined on war as it seems."

"Or that's what they want you to think," Uncle Winchester growled. Murchison and he were old sparring partners. "What do they actually *want*?"

The Prime Minister frowned. "They want recognition as a Great Power," he said, flatly. "Their control over both Vesy and Pegasus is to be recognised; they are to be effectively granted possession of those systems and the sectors beyond. In short, it is a land grab on an interstellar scale."

He shrugged. "If we accept those terms without further debate, the Indians will *graciously* allow us access to Vesy and the tramlines," he added. "But we will no longer control any of the systems ourselves."

"So the Indians expect us to just roll over and surrender those systems," the First Space Lord said. "We *can't* let this pass."

"No, we can't," Uncle Winchester agreed. "We do have allies."

"We don't," Murchison said, flatly. "The Great Power system is dead, Henry. It was killed by the war. Right now, the Americans are having their election; they won't risk getting involved unless the Indians do something they can't ignore. The French have their own internal problems; they're unlikely to get involved unless we make concessions to them instead. I rather doubt the Chinese will go to bat for us and the Russians...well, we believe the Indians have been making inroads with the Russians."

James winced. The Russians, during the height of the war, had attempted to deploy biological weapons against the Tadpoles, effectively committing genocide. Their commandoes had tried to take control of *Ark Royal* and launch the weapons, injuring James badly in the process. He cursed inwardly at the thought. If he hadn't been wounded, he would have been on the Old Lady when she made her final flight. It would have been better, perhaps, than surviving.

And Admiral Smith would have told you that you were being an idiot, he reminded himself sharply. *You have far too much to live for.*

"So we're alone," Uncle Winchester said. "We still have a considerable firepower advantage, don't we? Six fleet carriers to three?"

"Three of our carriers are deployed to the border," the First Space Lord said. "Concentrating an overwhelming force will take time."

"We can still take the offensive," Uncle Winchester said.

The Prime Minister tapped the table, sharply. "The question before us is simple," he said. "We have a choice between either conceding that the Indians have successfully captured some of *our* territory or going to war. Which choice do we make?"

Murchison cleared his throat. "Prime Minister," he said. "I understand the primal urge to just hit back at our enemies. There is no excuse for invading and occupying our territory, territory claimed by us in line with the various interstellar treaties; the Indians have committed acts of aggression and must be made to pay a price.

"*But*...we are not in a good position ourselves. The Royal Navy was gravely weakened by the war and there are endless demands on our resources. We could take the offensive against the Indians and beat them, only to discover that we've killed ourselves too. A long war might not only bring in other human powers, Prime Minister; it might weaken us to the point the Tadpoles see a chance to resume the war on their terms. They *have* to regard us as a dangerous enemy.

"We *have* denied the Indians recognition as a Great Power in the past, even though they probably deserved the title. Conceding that now will do us no harm; it may even serve as a bridge to opening other discussions. We gain little from Vesy; the system isn't worth fighting to keep. Let the Indians have it, if they wish. The only sticking points are Pegasus and Cromwell and I believe the Indians can be talked into withdrawing from both systems. It would be a clear breach of the international order to *keep* them."

James had his doubts. Yes, there was little to gain by keeping Vesy; the natives were primitive, barely crawling out of the Stone Age. But otherwise...rewarding the Indians for acts of aggression stuck in his craw. Maybe they *could* be talked into withdrawing from Cromwell and Pegasus...

Uncle Winchester cleared his throat. "It has always astonished me just how often the diplomats want to talk, talk, talk," he said. "In this case, there is nothing to talk *about*."

"Jaw-jaw is better than war-war," Murchison quoted.

"I doubt Churchill would agree with you," Uncle Winchester said. "There is literally nothing to talk about."

He held up a hand before Murchison could say a word. "There may - *may* - be some truth in the suggestion we unfairly denied the Indians recognition as a Great Power," he continued, his voice growing harder. "It wasn't our call. The Russians and Chinese were against it; the Americans and French didn't care enough to argue their case. Perhaps we *did* treat them badly. *But*...it doesn't serve as an excuse to kill our personnel, occupy our territory and demand - in the cheekiest of tones - that we kindly accept the *status quo*.

"Did we learn *nothing* from the Age of Unrest? Giving in to blackmail only leads to more demands! How many concessions were made to tin-pot dictators and religious fanatics during the Crazy Years that came back to haunt us when the entire global system hiccupped? How many of our people died because we tried to make nice with our irredeemable foes, instead of squashing them like bugs while we had the chance?

"So we surrender to the Indians? Let them get away with it? Maybe, if we grovel sufficiently, they will *kindly* allow us to reclaim Pegasus. And then what? What happens the *next* time someone decides they can take a bite out of our territory, in the certain knowledge we'll just let it go? We *cannot* allow the Indians to humiliate us! It will spell the end of Britain as a Great Power.

"The only acceptable outcome, the only one that maintains our current position, is recovering the territory the Indians occupied by force! And we must do it *alone*. There is literally no other alternative. The Indians *cannot* be allowed to get away with this."

He turned to face the Prime Minister. "I strongly suggest that we declare war on the Indians and do whatever it takes to recover our territory."

"India is not a rogue state," Murchison said, quietly. "We cannot send in the troops to give her a damn good thrashing. They may thrash us back."

"That's what they thought during the Crazy Years," Uncle Winchester said. "They were so scared of getting hurt, even if they could inflict far more harm on their foes, that they allowed threats to grow until they nearly proved lethal. The death of a single soldier was seen as grounds to surrender and walk away. And look how badly it cost them! The Troubles might have been averted if someone had stood up and said *enough*."

"India is not a rogue state," Murchison repeated. "And if we concentrate the level of force we would need to deal with her, we would leave the border gravely weakened."

"We may be able to convince the Americans or the French to move additional forces of their own to the border," the First Space Lord said, quietly. "They might not be willing to take overt steps to support us, but they'd understand what's at stake."

"The longer the Indians remain in possession of our territories, the harder it will be to dislodge them," the Prime Minister said.

"Then we seize their territories," Uncle Winchester said. "They have two Earth-type worlds we could capture."

"Neither of them is a worthwhile target," the First Space Lord said. "The bulk of the Indian shipbuilding industry is in the Sol System. Off-limits."

"This is war," Uncle Winchester said.

"The logic behind the Solar Treaty remains in place," the Prime Minister said. "We cannot afford to break it. *Everyone* would turn on us."

James nodded. Acts of aggression were banned within the Sol System, if only to preserve humanity's infrastructure and prevent collateral damage. It was one of the few treaties that *every* interstellar power honoured.

Or every human power, he thought, wryly. *The Tadpoles didn't sign the treaty before they attacked Earth.*

"Parliament will have to make the final call," the Prime Minister said, "but I will need to advise them. If we go to war, and Parliament may well vote for war, can we win?"

"Numerically, we have the advantage," Uncle Winchester said.

"They may have advantages of their own," Murchison insisted. "Most of their ships are post-war designs."

James felt his eyes narrow. Someone had been briefing Murchison...

"We have modern ships too," Uncle Winchester said. "The fact remains that we cannot let the Indians get away with this. If we fail to defend our interests now, when we have advantages, when *will* we start to stand up for ourselves?"

"And if we win, we win at a terrifying cost," Murchison snapped. "We could lose everything in the crossfire."

The Prime Minister looked at the First Space Lord. "Admiral Finnegan?"

"We have been looking at our options," the First Space Lord said. "Admiral Fitzwilliam's team has devised a number of potential operational concepts. With your permission, sir, he will brief you on them."

"Granted," the Prime Minister said.

James opened his briefcase, removed a datachip and plugged it into the processor slot beside his seat. The holographic starchart vanished. James took the control and opened the files, displaying another starchart. This one showed potential angles of approach to Pegasus, Vesy and Cromwell.

He took a breath and began.

CHAPTER THREE

10 Downing Street, London, Earth

"Time is not on our side, Prime Minister," James began, "but it may not be on their side either. We have to act fast before they can fortify their possessions; they have to secure recognition of their possession before the other interstellar powers bring pressure to bear on them. Accordingly, we have good reason to seek a quick decision and so do they."

He paused for effect before proceeding. "We believe, given the tram-lines, that they will have placed the main body of their fleet in Vesy," he continued. "That would allow them to determine our approach vector and concentrate their fleet against us. They would have pickets emplaced to watch for us, as well as human intelligence sources. They'd have time to redeploy before we arrived in the war zone. It is unlikely we could avoid a duel with their fleet.

"We have several possible choices. Variant One - Bulldog One - is to occupy their worlds and trade them for ours, although this would force us to deploy ground units to keep the local population under control. This might allow us to avoid a major fleet clash, but I regard that as unlikely. We believe the Indians will attempt to harass our forces on the ground while picking the time and place of a naval engagement. Besides, in the long term, we would have to make some hard choices concerning the local populations."

He saw the Prime Minister frown and nodded in agreement. Terra Nova had been settled by hundreds of ethnic and religious groups, back when no one had known just how many worlds there were for the taking, and it had been a complete disaster. If Britain kept the Indian worlds, they would either have to remove the settlers or accept a permanent ethnic mishmash, which would probably lead to war. And one round of the Troubles had been quite bad enough.

"Bulldog Two calls for us to proceed up the tramlines to Vesy," he said. "That would probably allow us to dictate the time and place of the battle, as we would be neatly positioned to block any enemy passage between Pegasus, Cromwell and Gandhi. However, the Indians would have plenty of time to prepare to meet us. We would also face the problem of fighting for a system we don't particularly want."

He tapped a switch, altering the starchart. "The third and final choice - Bulldog Three - is to proceed directly to Pegasus and force a battle there. That has a number of advantages; we'd be fighting for territory that is unquestionably ours, we'd be able to insert Special Forces onto the ground and our supply lines would be short. Well, shorter. Our logistics aren't going to be very good at the best of times. The Indians would also have the option of choosing to withdraw, if they didn't want to force a battle themselves. If they did, we would allow them to leave."

Murchison frowned. "Do you think they'll withdraw?"

"There's no way to know," James said. Diplomacy was outside his sphere of interest. "They may be running a giant bluff, in which case they'll back down when it's called, or they may be serious about keeping what they've taken. In *that* case, they will certainly have to fight at Pegasus. They won't have a choice."

"I see," the Prime Minister said. "Which option do you believe we should take?"

"I would prefer to choose either Bulldog Two or Bulldog Three," James said. "In an ideal world, we would proceed up the tramlines to Hannibal" - he tapped a star on the chart - "while deploying fast frigates or cruisers to spy out the terrain. At that point, the task force would either head to Vesy or Pegasus, depending on the Indian deployments. Bulldog One offers the least *risk*, but also the least potential gains. The Indian industries are effectively off-limits.

"Task Force Bulldog would be built around the *Theodore Smith*" - he couldn't help a twinge of pain at the ship's name - "and a hard core of escort carriers, destroyers and frigates. It would proceed to Hannibal, then advance onwards; ideally, we would attempt to tackle the Indian carriers separately. Both of their carriers are modern ships, after all; I'd prefer not to risk one of the pre-war carriers against them. The objective would be to secure Pegasus, land troops, recover the colony and then proceed to either Cromwell or Vesy. Once Cromwell was recovered, we could seek peace terms from a position of supremacy."

"We would have nothing to gain from kicking the Indians while they were down," Murchison commented.

"Except for the certainty they wouldn't be able to threaten us again," Uncle Winchester snapped. "We made damn sure that *Iran* couldn't do more than bluster during the Age of Unrest."

"The Indians could lose their colonies," the Prime Minister said, "but they couldn't lose their industries in the Sol System. Not unless we were prepared to throw the Solar Treaty out of the window. I think we must accept from the beginning that any victory we win will be limited in scope."

"And we may need their firepower if we end up fighting another war with the Tadpoles," the First Space Lord added.

And if we take the gloves off here, they'll do the same, James thought, privately.

The Prime Minister nodded, once. "How long will it take to gather the ships and assemble the task force?"

"We've already ordered the ships to prepare for redeployment," James said. "I believe it won't take longer than a month to ready the entire task force - maybe less, if we aim to deploy to Hannibal within the fortnight. The real problem will be logistics. I'd prefer to have our fleet train deployed with the task force, rather than risk having the freighters move in small convoys. The Indians will understand our weaknesses, Prime Minister, and will try to target the convoys where possible."

"I was under the impression that tracking a convoy in interstellar space isn't easy," Murchison said. "The Tadpoles didn't intercept many convoys, did they?"

"The Indians will have spies watching our bases," James pointed out. "The Tadpoles never had that sort of advantage. They shouldn't have too many problems noting departure times and then it wouldn't be too hard to calculate a rough location. In the longer term, we will need to pull additional smaller ships away from the border just to provide escorts to the fleet train."

"I imagine the Admiralty can handle it," the Prime Minister said. He looked James in the eye. "*Can* we win?"

"Nothing is certain in war, sir," James said. "However, I believe we have an excellent chance of whittling them down and defeating them. I do not believe they are willing to fight to the last."

"We would just need to weaken them badly," Uncle Winchester noted. "Their position is nowhere near as strong as ours."

"Unless we push them into a corner," Murchison countered.

"The point is that we cannot allow them to get away with this, as I keep saying," Uncle Winchester hissed. "This is not a dispute over who discovered a particular system first, but a schoolyard bully *nicking* your crisps and then kindly offering to give half of them back! We cannot compromise beyond allowing the Indians to leave without a fight. There's literally nothing *to* compromise."

He looked at the Prime Minister. "I propose telling the Indians to leave now or face the consequences," he said, flatly. "And then we assemble the task force and gird ourselves for war."

"We could always offer to concede their Great Power status if they left now," Murchison offered.

"That would still allow them to benefit from their crimes," Uncle Winchester said.

"People will die," Murchison snapped. "British *spacers* will die!"

Uncle Winchester's face darkened. "Yes, they will," he said, finally. "But how many more will die if we look *weak*?"

James kept his thoughts to himself. Privately, he agreed with Uncle Winchester; the Indians couldn't be allowed to benefit from their crimes. But, at the same time, he knew that war was a gamble. Victory would be costly and defeat was unthinkable. If there was a way to convince the Indians to leave, without using force, perhaps it should be taken.

Except they will start wondering what else they can force out of us, he thought. *And then we'll be blackmailed again.*

"So we ready the task force," the Prime Minister said. He glanced at the First Space Lord. "I believe Parliament will authorise readying for war, if the Indians cannot be convinced to withdraw now. They're due to meet in two hours."

"Yes, Prime Minister," the First Space Lord said.

"We'll work out the political objectives afterwards," the Prime Minister said. His gaze moved to James. "I assume you will be commanding the task force?"

"It's my plan, sir," James said. "Besides, *Theodore Smith* is my flagship."

The Prime Minister smiled. "You'll have orders once Parliament has met," he said. "But I dare say we'll meet again before you go."

"Yes, sir," James said.

"I don't like this," Murchison said. "We stand to lose an awful lot."

"We have no choice," Uncle Winchester said. "The Indians have seen to that, Neville."

The Prime Minister rose to his feet. "Henry, I imagine you and your nephew have a great deal to talk about," he said. "Sandra will show you to one of the private rooms. You'll be informed once Parliament has voted."

"Thank you, Prime Minister," Uncle Winchester said.

James sighed inwardly as the room emptied. He'd hoped to have a chance to visit the Cenotaph and the *Ark Royal* memorial before returning to Nelson Base, but it looked as though Uncle Winchester wanted to talk. It had probably been decided beforehand, almost certainly with the concurrence of the First Space Lord. James hadn't been *needed* to give the briefing, after all. The First Space Lord had minions to do that sort of thing.

Sandra led them to a small room, poured them both fresh cups of tea and left without a backwards glance. James watched the door closing behind her, then turned to stare at his uncle. Uncle Winchester looked tired, worn down by arguing; he hadn't looked so tired, James recalled, back when the Tadpoles had started the war. No one had really *believed* in aliens until Vera Cruz...

"You convinced the Prime Minister, I think," Uncle Winchester said, without preamble. "I dare say Parliament will vote for war."

James nodded. "They can't let it pass, can they?"

"Probably not," Uncle Winchester said. "Yes, there's a case to be made that we don't really need to worry about Vesy, but Pegasus and Cromwell are quite important. Parliament will understand that, I believe."

He rubbed his forehead. "When are you going to get married?"

"I haven't found anyone," James said, feeling his cheeks heat. It was an old argument. "Do we have to have this discussion every time we meet?"

"Yes," Uncle Winchester said, flatly. "You need to start raising the next generation of the family."

"I have Percy and Penny," James pointed out.

"Neither of whom are blood relations," Uncle Winchester said. "You cannot leave your titles to them."

James met his eyes. "There was a time when I believed that my birth made me superior to everyone else," he said. "I have learned hard lessons since."

"You were a little brat back then," Uncle Winchester agreed. "Locking the maid in the storeroom was particularly unpleasant. And then there was the time you gorged yourself silly on..."

"Uncle," James said. It wasn't something he wanted to remember. "Are you ever going to let me forget it?"

"I'll be telling your grandkids all about it," Uncle Winchester said. "And sneering at you when you complain about what awful brats your children are. You gave your parents quite a hard time."

He cleared his throat. "I have a bad feeling about this, James," he said. "The order we built after the Troubles is dead. It died with the war. Neville, the appeasing toad, is right about that, if nothing else. Either we fight the Indians, and risk heavy losses that may weaken us permanently, or we surrender and brace for the next round of demands. The universe isn't what it once was."

"I know," James said.

"We need time," Uncle Winchester added. "Time to rebuild the navy, time to incorporate the lessons of the war, time to rebalance the international order. Hell, maybe even time to make approaches to the Russians again."

"You know what they tried to do," James said.

"I also know we may need them in the future," Uncle Winchester said. He gave James a sidelong look. "Should I start looking for potential wives?"

James shook his head, firmly.

"Then start looking for someone yourself," Uncle Winchester said. "You're a war hero, moderately handsome, well-connected...you shouldn't have any problem finding someone willing to share your life. Or you can set up an arranged marriage and be...*friendly*, if not actual partners. There're quite a few marriages where the partners are homosexual and only married to produce children."

"I'm not homosexual," James said.

He sighed. Perhaps it would have been easier if he *had* been. No one gave a damn if someone happened to be homosexual, unless they were members of the aristocracy. *Then*, they had to produce children, even if it meant entering an arranged - and loveless - marriage with a woman who might have the same tendencies. But for him? He wanted someone he actually *loved*. And finding someone who loved him, instead of a gold digger, wasn't easy.

Perhaps I should have taken note of Prince Henry, he thought. The *Prince* had married for love, then taken himself and his wife to Tadpole Prime, well away from the media. *I could do that, couldn't I*?

"Then find someone," Uncle Winchester said. "The family needs you to get married, James."

"I'll start looking once I return to Earth," James said, reluctantly. "I imagine I'll have time to start a search then, if I must."

It was a bitter thought. He was still young, but it was unlikely he'd be promoted further. Promotion into the Admiralty was based on politics as much as competence and skill; his family, he suspected, already had too much influence in the Royal Navy. He was marginally surprised he'd been promoted to Vice Admiral, but then he *was* the senior survivor of *Ark Royal*. It made him the greatest living hero of the war.

"I can offer advice, if you like," Uncle Winchester said. "You're not *obliged* to marry a commoner, you know. There're quite a few young maidens in the aristocracy who'd know the score."

James scowled. It was tempting, perhaps too tempting. A young woman from the same social class as himself, someone safe...and boring. Sweet, soft-spoken - or good at hiding her true personality from her family. Pretty too, of course. The families worked hard to ensure that their children were at the very peak of health. There would be an understanding right from the start, an understanding that they didn't love each other... but that love would bloom, given a chance. She would manage his estates and raise their children while he tended to his career.

But she would be boring. And he disliked boredom.

"There aren't many other options," Uncle Winchester added. "I do have a list of potential commoners, ones with the ability to fit into the aristocracy, but they wouldn't have the same background."

"Of course not," James muttered.

He shook his head. The British aristocracy had learned the dangers of inbreeding the hard way. A commoner with a record of accomplishments - it crossed his mind that Admiral Smith would have qualified - could be invited to marry into the aristocracy, trading their genes for recognition. No one would look down on them or sneer at their children. Indeed, commoners who *became* aristocrats were highly honoured. It was the only way to keep the bloodlines fresh.

But a commoner wouldn't understand the hidden social rules of the aristocracy...

"It doesn't matter, not now," he said, firmly. "We can discuss it afterwards."

"Then we will go over your plan," Uncle Winchester said. "What do you plan to do if the Indians mass their forces?"

"Go elsewhere," James said, relieved. Military issues he understood. "Trying to defend everywhere is asking for trouble."

Uncle Winchester nodded, then questioned every detail with a thoroughness James could only admire. He'd known his uncle had helped design warships before the war, but he hadn't really grasped that Uncle Winchester had a level of tactical acumen too...something, in hindsight, that should have been blindingly obvious. And yet, his uncle had never really *bragged* about his achievements. He'd certainly never talked about them without being prompted.

And I asked for war stories, James recalled. His parents had sent him to Uncle Winchester's when they'd found the young James too much to handle. *I wasn't interested in the details.*

There was a rap at the door, which opened a moment later to reveal Sandra. "Sirs," she said, as she closed the door behind her. "The Prime

Minister wishes to inform you that the Houses of Parliament voted for war."

James let out a breath. It would be war.

He rose to his feet. "I'll need to return to Nelson Base," he said. "The task force will have to be assembled."

"Make sure you give them hell," Uncle Winchester said. "I'll speak to the Prime Minister; you'll probably have another discussion with us before you depart."

He held out a hand. James shook it firmly. "Good luck, James."

"Thank you," James said. A quick shuttle back to Nelson Base...he'd alert his staff on the way, get them to start sending out orders to the designated ships. They'd finalise the plan over the next couple of days, while the task force prepared for war. "We're going to need it."

CHAPTER FOUR

Nelson Base, Earth Orbit

"Captain Naiser," Admiral Fitzwilliam said. "Thank you for coming."

Captain John Naiser nodded once as the hatch closed behind him, then took the seat the Admiral indicated. It had been two weeks since *Warspite* had returned to Earth for the second time, leading a ragtag convoy of ships escaping Vesy. He'd spent most of that time sitting in front of various Boards of Inquiry, having every decision he'd made on Vesy dissected ruthlessly. Too many people had died for the Admiralty to do anything else.

He couldn't help feeling tense. His crew had been ordered to stay on the ship, save for the handful who'd been answering questions themselves; he'd been told to keep his ship ready for deployment, but he hadn't been ordered to attend any of the briefings or planning sessions he knew to be underway. War was looming and yet he'd had almost nothing to do, save for answering questions. If he hadn't been left in command of his ship, he would have wondered if he'd been made the scapegoat for the disaster. The Indians had organised the uprising, priming the Vesy and turning them against other human factions, but he'd been the officer on the spot.

But I was left in command, he reassured himself. *They must have another reason to keep me away from the planning sessions.*

"There isn't much time, so I'll be blunt," Fitzwilliam said. His voice was clipped, held under firm control. "As you know, Parliament voted yesterday for war. Task Force Bulldog - under my command - has been charged with recovering Cromwell and Pegasus and driving the Indians back to their own worlds. Your ship has been attached to Task Force Bulldog."

"Yes, sir," John said. Independent command of a small flotilla had been nice, but he was too junior to hold it indefinitely. "*Warspite* is ready to go to war."

"I'm glad to hear that," Fitzwilliam said. He leaned forward, meeting John's eyes. "I'm placing you and your ship on detached duty, Captain. I have a mission I want you to perform."

John lifted his eyebrows. "A mission?"

"On the record, *Warspite* will be assigned to Britannia," Fitzwilliam said. John felt a flicker of disappointment he ruthlessly suppressed. "There is a demand for small ships to provide additional security and *Warspite* would be perfect for the role. However, your actual orders - which will be sealed; you can open them once you enter the Terra Nova System - are to make a recon flight through the occupied systems. I need a full tactical survey to help plan our offensive operations."

"Yes, sir," John said. He felt a surge of brilliant excitement. A challenging mission against a deadly foe? It was what he'd signed up for. And he had a score to settle against the Indians. "You want us to find their carriers?"

"I doubt their dispositions will remain permanent," Fitzwilliam said. "They will almost certainly reposition their ships once they know where we're coming from."

He keyed a switch, activating the starchart. "Our best guess is that they will place at least one of their carriers in Pegasus and another in Vesy - assuming, of course, they're prepared to risk both of their carriers in the war. They may well have plans to cut their losses if we're ready to put up a fight."

He shrugged. "You are to start with Pegasus. First, I want a tactical sweep of the system; second, I want you to land a small commando team on Clarke III. We need up-to-date information on what the Indians are doing on the surface. So far, our analysts have concluded it could be anything from setting up defences to merely holding the moon in a very light grip."

"Because they can't hold Clarke III if we came knocking," John said.

"We don't know," Fitzwilliam said. "A SAS team - probably including a handful of Royal Marines - will be attached to *Warspite* just prior to your departure. They'll have a stealth shuttle for planetary insertion; you'll get them to the system, but they'll handle getting down to the surface themselves."

"We inserted the marines on Vesy," John said, quietly.

"There's more at stake here," Fitzwilliam warned. "You'll make sure you have a solid communications link with the troopers before heading through the tramlines to Vesy and Cromwell. Ideally, we want to set up stealthed platforms in the region, but that depends on local conditions. There's too much dust orbiting that damn gas giant."

"Yes, sir," John said. "Do you want to try to insert teams on Vesy and Cromwell?"

"I don't think so," Fitzwilliam said. "The diplomats" - his face twisted into a sneer - "believe that the Indians will probably concede Cromwell without too much of a fight. Cromwell is an Earth-type world, Captain, and our claim to possession is strong. They'd set a very distressing precedent if they chose to keep it."

John nodded. It had long been agreed, after Terra Nova had collapsed into civil war, that whoever settled a system's Earth-type world had unquestioned title to the remainder of the system. The Indians *might* be able to get their hands on Pegasus, if the Royal Navy failed to evict them, but the other interstellar powers would resist allowing them to keep Cromwell. It would definitely upset a number of apple carts.

"In any case, there's no point in trying to determine what's happening on Vesy," Fitzwilliam added, after a moment. "I think the general feeling on Earth is to pull back and let the Vesy come to terms with the cultural shock themselves."

"I agree, sir," John said. "The Vesy have been too badly traumatised by their first contact."

"So were we," Fitzwilliam pointed out.

"The Tadpoles were on the same level as us," John said. "I don't think the Vesy knew how to make gunpowder, let alone develop the scientific method, before the Russians stumbled across their world. They had no *concept* of space travel. We must have seemed like *gods*."

"That's a matter for a later date, if we win the war," Fitzwilliam said. "Ideally, Captain, we should have the task force at Hannibal by the time you return. You will rendezvous with us there. If we're not present, you will head back to Earth; hopefully, you will encounter us *en route*."

John nodded. Only an idiot - or a politician - expected starships to run on time. Something could easily go wrong, delaying them; the Indians could be expected to do whatever it took to delay the task force as much as possible. They'd have to be keeping an eye on Terra Nova too, he suspected. *Warspite* would have to enter stealth mode as soon as she entered the system and alter course to the tramline that would eventually take her to Pegasus.

"I may have another mission for you, once the first one is completed," Fitzwilliam added, after a moment. "However, your principle task is to serve as a scout."

"Yes, sir," John said. He couldn't help looking forward to the deployment. "*Warspite* was *built* for such missions."

"Good," Fitzwilliam said. "Under the circumstances, you will have first claim on anything you need from the stores. If any supply officers dare to complain, point them in my direction."

"Yes, sir," John said. He'd fought enough battles with supply officers to be glad of the chance to force them to check with an Admiral. They'd rapidly change their minds about objecting the moment they realised he wasn't joking. "I believe we don't need much, save for the SAS gear and other war stocks."

"Make sure you take all you can," Fitzwilliam warned. "You may not be able to return to Earth before the task force enters the war zone."

He smiled, rather thinly. "Is there anything else your crew needs?"

"They could probably do with some leave," John said. "It was a long deployment and there wasn't any real chance to stretch their legs and blow off some steam. But I don't think there's time."

"You can send a handful of crewmen to Island One, if you think you can afford to spare them for a couple of hours," Fitzwilliam said. "I want you on your way as soon as possible, Captain; handle it how you see fit, but don't delay your departure."

John smiled. Island One was tame, compared to Portsmouth, Southampton or Sin City, but it would give some of his crew a chance to relax for a few hours. He'd have to go through the duty roster with Commander Howard, his XO, and determine just who could be spared before departure. It was a pity he probably couldn't clear himself for a few hours of leave, but it would be an abuse of authority. Besides, there was just too much to do.

"Thank you, sir," he said.

"There is a price, of course," Fitzwilliam said. "You'll be carrying a couple of reporters with you."

"Oh," John said. He cleared his throat. "Sir, with all due respect, I thought this was to be a *secret* mission."

"The reporters will be informed, in no uncertain terms, that they are not to file any stories without permission from the Public Relations officers," Fitzwilliam said. "During your mission, Captain, they will be doing nothing more than recording and witnessing the deployment. They won't be allowed to send messages off the ship until the task force enters the Hannibal System."

John scowled. "We can keep them from sending messages, Admiral, but it will still be a security risk."

"The Prime Minister is very determined to make sure the war is presented in the best possible light," Fitzwilliam said, firmly. "You, at least, will only have one or two reporters. *I* will have a whole press corps on *Theodore Smith*. They'll all have signed the standard non-disclosure agreement and their stories will be checked prior to distribution. I understand your doubts, Captain, but we have our orders. We need to keep the press on our side."

John kept his face blank. *With friends like those, who needs the Indians*?

"The looming war has already started to dominate the newsfeeds," Fitzwilliam added. "Our press corps, at least, is being reasonably responsible, but foreign media sources are going crazy. We need to make sure we get our story out before the Indians have a chance to influence public opinion. They're already saying this is a war of choice."

"It isn't, sir," John said.

"Tell that to the reporters," Fitzwilliam said. He shrugged. "In any case, Captain, if they cause trouble you have authorisation to stick them in the brig until the war is finished. I believe that will be made clear to them too."

"Thank you, sir," John said.

"The reporters we had on *Ark Royal* were pretty damn bad too," Fitzwilliam added, with a thin smile. "I know *precisely* how you feel."

He reached into a drawer and removed a datachip. "These are your sealed orders, Captain," he added. "You'll receive the standard orders through the datanet; you will, of course, ignore them once you reach Terra Nova and open the sealed orders."

"Yes, sir," John said.

"I don't expect you to engage the enemy," Fitzwilliam said, as he rose to his feet. "Ideally, you should pass completely unnoticed. We don't want the Indians to know you're there, Captain; I'd like to have a *few* surprises to point at them. Don't go looking for a fight."

His expression hardened. "However...if you are forced into an engagement and you can't avoid it, I expect you to give them hell. Beat the living daylights out of them."

"Of course, sir," John said.

"Good luck," Fitzwilliam said. "Do you have any questions?"

"No, sir," John said. He rose and saluted. "Thank you."

"Thank me when you come back," Fitzwilliam said. "Not before."

John nodded and strode out of the hatch, down towards the docks. Nelson Base seemed to have come alive overnight; hundreds of officers and crewmen were transporting supplies from the stocks to the starships docked at the giant station. He pushed himself against the bulkhead as a pair of carts rumbled passed, pushed along by a pair of burly Royal Marines who had been pressed into service. Behind them, a couple of commanding officers strode past, probably heading for one of the innumerable briefings.

At least that explains why I wasn't invited, John thought. *The Admiral wouldn't want me to know too much if he was sending me into enemy territory.*

"Captain," a voice called. "How are you?"

John turned and smiled as he saw Commander Juliet Watson. She looked more confident than he remembered - but now, at least, she wasn't trying to serve as an XO. He couldn't help feeling pleased to see her again, even if she'd been an unintentional nuisance on his first deployment.

"I'm fine," he said. It would be nice to sit and have a drink with her, but he doubted he had the time. "I've just got to return to my ship."

"I was hoping Mike would be free this evening," Juliet said. "I've got a great deal to show him."

John concealed his amusement with an effort. Mike Johnston, *Warspite's* Chief Engineer, had a thing for Juliet, even when she'd been XO. It had probably worked in her favour - crewmen who would have ignored her wouldn't have dared trifle with the Chief Engineer - but it was skirting the boundaries of regulations. Now, after she'd been reassigned to Nelson Base, they'd seen each other fairly frequently. John was mildly surprised he hadn't heard of their engagement by now.

"I'll see if I can spare him," he said. It was hard to say *no* to Juliet. "But I can't make any promises."

He nodded to her and headed down towards the airlock. A pair of marines was standing on guard outside the ship, watching carefully while four crewmen carefully moved a truckload of supplies into *Warspite*. They saluted John as he approached; he saluted them back, then waited for them to confirm his identity before stepping through the airlock. It wasn't *likely* the Indians had spies trying to creep onto the ship, yet the possibility couldn't be discounted *completely*. The Great Powers might have agreed not to wage war on one another, at least before the Tadpoles had shown themselves, but there had been no shortage of attempts to penetrate security systems and steal intelligence and technological data.

And the Indians might have spies of their own, he thought. *No, they will have spies of their own, watching and waiting to see what we do.*

It wasn't a cheerful thought. The Royal Navy needed to trust its personnel, not start a witch-hunt for Indian spies. Hell, quite a few crewmen were of Indian descent, although most ties to motherlands had been cut during the Troubles. Who knew what would happen if they were specifically targeted by the counter-intelligence staff? The paranoia might do more damage than Indian weapons.

He keyed his wristcom as he entered his ready room. "Commander Howard, report to my ready room as soon as possible."

"Aye, Captain," Howard said. "I'm on my way."

John sat down behind his desk and opened his terminal. The official set of orders was already waiting for him; he skimmed them briefly, then placed the sealed orders in his secure drawer. They'd remain there until they reached Terra Nova, where he'd need to show them to the XO. Howard would probably guess their existence once the SAS troopers came onboard - there was no need to transport the SAS to Britannia - but until then the sealed orders had to remain a secret. It wasn't particularly clever - John trusted his XO completely - yet there was no choice. The more people who knew, the greater the chance of an accidental leak.

The hatch opened. "Captain," Howard said.

"Take a seat," John ordered. He glanced through the list of messages and frowned. The SAS would be arriving an hour before the planned departure time, something that bothered him more than he cared to admit. A handful of troopers wouldn't pose a problem, but their shuttlecraft would have to be stowed away somewhere safe. "We're departing for Britannia in two days."

Howard raised his eyebrows. "Britannia?"

"We will also be transporting an SAS detachment - probably one or two troops, around sixteen men apiece," John added. He'd let Howard draw his own conclusions. "They'll have at least one shuttlecraft with them - a non-standard design. They want her to remain secure."

"Yes, sir," Howard said. "We could plug her to the hull and cover her in camo fabric. She'd remain completely out of sight."

"Good idea," John said. "Make the arrangements; verify the straps yourself, rather than asking anyone else to handle it. Officially, we're taking on additional marines rather than anything more...interesting."

"Of course, sir," Howard said.

John smiled. "We also have permission to take what we need from the stores, so put in requests for everything," he added. "Just make sure we have enough room to get through the corridors in case of emergency."

"I was on *Courageous*, sir," Howard said. "I remember."

"Me too," John said. He'd served on *Canopus*...and the escort carrier had been so crammed with supplies that making one's way through the ship had been difficult. And, in the end, it hadn't been enough to save her when the Tadpoles came knocking. "We'll need everything we can get."

He took a breath. "We also have permission to offer shore leave to deserving crewmen," he added. "They're authorised to visit Island One for a couple of hours at a time. Put together parties of suitable candidates and remind them that anyone who fails to report back will be listed as a deserter. We can't afford to delay our departure."

"Yes, sir," Howard said.

"And tell the Chief Engineer that he has an hour's leave tonight, if he wants to use it," John added, after a moment. "I think we can spare him that long."

"Of course, sir," Howard said.

"I'll deal with the paperwork now," John concluded. He'd be surprised if Howard didn't have a good idea of where they were going, but it wouldn't matter as long as he kept his mouth shut until departure. "Let me know if there are any problems."

"Yes, sir," Howard said.

John smiled to himself as his XO left the compartment. There *was* no shortage of paperwork, but he couldn't help a thrill of excitement. After so much, after so many defeats, it felt good to be going back to war. This time, it was going to be different. No civilians, no diplomats, no aliens...just a mission and a chance to test themselves against a peer power. It would be *very* different.

This time, he thought, *we're ready for war.*

CHAPTER FIVE

SAS Headquarters, Hereford, Earth

"Welcome to hell, Lieutenant."

Lieutenant Percy Schneider sucked in his breath as he was escorted through the heavily-guarded gate and into one of the most secretive military bases in Britain. It looked, on the surface, to be quite similar to a number of other bases he'd visited, but he couldn't help a thrill of excitement. Hereford was the home base of the Special Air Service, the toughest Special Forces unit in the world. *Every* serving soldier - at least, every front-line soldier - hoped to become an SAS trooper or serve in one of the other SF units. Percy had hoped, one day, to try out for the Special Boat Service, but he'd never expected to visit Hereford until then. The base was rarely open to visitors.

"Take a long look," his escort advised dryly. "There's nothing really to see here."

Percy nodded in agreement. The important parts of the base would be behind a second line of fencing or deep underground, well away from prying eyes. He might have been asked - ordered - to visit, but he wouldn't see anything above his pay grade. There weren't even any troopers in view, although the driver - when he'd been picked up from the railway station - had told him that they spent most of their time training when they weren't actually on active duty. They wouldn't show off for *him*.

He sighed inwardly, then followed his escort through a set of doors and into a barracks that looked remarkably similar to the barracks in Edinburgh. The only real difference was a long line of framed newspaper cuttings hanging from the walls, each one talking about the SAS or another SF unit. He paused long enough to read one dating all the way back to the famed Iranian Embassy Siege before his escort coughed impatiently and led him onwards. There wasn't anyone else in view until they entered the antechamber, but he could feel unseen eyes watching him. The base was carefully monitored in case of trouble.

"Captain Drake will see you now," the escort said, nodding to a door. "Good luck, Lieutenant."

"Thank you," Percy said.

He braced himself and stepped through the door. His orders had been clear - he was to make his way to Hereford and report to Captain Drake - but they hadn't told him why. He didn't think he was in trouble - he hadn't been in command of the base on Vesy when the final battle had begun - yet it was still odd. It wasn't as if he'd thrown his cap in the ring and applied for SAS Selection. Offhand, he couldn't recall anyone ever being invited to Hereford merely to speak to one of the SAS officers.

"Lieutenant Schneider," Captain Christopher Drake said. His voice was oddly unaccented, but Percy thought he could detect traces of Lancashire. "We don't stand on ceremony here, so please take a seat."

Percy obeyed, studying Drake carefully as he sat down. He was a tall man, wiry rather than muscular; his eyes were warm, but sharp. The uniform he wore was completely unmarked, save for a single rank badge; he carried a pistol at his belt, the flap open so he could draw it in a second. Percy puzzled over it for a long moment, then recalled the number of terrorist threats against military bases during the Age of Unrest. The bombardment of Earth during the war had unleashed a whole new wave of terrorism.

"I apologise for summoning you here at such short notice," Drake said. "Do you know why you are here?"

"Vesy," Percy guessed.

"Not quite," Drake said. "Pegasus. Specifically, Clarke III."

Percy nodded slowly. He'd been on the surface while *Warspite* had been supporting the colony effort, practicing military deployments in utterly alien - and completely inhospitable - terrain. Clarke might have been fun, if the atmosphere hadn't been poisonous; they'd joked, at the time, about setting up ski resorts and charging admission. But now, of course, the Indians were in possession of the gas giant's moon. They'd have to be evicted before the colony could resume normal development.

"I read your file," Drake said. "It was quite an interesting read. You joined the marines four years ago; you were assigned to *Warspite* as a Corporal one year ago and took part in the liberation of Vesy from the Russians. Captain Naiser left you behind, in command of Fort Knight; you served as a combination of outpost commander and diplomat until you were relieved. Quite an achievement for one so young."

"Thank you, sir," Percy said.

"You were promoted to Lieutenant and placed in command of the QRF," Drake continued, calmly. "You were on the spot during the troubles on Vesy - eventually, you helped defend Fort Knight long enough to get the civilians off-world before it was too late. And you've been nominated for a couple of medals..."

Percy frowned, inwardly. He'd tried to look up Drake's record on MILNET, only to discover that anything beyond a bare acknowledgement of Drake's existence - a standard precaution against walts - was classified well above his security clearance. But someone who held the rank of Captain in the SAS *couldn't* be dismissed. He'd have more practical experience on active duty than just about anyone Percy knew, save - perhaps - for Sergeant Peerce. It was unlikely - very unlikely - that Drake was genuinely impressed by Percy's record. He'd have to wonder if Percy had been promoted too far, too fast.

"I shall be blunt," Drake said. "You've been detached to my troop, Percy. I'm afraid you don't have a choice."

"Yes, sir," Percy said, automatically.

"We're going to be deploying to Clarke," Drake explained. "It won't be the first planetary insertion we've done, Percy, but none of us have actually visited Clarke itself. You're one of the few people we can tap for support. Your CO already approved the transfer before you came here."

Percy had to smile. "Does this make me a trooper?"

"Not until you pass Selection," Drake said. He smiled, openly. "But you will be fast-tracked through Selection when you get home."

If I get home, Percy thought.

The thought sent chills down his spine. He'd heard stories of SAS deployments, including a number of stories that couldn't possibly have been turned into movies. No one would believe that such operations had ever taken place. Slipping undetected through a planet's atmosphere was sanity itself compared to some of the crazier stories he'd been told. He looked at Drake and wondered, suddenly, just how many of them were true. Drake didn't look to be the sort of person who ever gave up.

"You're better placed than some of the people we've had to take along," Drake said. "You actually went through training, which is more than can be said for some of the intelligence officers. I assume you know how to fire a gun?"

"Yes, sir," Percy said, stiffly. He knew it sounded as though he was being teased, but it was a *very* silly question. "I came first in my class of shooters."

Drake smiled. "You'll find we're held to even greater standards," he said. "We'll be testing you out on everything from pistols to sniper rifles. Did you have any problems operating on Clarke?"

"Our weapons and equipment had to be cold-proofed," Percy said. "They *were* designed for unpleasant environments."

"Always good to check," Drake said.

Percy couldn't disagree. There had been cases where weapons had worked perfectly in the laboratory, or out on the training fields, and then jammed up on active service. The oil had dried, or frozen solid...it had cost lives, in the past. He'd been warned to be careful when he'd been deployed to *Warspite*; their equipment *was* rated for all environments, but it was well to be *sure*. Their weapons could not be allowed to fail when they were advancing on an enemy position.

"I won't lie to you," Drake said. "This will be the hardest thing you've ever done. If it was completely up to me, you'd have weeks to prepare yourself for insertion, but we don't have weeks. You'll have a day with us now and then we're transferring to *Warspite*."

Percy brightened. "Yes, sir."

"You'll be in lockdown, though," Drake added. "If you want to write letters or emails, you'll have to send them through me. I would advise you not to send anything too explicit, but I could do with a laugh."

"I'll try to be blatant," Percy said, dryly. "Or would you like me to download a romance novel and copy the interesting parts into an email?"

Drake laughed. "As long as it's an *interesting* romance novel."

Percy snorted. He'd always detested the thought of someone reading his private mail, but military security came first. *That* had been made very clear during his first deployment. The censors didn't really mind if a squaddie spent hours writing a letter to his girlfriend that detailed precisely *what* he intended to do with her when he got home, but they'd be furious if he accidentally revealed operational details. It would lead to an unpleasant interview with the soldier's CO and perhaps an immediate flight home.

"I'll pick something very amusing," he said. Penny had given him a copy of one book featuring a Royal Marine for a joke and he'd been left with the impression that the writer had never set eyes on a soldier. But it had been funny, in a morbid kind of way. "Or maybe not write anything at all."

"Good," Drake said. "Once the ship is underway, you can meet your friends if you wish, provided you keep up with the training. I suggest, however, that you concentrate on working with us. We're going to need to rely on you once we hit the surface."

"Yes, sir," Percy said.

Drake rose. "For the moment, you're attached to B Squadron, 5 (Space)Troop," he said, as he led the way towards the door. "You *won't* be a Lieutenant, I'm afraid. I hope that won't be a problem?"

"No, sir," Percy said. He didn't hold *any* rank in the SAS. It was unlikely he'd be called upon to take command, or do anything other than share his expertise and serve as a footsoldier. Hell, if he *did* have to take command, there would be no one left to follow his orders. "I understand."

"That's a relief," Drake said. He didn't bother to look back as he headed down the corridor. "Every so often, we get someone who wants to cling to his old rank."

Percy wasn't really surprised. It hadn't been *easy* to get promotion - and he'd been lucky. He would have had to give up his rank if he applied to join the SAS, but officers attached to the SAS - willingly or unwillingly - might not be so keen to surrender something they'd worked to achieve. And yet, he was fairly sure he'd be allowed to keep his rank once he returned to his original unit.

He heard the sound of gunfire as they passed through a set of heavy metal doors and walked down a long staircase. The sound of shooting was growing louder; they stopped outside a second set of doors and donned ear protection before opening the doors. Inside, there was a shooting range, with a dozen men in black uniforms systematically firing their weapons towards a series of holographic targets. Four more men were kneeling on the floor, dismantling and reassembling their weapons; it looked very much as though the troopers were test-firing everything they had before boarding the shuttle for *Warspite*.

Drake put his fingers in his mouth and whistled, loudly. Percy watched with interest as the troopers turned to face their commander. They had nothing to prove, he noted; they weren't showing off their weapons or thrusting forward, trying to dominate the surroundings. There was something about the way they moved, an easy confidence in themselves, that was more impressive than any shouting or screaming.

They've already been through hell, he thought. He'd looked up SAS Selection when he'd completed the Commando Training Course and he'd been impressed. *And then they went out and did the impossible.*

"This is Percy Schneider," Drake said, without preamble. "He visited Clarke III last year, which makes him the closest thing to an expert we have. He's a Royal Marine with genuine experience, so don't expect him to ask which end of a rifle fires the bullets. Sergeant?"

A tall man stepped forward. "Captain?"

"Check Percy out on our equipment - everything from environmental suits to weapons and communications gear," Drake said. "We'll be leaving tomorrow morning; I want him ready to go by then."

"Yes, sir," the Sergeant said.

Percy braced himself as the Sergeant studied him, forcing himself to meet the Sergeant's eyes. Platoon Sergeant Danny Peerce had mentored him, first on *Warspite* and then on Vesy, but *this* Sergeant looked a great deal nastier. He'd have to worry about Percy's qualifications, no matter what the files said. Percy hadn't gone through Selection and so there would be a question mark over his abilities.

"I am Sergeant Dale Lewis," the Sergeant said. "You've seen active service, right?"

"Yes, Sergeant," Percy said.

"Then you will have no trouble with our training," Lewis said, with an evil smile. "Let's go."

The next few hours proved to be hellish. Percy knew he was in pretty good shape - he'd kept up with his training on Vesy - but running around after Sergeant Lewis felt like going all the way back to the Potential Royal Marines Course and starting again. Many of the weapons he was shown - and forced to fire time and time again until the sergeant was satisfied - were familiar, yet some were clearly unique to the SAS. It was lucky, he decided, as they moved to survival gear, that he'd had time on Clarke *and* Vesy. He had enough experience in using hardsuits to please even Sergeant Lewis.

"There isn't time to fit you out with booster implants," Lewis said, as he led the way into the medical bay. A grim-faced doctor was standing there, holding a datapad in one hand and a pocket scanner in the other. "You may be at a disadvantage if you have to run after us."

Percy nodded, curtly. "I'll try and serve as the rearguard then," he said. He'd heard that the SAS had booster implants - as well as implanted weapons and communications devices - but details had been sparse. However, if they were anything like the civilian models used by spacers, it would take weeks to learn how to use the implants. "How do your implants work?"

"That's classified information," Lewis growled. "Pass Selection and you'll find out."

The Sergeant didn't let up. As soon as the doctor had pronounced Percy physically healthy, he'd led Percy into a sparring room and tested him, ruthlessly. Percy had been trained in hand-to-hand combat, but the Sergeant was astonishingly fast and terrifyingly strong. It was a surprise, when the sparring came to an end, when the Sergeant reluctantly cleared Percy to accompany the troop and led him to meet the rest of the troopers.

Or maybe it shouldn't have been, Percy thought, feeling his body aching. *If Drake wasn't joking about officers who didn't know how to fire a gun...*

"We operate on a first-name basis here," Lewis explained. The SAS common room didn't look *that* different to the one he recalled from Edinburgh, although it was cleaner than anything *civilian*. "And we have zero tolerance for bullshit."

"Quite right," a trooper said. He stuck out a hand for Percy to shake. "I'm Jimmy. I read your file. What was it like on Vesy?"

Percy hesitated. "Tricky," he said, finally. "Hot, sticky and remorselessly political."

Jimmy laughed and slapped Percy's shoulder. "Sounds like fun," he said. "And Clarke?"

"Cold, icy and deadly," Percy said. "You wouldn't last a minute without protective gear."

"But at least it's a free-fire zone," Jimmy said. "There won't be any aliens or civilians to get in the way when we engage the Indians."

He waved Percy to a seat and passed him a can of Panda Cola. "Tell us about it."

Percy nodded and started to talk. The troopers listened intently, without the jokes he would have expected from a rival branch of the military. But then, the troopers didn't have anything to prove; hell, some of them might have been *drawn* from the Royal Marines or had friends who'd served on Vesy too. They didn't need to engage in horseplay to prove themselves.

"If you want to update your will, make sure you do it now," Lewis said, an hour later. He'd listened quietly, sometimes asking questions to parse out more of the story. "Or check your email - remember, anything you send will be held in the buffers until someone's had a chance to take a look at it. This is pretty much the only piece of downtime you'll get, so enjoy it."

"Aw, Sergeant," Jimmy said. "We were hoping to take him to the pub."

Lewis lifted his eyebrows. "Would *you* care to explain to the Captain while you're all rolling drunk or puking during the shuttle flight?"

"Um...no, Sergeant," Jimmy said.

"Right answer," Lewis said. "You're in lockdown anyway, so behave yourselves. Percy, you have a bunk with the lads. Don't worry about standing guard tonight - you'll do enough of that on the ship."

Percy nodded. He'd have to email Canella before departure - and Penny. She'd made it back to Earth - the Indians had returned her without delay - but he hadn't had a chance to talk to her. God alone knew what she was planning to do, apart from writing the full story of the disaster on Vesy. It might make interesting reading.

And I'd better hope no one here learns she's my sister, he thought, as he headed for the nearest terminal. *The media is the enemy of secrecy and security.*

CHAPTER SIX

HMS Warspite, Earth Orbit

"They do feel the urge to be melodramatic, don't they?"

Penny Schneider had to fight down the urge to roll her eyes. It had been an hour since they'd boarded the shuttle and set off for an undisclosed destination and Darrel Stevenson had spent most of the time complaining about it. If he hadn't wanted to agree to the terms and conditions for being embedded with the military, she asked herself, why had he signed up in the first place? *She*, at least, had known what she was getting into when she'd signed on the dotted line. There might be a number of irksome security regulations - and the promise of a hefty jail term if she deliberately broke them - but there was also the prospect of a scoop. It was something she needed desperately to boost her career.

Because my stories weren't unique when I was returned to Earth, she thought, sourly. The Indians had held her prisoner just long enough to devalue her experiences and allow other reporters - who'd escaped with the Royal Navy - to undercut her. *I need something new as soon as possible.*

She ran a hand through her long blonde hair as the shuttle rocked one final time. The gravity field shimmied, suggesting that they'd docked with a starship. She couldn't help a flicker of fear despite the anticipation, fighting the urge to request - demand - that she be taken back home. It wouldn't be the first time she'd travelled on a military ship, but it wouldn't be the same. This time, they were going to war.

I could die here, she told herself. She'd faced death before - on Earth, during the war - but this was different. *Someone might blow the ship to atoms and take me with it.*

The hatch opened. She rose to her feet and picked up her carryall, walking through the hatch and into a small airlock. The logo on the inner hatch was familiar, *very* familiar. She had to choke off a laugh as she realised she'd been assigned - again - to *Warspite*. Was Percy back onboard? He'd been on Vesy, the last time they'd met, but Fort Knight was no longer in existence. She knew he'd survived - she'd checked the records as soon as she'd been returned to Earth - but she hadn't been able to organise a meeting. Her sources had told her, in confidence, that everyone who'd had anything to do with the disaster were being interrogated by various Boards of Inquiry to find out just what had happened. She could only pray that Percy hadn't been singled out as the scapegoat.

She smiled, despite her fears, as the inner hatch opened to reveal Commander Howard. She'd met him during the first trip to Vesy - as XO, he'd been responsible for supervising the reporters as well as his regular duties - and she rather liked him, although she knew he'd been careful what he'd shown her. She didn't fault him for that, but it was rather annoying. Naval personnel tended to stay firmly on-message whenever they thought they were being monitored by their superiors.

"Commander," she said. "*What* a surprise to see you again."

"There *was* a need for secrecy," Howard said. He looked past her. "Mr. Stevenson. Welcome onboard *Warspite*."

"Thank you," Stevenson said. "Was it really necessary to hide the destination from us?"

"I'm afraid so," Howard said. "I assume you paid close attention to your briefing?"

"Of course," Stevenson said, irked. "It was very interesting."

"Operational details have to remain a secret, for the moment," Howard said. He turned, motioning them to follow him. "I know it's a burden, but we cannot afford to take risks."

He said nothing else until they reached their suite. It was larger than Penny had expected - one small living compartment and a single bedroom - but she had the very definite impression that Stevenson was disappointed. She dropped her bag on the sofa, checked inside the bedroom and smiled to herself. The compartment was much bigger than the quarters she'd used last time she'd been on the ship.

"You'll have the bedroom, we assume," Howard said. "Mr. Stevenson will have the sofa. The head" - he jabbed a finger towards the bathroom - "is shared. I'm afraid there isn't anyone assigned to keep the room tidy, so you'll have to handle it yourselves. The door will need to be keyed to your fingerprints if you want to keep everyone else out; you'll be able to handle that through the room's terminal, over there."

Penny followed his pointing finger and nodded. "When will we depart?"

"Tomorrow morning," Howard informed her. "As we're moving vast amounts of supplies through the ship, the two of you are to remain in your compartment for the moment. You will be escorted to the mess when dinner is ready; until then, there's a small stockpile of food and drink in the fridge."

"It's a tiny fridge," Stevenson complained.

"I *assure* you that this is the second-largest cabin on the ship," Howard said. "This isn't exactly a fancy hotel."

Stevenson looked disbelieving, but Penny nodded in understanding. She'd seen the junior enlisted quarters during her first cruise and they were *tiny*. There was nowhere near enough room to swing a cat and privacy was a joke. She'd endured the refugee camps on Earth, but she honestly doubted she could have tolerated such close quarters for very long. If the crewmen had fallen out or started fights, it would have been intolerable.

"We understand," she said. "It *was* in the briefing notes."

Howard smiled, very briefly. "You can compose or record messages, if you like, but they will be held in the buffer until a censor can inspect them or we return to Sol," he reminded her. "And I'll see you tonight, for dinner."

"Thank you," Penny said.

She watched Howard go, the hatch hissing closed behind him. "Well," she said. "All we can do now is wait."

"I suppose," Stevenson said. He bent down to inspect the sofa carefully. "How do you think you turn it into a bed?"

Penny examined it for a moment. "I don't think you do," she said. The sofa wasn't very big - Stevenson was in for a few uncomfortable nights - but it was better than sleeping on the deck. "You'll probably find blankets in the drawers underneath."

Stevenson sighed. "The things I do..."

"Just go embed yourself with the troops," Penny said. Her mentor during her first year as a reporter had been an embed, someone who'd lived and worked with a military unit while being a reporter. His stories had always been hair-raising. "You'll be sleeping in mud, eating dung for dinner and dodging fire from people who are trying to kill you."

"Reporters shouldn't be killed," Stevenson objected.

Penny snorted, rudely, as she picked up her carryall. Reporters *were* targeted; sometimes, they looked like soldiers, if seen from a distance. Or they were targeted because the insurgents saw them as the enemy, the men and women who encouraged the British population to support punitive strikes against rogue states and terrorist groups.

And if this ship gets destroyed, she thought, *we'll be blown to atoms, without the enemy ever knowing who they killed.*

She pushed the thought aside as she stepped into the tiny sleeping compartment and opened her carryall, dumping her clothes into the drawer beneath the bed. She'd been told not to bring any more than the bare essentials, something that bothered her more than she cared to admit. A suitcase of clothes wouldn't be that bad, would it? But her editor had made it clear that he expected her to abide by the military's rules. There was no profit - and no scoop - to be had if she spent the trip in the brig, being fed bread, water and ration bars.

"You've been on this ship before," Stevenson called. "What do you do when you're bored?"

"There's a games compartment," Penny said. "And a couple of entertainment rooms where you can watch movies. But I suggest remaining here until the Commander comes back for us. You don't want to get in the way."

She pulled her datapad out of the carryall and pressed her thumb against the sensor. It lit up, a pop-up reporting that it was unable to establish a datalink to Earth's giant datanet and send messages to her editor. Somehow, Penny wasn't surprised. The datapad would need to link to the ship's internal communications network and it would be off-limits, without the right passwords and authorisations. She doubted she'd get them either, at least until they were allowed to send messages back home freely. The military wouldn't be taking chances.

"You should have downloaded a few books or movies," she said, as she opened her reader and thumbed through the options. The latest in a long-running series about a young witch attending a school for magicians was out; it had automatically downloaded, the last time she'd connected to the datanet. "Watch something if you don't have any work to do. Or try and get some sleep."

Stevenson snorted. Moments later, she heard the theme music from a particularly irritating soap that hadn't yet managed to be taken off the air, despite the Troubles and the First Interstellar War. Quite how the BBC had managed to keep it going was something of a mystery. She sighed, pulled the hatch closed and lay back on the bed. If there was nothing to do until the ship was underway, she might as well spend the time reading. She'd have to go to work soon enough.

———

Percy couldn't help feeling annoyed as he followed Lewis and the troopers onto the heavy-lift shuttle. He'd sent a message to Canella the previous night, before he'd bedded down with the troops, and made the mistake of checking his email the following morning. Canella's message had been apologetic, but she'd made it clear that she'd found someone else after his assignment to *Warspite* and departure from Earth. Percy had hit the table in anger and then forced himself to bury his feelings as deeply as he could. They'd only prove a distraction on the voyage.

And on the deployment, he thought. Lewis had made it clear that they'd be exercising constantly on the ship, as well as training with the Royal Marines. *I can't afford to be distracted.*

He found his seat and sat down, waiting for the shuttle to take off. The other message he'd found, from Penny, had been equally worrying; she'd been offered a chance to embed with the military and taken it. By the time he'd seen it, going by the timetable she'd provided, she would already be in lockdown. He'd fired off a quick message anyway, warning her to be careful. She was, as far as he knew, the only blood relative he had left.

Unless mother is still out there somewhere, he thought, as the shuttle's hatches banged closed. *But it's been nearly six years since the war.*

It wasn't something he wanted to think about, not really. Their mother hadn't been in the house when the aliens had attacked Earth; Penny, Percy and Gayle Parkinson had been alone, forced to escape to higher ground on their own. God alone knew what had happened to her; Percy wondered, sometimes, if she'd been drowned in the tidal waves and her body swept out to sea, or if she'd taken the opportunity to disappear and start a new life. Either one was possible...

The shuttle rocked and took off. Percy closed his eyes and tried to relax, knowing there would be nothing to do until they reached *Warspite*. It didn't work; his thoughts kept buzzing through his head, reminding him that Penny was missing and Canella had left him for someone else. He'd been warned, when he'd signed up for training, that long deployments could ruin relationships - no matter how strong they were - but he hadn't really believed it. How could he have? He hadn't really had any real relationships in the past.

A romance at school doesn't count, he told himself firmly. In hindsight, it was embarrassing to admit just how badly he'd mooned over a particular girl, then cried when she'd broken up with him. It had felt like the end of the world...which proved his father had been right, more than once, when he'd insisted that teenagers were stupid. *You grew out of it.*

He must have fallen asleep, because the next thing he knew was being shocked awake by a sudden twist in the gravity field. Lewis glanced at him sharply as he opened the hatch, then motioned for the troopers to file out into the cruiser. Percy picked up his carryall - there wasn't much in it, apart from a couple of uniforms and a datapad - and brought up the rear. It felt odd not to be taking the lead, but Lewis had made it clear that he was to remain firmly in the back. The troopers knew what they were doing; Percy, who hadn't passed Selection or trained with them, couldn't put himself beside them.

Unless the shit really does hit the fan, he thought. The stealthed shuttle *should* be able to make its way through the planet's atmosphere without being detected, but the first flights down to the surface had been nightmarish even without trying to hide. *We could be blown down by a snowstorm and forced to crash - or be detected and shot down at the worst possible moment.*

"Percy," a familiar voice said. He looked up to see Captain Darryl Hadfield, standing at the hatch to Marine Country. "Fancy meeting you here."

"Sir," Percy said, awkwardly. He wasn't quite sure where he fit in any longer, not while he was under Drake's command. "It's good to see you again."

"Likewise," Hadfield said. He looked at Drake. "We're putting your men - and Percy - in Compartment C. It'll be cramped, but there should be enough room for all of you."

"It will do," Drake said. "Did you get the training schedule?"

"We'll be happy to make your lives miserable, once we're underway," Hadfield said. Percy could *hear* the competitiveness in his voice. Embarrassing an SAS Troop would be a feather in Hadfield's cap. "For the moment, half of my unit is on guard duty and the other half is confined to Marine Country."

"Brilliant," Drake said. He nodded to the hatch. "Shall we proceed?"

Hadfield opened the hatch, allowing them to enter. Percy felt almost as if he were coming home. A handful of marines were sitting in the common room, either reading from their datapads or watching a movie; a couple waved to Percy, who waved back. Lewis tossed him a sharp look - an unspoken reminder that, for the duration of the mission, he belonged to the troop - as they walked past the room and into Compartment C. Cramped was an understatement, Percy decided. There was barely room for twenty burly men.

"Ah, we've had worse," Lewis said. He probably had. If some of the stories were to be believed, an entire troop of SAS operators had once been stuffed into a tiny tent in hopes of finding protection from the snow. "Get your kit stowed away and we can start exercising - again."

"Percy," Hadfield said. "A word with you."

Percy glanced at Drake, who nodded. "Go."

He followed Hadfield back into the corridor and watched for the hatch to hiss closed. "I heard you'd been reassigned, again," Hadfield said. "Congratulations."

"Thank you, sir," Percy said.

"I've worked with Drake," Hadfield said. "He's a good man to have at your back in a firefight."

He shrugged. "There's something else you should know, though," he added. "Your sister has managed to get herself embedded on this ship."

Percy felt his blood run cold. He knew the mission, at least in general terms. It wasn't hard to fill in the remaining details. In order to reach Clarke III, *Warspite* would have to pass through enemy-held territory, with at least one Indian carrier and innumerable smaller ships on the prowl. If there was a single mistake - or if the Indians got lucky - they might be detected, hunted down and destroyed. He'd accepted the prospect of his own death, but he didn't want to think about the risk of losing *her*.

"Shit," he said. It didn't seem strong enough, somehow. "Where *is* she?"

"She's in lockdown at the moment," Hadfield said. "There are...*details* of the mission that aren't common knowledge, not yet. You can see her once we're underway."

"I will," Percy said. It would be too late to convince Penny to go elsewhere. Even if she *was* allowed to leave the ship, she'd go straight into lockdown on Nelson Base. "I thought she'd want to stay at home after..."

Hadfield cut him off. "Would you want to stay at home after Fort Knight?"

"That's different," Percy said.

"How?" Hadfield asked. "You returned to Earth with us and now you're setting off, back to the war front. Your sister was returned by the Indians; now, Percy, she wants to return to the fray."

"She isn't a soldier," Percy protested.

"But she does have a job to do," Hadfield told him, bluntly. "I think it's a little late to be overprotective."

"I suppose," Percy said. "How much can I tell her?"

"Everything, once we're underway," Hadfield said. "The Captain will make a ship-wide announcement."

Percy smiled. "So who knows and who doesn't?"

"Just stay here and keep your mouth shut," Hadfield advised. "Drake will keep you busy, I think. It's quite a honour to serve with the SAS."

"Yes, sir," Percy said. It was, he knew, although he would have preferred more training before departure. "Would you countersign my application to Selection, when this is over?"

"If you like," Hadfield said. "But you'd better come back alive."

CHAPTER SEVEN

HMS Warspite, Earth Orbit

"I received your final report, Captain," Admiral Fitzwilliam said. He peered out of the viewscreen, his eyes suddenly very hard. "You're ready to depart on schedule?"

"Yes, sir," John said. "The crew has been reassembled, we've crammed our holds with spare parts and weapons, the troopers are onboard and the reporters are locked in their cabin. We can depart in half an hour, as planned."

"Very good," Fitzwilliam said. "You've received the updated Rules of Engagement?"

"Yes, sir," John said. He paused. "Am I to assume that the diplomats are still hoping for a peaceful solution?"

"I think we're way past that point, but the Prime Minister needs to conciliate certain parties in Parliament," Fitzwilliam said. "The Indians will have ample opportunity to withdraw from the occupied systems, Captain. They have already been given the response to their ultimatum."

John nodded. He rarely listened to political speeches, but he'd watched the Prime Minister's address to the nation, knowing that it was *really* aimed at the Indians. They'd been told, in no uncertain terms, to withdraw from Pegasus and Cromwell or be forced out. By now, John was sure, messages would already be heading from Earth to Pegasus, warning the Indian commanders to prepare for war. He'd be surprised if the Indians hadn't taken the possibility of a violent response into account, but stranger things had happened. They might well have believed that Britain would just roll over and take it.

"The current ROE will remain in effect until the task force sets out," Fitzwilliam said. "At that point, we will assume that we have to fight - and take the offensive. Until then, you are to try to avoid contact. But if you are detected, you are authorised to open fire if you feel your ship is in serious danger."

"Good," John said. He wasn't entirely happy with the ROE, but he doubted they would get any better until the task force departed. At least he didn't have to wait for the Indians to open fire before he could fire himself. It wasn't ideal, but it would have to do. "We'll see you when we see you."

"In Hannibal," Fitzwilliam said. "Good luck, Captain."

His image vanished from the display. John took a moment to gather himself - they were going to war - and then rose, walking out of the door and onto the bridge. His crew were already preparing the ship for departure, testing and retesting everything before they left the safety of Earth. The last thing they needed was *another* catastrophic failure in the middle of a war zone. It wasn't a pleasant thought. Once the Indians had finished laughing, they'd blow *Warspite* to atoms.

"Captain," Commander Howard said, rising from the command chair. "You have the bridge."

"I have the bridge," John confirmed. "Status report?"

"All systems are fully functional," Howard reported. "The hatches are closed, the shuttles are stowed away and all crewmen have been accounted for."

John sat down, bracing himself. "Do we have an updated intelligence report from MI5?"

"Yes, sir," Howard said. "But it wasn't conclusive."

"I see," John said.

He sighed, inwardly. It wasn't really a surprise - the Indians would hardly have bothered to fit their spy ships with IFF transmitters that betrayed them - but it was annoying. Had there ever been a war where both sides had *shared* a shipyard? Nelson or Drake - even Woodward - would have reacted with horror to the thought. But the Indians had dozens of facilities orbiting the Earth, easily close enough to Nelson Base to keep an eye on the British deployments. They'd be able to watch from a distance as *Warspite* headed towards the tramline.

We'll just have to evade contact as soon as we enter the Terra Nova System, he thought, grimly. If nothing else, the Indians would have real problems keeping up with *Warspite*. She wasn't the fastest thing in space, but it would be hard for a stealthed ship to follow her without revealing its presence. *Launch a drone towards the first tramline and alter course to the second ourselves.*

He keyed his console. "Engineering?"

"We're ready, Captain," Chief Engineer Mike Johnston reported. He sounded happy; John knew, from Howard, that he'd spent quite a bit of time on Nelson Base. "All systems are online."

"Good," John said. "Helm, power up the drives."

"Aye, sir," Lieutenant Carlos Armstrong said. A dull thrumming echoed through the cruiser as the drives came to life. "No problems, Captain; I say again, no problems. Power curves are normal."

"Set a least-time course for Terra Nova," John ordered. "Tactical?"

"No Indian warships within scanning range," Lieutenant-Commander Tara Rosenberg reported. "There are, however, a number of watching ships from other nations."

John sucked in his breath sharply as the holographic display came to life. The Turks and Brazilians - like the Indians - wanted Great Power status for themselves. They'd be watching with great interest, perhaps even covertly supporting the Indians, as the Royal Navy readied itself for war. And there were no Indian warships near Earth...they'd left their homeland wide open, save for the protection of the Solar Treaty.

And they're right, John thought. *We don't dare break the treaty, even though that frees up more of their warships to hold the territory they seized.*

It was a galling thought. He understood the logic behind it - the human race would need the Indians if the Tadpoles restarted the war - but it was frustrating as hell. No matter what happened, the Indians couldn't be defeated completely. And they could keep producing war material and sending it out to the front, in the certain knowledge that Britain wouldn't dare to try to intercept the convoys while they were in the solar system. The consequences would be incalculable.

We don't even dare risk sending in the Special Forces, he thought. *Who knows where that will end?*

He pushed the thought aside, irritated. "Inform Nelson Base that we are ready to depart," he ordered. "And then disconnect from the station."

"Aye, sir," Lieutenant Gillian Forbes said, briskly. There was a pause as she worked her console. "We are cleared to depart, sir."

John sucked in his breath, feeling a flicker of the old excitement. He was now in sole command of a warship, master of all he surveyed. Even the grim awareness that they were going to war didn't defuse his pleasure at returning to interstellar space. No more boards of inquiry, no more endless debriefings...just a cruise well away from the Admiralty, preventing it from looking over his shoulder.

"Take us out," he ordered, quietly.

He sat back and watched the display as *Warspite* slowly pulled away from Nelson Base, passing a handful of supply ships making their slow way towards Island One. A giant supercarrier - the *Theodore Smith* - hung close to the base, ready and waiting for the task force's departure. Behind it, a dozen frigates and destroyers were hastily preparing themselves for war. He felt a flicker of nostalgia when he saw HMS *Petunia* - an escort carrier of the same class as *Canopus* - taking up position behind *Theodore Smith*. It had been over five years since he'd served on a similar vessel...

"We're clear of orbital space, sir," Armstrong reported.

"No sign of pursuit," Tara added.

"It wouldn't matter, not so close to Earth," John said. The Indians had a communications chain leading all the way to Gandhi. It might be worth arranging for something to happen to that chain before the war began in earnest. "Helm, ramp us up to full military power and take us to the tramline."

"Aye, sir," Armstrong said.

Warspite quivered again as the drives thrust her forward into interplanetary space. John glanced at the display, then hastily keyed out a message for Admiral Fitzwilliam. It was quite likely the Admiral's staff had already considered the possibilities - he could see why they might want the chain to remain intact - but it was well to be sure. He finished the message and turned his attention to the display, watching the hundreds of freighters buzzing to and from the tramlines. How many of them were carrying military-grade sensors, monitoring *Warspite's* movements for the Indians?

He scowled at the thought. The First Interstellar War had taught humanity the danger of placing all its eggs in one basket. Every spacefaring nation was working desperately to build up its out-system colonies, including Britain. John had even been tempted by some of the settlement grants on Britannia or Nova Scotia, although he wouldn't leave the Royal Navy unless someone dragged him out with wild elephants. The only way to secure humanity's place in the universe was through settlement and maintaining a powerful military machine, both of which were being risked by the confrontation. In hindsight, if the Indians had claimed Great Power status at the end of the war, they might well have got what they wanted without a fight.

But if the key to being a Great Power is being so strong that no one can stop you without being destroyed themselves, he thought, *the Indians wouldn't need acknowledgement to make them a Great Power. They'd have everything they needed themselves.*

The minutes ticked by slowly. John kept a close eye on the status display, hoping that any problems would reveal themselves before they jumped through the tramline. But nothing happened as the tramline grew closer, a handful of starships flickering into existence ahead of *Warspite* as they returned from colony missions. It was quite likely that some of them were Indian...

"Ready a drone," he ordered, coolly. "It is to be launched the moment we pass through the tramline on an evasive course to Tramline B."

"Aye, Captain," Tara said.

"We will go into stealth mode and make our way to Tramline E," John added. "Our change in course should not be noticeable."

Unless there's something sitting far too close to the tramline, he thought. It was paranoia, but being paranoid was the smart option when a war was underway. *The Indians might have a watcher lying doggo.*

Howard glanced at him. "Tramline E?"

"Yes, Commander," John said. "Tramline E."

He cursed the security games under his breath as the tramline grew closer. If Howard hadn't already pieced together the true nature of their mission, he'd be able to do it now. Commander Howard was his XO, his strong right arm - and his designated successor. Keeping information from him was dangerous when he might have to assume command of *Warspite* if something happened to John. Who knew? Howard might take the ship to *Britannia* on the assumption that those were the *actual* orders. It wouldn't be the first time security regulations keeping officers in the dark had caused serious problems.

It was a great deal easier, he reflected morbidly, *when we didn't have to worry about human spies.*

"Captain," Armstrong said. "We're approaching the tramline."

"Drone ready," Tara added.

"Take us through," John ordered.

He braced himself for the brief moment of disorientation as the starship hopped through the tramline, vanishing from the Sol System and reappearing in the Terra Nova System. The display blanked out for a long chilling moment before rebooting, displaying the local star and countless energy signatures from semi-rogue mining operations and a dozen quasi-legal settlements. It definitely *looked* as though the activity was starting to taper off a little, but it would be a long time before the system was under a single government. Terra Nova's strongest export remained people in search of a more peaceful life.

"Local space is clear," Tara reported.

It proved nothing, John knew. A starship with her drives and active sensors shut down would be completely undetectable, except at very close range. The Indians *could* have a watchdog spying on the tramline...but they'd have to know, in advance, the precise coordinate where *Warspite* would materialise. It wasn't impossible, he knew. Just merely very unlikely.

"Launch the drone," he ordered. "Take us into stealth mode...*now*."

"Aye, sir," Tara said. There was a long pause. "The drone is on its way to Tramline B."

John nodded, once. The beancounters would make a fuss - they never let a war get in the way of keeping costs as low as they could - but it didn't matter. All that mattered was the simple fact that anyone watching *Warspite* from a distance would track the drone on its course to Tramline B, where it would deactivate itself. They'd think that *Warspite* had left the system, rather than altering course to head to Tramline E. If everything went according to plan, the Indians would never know that *Warspite* was on her way to Pegasus.

"Set course for Tramline E," he ordered.

"Aye, sir," Armstrong said. "Course laid in."

"Engage," John ordered.

He smiled to himself. Armstrong would, of course, have plotted out the course as soon as John had mentioned where they'd be going, then stored it in his console until the time came to bring it out. It was a common technique. *Warspite* thrummed again as she picked up speed, thrusting away from the tramline before anything else could come through and detect their presence. He sat back in his command chair and forced himself to wait, keeping a sharp eye on the passive sensors. If anyone *was* close enough to watch them without being detected, they'd have to reveal themselves now or lose track of *Warspite*.

"Commander Howard," he said. "You have the bridge."

"Aye, sir," Howard said. "I have the bridge."

John nodded, stepped into his office and opened the secure drawer. The sealed orders were where he'd left them; he plugged the datachip into his terminal, waited for the verification program to confirm that they had left Earth far behind and then sat down to read through the orders as soon as they were unlocked and displayed. They were nothing more than a more detailed version of Admiral Fitzwilliam's verbal instructions, he was relieved to note. It wouldn't be the first time sealed orders had differed markedly from whatever the recipient had been told beforehand.

He uploaded the orders onto the datanet, rose and walked back onto the bridge. Howard rose to his feet; John sat back down, motioned for Howard to read the orders quickly, then keyed his console. It was time to inform the crew.

"All hands, this is the Captain," he said. Everyone would hear him, from the reporters to the SAS troopers in Marine Country. "As some of you will have surmised, we are *not* heading for Britannia. Our orders, instead, are to make our way to enemy-held territory and conduct a full tactical survey of their positions. This is, of course, a somewhat more challenging mission than you may have expected."

He smiled at the thought before continuing. "We will proceed immediately up the tramlines to Pegasus and commence our mission," he said. "As it is imperative that we remain undetected, we will remain in stealth mode from this moment on. We will *not* be opening communications links to anyone until we rendezvous with the remainder of the task force after completing this mission. They are *depending* on us to succeed.

"This is not our first operation where we had to sneak through enemy territory, but it will be the most difficult," he added. "And yet, we have the experience to make it work. The Indians will not even catch a *sniff* of us before we return to the task force. I have faith in our ship - and in each and every one of you. We will complete our mission and lay the groundwork for recovering our territory."

He keyed his console again, closing the channel. "Commander Howard," he said. "You have read the orders?"

"Yes, sir," Howard said. He didn't sound very surprised. "I will make a note of it in my log."

"Thank you," John said. He had to fight down the urge to ask just how much his XO had guessed before the sealed orders were revealed. Howard was smart; he'd probably guessed the truth long before the SAS had arrived. "Note also that the sealed orders were not disclosed ahead of time."

"Aye, sir," Howard said.

John settled back in his command chair and forced himself to relax, as completely as he could. It would take a fortnight, at the best speed they could manage while remaining in stealth mode, to reach Pegasus. The Indians might have pickets watching for them, he knew; if he was in command of their fleet, he would have placed at least one watching scout in J-34, one jump from Pegasus. An enemy ship advancing from Earth, thanks to the tramlines, would *have* to pass through that system. There was simply no way to avoid it.

But we're very tiny and space is very big, he reminded himself. *They won't be able to spot us unless we get unlucky - or careless.*

"Inform the crew that one deck is to be put aside for the SAS, once they start training," he ordered, curtly. The presence of the SAS had been meant to be secret, although he suspected some of his crewmen had probably guessed who they were. "And make sure it's completely sealed off."

"Aye, sir," Howard said.

"We'll discuss other aspects of the mission tonight," John said. He'd have to meet with the reporters at least once, even though he would have preferred to avoid it. "But it can wait for the moment."

He took one final look at the display, then forced himself to think about the future. The voyage would be the easy part. Hell, it would be boring once they slipped out of settled systems and away from watching eyes. But once they reached Pegasus, the real fun would begin...

...And if the Indians were on the prowl, he knew, getting close enough to deploy the stealth shuttle would be far from easy.

CHAPTER EIGHT

HMS Warspite, In Transit

"There's someone at the door," Stevenson called. They'd been told they could leave their cabin, once the starship had left Earth, but he'd spent most of his time just lying on the sofa. "He wants to see you."

"Oh," Penny said. She stood and peered out of the cabin. "*Percy*?"

"Penny," Percy said. He didn't sound pleased. "Can we talk?"

Penny nodded, slowly. She had known he'd been assigned to *Warspite* for her first cruise, but she hadn't realised that he'd be returned to the ship after the disaster on Vesy. Meeting him was a shock...she hesitated, wondering if they could use the bedroom, then walked out of the cabin. Percy would have to know somewhere they could go for a private chat.

"I suppose we can," she said. "Do you know anywhere private?"

Percy nodded and led her through a maze of corridors into the observation blister. It was empty, thankfully; she ran forward and pressed her face against the transparent material, staring out into the vastness of interstellar space. Countless stars burned steadily in the darkness, their unblinking gazes calling to her. She knew, intellectually, that *Warspite* was making her way through space at unimaginable speeds, but it looked very much as though they were standing still. The stars didn't seem to be moving at all.

"I was surprised to see you," she confessed, once the hatch was firmly closed. "Did you *know* you'd be returning to *Warspite*?"

"I was surprised to see *you*," Percy said, gruffly. "What are you doing here?"

"My job," Penny snapped. There were times when having an overprotective brother came in handy, but this wasn't one of them. "Witnessing living history and sending reports back home."

"So the enemy can read them with great interest," Percy sneered. He had never really approved of her career choice. "Are you sure you won't accidentally betray us?"

"Everything I write has to pass through the censors," Penny snapped back. "It's not my fault if they miss something that might help the Indians!"

"They'll probably overlook *tons* of useful information," Percy muttered. "I doubt they know which end of a rifle fires the bullets."

"I'm sure the Indians do," Penny said. "Unless you're expecting them to commit suicide when you land on Clarke."

Percy tensed, slightly. It would have been unnoticeable if she hadn't known him so well.

"I'm expecting hard fighting," he said, finally. Was he *planning* to land on Clarke? She didn't like the thought, but it was his job. "You could get yourself killed out here."

"*You* could get yourself killed out here," Penny said. She crossed her arms under her breasts, scowling at him. "This isn't a refugee camp, Percy, and I'm not a teenager any longer."

"Thanks be to God," Percy said. "You were hellish as a teenager."

Penny smirked. "I could tell Canella all sorts of stories about *your* teenage years..."

Percy's expression darkened. "She broke up with me."

"I'm sorry to hear that," Penny said, sincerely. She'd only met Canella once, but she'd liked the girl. "Did the deployments get to her?"

"Yeah," Percy said. "I think she must have had second thoughts from the moment I said goodbye to her. Being on a starship is a far cry from serving on the other side of the world."

Penny nodded in agreement. It only took seven hours to travel from one side of the world to the other - or it had, before the war. The hypersonic jets that had once bound Earth together had largely been grounded, all services cancelled as the human race struggled to survive and rebuild. Percy could have returned to Edinburgh every couple of months when he went on leave, if he wished; it was a great deal harder to travel between Earth and Vesy. Canella hadn't seen him for over a year.

"Well, I'm sure you will find someone else," she said, briskly. "Are there any young women on the ship you might like?"

"If I have time," Percy said. "Do you know how hard it was to get a chance to come see you?"

Penny gave him a sharp look. "No," she said. "What are you doing?"

"Training," Percy said. He held up one hand. "And it's classified, so please don't ask about it."

"I won't," Penny said. She had a feeling that she was right, that Percy was going to land on Clarke, but she kept that thought to herself. "It's good to see you again, even if it is...*here*."

"I suppose," Percy said. "I'd be happier if you were safer, Pen-Pen."

Penny felt her cheeks heat. "I'm not a child any longer, Percy," she said. "And is there *anywhere* safe these days?"

It wasn't a pleasant thought. They'd grown up in a safe environment; their father hadn't been wealthy, but he'd earned enough to give the family a security blanket and ensure that his children received a good education. And then their father had gone off to war, their mother had vanished during the bombardment and they'd had to flee the onrushing waters in hopes of finding a safe place to rest. She'd gone back to their home town later, after the area had been declared safe, only to discover that their home had been looted. Everything they'd owned had been either stolen or destroyed by the waves.

They'd been lucky, she knew. Admiral Fitzwilliam had taken them in, after the war; they'd had a measure of safety that few others had enjoyed. And yet, there had been no guarantees of anything. They'd worked in the Reclamation Corps before Percy had gone into the Royal Marines and she'd found work as a reporter, but it could easily have been worse. She'd seen the bodies recovered from the waters and known she could have died there too.

"I suppose there isn't," Percy said. "But a war zone is even less safe than anywhere else."

Penny rolled her eyes. "Like I said, I'm not a child any longer," she said. "I knew the job was dangerous when I signed up for it."

She cleared her throat. "So...do you have your eye on anyone?"

"Not yet," Percy said. "Who's the milksop in your cabin?"

"A fellow reporter," Penny said. "He gets the sofa, I get the bed."

"What a fair division of labour," Percy murmured. "So...not a boyfriend then?"

"No," Penny said. "I'm still writing to Hamish, but..."

"A Para," Percy said, with mock horror. "You're dating a Para. I'll never be able to hold my head up in public again."

Penny stuck out her tongue. "Does it really matter who I date?"

"I just don't want you hurt," Percy said. He sighed. "Our parents had problems because dad was away, fighting the war."

"I know," Penny said. She had no idea if Percy knew - she was damned if she was going to tell him, if he didn't - but she was sure their mother had been having an affair. And their father too, perhaps. "I'm only writing to him, Percy. There's no guarantee of *anything*."

"I suppose not," Percy said. "3 Para was earmarked for deployment, the last I heard, but they're currently reforming after Vesy. They may wind up being held back while 2 Para joined the task force."

"His last message wasn't too clear," Penny said. "I had to tell him that I'd been accepted as an embed and that I wouldn't be able to email him for a while."

"I have no idea what he'll make of that," Percy said. "Some of the lads I served with were married. They liked the thought of coming home to a wife and kids."

"I suppose it would have its charms," Penny said. "Does it always work out?"

"We're encouraged not to marry until we've completed our first deployments," Percy said, softly. "It can play merry hell with marriages."

Penny gave him a sharp look. "How would you know about that, Percy?"

"It's one of the things we're told in training," Percy said. "Being a marine means that your life no longer belongs to you. Your service to the company comes first."

He glanced at his watch. "There isn't much time left," he admitted. "I'll try to see you again before the shit hits the fan."

"It can't be worse than Vesy," Penny said. She'd come far too close to death on the alien homeworld. She still had nightmares, sometimes, about alien mobs closing in on her. "Can it?"

"I hope not," Percy said. He shrugged. "How did the Indians treat you?"

"They were decent enough," Penny said. "Once they had us, they tended to our wounds - those of us who were wounded - and then shipped us back to Earth. I was half-hoping they'd give me a chance to embed with their forces, but they evidently thought better of it."

"They'd have turned you into a propaganda mouthpiece," Percy said. "You wouldn't have been able to hold your head up in public again."

"I imagine it would have been embarrassing," Penny agreed, dryly. "The Admiral would not have been pleased."

She sighed. "Did you have a chance to talk to him?"

"Not properly," Percy said. "I only saw him at a couple of debriefings, where he listened without speaking. There was no chance for a private chat."

Penny winced. The Admiral was, perhaps, the only person they knew who could tell them how their father had died, but he'd refused to be drawn on the subject. She'd researched it as best as she could, yet no matter what she did she kept running into stone walls. There was a great deal of information in the public domain about the final flight of *Ark Royal*, but it only made it clearer just how much had been hidden. How and why had their father died?

If he'd died in the final battle, he would have been memorialised as such, she thought. There had to be *some* mystery surrounding his death. An accident - or a suicide - wouldn't have been covered up. *Did he die on the Old Lady herself?*

"I haven't seen him for years," she said. "I actually turned down an invitation to the Christmas Ball because I was busy."

"Go interview him," Percy suggested. "You're a reporter, aren't you? I'm sure he'll be delighted to give you a proper interview."

"I doubt it," Penny said. Apart from the PR officers, who could talk for hours on end about nothing at all, she had yet to meet a naval officer who was glad to see a reporter. Percy probably didn't count. "What would you say if I tried to interview *you*?"

Percy smirked. "Just remember to describe me as a handsome, strong, clever, sophisticated, cunning, smart, snarky, alpha male..."

"Oh, piss off and eat a dictionary," Penny said. She struck a writing pose. "Corporal Percy is a smug conceited git..."

"Lieutenant," Percy said. "I'm a Lieutenant now."

"I notice you didn't deny the rest of it," Penny said. She smirked at his expression, then sobered. "I don't think the Admiral would be too pleased to get an interview request from me - I'd either have to be tough, which would irritate him, or soft-pedal. And *that* would be held against me later."

Percy frowned. "It would?"

"He's our guardian," Penny reminded him, sarcastically. "All right, we're both adults now, but we haven't broken the connection. People will expect me not to be too hard on him."

"So they'll assume the worst," Percy mused. "That could be a problem."

"Yeah," Penny agreed. "It could."

She shook her head. "I think we should probably ask him after the war," she added. "But if it's been classified, Percy, it may have been classified for a reason."

"I know," Percy said. "But I still want to know."

He glanced at his watch again. "It's time to go back to training," he said. He swept her into a brief hug. "I love you, little sister."

"I'm not that little," Penny said, hugging him back. "Good luck with your training."

Percy's face darkened. "I'll need it."

Penny watched him go before turning to look back out at the stars. Their father's body was lost somewhere in the darkness, she knew; it had certainly never been recovered and shipped home to Earth. That was true of most of the crewmen who'd died on *Ark Royal*, but she'd tracked down as many death reports as she could and they'd all been listed as going down with the ancient carrier. Hell, most of the starfighter pilots had died there too. There was simply no reason to assume their father *hadn't* died there, save for the simple fact that he *hadn't* been included on a list of the dead...

And for the fact that Rose Labara and Prince Henry were listed as commanders of the starfighter squadrons, she thought. *That should have been dad's job...which suggests, very strongly, that dad died before the final battle.*

She shook her head in irritation and turned to walk out of the hatch. A pair of crewmen nodded politely to her as she left, manhandling another cart crammed with supplies down the corridor towards the tactical compartment. Penny briefly considered trying to ask them a few questions, but knew it would probably get her in trouble. Instead, she kept walking until she was standing at the hatch leading into the mess. A handful of crewmen were sitting at tables, hastily eating as much as they could before going on duty or returning to their quarters to sleep.

"Hey," the cook called. "You come to eat something nice?"

Penny smiled. The cook had been happy to chat with her during the first deployment, joking that he'd undertaken the hardest training course in the Royal Navy. He hadn't passed, of course; apparently, *no one* passed the catering course. Penny had to admit the food wasn't five-star, but it was filling and there was plenty of it. No wonder the cook was overweight...

But then, she thought as she walked over to join him, *who'd trust a skinny cook*?

"I could do with it," she agreed. "What do you have?"

The cook smiled. "Suspicious sausages, questionable potatoes, portable human-methane converters...or fruit and vegetables, if you feel like being picky."

Penny had to smile. "Do we have any fresh fruit?"

"Yeah, but not for long," the cook said. "Better get your fair share before it's all gone."

"Give me some sausages, chips and beans," Penny said. She'd have to work it off later, but thankfully they had free access to the exercise compartment. "Do you have a few moments to chat?"

"Only off the record," the cook boomed. He picked up a pair of sausages and dropped them onto a plate, then added the chips and a healthy serving of beans. "Unless you want to gripe about the food. There's no way we can serve fresh food throughout the voyage."

Penny nodded as she took her plate. "I have travelled in space before," she said. She didn't like to think about where the reprocessed food came from - no one did - but it was just something that had to be endured. "As long as the supply of hot sauce holds out, we should be fine."

"Ah, we lost a bottle last night," the cook said. "One of those new guys from Marine Country came in, pinched a bottle and downed it like cheap beer, right in front of us. His poor girlfriend!"

"He actually managed to drink a whole bottle?" Penny asked. She'd tasted navy-issue hot sauce in the past, during her first cruise. It probably violated international laws against chemical weapons just by existing. *She* had certainly not been able to tolerate more than a drop or two at a time. "Why?"

"Ah, some stupid contest between them and the marines, I imagine," the cook said. "We had a bunch of Paras on *Hamilton* and they spent half their time trying to one-up the marines."

Penny considered it as she tucked into her food. A new group of soldiers? They couldn't be marines...which meant *what*? If they were Paras, Percy would probably have mentioned them when she'd talked about Hamish. And that meant they had to be Special Forces.

"I'm sure you have at least a hundred more bottles," she said, finally. "Or did they take them back to their lair to drink too?"

"I hope not," the cook said. "It's bad enough catching crewmen who are trying to raid the galley."

He grinned. "But enough about them," he said. "How are *you* feeling about going to war?"

"I was on Vesy," Penny said, automatically.

"This will be different," the cook said. He made a show of stirring the beans. "The Indians will be shooting at us, if they catch wind of our presence. Perhaps serving beans was a bad idea."

"I'm torn between excitement and fear," Penny admitted. It wasn't something she'd want to admit to Percy. *He'd* just point out that she could have stayed on Earth. "Is it always that way?"

"I was an assistant cook during the first war," the cook said. He slapped his belly meaningfully. "I didn't actually fight; I just kept the fighters fed and watered. And I learned there was no point in stressing out, even in the middle of a war zone. If a missile has our name on it, we're dead; if it doesn't, we'll live to see another day. That's all that's important."

"Very profound," Penny said.

"We can't all be starship commanders or starfighter jocks," the cook said. "Some of us merely keep the rest of the crew alive. We just do our duty and leave the rest in God's hands."

"True," Penny agreed. She finished her meal. "And thank you for the food."

"I must have done something wrong," the cook muttered. He eyed the plate suspiciously. "You're the first person who actually thanked me."

Penny laughed and left the compartment.

CHAPTER NINE

Nelson Base, Earth Orbit

"That's the latest report, Admiral," Commander Sally Acorn said. "Captain Tracy states that HMS *Lillian* should be ready for departure along with the rest of the task force."

"I trust you inspected the report carefully," James said. "*Lillian* was in the repair yards last week, wasn't she?"

"Yes, sir," Sally said. "However, it was only routine maintenance and she *has* been cleared for active service. The only downside is that some of her crew were drawn from the reserves and need time to work up for duty."

"Then add her to the fleet list and make sure she's slotted into the training schedule," James said, after a moment. He understood Captain Tracy wanting to get into the fight; James would just have to hope that Captain Tracy hadn't been so determined to be involved that he'd creatively edited his readiness report when the CVE left the yards. "Give him copies of the security codes and inform him that I'll expect him to attend the final briefing before departure."

"Yes, sir," Sally said. She cleared her throat. "Mr. Oswald requested an appointment to speak with you, later in the day."

"Joy," James said. "Inform him that I will see him" - he glanced at his schedule - "at 1500 precisely, on Nelson Base. I can't afford to take time off to go to London or Luna Nine right now."

"I'll see to it," Sally said. James didn't envy her. The intelligence services - MI5 and MI6 - tended to be pushy. "There was also an update from the Foreign Office. The Americans will be dispatching another carrier to the border, allowing us to pull one back to reinforce the task force."

"Good," James grunted. It would be at least two months before the carrier arrived, but by then he had a feeling he'd welcome the reinforcements. "Is there anything else?"

"Not at the moment, sir," Sally said.

She saluted and withdrew, leaving James alone. He shook his head tiredly; civilians might expect spacers to study tactics, but the blunt truth was that he spent most of his time studying logistics. The old saying still held true, even in the twenty-third century; there was no point in coming up with cunning battle plans if one couldn't get the ships out and support them. It had seemed so much easier when he'd served on *Ark Royal.*

And it was still a pain keeping the task force supplied, he thought, ruefully. *We had real problems during Operation Nelson.*

He pushed the thought aside as he checked the latest set of updates. The task force was taking shape, the ships slowly assembling in orbit near Nelson Base. He'd considered various ways to try to hide a ship or two, but he rather doubted they could prevent the Indians from making some very good guesses about the task force's size and composition. Beyond the warships, a dozen freighters waited, crammed with the supplies they'd need to fight the war. Losing them, in some ways, would be just as bad as losing the carrier.

But if we do lose the carrier, we lose the ability to take the offensive, he thought, sourly. *The Indians will know that as well as we do.*

It was a galling thought. Seven years ago - when aliens were nothing more than a figment of human imagination - the Indians wouldn't have had a chance. The Royal Navy could have squashed their entire military in a single battle and that would be that. But now, between the losses caused by the war and the advancements in military technology, the odds would be far more even. The Indians, if they took out the carrier, might win by default.

Five years from now, we'll have a whole fleet of modern carriers, he thought. *They picked their time very well.*

His intercom buzzed. "Admiral," Sally said. "Admiral Soskice has arrived. He's requesting an immediate meeting."

Tell him to go away, James thought. He wasn't sure he *wanted* to speak to Admiral Soskice, not now. *Tell him to make an appointment...*

He pushed temptation aside. "Send him in," he said. He had at least half an hour before the next scheduled meeting, unless something came up beforehand. "I'll speak to him now."

The hatch opened, revealing Admiral Soskice. James had always cordially disliked him - Admiral Soskice had never commanded a ship at war, which made all of his experience theoretical at best - and they'd been rivals over the past two years. Soskice's position as head of the Next Generation Weapons program had given him a yen for developing new technology and pushing it into active service, often before it had been properly tested. James would be the first to admit that *some* of Soskice's ideas had worked well - the starfighter-mounted plasma cannons, for example - but others had been asking for trouble.

"Admiral," Soskice said. With his balding dome and unshaven face, he didn't even manage to *look* like a naval officer. James couldn't help thinking of him as an academic who was somewhat out of his depth. The horn-rimmed spectacles only added to that impression. "Thank you for seeing me."

"I wasn't aware you had an appointment," James said, dryly. "Doubtless my aide made a terrible mistake."

"You're going to be in command of the task force," Soskice said, sitting down without being invited. "Do you intend to fight a conventional war?"

"I believe we have little choice," James said. "This isn't a war against an alien foe."

"The balance of technology has shifted," Soskice said. "You know that as well as I do."

"It has changed," James conceded, reluctantly. He'd been a mere commander when the Tadpoles had obliterated a multinational naval force - including two British carriers - at New Russia, but he still remembered the shock that had run through the entire navy. It had been the most one-sided battle since kinetic weapons had been dropped on Argentina during the Third Falklands War. "But the essentials remain the same."

"The Indians have been learning from our troubles," Soskice pointed out. "Their carriers are armoured with modern plating..."

"So is the *Teddy*," James countered.

"And their fleet mix isn't so dependent on starfighters," Soskice added, ignoring the interruption. "You know as well as I do, James, that starfighters are no longer the queens of the battlefield."

"That's debatable," James said.

"We've run countless simulations that prove it beyond all doubt," Soskice snapped. It was an old argument, one they'd had many times before. "You know that as well as I do."

James felt his temper flare. Somehow, he put firm controls on it.

"*You* know as well as *I* do that those simulations depend on what assumptions are programmed into the machines," he said. "Your assumptions are always hopelessly pessimistic."

"And yours are hopelessly optimistic," Soskice said. "Are you truly that wedded to the concept of the carrier and her flocks of starfighters?"

"I'm a carrier officer," James said, curtly.

He glanced at the picture he'd hung on the bulkhead - *Ark Royal's* command crew on the eve of her departure for Alien-Prime - and felt a stab of guilt. He'd tried to ease Commodore Smith out of his command in the hopes it would allow James to claim to have commanded a carrier at a very early age. Perhaps it would have worked, too, if Smith hadn't cleaned up his act. There were moments when James wanted to go back in time and punch his younger self in the nose.

"The carrier is a dying breed," Soskice said. "There are limits to how much we can protect them against the new developments in weaponry."

"Defensive technology has also advanced," James pointed out.

"And starfighters themselves are easy targets for plasma cannons," Soskice said. "Their aim may not be perfect, but they can pump out a hell of a lot of fire. The Indians have *crammed* their ships with plasma cannons."

"So have we," James snapped.

"But they're the ones on the defensive," Soskice said. "They have other advantages too."

James looked him in the eye. "Do you have a wonder weapon that will blow the enemy ships out of space with the push of a button?"

"No," Soskice said. "The closest we have to it is the heavy plasma cannon."

"Which you mounted on *Warspite*," James said. He had to admit that it had proved its value, but only against a target that hadn't been expecting it. "We may be able to use it against one of the Indian ships."

Soskice tapped his knee, impatiently. "James, the blunt truth is that the pre-war fleet mix is no longer suitable," he said. "We had a number of massive carriers and hundreds of tiny frigates and destroyers. Now...we need to start work on middling ships."

It was, James knew, an old problem. The Royal Navy *needed* carriers to serve as command ships and starfighter platforms, but the huge carriers were extremely big targets. Smaller ships - the frigates - were tiny, small enough that they could be built in vast numbers without breaking the budget. But they too had relied on the carriers for logistics support. Now, with the war exposing weaknesses in humanity's concepts, there was a need for a whole new class of mid-sized ships, starships that combined the range of a carrier with the mobility of a frigate.

Warspite did well, he thought, as much as he hated to concede anything to Soskice. *But it's dangerous to build a whole new fleet without testing the concepts thoroughly first.*

"Right now, we are going to war," he said, instead. "And we're going to war with the ships we have on hand. There's no way to avoid it. The Indians aren't going to let us wait for five years, or ten, or however long it takes to put a whole new fleet mix together."

"True," Soskice said.

"*Warspite* is currently on a mission," James said. "Do you have anything else we can use *now*?"

"We've been updating the penetrator heads on missile warheads," Soskice said. "One of them produces a very weak EMP. It's useless against starships, of course, because they're always hardened, but it may cause the plasma containment fields to overload."

"Useful," James said. They'd killed a number of Tadpole starfighters that way. "Does it actually work in the field?"

"It hasn't been tested," Soskice said. "But the lab reports are very promising."

"They always are," James said.

He'd wondered why Uncle Winchester had taken early retirement, right up until the time he'd spent a year in the Ministry of Defence, London. *Every* corporation that produced weapons and technology for the military was determined - very determined - to convince the MOD to buy its products. A fat military contract could be worth billions of pounds over the next few years. Naturally, the salesmen went all-out to convince the MOD that the latest gadget would utterly revolutionise the face of war.

And they're mostly wrong, he thought. *And when we say no, they start whining to the Members of Parliament.*

"We can take a handful along and give them a try," he said. The Indians would know the dangers - it wasn't as if the use of EMP in war was a secret - but it was worth adding a couple to the missile load. "Anything else?"

"Modified drive field launchers," Soskice said. "And improved ECM for missile warheads."

"It's the drive fields that are the real problem," James pointed out.

"That's something we're working on," Soskice said. "We're actually looking at plans for a battleship, rather than a carrier."

James's eyes narrowed. "Wouldn't that have all the disadvantages of a carrier with none of the advantages?"

"No, because we could scale up the drives," Soskice said. "Given the latest improvements in power and weapons technology, we could also rig the ship with solid armour and heavy energy weapons. It would be on a very different scale to anything we currently have."

"I'd like to see the plans," James said. "But for the moment, we won't be able to deploy it against the Indians."

"It isn't anything more than a concept," Soskice admitted. "The real question, of course, is just how far the *Indians* have advanced."

James sighed. There were several different intelligence assessments of just how far the Indians had advanced, all of which came to radically different conclusions. One had asserted that the Indians simply didn't have anything more advanced than the pre-war Royal Navy; another had claimed that the Indian Navy was composed entirely of modern ships and had the firepower to even the odds against the British. James was inclined to believe the truth lay somewhere between the two, but where? He knew the Indians had at least one modern carrier, and presumably a number of smaller modern ships, yet just how capable *was* it?

They never trained with us, after the war came to an end, he thought. *Their government must have been plotting the war as soon as they realised we were gravely weakened; they wouldn't have wanted to give us any insight into their capabilities.*

"There's no way to know until we actually engage them," James said. He rather doubted the Indians would withdraw, even though they had to know the task force was gearing up for war. Instead, MI6 reported that they were working on shoring up their diplomatic position and preparing to hold the territory they'd stolen. "Unless you have any insights...?"

"They will be looking for a silver bullet themselves," Soskice noted. "I expect they'll have poured more resources than us into finding ways to counter starfighters."

"But you don't know," James said. He cursed the simulations under his breath. Was it not possible, really, to hold a simulation without politics becoming involved? War games made more sense...but then, there *had* been war games in the past when the winning party was known in advance. "No one knows."

"Of course not," Soskice said. "But we have to assume the worst."

"And try not to fall into the *Superiority* trap at the same time," James said. "They *did* make you read it, didn't they?"

"The people in the story were idiots," Soskice said. He leaned forward as he spoke. "They *already* held the whip hand when they started fiddling with their weapons mix and coming up with new ideas. The story makes it clear that their victory was just a matter of time."

"True, I suppose," James said. "One could make the same argument about the First World War, Admiral. It doesn't mean that sending wave after wave of men across No Man's Land to be mowed down by machine guns was particularly bright."

"*We* are not in that situation," Soskice continued, ignoring the comment. "You served during the war, Admiral. The Tadpoles held the whip hand and we would have been defeated, *easily*, if we hadn't kept an ancient carrier in service. They had more advanced weapons, more advanced ships and knew us far too well. We knew nothing about them until we recovered bodies and a semi-intact ship during the war."

"I was there," James snapped.

"That's my point," Soskice said. "We *cannot* afford to stop pushing the edges and researching newer weapons, because we *cannot* rest on our laurels. The Tadpoles will advance further now, as will the smaller human powers. We simply do not have enough of a margin of superiority - no margin at all - to relax. Pushing the edges is our only hope of remaining in the lead."

"You assume there *will* be future developments," James said.

"From a modern-day perspective, *Superiority* is laughable," Soskice pointed out. "They build a colossal tactical computer so large they have to carry it in a giant space liner. *We* can produce something with far more computing power easily, something so small it can sit on your desktop. Clarke simply couldn't imagine some of the developments that took place during his lifetime. *We* didn't master the use of plasma weapons until the Tadpoles showed us the way."

James scowled at him. "The *principle* remains unchanged."

Soskice shrugged. "Yes, there *will* be new developments," he said. "And yes, some of them will not be as useful as we might hope, at least on first blush. But we have to be ready to take advantage of them. Or the Indians will do it instead."

"We don't have time," James said. "And we are reluctant to give up the weapons mix we *know* works in exchange for something we don't trust."

"The Indians have every incentive to innovate," Soskice said. "It's not easy to predict the future, James, but I ran a set of simulations."

"Psychohistory was discredited a long time ago," James said.

"With good reason," Soskice said. "It could not predict the Tadpoles, for example, or the slow avalanche of changes caused by unpredictable human decisions. But you can predict *some* things reasonably well. Assuming there isn't a second war, or a series of natural disasters, our productive capability will continue to rise sharply. The Indians simply don't have the groundwork to match us. In ten years, we'll be well ahead of them."

"Good," James said.

"But that doesn't take into account new developments," Soskice added. "What if the Indians develop something *new*? Like I said, they have every reason to innovate."

"Which would be inherently unpredictable," James said. "We have to deal with things as they are."

He shook his head. "I understand your concerns, Admiral, but I have a great deal of work to do," he said. "My next appointment is due at any minute."

"This is a serious matter," Soskice said.

"I know," James said. He *did* understand Soskice's position. Hell, he even *agreed* with it to some extent. "But there's no way to improve our weapons within the week, is there? We have to challenge the Indian positions with what we have on hand, not what we'd like to have. The future will have to take care of itself."

CHAPTER TEN

Clarke III, Pegasus System

"General," his aide said. "A courier boat just jumped into the system and made contact. There is a secure message for you."

General Anjeet Patel nodded, shortly. "Have it relayed to my office," he said. "I'll decrypt it there."

He stood, taking the opportunity to look around the CIC. INS *Viraat* was the most modern carrier in the navy - perhaps the most modern carrier in the human sphere - but it was the first time she'd gone into a war zone. Her crew had never been truly tested, despite endless exercises; it galled him, sometimes, that the Indian Navy hadn't been a big player in the First Interstellar War. The British, whatever else could be said about them, had amassed a staggering number of experienced officers to command their ships.

And the British had plenty of time to rebuild their starfighter arm, he thought, as he stepped through the secure hatch into his office. *Viraat* had more than enough space for his staff, as well as the two thousand officers and men who made up the crew. *They'll have learned a great deal from the war.*

He closed the hatch behind him and strode over to the table. The message was already blinking up on the terminal; he pressed his hand against the scanner, allowing it to read his ID implant, as he sat down on the chair. A steward appeared from the side hatch, offering coffee; Anjeet shook his head firmly and dismissed the steward as the message finished decrypting itself. It should be secure, he told himself, but there was no way to be sure. If there was one form of international warfare that had never abated, even during the Age of Unrest, it was the endless contest between intelligence agencies. The British would have been trying to crack India's codes long before they knew there would be war.

The Prime Minister's face popped up in front of him, looking grim. "General," he said, without preamble. "The British have flatly refused to accept our terms. They will not recognise our conquests and will not consider our other demands until we withdraw from the occupied star systems. There is, in short, no reason to assume they will concede some points in exchange for our submission."

Of course not, Anjeet thought, wryly. *If we backed down, they'd take it as a sign of weakness.*

"Instead, the British are assembling a task force to recapture the occupied systems," the Prime Minister continued. "Details are attached; intelligence believes there will be at least one fleet carrier, two escort carriers and at least a dozen smaller ships. The British have been quite successful in concealing precisely *which* ships have been assigned to where; we believe there will be several more ships added to the task force, but we don't know for sure. There will be talks and more talks, no doubt, none of which will get anywhere. There are no reasonable grounds for compromise.

"Accordingly, you are ordered to move to phase two. Defend the occupied territories; prevent, if possible, the British from gaining a foothold in either Pegasus or Cromwell. The ROE have been updated, allowing you to fire first if you believe the British threaten your positions. However, we do *not* want any atrocities. The war is to be conducted in as civilised a manner as possible."

Anjeet nodded, curtly. *He* had no interest in any atrocities either.

"I don't think I have to remind you that the world is watching like an elderly relative who *knows* you did something rude, even if she isn't quite sure," the Prime Minister warned. "Do everything you can to protect the British civilians; keep the POWs separate, if you don't want to spare the shipping to return them home, and treat them in line with the standard conventions. The other interstellar powers may become involved if we do otherwise."

He paused for a long moment. "We need to slap the British back as hard as possible, once their task force arrives," he concluded. "Should open shooting commence, the gloves are to come off completely; you are to switch to ROE-3. At *that* point, General, you may take the offensive down the tramlines."

"Brilliant," Anjeet muttered, sarcastically.

"I'll keep you updated to the best of my ability," the Prime Minister said. "Good luck."

His image vanished, revealing a handful of encrypted files. Anjeet cursed under his breath as he opened them, one by one, and skimmed through. He'd wanted to place pickets in Hannibal and the other systems between Terra Nova and Pegasus, in hopes of attacking the British Fleet Train, but the Prime Minister had vetoed the plan. As long as there was hope of a peaceful solution, he'd be reluctant to take the gloves off ahead of time.

"Which will give the British time to mass their forces and take the offensive," he said. "They'll get to choose the time and place of the first engagement."

He finished skimming the files and sighed again. There was a second carrier in Vesy, but he didn't dare bring her through to Pegasus for fear the British would take the offensive towards Cromwell instead. It wouldn't change the balance of power, he was sure, yet it would be embarrassing. He needed to keep his forces in place to react quickly to any British moves.

And they may be capable of jumping one of our carriers, he thought. *That would even the odds quite sharply.*

He keyed his terminal, sending the files to the intelligence staff. They'd go through them, teasing out all the nuggets of information and making educated guesses about which ships the British would add to their task force. Not, he knew, that it would matter. They'd probably be able to track the British once they entered Hannibal...unless, of course, the British decided to take the war to the Indian worlds instead. It was quite possible.

Shaking his head, he looked down at the display. The troops were still landing on Clarke, setting up a whole network of defences. If the British took the offensive, they'd get a bloody nose; it was possible, quite possible, that they wouldn't even realise the danger until they got too close to avoid the mass drivers. Civilised nations disliked them, but the war had removed all taboos concerning their use. A single hit would be enough to cripple a carrier beyond repair.

"And if they do recognise the trap," he mused to himself, "they will still have to spring it if they wish to recover their territory."

He rose to his feet. The command staff would have to be briefed, now they knew there *would* be war. They'd have to dust off the contingency plans, update them as best as they could and then place their forces in the best position to repel attack. And earmark ships for later raiding, if the British took the offensive. Knocking out the British supply lines would make winning the war easier.

Of course, he reflected as the hatch hissed open in front of him, *they will feel the same way too.*

"I think this compartment is safe," David Majors said. "They certainly haven't bothered to *look* into it."

"You *think* this compartment is safe," Doctor Sharon Henderson echoed. "Are you *sure*?"

"There's no such thing as surety," Lillian said. She'd been surprised to be invited to the covert meeting, but she supposed there weren't many others with genuine naval experience on the colony. "If the bug sweep turned up nothing...?"

"It didn't," Majors confirmed. He wasn't an electronics expert, but he'd admitted to serving a term in the Royal Signals during the war. "However, the Indians may have developed something new."

"They could be listening through the datanet," Sharon said, nervously. "We're not *spies*."

"I took the precaution of isolating this sector," Majors reassured her. "The Indians *have* installed monitors in the datanet, true, but they won't actually be able to peer into this compartment without actually reconnecting the system. We'd know if they did."

"And what will happen," Sharon asked, "if they catch us?"

"They said it themselves," Lillian said. "We'll be treated as insurgents, who can be shot on sight - perfectly legally."

"So we keep our heads down and wait for the navy," Sharon said. "Getting involved now might be pointless."

"The problem is that the navy will need intelligence," Majors said, tartly. "Like...what are the Indians doing on the surface?"

"They're building defences," Lillian said. She scowled in bitter memory. "I'm not sure what they are, but I overheard two of the guards talking about being able to hit ships in orbit."

"That would make them mass drivers," Majors said. "Unless they *have* managed to solve the problem of creating a plasma containment field that lasts for more than a few seconds."

"Mass drivers seem more logical," Lillian said. "Combined with an orbiting sensor network, they could seriously upset anyone trying to approach the planet."

"Right," Majors said. "Is there anything we can do about them?"

"Not now," Lillian said, after a moment's thought. "They don't seem to care about us going outside, but they sure as hell object to us going anywhere near their fortifications without permission."

"They had you driving a vehicle for them," Majors said. "Are they going to keep expanding the colony?"

"I believe so, but it's still nowhere near their positions," Lillian said, flatly. "And they may be planning to wait until the end of the war."

Sharon leaned forward. "Can't you sneak a signal into the communications net?"

"I doubt it," Lillian said. "They took over the entire command network the day they arrived."

"We'd find it very hard to insert a signal without the new command codes," Majors agreed, softly. "One of you *could* try to seduce the local commander..."

Sharon bunched a fist. "Are you serious? I'm a doctor, not Mata Hari."

"I don't think the Indians would be seduced," Lillian said, quickly. "They rarely spend time with any of us, save for when they're issuing orders."

"True," Majors agreed. "Could one of us sneak out of the colony?"

"You'd have to survive on your own," Lillian said. "I don't see how you could do it..."

"Take a tractor," Sharon suggested. "Strip the life support system, then destroy the rest of it so they find nothing, but wreckage. It wouldn't be the first time there's been an accident that caused an explosion."

"And even if you did," Lillian added, "what then?"

Majors shook his head. "I don't know," he said. "I just...I just hate being helpless!"

Lillian understood, but she also knew that the Indians were firmly in control. The colonists had no weapons, no secure access to the datanet and no control over the life support. And even if they *did* manage to throw the Indians out, the orbiting starships could simply bombard the moon from orbit, flattening the colony into rubble. It might be *neat* to get someone outside the colony, to fake his death so the Indians had no idea he was on the loose, but what would be the *point*? None of them were soldiers!

"I think the only thing we can do is gather information and hope there will be a chance to use it," she said, finally. She wished, suddenly, that she'd paid more attention in the brief Conduct After Capture course, although it hadn't been designed for living under enemy occupation. They had a moral duty to resist, if they could, but how? "The Royal Navy *will* be coming, I'm sure."

Sharon snorted. "And what if it doesn't?"

"Then we get to decide if we want to stay here under their rule or go somewhere else," Lillian said. She rose to her feet as her watch beeped an alert. "I have to go."

"We'll meet up tomorrow; same time and place," Majors said. "See what you can glean from their supplies."

Lillian nodded and hurried from the room, heading through a maze of stone corridors and up a flight of stairs into the engineering section. The Indians had searched it thoroughly, then placed a guard at the hatch; the guard eyed her coldly before stepping aside to allow her to pass through and into the giant compartment. She picked her environment suit off the wall, pulled it on over her shipsuit and checked the telltales before heading out to where the tractors were waiting. A pair of Indian officers stood next to one, waiting for her.

Shit, Lillian thought. Did they *know* she'd been talking with others, discussing ways and means to resist? She felt a cold pit in her stomach, yawning wider as she approached the Indians. No one had been executed - yet - for insurgency, or even passive resistance, but the Indians *would* have every right to kill her if they knew what she'd done. No one was tolerant of insurgents these days. *What do they want*?

"You'll be transporting pallets from the shuttles today," one of them said. "Get them over to the dumping ground and leave them there."

"Understood," Lillian said. She was tempted to offer to take them further, but they might have smelled a rat. So far, no one had done more than the bare minimum to help, despite quite a few inducements. "I'll get on my way."

She climbed into the tractor, allowing herself a moment of relief as the hatch slammed down and the engine hummed to life. The Indians hurried backwards as she turned the tractor around and headed for the airlock, which opened at her approach. She linked into the outside communications grid, informing the command centre that she was leaving the colony, then smiled as the airlock closed behind her. The second hatch opened a moment later, revealing the frozen terrain beyond. No matter what was happening behind her, it still took her breath away.

Clarke, an immense blue-green orb, hung in the sky, utterly dominating the surrounding landscape. She'd heard that some people had problems living on Io or another of Jupiter's moons because of the Great Red Spot, but she'd never really believed it until living on Clarke III. Clarke was an awe-inspiring sight; the Great Red Spot, however, would look like an enormous red eye glowering down on anyone below it and reminding them of just how tiny they were, against the vastness of the universe. She smiled at the thought, then forced herself to look at the ground as she gunned the tractor forward. The vehicle hummed to itself as it crawled over the snow towards the Indian shuttles.

They looked *very* like British designs, she noted, although there were quite a few more of them than she'd expected. She parked the tractor next to the closest and waited for orders, then watched as a handful of suited men transferred pallets from the shuttle to the rear of the tractor. None of the pallets were marked by anything apart from a number; the Indians, she assumed, had decided not to take the risk of labelling them in English or Hindi. The tractor lurched back to life as soon as the Indians were ready, transporting the goods towards one of their new installations. They'd set up *something* quite close to the colony, yet several of their other installations were much further away. She tried to see what it was as the tractor drew closer, but no matter how she stared it was impossible to be sure.

Maybe it is a mass driver, she thought. She'd seen the giant mass drivers on the moon, the ones that kicked buckets of raw materials to Earth, but there was no reason why a mass driver on Clarke had to be so large. Technology had advanced since the moon had been settled in 2050. *And if it is, they could hit anything they can see.*

She pushed the thought aside as she stopped the tractor and waited for the Indians to unload her cargo. They didn't seem too interested in chatting with her, something that surprised her more than she cared to admit. The marines on *Warspite* had always flirted with her and any other attractive female crew. But then, none of the Indians seemed interested in socialising with the British colonists. She had a feeling they'd been warned to keep themselves strictly to themselves.

Her radio buzzed. "Thank you," an Indian voice said. "You may now return to the shuttles."

Lillian sighed, but did as she was told. There was no escaping the fact that it *was* collaboration, at least in some form. It was quite likely she'd be in trouble if she ever returned home...apart, of course, for whatever consequences there were for breaking her parole. And yet, she *was* spying on them...if, of course, she had any way to get the information to anyone who needed it. She looked up, tracking the lights in the sky; one of them was an Indian carrier, but the others? Might one of them be a British ship?

Probably not, she thought, as a new flight of shuttles swooped overhead and landed near the colony. *The Indians chased the tin-cans out of the system.*

It was nearly two hours before she was finally told to go back to the colony and pass the tractor to someone else. Lillian headed back and headed towards the communal showers, where she washed herself as quickly as possible. Water wasn't exactly scarce on Clarke, but the plumbing was nowhere near complete. And besides...

She looked up as Sharon entered the shower compartment, a towel wrapped around her. The doctor tapped her lips before Lillian could say a word, then lifted her eyebrows. Lillian shrugged, expressively. She'd learned nothing of any use.

"There have been a handful of new patients in sickbay," Sharon said, as she started to wash herself thoroughly. "Indian workers with minor injuries."

They're moving fast, Lillian thought. She knew from experience that working fast tended to lead to more accidents, although Clarke's atmosphere tended to make them worse. *They must be expecting trouble.*

Oddly, the thought made her feel a great deal better.

CHAPTER ELEVEN

HMS Warspite, In Transit

"This," Lewis said, "would be a very bad time to tell me you're agoraphobic."

Percy gave him an odd look as they donned their spacesuits. "I'm a Royal Marine," he said, crossly. "You've seen my service record."

"And you do have experience in deep space work," Lewis agreed. "But not everyone likes crawling around on the hull."

"I do," Percy said, truthfully. "There's just *something* about the vastness of space that appeals to me."

Lewis gave him a sharp look, obviously suspecting that Percy was taking the piss. Percy fought to keep his expression as bland as possible. He was getting more than a little annoyed of the constant testing. There was no way he could have been cleared for shipboard duty if he hadn't been able to go out on the hull without a panic attack and Lewis would know it. But then, he was far too aware that his responses to the probing would be held against him, if he snapped back at the Sergeant. He'd undergone enough tests during basic training to know the score.

"I'm glad to hear it," Lewis said. He turned, allowing Percy to see his back. "Check my suit."

Percy checked the telltales and frowned. The reserve oxygen cylinder wasn't connected to the life support unit. Lewis would have been fine, he thought as he reconnected it, as long as he didn't try to stay outside for more than an hour. The central processor might need to be replaced too.

It should have sounded the alert when Lewis activated the suit without clipping the oxygen supply into place.

"You should probably get a new suit," he said, once he'd checked the rest of the telltales. "I think this one probably needs to go back to engineering."

"I deactivated a few systems," Lewis said. He started to click the components back into place. The telltales turned green, one by one. "I'll just go out like this."

Another test, Percy thought sourly. *But at least I already know the answer.*

"You need to change suits," he insisted, firmly. "You'd be taking your life in your hands."

Lewis smiled, so briefly that Percy almost missed it. "And you're willing to contradict me on it?"

Percy stood his ground. "Yes, Sergeant," he said. "I am."

"Good," Lewis said.

He removed the suit quickly, then pulled another one from the rack and started to don it. Percy took the old suit and placed it in the locker for later examination and repair, making sure to log it on the terminal. He had a feeling the whole test had been rigged, but it was well to be sure. Disconnecting a number of settings could easily make the whole suit actively dangerous. Lewis checked Percy's suit, pronounced himself satisfied and then allowed Percy to check the new suit. This time, there were no red lights.

"Follow me," Lewis said, as he opened the airlock. "Keep yourself tethered at all times."

"Yes, Sergeant," Percy said. "Being lost in space would be embarrassing."

He shivered at the thought as the second hatch opened. It was an old nightmare, one shared by all spacers; falling into the inky darkness of space, trapped in a spacesuit, the oxygen steadily running out...and no hope at all of rescue. Civilian spacesuits were over-engineered to ensure their beacons were always functional, but military suits were far more limited. The cruiser's stealth mode would be fatally compromised if he started screaming for help.

Lewis led the way out into space, his magnetic boots allowing him to walk normally. Percy followed, keeping his eyes firmly fixed on the hull.

There was no time to get distracted by the stars. He tethered himself to the railing, then walked towards the concealed shuttle. It was hidden under camo netting, but he could make out the details easily. The stealth shuttle simply didn't *look* normal.

Let's just hope no one gets a visual of the hull, he thought. The shuttle was odd enough to catch the eye. Unlike a normal craft, it looked almost like a flattened brick. He honestly wasn't sure what material they'd used to make the hull, but it sure as hell didn't *look* like metal. The tiny drive unit at the rear looked even odder, like something out of an alien-contact movie. *They'd know there was something weird about the hidden object.*

Lewis opened the hatch and climbed into the shuttle. Percy followed, blinking in surprise as the lights came on, revealing a handful of seats and a tiny cockpit. The SAS troopers were big men; he honestly wasn't sure there was room for all of them in the single shuttle, particularly when they had to wear suits. He followed Lewis to the front of the craft and frowned as he took in the controls. They looked almost ridiculously simple. He couldn't help thinking of the *Thunderbird 2*-themed car he'd been given for his seventh birthday.

"There wasn't time to check you out on this earlier," Lewis said. He pointed a hand towards the pilot's seat. "Sit down, Percy. I'll be with you in a moment."

Percy nodded and sat. The controls still looked odd, but it wouldn't have been easy to fly a standard shuttlecraft while wearing a spacesuit. Indeed, the more he looked at the design, the more he realised that the stealth shuttle wasn't intended to be flown *without* a spacesuit - or, for that matter, an armoured combat suit. He was tempted to take the stick and start moving it, but he knew better. He'd flown shuttles during basic training - Royal Marines were expected to cross-train as much as possible - yet he'd never flown anything like the stealth shuttle. He hadn't even *heard* of them before he'd been ordered to Hereford.

But they're probably highly classified, he thought, as Lewis returned to stand behind him. *If they can really get through a planet's atmosphere without being detected, they'd be a priceless asset.*

"Welcome onboard," Lewis said. He sat on his haunches, watching Percy carefully. "This is a *Chameleon*-class lander, designed specifically for covert insertion. You may have noticed quite a few oddities about the design. What do you think those mean?"

Percy hesitated, thinking hard. The design wasn't particularly aerodynamic...

"It's a one-shot craft," he said, finally. "There's no way to take off again."

"Correct," Lewis said. "Once we're down on the surface, we're stuck until we get picked up by the navy or captured by the Indians. There's no way for us to leave under our own power."

He sat back, but his eyes never left Percy's face. "The hull is composed of a material that is highly classified," he explained. "It is almost completely transparent to radar; an active sensor sweep will show nothing, even if the shuttlecraft is very close. Furthermore, it is capable of absorbing and safely dumping a considerable amount of heat. Our passage through the atmosphere will be almost unnoticeable."

Percy nodded in understanding. It was easy to hide a starship, even an entire supercarrier, in the endless wastes of interstellar space, but it was a great deal harder to slip into a planet's atmosphere without being detected. Even something as small as a single man making an orbital jump would leave a heat trail behind, leading the enemy right to him. *Warspite's* marines had sneaked down to Vesy, when they'd first stumbled across the alien world, but the Russians hadn't had a proper monitoring network. The Indians, by contrast, definitely *would.*

"The greatest downside is that she makes a fleet carrier look nimble," Lewis added. He keyed a code into the console, bringing it to life. "You were checked out on helicopters, I assume? This craft is far harder to fly than a helicopter. The best we can really do is control our fall to the LZ. There won't be any way to alter our final landing point beyond a few kilometres."

"And if the enemy sees us coming, they'll have plenty of time to catch us," Percy said, slowly. "Were these craft ever tested against a modern network?"

"We did two combat drops against the UKASDR," Lewis said. "The first time, we didn't tell them what we were doing; the second time, we offered a reward to the controller who saw us coming and scrambled a response team. We weren't spotted, either time."

Percy felt a flicker of admiration. The United Kingdom Air Space Defence Region was heavily guarded. *No one* was meant to be flying through the electronic fence guarding Britain without permission. These days, after the war, the defenders would be likely to shoot first and ask questions later. The SAS could have been shot down by their own side, quite by accident. But the fact they'd made it through had to have worried a few officers in the MOD.

"We did have some advantages," Lewis admitted. "The pilot was very familiar with British weather - we got to choose the time and place of our insertion. It might not be so easy to land on Clarke."

He paused, dramatically. "There's another weakness," he warned. "The hull is *alarmingly* fragile. We hit the ground; it starts to break up. What doesn't shatter into fragments will be destroyed by the self-destruct system. The computer" - he jabbed a finger at the console - "will be reduced to dust."

"Shit," Percy said. He glanced at the bulkhead. What *was* it? A new composite? He'd never been particularly interested in chemistry, but he was curious. "I'd better not punch the hull."

Lewis smiled, coldly. "Quite," he agreed. "I want you checked out on this craft before we plunge into the Pegasus System. You shouldn't be flying her, but I want to be sure you know what you're doing."

And understand the limitations of the system, Percy added, silently. He'd been astonished to discover that the SAS held open planning sessions. *Everyone* was free to contribute a suggestion and, while the discussions had turned heated at times, they'd never broken down into violence. *You want me to know what's possible before I start offering dumb suggestions.*

He took the stick in his hand as the simulation began. Lewis, he rapidly discovered, had underestimated the case. The stealth shuttle handled so badly that he lost control the first time and had to cancel the simulation as the craft plummeted into the ground. Lewis made a number of sarcastic remarks, then ordered him to try again. This time, Percy managed to land, but landed so hard that it was unlikely anyone could survive. By the time he thought he'd mastered landing in perfect conditions, he was tired and cranky.

"I don't envy the pilot," he said, as he reset the simulator once again. "How close can we get to the planet before we're committed?"

"There isn't much reaction mass in the tanks," Lewis said. "We could abort and drive into interstellar space, if we had no alternative, but it wouldn't be easy for *Warspite* to pick us up without being detected."

"They'd have problems *finding* us under perfect conditions," Percy agreed. "They'll need us to turn on a beacon."

"Which the Indians could hardly fail to detect," Lewis said. "Still want to come with us, Percy?"

"I was under the impression I didn't have a choice," Percy pointed out.

"You've told us plenty," Lewis said, suddenly serious. "I've never had someone *conscripted* into my unit before. If you want to back out, if you want to go back to your old unit, you can. There isn't a security risk any longer."

Percy hesitated before shaking his head. "I'll see it through to the finish," he said. He didn't have it in him to back out, not now. Besides, he was *still* the only person on the team who had any knowledge of Clarke. His experience might make the difference between life and death. "But thank you for the offer."

"Good," Lewis said. He pointed to the console. "Get back to work. This time, you're going to be plummeting into a snowstorm."

Percy groaned.

"Captain," Penny said. "Thank you for granting me this interview."

"It's a pleasure to see you again," Captain Naiser said. If he was being untruthful, Penny couldn't tell. She doubted he was *really* pleased to see her, let alone submit to an interview, but at least he was trying. "Still, I may be called away at any moment."

"I understand," Penny said. She glanced around the cabin with some interest. "Is this really the largest cabin on the ship?"

"I'm afraid so," the Captain said. "*Warspite* wasn't designed to hold more than a couple of hundred crewmen at most, really. We're actually pushing life support to the limits right now."

Penny swallowed. "I don't think I wanted to know that," she said. "Are we in any danger?"

"We probably couldn't take on many more passengers," the Captain said. "Our life support systems are heavily over-engineered, though. We could lose half of the atmospheric reprocessors and still be fine. The only real threat would be the air getting a little smelly."

"Oh," Penny said. She'd noticed that starships tended to smell, although she'd grown accustomed to the stench after two or three days of breathing nothing else. It wasn't a *bad* smell, not really, but it wasn't always pleasant. "And if we lost the rest of the life support?"

"We'd probably have lost the entire ship," the Captain said briskly. "In that case, we'd be dead anyway. There would be no need to worry about it."

"I suppose," Penny said. She glanced around the cabin again. It was bare, save for a handful of pictures hanging on the bulkhead. There were no signs that the Captain had any interests beyond being a Captain. "I'm supposed to do an in-depth interview of you, but I don't know what I can ask that hasn't already been dug up."

"There were too many interviews after my first return from Vesy," the Captain agreed. He cocked his head, slightly. "You could always just talk, I suppose."

Penny had to smile. "Do you believe we can beat the Indians?"

"I believe we can," the Captain assured her. "But I wouldn't say anything else, would I?"

"I suppose not," Penny agreed. "Are you confident that you can carry out your mission?"

"If I thought it was impossible, I would have said so when I was briefed," the Captain said, frankly. "It will be dangerous - there's no doubt about that - but it's doable."

Penny frowned. "But it could go wrong?"

"Of course it could," the Captain said. "War is a democracy, unfortunately. The enemy gets a vote too. Very few things *ever* go according to plan. We can cover all the bases, check out everything we can in advance and *still* run into trouble."

"That sounds pessimistic," Penny observed.

"It is," the Captain said. "Nothing is certain in war. We may run into superior force and be destroyed. We may make a terrible mistake and be destroyed. We may encounter something right out of left field and be destroyed. There's just no way we can prepare for everything."

He shrugged. "Back during the Crazy Years, politicians used to insist that nothing - absolutely nothing - had to be allowed to go wrong. The death of a single soldier was used as an excuse to end the war. Even a partial success was not good enough. They wanted everything to be perfect; the troops deployed on day one, the enemy capital taken on day three, the troops brought back home on day five.

"But war isn't predicable. No matter what you do, you take losses; no matter what you do, it will cost you. You can do the right thing and it will *still* cost you. And it will certainly not look perfect."

"I was on Vesy," Penny said. "Do you think things could have been different?"

"I think we needed a better approach to the aliens from the start," the Captain said. "If we had approached them as a united body, we might have been able to prevent the uprising. But politically, there was no hope of doing anything of the sort. And then...the technology they gleaned from us, even something as simple as gunpowder, would change their society in unpredictable ways. We would be surprised no matter what happened."

Penny nodded in agreement. "You think the situation couldn't have been controlled?"

"I think our sense of control was an illusion," the Captain said. "And I think that's true of war too. You don't get to have control over how things go, merely...the ability to influence it."

He shrugged. "I was always taught it was better to do something - anything - rather than let the other side take the initiative," he added. "In this case, the Indians took the initiative from us and ran with it. We have to take it back."

"Like playing chess," Penny said. "The person playing white has an advantage because they get to make the first move."

"They can lose it pretty quickly," the Captain said. "But yes, you're right. The Indians got to pick the time and place the war started. That gave them the advantage at the start. Now...*we* have to undermine them."

His intercom buzzed. "Captain," Howard said, "we're approaching the tramline to J-35."

Penny shivered. J-35 was the final system between Earth and Pegasus. The long and boring cruise was about to come to an end.

"Thank you for your time, Captain," she said, seriously. "It was very informative."

The Captain smiled. "I hope you'll have something more to write about soon," he said, dryly. "I don't think I told you anything particularly useful - or interesting."

Penny shrugged. She'd done a hundred interviews; officers, crewmen, marines...the only people who had refused to talk to her had been the newcomers, the soldiers she was sure were SAS. But there hadn't been any *real* scoops...

But now? She was sure that was about to change.

And, assuming I make it home, she thought as she rose to her feet, *I can write my own ticket.*

CHAPTER TWELVE

HMS Warspite, In Transit

"All systems report ready, Captain," Howard reported, as John took the command chair and studied the display. "There's no sign of watching ships."

"Understood," John said. The tramline lay ahead of them, ready and waiting. He doubted they would run right into an Indian starship, but the crew was ready to repel attack anyway, just in case. "Take us through the tramline."

"Aye, sir," Armstrong said. "Jump in five...four...three..."

John braced himself as the display blinked out, then rebooted. J-35 was a useless system, at least by pre-war standards; the red star was alone in space, save for a handful of asteroids and comets. A small settlement might be able to survive, with a great deal of careful planning, but there would be little room for expansion. It wasn't even *claimed* by any interstellar power, let alone a religious or isolationist group who might be interested in permanent settlement. But an Indian starship might be lurking, watching and waiting for any intruders from Earth...

They'll be hiding near the tramline, if they're there, he thought. The hell of it was that there was no way to *know* if there was a watching ship or not. It was quite possible that *Warspite* would slip past the picket and jump through the tramline without either of them having the slightest idea the other was there. *They couldn't hope to pass on a warning without being close to the tramline.*

"Passive sensors are clear, Captain," Tara reported. "There's no hint of any enemy presence."

Which proves nothing, John thought. *The Indians could be pretending to be a hole in space.*

"Set course for Tramline B," he ordered. He took a moment to consider his options. "We'll slip through at Point Delta."

"Aye, Captain," Armstrong said.

Howard gave him a sharp look - travelling to Point Delta would add an extra seven hours to the journey - but said nothing. There was simply no way to predict where the Indians would be lurking, if indeed there *were* any Indians. All they could do was crawl from one tramline to the other, every passive sensor primed for the slightest *hint* of an enemy presence. It was unlikely in the extreme they'd reach point-blank range without realising how close they were, but the possibility couldn't be ruled out. He'd just have to pray.

The Indians could have seeded the system with recon platforms too, he thought. *He* wouldn't have wasted the money, but the Indians would need as much advance warning as possible before the Royal Navy arrived. *And they're even stealthier than a starship.*

"Course laid in," Armstrong said.

"Engage," John ordered.

The display didn't change as *Warspite* made her way towards Tramline B. John kept a sharp eye on it, even though he knew there would be an alarm if something popped up. In hindsight, perhaps it would have been better to formally claim the system, even though it *was* useless. They would have legal grounds for engaging any Indian starship they encountered within J-35. But, technically, it was neutral space.

These ROE will be the death of us, he thought, grimly. *It was so much easier when we were fighting the Tadpoles.*

He forced himself to sit back and check through the latest set of reports from the SAS. Drake - he wasn't called a Captain onboard ship, where both Hatfield and John himself shared the same rank - had updated his deployment plan, confirming that they intended to make their way to Clarke and land on the icy moon. John was privately impressed - he'd seen the stealth shuttle and knew it would be a bitch to fly - but he knew they'd have to wait and see what the Indians were doing before they risked allowing the SAS to go in. Even a stealth shuttle could become visible if something went badly wrong.

"Commander Howard, get some sleep," he ordered. "It'll be fourteen hours before we're ready to jump. Report back at 2100."

"Yes, sir," Howard said, reluctantly.

John didn't blame him. The sensation of being watched was growing stronger as they made their way further into the system. Sleep wouldn't come easy for either of them. But there was no choice. They had to be reasonably fresh and alert when they jumped through the tramline to Pegasus. Or, for that matter, if they encountered an Indian warship. He nodded firmly towards the hatch - Howard saluted and walked off the bridge - and turned his attention back to his console. Whoever had said that war was long hours of boredom, broken intermittently by moments of screaming terror, hadn't known the half of it.

The display bleeped. "Captain," Tara snapped. "One starship just jumped into the system, Tramline B."

Which means she actually arrived an hour ago, John thought. FTL communications were still a pipe dream and FTL sensors even more so. *What is she*?

He looked at the tactical officer. "Can you ID her?"

"I think she's a courier boat," Tara added. "She's not making any attempt to hide, sir; she's just blazing across the system to Tramline A. I think she's actually pushing her drives to the limit."

John felt a flicker of paranoia. Had they been detected after all? Had an unseen picket ship jumped through to Pegasus and sounded the alarm? Or was it just a coincidence? It shouldn't have been possible for the enemy to detect their presence, but the Battle of New Russia had taught the Royal Navy that its assessment of what was technologically possible was rather inadequate. But if the Indians *had* developed some form of FTL sensor, the war was within shouting distance of being lost anyway.

"Project her course," he ordered. "Is she going to come anywhere near us?"

"No, sir," Tara said. "She's on a straight-line course for Tramline A. She shouldn't come anywhere near us."

"Keep an eye on her," John ordered. Courier boats were really nothing more than drives and tiny living quarters - their crews tended to be a little weird, even by spacer standards - but it was possible the Indians had outfitted their ships with enhanced sensors. The Indians didn't have enough ships to risk over-specialisation. "Let me know if she changes course."

"Aye, sir," Tara said.

John briefly considered trying to intercept the ship, but rapidly dismissed the idea as pointless. Even if he managed to catch up with her - the courier boat was faster than *Warspite* in stealth mode - the mere act of intercepting her in J-35 would tip off any watching starships. They might succeed in capturing a tiny courier boat, but the *real* mission would be hopelessly compromised. Instead, he watched the courier boat on the display until she reached the other tramline and vanished. Wherever she was going, he knew all too well, she was definitely on her way.

It was odd, though; he brought up the starchart and puzzled over it. The Indians would need to send messages to Earth - that was a given - but they could do it quicker by sending them through the tramline to Vesy and then to Gandhi. At that point, the messages could be sent through the communications chain, shortening the trip by a week. Had they sent something so secret they hadn't wanted to take even the slightest risk of being intercepted...or were they trying to force him to reveal his presence?

But it doesn't make sense, he told himself. *They would have needed to slow down if they wanted to tempt us into an interception.*

He looked up, five hours later, as Howard stepped back onto the bridge. The XO looked disgustingly fresh; he'd clearly taken the opportunity to have a shower, don a clean uniform and get something to eat before reporting for duty. John didn't blame him in the slightest, but it was still irritating. There was no way *John* wanted to leave the bridge, yet he needed his rest too. They had to be fresh, he reminded himself again, for when they jumped into Pegasus.

"Inform me the moment anything changes," he ordered, as he rose. "You have the bridge."

"Aye, sir," Howard said. "I have the bridge."

John walked through the hatch and down to his cabin. The hatch opened when he touched his hand against the sensor, allowing him to step inside. A pot of coffee was steaming merrily on the side table; he resisted the temptation to pour a cup and drink it as he undressed rapidly and climbed into bed. He didn't really expect to sleep, but darkness fell the moment he closed his eyes. It felt as if no time at all had passed before the alarm buzzed, jerking him back to wakefulness. When he glanced at his watch, it told him that six hours had passed.

I need a proper rest, he thought, as he pulled himself out of bed and checked the ship's status display. He'd hoped to have a chance to visit Sin City and find some non-judgemental company for a couple of days, but between the debriefings and getting *Warspite* ready for departure there simply hadn't been time. *I could book a hotel room on Earth and just sleep in it for a week.*

He pushed the thought aside as he keyed the intercom, ordering breakfast, and then stumbled into the shower and lowered the temperature as far as it would go. The cold water jerked him awake; he washed himself hastily before stepping back out of the shower and drying himself as fast as possible. His old uniform would need to be cleaned; he pulled a new one from the locker and donned it hastily. The hatch chimed; he tapped a switch to open it, allowing the steward to enter with a small tray of food.

"Cook says this is the last of the waffles, Captain," the steward said. "We'll be on reprocessed foods from now on."

"Thank you," John said. Most civilians preferred not to think about what went into reprocessed food. Hell, it had taken him weeks to get over it, back when he'd entered basic training. There were candidates who never did. "It can't be helped."

The steward saluted and retreated. John poured himself a cup of coffee, sat down and started to eat. The waffles wouldn't have been considered particularly good on Earth, but in space they were heavenly. He drank the coffee, checked the status display for the second time and then headed back to the bridge. Howard would have made sure the remainder of the crew had their own chance to sleep.

"Captain," Howard said. "We are within an hour of Tramline B. No enemy contacts; I say again, no enemy contacts."

"Thank you," John said. "I relieve you."

"I stand relieved," Howard confirmed.

John sat down and checked the near-space display. It was empty; the only cause for concern the ship's sensors had noted was a handful of flares on the surface of the sun, brief discharges that might cause problems for any starships that slipped too close. *Warspite* was well away from them, he noted; there shouldn't be any danger. But it wasn't uncommon for astronomers to take their ships too close to a particularly interesting cosmic event and end up dead.

"Captain," Armstrong said. "We should be heading through the tramline at Point Delta within forty minutes. Do you want to alter course."

"Negative," John said. "Steady as she goes."

He braced himself as the tramline moved closer, feeling the tension rising on the bridge. Logically, there was no reason to expect the Indians to know *precisely* where to put their watchdogs to intercept *Warspite*, but it didn't matter. The sense they were being watched was growing stronger all the time. If the Indians had scattered a handful of recon platforms around, they'd be completely undetectable. Unless, of course, they made a deadly mistake and went active.

Or if they opened fire, he thought, morbidly. *They'd be quite visible when they started spitting missiles towards us.*

"Prepare for jump," he ordered. "Ship's status?"

"All systems go," Howard reported. "Stealth mode has not been compromised."

John hesitated. They could run a sweep around the tramline, but there was no way to be *entirely* sure there were no watching eyes. It had been easier - much easier - during the first war, when he'd been a lowly starfighter pilot. He hadn't been responsible for an entire ship and crew, not back then.

"Take us through the moment we enter the tramline," he ordered.

"Aye, Captain," Armstrong said. "Jump in seventy seconds and counting."

John took one final look at the display. It looked empty, too empty. He knew he was being silly, but part of him would almost have preferred to see a fleet of advancing warships. Then, at least, he would have *known* what the enemy was doing. Instead, he had no way to know what - if anything - was lurking within J-35. The only certainty he had was that the Indians *would* be firmly entrenched in Pegasus.

"Jump in ten seconds and counting," Armstrong said.

"Understood," John said. He watched the last seconds tick away. "Take us through."

He took a long breath as the display blanked out and reformatted itself, again. This time, it showed Pegasus, where it had all begun. John remembered escorting the first colonists to the system, back when he'd first been assigned to *Warspite*; he'd walked on the icy surface of Clarke III and admired just how quickly the colonists had started to make the world home. Governor Brown - he wondered, briefly, what had happened to the man - had even planned to start the long process of terraforming Wells. The Mars-type world would become a new jewel in the British crown...assuming, of course, they managed to drive the Indians out of the system.

"Jump complete, sir," Armstrong said.

"Take us away from the tramline; go passive once we're at a safe distance," John ordered. There was nothing to be gained by rushing in, not when the Indians would definitely have prepared the system to repel attack. "Status report?"

"I'm picking up a handful of transmissions from Clarke, but nothing solid," Tara reported, grimly. "At this distance, sir, we wouldn't see much unless they power up their drives."

John nodded. "Inform me the moment you locate that carrier," he ordered. "That's the most dangerous ship in the system."

The display kept updating, new icons flickering into existence. It didn't *look* as though any of them were artificial, although it was hard to be sure. The system had always had a great deal of space junk, one of the reasons why it had been claimed so fast. There was literally no shortage of raw materials to be turned into everything an industrial society would need.

"They're setting up a cloudscoop," Tara said, suddenly. The display focused suddenly on a structure orbiting the gas giant. "I don't think it can be anything else."

"They're serious about moving in to stay," Howard commented. "That's not a small investment."

"They'd need to start shipping fuel to Vesy if they want to uplift the natives," John said. He wasn't sure if the Indians were sincere about helping the Vesy to reach the stars, but if there were any gains to be had from uplifting aliens the Indians would be in a good position to benefit. "The sole gas giant in the Vesy System is highly radioactive and impossible to mine."

"They're also lobbing ice asteroids towards Wells," Tara added. "They must have dumped a terraforming package onto the planet too."

John swore, inwardly. It was generally agreed that whoever settled the Earth-like world received title to the rest of the system. But Pegasus didn't *have* an Earth-like world, unless Wells was reshaped into something habitable. It would take decades, at the very least, for the world to develop a breathable atmosphere, but if the Indians kick-started a terraforming project they might be able to lay claim to Wells itself. They'd certainly manage to muddy the political waters still further.

But it will take them decades, he reassured himself. Wells was a long-term project. *The war will be over by then, one way or the other.*

"They might also have dumped colonists on the world," Howard mused. "They could certainly do it on Cromwell."

"We'll cross that bridge when we come to it," John said. It wouldn't be the first time a problem had been solved by forced relocation, but doing it on an interstellar scale would be a logistic nightmare. Cromwell had only a few thousand colonists; the Indians could overwhelm them easily, just by shipping in ten thousand volunteers from India. "For the moment, we won't worry about it."

"Aye, sir," Howard said.

A red icon flashed to life on the display. "Captain," Tara said. "I've located the carrier."

John sucked in his breath. The carrier - INS *Viraat* - was holding position near Clarke III, but keeping her distance from the rocks orbiting the gas giant. There would be a handful of smaller ships nearby, he was sure, but so far they weren't showing up on the display. It didn't matter. He'd seen the intelligence reports - and the carrier herself, back at Vesy. INS *Viraat* was a deadly threat.

"Her drives are stepped down, as far as I can tell," Tara added.

"It won't take them long to flash-wake their systems," Howard warned. He frowned, considering the possibilities. "If their designs are anything like ours, they could be at battlestations within five minutes."

"We'll keep our distance," John said. He studied the display for a long chilling moment, then tapped a command into the system, sending an update to Drake. "Designate this point" - he tapped a location on the display - "as Point Alpha, then set course for it."

"Aye, sir," Armstrong said. "Course laid in."

John took a breath. Now, the *real* work would begin.

"Take us in," he ordered.

CHAPTER THIRTEEN

HMS Theodore Smith, Earth Orbit

"She's magnificent," Commander Sally Acorn breathed.

"Yes, she is," James agreed, as HMS *Theodore Smith* slowly came into view. "The most powerful supercarrier designed and launched by the Royal Navy."

He'd seen the mighty carrier before, but he drank in the details as the shuttle swooped towards the VIP airlock. The carrier was over three kilometres long, a flattened rectangle flanked by no less than four starfighter launching tubes. Her hull - lined with modern armour that was actually tougher than the solid-state armour of *Ark Royal* - was studded with point defence weapons, sensor blisters, mass drivers and external missile racks. She might not be the most agile of starships, but she was definitely faster than the average fleet carrier.

And Ark Royal handled like a commercial megaton freighter four times her size, he reminded himself. It felt disloyal to make the comparison, but he couldn't help it. *Theodore Smith could kick the ass of the fleets we faced without breaking a sweat.*

He smiled at the thought as the shuttle docked, the hatch hissing open to reveal a tall dark-haired woman waiting for him. James smiled in genuine pleasure and saluted, first the flag and then the woman. She saluted him back at once.

"Admiral Fitzwilliam," Captain Susan Pole said. She stuck out a hand in greeting, which James shook firmly. "Welcome onboard."

"Thank you, Captain," James said. *Theodore Smith* had been his flagship ever since she'd entered service, but he'd spent very little time on her over the past two months. "It's a great pleasure to be back."

Susan smiled. "I can imagine," she said, as they turned to head down the long corridor to the CIC. "I caught the interview last night."

James made a face. The media, of course, had been demanding interview after interview, all of which he'd managed to duck until now. He'd had to go in front of the cameras and answer questions from a whole panel of reporters, none of whom understood the first thing about space warfare. They certainly didn't seem to realise that it would take at least a fortnight for *any* news to come back from the front; hell, they seemed to imagine that the MOD intended to sit on any messages - sent, no doubt, by FTL transmitter - until they'd been spun into declarations of complete victory.

"All lies, Captain," he said. He glanced at Sally, dismissing her to her duties, then turned his gaze back to Susan. "I trust your ship is ready for departure?"

"Yes, sir," Susan said. There was nothing, but confidence in her voice. "We finished loading the war stocks last night. There shouldn't be any problem meeting the scheduled departure date."

James nodded. He'd met Susan shortly after his promotion to Commodore, after the final flight of *Ark Royal*. Like many other officers in the post-war navy, she was young for her role, but there was no doubting her competence. Indeed, he had a feeling he'd been competing with her for carrier command before the war had started and he'd managed to get himself transferred to *Ark Royal*. Now, she was his strong right arm.

"The Old Man would be proud," he said, remembering the struggle to get *Ark Royal* ready for space. "And he'd be proud of his namesake too."

"Of course, sir," Susan said. "We incorporated a great many lessons from the war into her hull."

James said nothing else until they passed through the CIC - his staff had arrived earlier, once he'd been able to spare them from Nelson Base - and into his office. It was larger than he thought he had any right to expect, but the Royal Navy was determined to ensure that flag officers received the very best of everything. James wasn't sure he approved - he knew that Admiral Smith would *not* have approved - yet it was something he hadn't been able to change. There were limits, clearly, to the powers of a Vice Admiral.

"I assume you've read the classified briefings," he said, once the hatch was firmly closed behind them. The compartment had been swept for bugs before a Royal Marine had taken up position outside. It was as secure as modern technology could make it. "We have our final orders."

"Yes, sir," Susan said.

"Commodore Nigel Blake will assume command in the event of something happening to me," James added. "Commodore Pollock was earmarked for the role, but he has health problems and the doctors believe he'd be better off in a desk job."

"Yes, sir," Susan said. She ran her hand through her short dark hair. "If something happens to you, it'll happen to the whole ship."

"I know," James said. Susan would technically be the third in line to take command, if something happened to James and Commodore Blake, but she would almost certainly go down with her ship. It might not matter; if the carrier was lost, the war would be lost along with it. "We'll need to take the time during the voyage to work out the kinks in our arrangements."

"Not all of us have served together before," Susan agreed. She sounded rather frustrated. It could take months to work a fleet up for combat, yet they were expected to be ready to deploy in a matter of weeks. "I've been running drills with the carrier battle group, sir, but we didn't have the entire task force to play with."

"We'll see to it once we're underway," James said. They'd just have to learn on the go, despite the inconvenience. "Nine more ships will be meeting us in Terra Nova, Captain. The politicians finally agreed to pull our flotilla out of the system. The French will be handling rescue duties for British civilians in exchange for political favours."

"Good," Susan said. "The flotilla was a waste of resources from start to finish."

James nodded in agreement. "We're due to depart in seven hours," he said. "My staff should have time to complete the first set of arrangements - I need to make a whole series of calls - but please let me know if there are any problems."

"I've worked with your staff before," Susan said. "I don't think we'll have anything to worry about, sir."

"I hope not," James agreed. An Admiral had his own command staff, which sometimes ended up picking fights with the *starship's* command staff. James trusted his people - Susan was right; they *had* worked together for years - but he knew there could be problems. "If there *are* problems, we'll work them out in the first week of sailing."

He watched her go, then keyed his console, linking into the secure datanet and requesting a conference with the Prime Minister. It could be quite some time before the Prime Minister answered - there was no way to know where he was at any given time - so James opened his terminal and began scanning through the long list of reports. His staff was meant to handle as many of them as possible, yet they tended to be quite conservative about what actually required his attention. James didn't really blame them for being careful - he would prefer to waste his time than overlook a tiny detail that would turn out to be important later - but it could be annoying. By the time the communications link lit up, he was more than a little annoyed at whoever had sent a report on projected ammunition expenditures to his terminal.

We always shoot off more ammunition than projected, he thought, crossly. He'd learned *that* lesson during his time as an XO. *Haven't they noticed that by now*?

"Admiral," the Prime Minister said. He sounded tired. Unlike James, he hadn't been able to avoid either the press or hordes of MPs. "I apologise for the delay."

"Thank you for taking the call," James said. There were only a handful of people who could call the Prime Minister without clearing it first; he'd known he'd been put on the list after he'd been placed in command of the task force, but he had never taken advantage of it. "The task force is ready to depart on schedule."

"That's good," the Prime Minister said. "Parliament wants a victory, Admiral. It wants it very much."

James nodded. Uncle Winchester had briefed him thoroughly, both personally and through his team of political agents. Parliament was furious about the insult to both British prestige and the global order, but a number of MPs were worried about the cost of the war. They'd take any opportunity they could to cancel the task force and rely on political pressure to drive the Indians out of Pegasus.

Which won't work, he thought. *They'll think they've won and dig in harder.*

"You have your orders, covering all the contingencies we anticipated," the Prime Minister continued. "You also have authority to negotiate a ceasefire if the Indians agree to vacate the system without any further ado. I've included written authorisation naming you a diplomatic representative, within certain strict limits."

James nodded, curtly. Parliament had wanted to send a political representative to accompany the task force, but the Prime Minister had been adamantly opposed and the bill had died in committee. A diplomatic representative who *wasn't* tied to the military - or at least lacked a solid grasp of military realities - would be more of a hindrance than a help. There was simply no room for negotiations. Either Britain recovered the captured systems or lost them to the Indians. There was no middle ground.

"I won't give away the store, sir," he said.

"Glad to hear it," the Prime Minister said. "There hasn't been any formal communications from the Indians, but back-channel messages are still being exchanged. They're determined to hold the systems until forced to withdraw. MI6 has been unable to establish what orders have been given to the enemy commander, Admiral. However, if they are determined to remain in possession of the stolen territory, the orders will boil down to 'hold at all costs.'"

"We'll just have to convince them otherwise, Prime Minister," James said. He glanced at his terminal. "Everything is loaded, even the reporters."

The Prime Minister smiled, tiredly. "You have all the authority you need to keep them under control, Admiral," he said. "I'm sure a few months in the brig will be enough of a threat if necessary."

"I hope so," James said. Susan had already made it clear to the reporters that certain parts of the carrier were off-limits, but they were the compartments the reporters wanted to visit. "I think we'll be feeding them ration bars rather than bread and water."

"I'm pretty sure there are laws against cruel and unusual punishment," the Prime Minister said. He smiled. "Good luck, Admiral. The King will be addressing the nation just before your departure. Princess Elizabeth has already been earmarked for visiting the ships when you return."

"Thank you, sir," James said.

He sighed, inwardly. There was a need for the Royal Family to at least *pretend* to be involved, but he doubted it would be a pleasant visit. He'd *met* Princess Elizabeth and decided, in the privacy of his own mind, that if she had a single brain cell in her head it had been turned to mush long ago. Her brother, at least, had been a starfighter pilot during the war, but he'd headed off to Alien Prime after the final battle to serve as Ambassador. James rather suspected, from the rumours he'd heard, that Prince Henry had told his family - flatly - that he had no intention of ever taking the throne. The young man he recalled had been so determined to seek his own destiny that he'd even signed up at the Academy under a false name.

The Prime Minister nodded. "I'll see you when you get back, Admiral," he concluded. "I wish there was more time to organise a proper departure."

"We don't need bands playing, Prime Minister," James said. In all honesty, the crews had worked so hard they needed a rest, not a formal departure ceremony. "There will be time for that when we get home."

"Good luck," the Prime Minister said.

James watched his face disappear from the display, then rose to his feet and headed out into the CIC. It was considerably larger than the CIC on *Ark Royal*, crammed with consoles, holographic displays and a dozen crewmen. He took a moment to inspect the near-space display - there was no avoiding the handful of foreign warships in orbit around Earth, watching as the task force took shape - and then left the CIC, heading down to the engineering compartment. Admiral Smith had always toured his ship before departing and it was a tradition James intended to honour.

He paused, for a moment, outside the memorial in the exact centre of the giant supercarrier and bowed his head. Had it really been six years since he'd first set eyes on Admiral Smith - and five since his death? It had seemed so easy to unseat the older man from his command chair, to take *Ark Royal* for himself. No one had seriously expected the ancient museum piece to be the only starship actually capable of facing the Tadpoles in open battle. James had honestly thought he'd spend a year in command, then use it as a footstep to command of a modern fleet carrier.

And if I had kept command, he thought, *it would have been disastrous.*

His cheeks burned as he remembered the very first meeting. He'd thought Smith a drunkard; he'd thought the meeting a formality before Smith was shuffled off somewhere even more harmless than a decaying supercarrier. Instead, Smith had coolly pointed out that *James* was utterly unready to command the Old Lady - and succeeded in retaining his command. He'd been right, James had to concede. His younger self had been an idiot.

He saluted the portrait - he couldn't remember Admiral Smith ever looking so good in real life, but the artist had probably never seen him in person - and then headed onwards, visiting compartment after compartment. He'd helped to design the ship, yet there had been quite a few changes as the yards struggled to turn the concept into reality. The combination of modern drives and older-style armour alone had caused a whole string of problems.

His wristcom buzzed. "Admiral," Susan said. "We're ready to depart. Do you wish to watch from the bridge?"

James hesitated. *He'd* commanded *Ark Royal* during Operation Nelson and he'd been irked at how Admiral Smith had watched over his shoulder. It had been understandable - Smith had served on *Ark Royal* longer than James had been in the Royal Navy - but it had been annoying. The Royal Navy had long established that the ship's captain held final authority while a starship was in transit, yet few commanding officers would have the nerve to tell off an admiral. It didn't help that the commander of a shuttle, who might be a lowly midshipman, would technically have the right to issue orders to a senior officer.

"No, thank you," he said, finally. "I'll watch from CIC."

A dull tremor ran through the giant ship as he turned and slowly walked back to the CIC, taking his seat underneath the main holographic display. It was standardised - he'd used one like it during his first command along the border - but he made a mental note to start working through all the possible scenarios once they were underway. Another quiver ran through the ship - the drivers coming online - and he smiled. The temptation to just take the intership car up to the bridge was almost overwhelming.

Better let Susan handle it, he told himself, firmly. *She doesn't need you in the way.*

"Admiral," Commander Eland said. He was a newcomer, hastily reassigned from HMS *Victorious*, but he'd worked hard to fit into the command staff. "Nelson Base has cleared the fleet for departure."

"Good," James said. "Has the rest of the task force checked in?"

"Yes, sir," Eland said. "There are no problems."

James settled back in his chair. Fifteen warships - with nine more waiting to meet them at Terra Nova - three assault ships, three RFA support ships and ten freighters crammed with supplies. There would be more on the way, he knew, once several more warships had assembled at Nelson Base to provide an escort. Unless the Indians rolled over the moment the Royal Navy arrived, which he doubted, they'd have to burn through their supplies at a terrifying rate.

But it's the most formidable task force the Royal Navy put together since the war, he thought, grimly. It seemed impossible that the Indians could make a stand against it, yet Soskice - damn the man - had awakened a kernel of doubt. *If we lose, here and now, there will be no second chance.*

It wasn't a pleasant thought. They'd assumed, right up until the end, that the Tadpoles had wanted to exterminate the human race. Some of their factions, certainly, had been determined to do just that, wiping out the threat they thought humanity was to them. There had been no way to back down, no way to avoid the fight; they'd thought the choice was between fighting to the last or utter extinction.

But the Indians can't defeat us completely, any more than we can defeat them, he thought, sourly. *The politicians might just decide to swallow the insult rather than go back to war.*

Susan's face appeared in front of him. "Admiral," she said. "We will be leaving orbit in five minutes."

"Good," James said. There was no point in trying to hide. Indeed, he expected a number of other foreign warships to shadow the task force. Some of them would be covertly supporting the Indians, he was sure, but others would be trying to learn what they could from the first human-on-human interstellar war. "You may take us out on schedule."

CHAPTER FOURTEEN

HMS Warspite, Pegasus System

"Two new starships detected," Tara said, softly. "They're either destroyers or frigates."

John nodded, feeling the tension rising again. There were fifteen Indian starships within detection range - and more, perhaps, lurking in stealth mode. A handful was near the carrier, covering her against incoming threats, while the remainder were orbiting Clarke III or surveying the system. John wasn't sure why they thought they needed to bother - they'd certainly have obtained copies of the Royal Navy's survey results - but it did have the advantage of keeping a number of ships away from the danger zone. They wouldn't be able to intervene if the shit hit the fan.

Not that it would matter that much, he thought, as he silently worked through the vectors in his head. *They'd have plenty of time to concentrate their forces before the task force arrives.*

"The carrier is running a regular active sensor sweep," Tara added. "I don't think we can slip into weapons range without being detected."

"They'd be worried about space junk," John said. There was no shortage of tiny pieces of debris orbiting the gas giant. The last time he'd been in the system, the scientists had speculated that a moon had broken up millions of years ago and most of the remains had entered stable orbits. There'd even been an interesting argument over just *why* the moon had broken up in the first place. "But it does make it easier for us to keep tabs on where they are at any given time."

"Unless that's what they want us to think," Howard offered. "We don't have eyeballs on the target."

John nodded. The Indians could fake a carrier, if they wanted; the *real* carrier could be concealed under stealth mode while the fake carrier drew fire from any incoming ships. There was no way to tell the difference, save for watching the carrier launch starfighters or move out of orbit. And even the latter could be faked, if the Indians were prepared to put in the effort. Given the value of a supercarrier, John wouldn't have cared to bet against it.

"We'll slip a platform as close as possible to the carrier on the way out," he said. The original settlement hadn't included any stealthed platforms; there'd seemed no reason to prepare the system for enemy occupation. But really, who would have imagined the chain of events that led to the war? "Helm?"

Armstrong looked up. "Yes, sir?"

"Keep us inching towards the moon," John ordered. "We'll deploy the first set of platforms once we get close enough."

"Aye, sir," Armstrong said.

John keyed his console. "Major Drake" - the SAS officer had been granted a courtesy promotion while onboard ship - "we should be at the deployment zone in two hours. Is your team ready for deployment?"

"We're ready to man the shuttle," Drake confirmed. "I've just got the lads having a brief rest until the mission commences. All we need to do is get out there and cast off."

"Good," John said. He'd thought himself a brave man - he still had nightmares about the final desperate attack on a Tadpole ship, just after *Canopus* had been destroyed - but the planned deployment to Clarke III sent chills down his spine. "We'll alert you thirty minutes prior to shuttle launch time."

He closed the channel and turned his attention back to the main display. A handful of automated miners were coming into view, marking yet another Indian effort to assert their control over the system. It would probably take months, at the very least, to set up a full-scale mining operation - and *that* would raise the question of just what they intended to do with it - but it was a potential nuisance. Besides, as *Ark Royal* had proven, mining asteroids for raw materials that could be turned into mass driver ammunition wasn't particularly hard.

And that carrier will be bristling with mass drivers, he thought, coldly. *They'll have been planning to fight the Tadpoles, if necessary.*

It wasn't a pleasant thought. Mass drivers didn't throw their projectiles at the speed of light - it was impossible for *anything* with mass to travel at the speed of light - but there would be very little warning before a mass driver shell slammed into *Warspite*. His ship was nimble - certainly when compared to a carrier - yet it would be hard to evade the projectile before it was too late. The only other countermeasure, besides moving the ship, was hitting the projectile with something hard enough to destroy it and taking the shot in time would be difficult. He couldn't recall it ever having been tried outside simulations.

Wonderful, he mused. *We're going to be testing all the war-fighting theories of the past five years for the first time.*

John forced himself to relax as the moon grew closer. The Indians were clearly establishing an orbiting station, rather than relying on their ships; it looked, very much, as though they were planning to establish a habitable asteroid too. They were *definitely* planning to stay. John was surprised they were prepared to make the investment, but overshadowing the British commitment would be one way to make their control stick. Even so, it was about as odd as setting up a mining operation. The investment might be completely wasted, if the Royal Navy took the system...and, if the Royal Navy was defeated, it would still be a long time before the investments started to pay off. It was quite possible the Indians would be going into debt, even if the war ended with them in control of both Pegasus and Cromwell...

They must be very confident of victory, he told himself. *Or are they holding out for a share in the system regardless of who wins the war*?

He considered the point for a long moment. Terra Nova was the only human-settled star system where the locals didn't exert any control beyond their planet's atmosphere. Even if they did manage to unite their world and start building a navy, the other interstellar powers would object. There wasn't a single nation that didn't have interests, directly or indirectly, in the Terra Nova System. The standard rules of ownership simply didn't apply. But Britain owned the rights to Pegasus...

Unless they plan to assert that their investments aren't connected to the war, he thought. *And that capturing them would be naked theft.*

He made a mental note to discuss the possibility with the Admiral - it was well above his pay grade - and then turned his attention to reports from engineering. The recon platforms were ready for deployment, each one crammed with passive sensors and completely undetectable unless the Indians got *very* lucky. Once emplaced, the Royal Navy would have a record of every Indian starship that went active, as well as shuttles flying to and from the colony on Clarke. The intelligence staff would be able to make a number of very good guesses about just what the Indians were planning...

"Captain," Armstrong said. "We have reached the first deployment point."

John took a breath. "Deploy the first platform," he ordered. In theory, the Indians shouldn't be able to detect them, but it wouldn't be the first time someone accidentally radiated a betraying emission. "Now!"

"Aye, Captain," Tara said. There was a long chilling pause. "Platform deployed, sir. Laser link established; coordinates set."

"Recheck everything," John ordered, tersely. There was no room for errors. The first platform could *not* be lost without risking the entire network. "Confirm status."

"All systems go," Tara confirmed. "Live feed coming through the network now."

"Good," John said. "Helm, move us to the second deployment point. Prepare to launch the second platform."

"Aye, sir," Armstrong said.

It was nearly an hour before all seven recon platforms were deployed, two stealthily making their way towards Clarke III while the remainder held position in orbit around the gas giant, linked together by pinpoint laser beams. There would be almost no chance of the Indians detecting them, John was sure, and in the unlikely event of a miner stumbling across them the platforms would self-destruct, ensuring that nothing fell into enemy hands. The boffins had been very insistent on that, pointing out the dangers of allowing the Indians a good look at British stealth and recon technology. John suspected the Indians weren't far behind - if at all - but there was no point in arguing. Trying to prevent the Indians from gaining any insight into British capabilities was worth any effort.

Not that it matters, he thought, glumly. *If they stumble across a platform, even if it destroys itself, they'll know they're being watched.*

"Move us to the final deployment point," he ordered. "Keep a direct laser link to Platform One."

"Aye, sir," Armstrong said. "We're on the move."

John nodded, feeling sweat running down his back. He didn't dare take *Warspite* any closer to Clarke III, not when the Indians had presumably scattered recon platforms of their own around the tiny moon. The SAS would be running a gauntlet...and, from what he knew of the stealth shuttles, they'd be dead if the Indians got a sniff of their presence. They were simply designed for nothing more than being undetectable. A single plasma burst would be more than enough to swat them out of existence.

"Captain," Tara said. "The carrier is launching a flight of starfighters."

John braced himself. The carrier was *real*. It *had* to be real, unless the Indians had managed to fake a flight of starfighters. "Are they coming towards us?"

"No, Captain," Tara said. "It looks like a standard training flight."

"Keep watching them," John said. He studied the formation for a long moment, then nodded slowly. It *did* look like a training formation. The Royal Navy - and God knew there was no sign the Indians disagreed - believed in regular training fights and exercises, even during deployments. It was vitally important to keep the pilots at their best. "Let me know the moment anything changes."

"Aye, Captain," Tara said.

John watched the Indians for a long moment as *Warspite* made her way towards the final deployment point. The starfighters would have no trouble catching up with his ship if they detected her presence, which would force him to test Admiral Soskice's theories in real life while he tried hard to put as much distance as he could between *Warspite* and the Indian capital ships. His ship was crammed with point defence weapons, but how well would they work in practice? The simulations changed depending on what assumptions one fed into the system.

We may be about to find out, he thought. Another flight of starfighters launched from the Indian carrier, falling into a very definite exercise formation. No one in their right mind would fly in a predictable pattern during wartime, no matter how elegant it was. They'd be blown out of space before they could realise they were in trouble. *And then we'd know just which theories actually work.*

The Indian pilots looked to be good, although he thought he could see a certain lack of *real* experience that would cost them, in a real battle. Exercises, no matter how realistic, were rarely as unpredictable as real combat...but then, there hadn't *been* any real combat since the war. And the Indians had only had a handful of officers and men who'd fought in the Battle of Earth. They certainly hadn't joined the Great Powers in planning ways to take the offensive.

And no Indian carrier took part in Operation Nelson, he thought. *Did they have something planned even as far back as then*?

He shook his head. In hindsight, it might have been a mistake not to take the Indians seriously, but there was nothing to be done about it now. Once the war was over, there would be time to place international affairs on a whole new footing. And that, too, was well above his pay grade.

"Steady as we go," he ordered, quietly. Thirty minutes to the final deployment point, then the SAS would be on their way. "There's no reason to panic just yet."

———

"Percy," Penny said, as Percy popped his head into the observation blister. "Are you alright?"

"I always feel nervous before deployment," Percy said. His face was so pale that Penny seriously considered dragging him to sickbay. "I'll feel better as soon as we're on the way."

"You're going down to Clarke," Penny said. She hesitated, then told him what she'd found out. "You've joined the SAS."

"I'm....just working with them," Percy said. His eyes narrowed. "How did you find out about them?"

"Everyone on the ship knows," Penny said, sarcastically. It hadn't taken her long to discover that there were no secrets on a small warship. "And they know I'm your sister too."

"As long as they're not sharing nude photographs of you," Percy muttered. He cleared his throat before she could demand to know what he meant. "Don't put that in your reports, ok? The censors will not be amused."

"I won't," Penny said. She'd written a handful of articles, but most of them had been puff pieces. Neither she nor Stevenson had been permitted to watch from the bridge as *Warspite* made her approach to Clarke. She was tempted to complain it wasn't the full access she'd been promised, but she had a feeling that complaints would get her nowhere. "You owe me an interview when you get home."

"If I do," Percy said, morbidly. "Penny..."

He shook his head. "This could be the last time we see each other," he said. "I wish you hadn't come."

Penny felt her temper flare. "Would it have been better if I'd stayed on Earth and only heard about your death months or years after it happened?"

She glared at him. "At least this way I'll know what happened!"

Percy smiled. "But you could make up something far more impressive to tell your children," he pointed out. "Percy, my brother, who died in the arms of a dozen women after ingesting a large meal of oysters and injecting himself with super-boost. We should all try to pass that way."

"I hate you," Penny said. "And I wouldn't tell my children that you died in bed like *that*. I'm not Uncle Al."

"I'm pretty sure Uncle Al was making up most of his stories," Percy said. "Mum always said he was a braggart, a liar and a pain in the ass."

Penny had to smile. Uncle Al had been their mother's brother; he'd died two years before the war. He'd been fun, she had to admit, although the tales he told of adventures in faraway lands had been completely unsuitable for children. Their mother had regularly shouted at him for telling Percy and Penny about how he'd met strange women and courted them. Percy had once made the mistake of telling their mother that he wanted to be like Uncle Al and wound up grounded for a week.

"I'll tell them they should be proud of you," Penny said. "But I think you'll be fine. You're like a cockroach. You just don't die even when you get smacked with a shoe."

Percy shuddered. "Don't joke about cockroaches," he said. "The barracks in Malaysia were *full* of the damn things. We had to resort to a flamethrower just to keep them from crawling on our bunks."

"I hope you're joking," Penny said. Burning down a barracks was probably worthy of a court martial, not reassignment to Edinburgh. "I didn't hear anything about you being booted out of the military for gross stupidity."

"It could be worse," Percy said, refusing to rise to the bait. "We were doing battle with *huge* scorpions in the Middle East. Some of them were so large and nasty we used to joke they'd been mutated by radioactivity. There was a Yank base next door and we pitted our scorpions against theirs in duels to the death..."

His wristcom bleeped, once. "I have to go," he said. "Penny, take care of yourself, all right?"

"I'll try," Penny said. She gave her brother a hug. "And good luck, Percy. Come back alive."

She watched him go, feeling cold ice crawling through her heart. Percy...had always been strong and confident, even before he'd joined the military, but now...he'd always been overprotective, yet now he was overdoing it. Had her near-death on Vesy affected him so badly? She was the only blood relative he had, after all. And they'd been forced to struggle together to escape the floodwaters during the war.

"I'll see you again, Percy," she whispered. "But I can't stay out of danger."

"We're holding position at the final deployment point," Armstrong reported.

"There are no signs we've been detected," Tara added. "The SAS should be able to deploy without problems."

John nodded. Getting out wouldn't be hard, unless the Indians decided to radically expand their exercise schedule. It looked as though they were practicing dogfighting rather than search and locate patterns. They didn't seem to be doing too badly, as far as he could tell; he was already making notes in a file for the Admiral's tactical staff. But any weaknesses he saw in their formations would probably be corrected by the time the task force arrived.

"Very good," he said. He keyed his console. "Major Drake?"

"We're ready, Captain," Drake said. "Thank you for the lift."

"You're welcome," John said. He wanted to tell the SAS officer to make sure he kept a laser link to the platforms, but he knew Drake would know his job. No one passed Selection without being *very* capable, even at the start. "Have a good one, Major. You may undock at leisure."

"Just make sure you get home alive," Drake said. "The task force is going to need your intelligence too."

John nodded. The connection broke.

"Captain," Tara said. "The shuttle has undocked."

"Hold our position," John ordered. "We'll let them get some distance before we take our leave."

CHAPTER FIFTEEN

Stealth Shuttle Sneaky Bastard, Pegasus System

"You know," Jimmy said, as he sat down in the stealth shuttle. "This ship needs a name."

Percy shrugged and connected his suit to the shuttle's support system. Oddly, he'd done a handful of covert insertions himself, although not in a first-class stealth shuttle. They couldn't risk any transmissions, even very low-power microbursts. Flying in the suits would be bad enough, but being detected by the Indians would be worse. The shuttle might as well be made of glass for all the protection it would give them against incoming fire.

"It *has* a name," Corporal Ed Hill said.

"It has a set of numbers," Jimmy said. "There isn't a proper name. It's bad luck for a ship not to have a proper name."

"We're not smacking a bottle of bubbly into the hull," Lewis said. The sergeant smiled in a manner Percy found more than a little alarming. "I'm not going home to explain to a court martial board precisely how we managed to break an expensive shuttle."

"We're going to break it anyway," Jimmy pointed out.

"You flew in helicopters and none of them had names," Lewis snapped.

"Yes, they did," Hill said. "No one dared write them down, but they did have proper names."

"Pick a name," Drake said, as he took his seat next to the pilot. "Something we can be proud of when we read it in the history books."

"*SAS Rules*," Rupert offered. He snickered. "Or *Fuck Off*."

"I was going to suggest *Sneaky Bastard*," Jimmy said. "It suits her, doesn't it?"

"Very well," Drake said. "I hereby name this ship the *Sneaky Bastard* and may God help all who fly in her. Now, take your places and prepare for departure."

Hill smiled. "The flight to some godforsaken patch of rock is about to depart," he said, in shrill falsetto. "In line with our standard policies, the food served will be anything but edible, no matter how much you harass the stewardesses. The pilot is drunk" - Percy had to conceal a smile as Corporal Cook, the pilot, made a one-fingered gesture without looking round - "the co-pilot is mad and the stewardesses all got engaged last week to the same Para."

"The lucky bugger," Jimmy said.

"And the guy sitting next to you is so fat you'll be squashed against the window and you'll want to hurl every time you look at him," Hill continued. "And..."

"That will do," Drake said. He glanced over his shoulder. "Is everyone suited, buckled and ready to go?"

"Yes, sir," Lewis said. The troopers rapidly checked and rechecked their equipment; Lewis inspected Percy's gear carefully before reluctantly nodding. "All checked and ready to go."

A quiver ran through the shuttle as she undocked from *Warspite*. "We're on our way," Drake said. "Get some sleep. You'll need it."

Percy sighed inwardly as he closed his eyes. Lewis had told him, in no uncertain terms, that electronic players, e-readers and music boxes were strictly forbidden. They simply couldn't risk using *anything* that might produce an electronic signature the Indians could detect. He would have liked to bring a book, but it would be impossible to handle one in his suit. And taking off the suit, even for a brief moment, was also forbidden. They would have no other protection if the shuttle sprung a leak.

"I could always tell a story," Jimmy offered. "There was this girl back in Las Vegas..."

"Which ends with you fleeing the city ahead of a hundred policemen and a dozen outraged fathers," Lewis interrupted. "Don't you have any stories that aren't about sex, drugs and rock and roll?"

"I'm hurt, Sergeant," Jimmy said. "To think that I would waste time talking about drugs and rock and roll. Honestly!"

Lewis snorted. "Just get some sleep, Jimmy," he ordered. "There's a long walk ahead of us."

Percy smiled to himself - Jimmy's stories were even less plausible than Uncle Al's - and forced himself to sleep. There was no point in remaining awake for the five hours it would take to reach the moon's atmosphere - and besides, there was nothing they could do if the Indians happened to detect them. He wasn't sure quite what the Indians would do, but they'd either be killed out of hand or forced to surrender. Either one would bring his war to an undignified end.

The alarm jerked him awake, hours later. He glanced around in shock, cursing the spacesuit under his breath; four and a half hours in the suit hadn't done wonders for the smell. Lewis was talking quietly over the network, briefing the troopers on the atmospheric conditions ahead of them. They didn't sound pleasant. Percy allowed himself to feel relieved that Corporal Cook was flying the shuttle, instead of him, even though it would leave him and the others feeling utterly helpless. There was something about flying through turbulence that unnerved him, no matter how many times he'd been in more danger on the ground. The risks of dying were considerably higher in a war zone...

He forced the thought out of his mind as the shuttle altered course slightly, banking towards the moon. Clarke III didn't look any different, he noted; it was still an icy world, reflecting the light of the gas giant back into space. He silently calculated the location of the colony, hoping that Cook didn't make a mistake and put them down in an ocean, or the other side of the moon. Either one would prove fatal.

"We'll be entering the atmosphere in twenty minutes," Cook informed them. His tone turned mischievous. "If you want to go to the toilet, now is the time."

Percy rolled his eyes, safe in the knowledge no one could see him behind his visor. They were in suits, not uniforms; if they needed to go, they had to go inside the suits. It wasn't a very pleasant process, but it beat trying to get out of the suits in the cramped passenger compartment. And yet...he understood why the troopers kept joking, even as they drew closer to their destination. If they started to think about just what they were doing, they might freeze up...

And in the middle of combat, he thought grimly, *freezing could prove fatal.*

"Get into landing positions," Lewis ordered. "Captain?"

"It will be a rough landing," Drake confirmed. "And we'll have to move out as soon as we're down."

Percy sucked in a breath as he shifted position. The last time he'd flown through the moon's atmosphere, it had been on a standard shuttle, without any need to hide. They'd been able to alter course as necessary, just to avoid threats from snowstorms and other high-altitude disturbances. Now...*Sneaky Bastard* wouldn't be able to avoid anything unless Cook wanted to run the risk of being detected. They'd just have to hope that the preselected flight path was clear of anything that might make the flight more interesting than any of the troopers would have preferred.

"Here we go," Cook said. "Try not to be sick."

Percy swallowed hard as the shaking began. *Sneaky Bastard* shuddered violently, as if she was slamming into a body of water rather than the moon's thin atmosphere. The sensation only grew worse as they plummeted further down towards the surface; he swallowed again and again, refusing to be sick inside the spacesuit. It would be uncomfortable, he knew from bitter experience, and he would just have to endure until they finally set up camp near the colony. There was nothing else he could do. Somehow, he managed to keep his gorge down as the shuttle levelled out, then started to shake again.

"Cookie," Hill called. "Are you *trying* to hit every last patch of turbulence?"

"Stop bitching," Cook called back. "You couldn't do a better job!"

Sneaky Bastard rang like a bell; Percy braced himself, convinced for a long second that they'd slammed into something solid. Had they landed? The shuttle dipped again, convincing him that they'd merely hit a rough patch of air. He grabbed hold of the makeshift seat and held on for dear life, promising himself he'd never make fun of anyone on a commercial airliner ever again. His mother had been *very* nervous the first and last time they'd flown together.

"We need to turn around," Jimmy said. "I left my stomach somewhere back there!"

Percy laughed. He wasn't the only one.

"It's your own stupid fault for letting go of it," Cook called. "I hope you had it insured."

"There was this bunch of girls in a bus," Jimmy said, "and we were driving alongside them, wearing our uniforms. And they started waving and flashing their tits at us. It was great fun. We followed them into a service station and got laid there..."

Percy didn't believe a word of it, but the story was a welcome diversion. It grew filthier and filthier as the shuttle levelled out again and flew straight for several minutes, then fell further into the atmosphere. Jimmy had just reached the conclusion when Cook shouted for them all to brace themselves; Percy covered himself, just as there was a final terrifying crash. The shuttle hit the ground hard enough to do real damage. Pieces of debris fell all around them.

"Get up," Lewis snapped, as one bulkhead caved in. "Grab your packs and go!"

"There's nothing overhead," Cook confirmed. "The next starship entering visual range of this location will be overhead in fifteen minutes; I say again, we have fifteen minutes to hide the evidence."

Percy unsnapped his suit from the chair and ran, snatching up his pack on the way out. The landscape looked just as he remembered; white snow on the ground, twisted mountains in the distance...and, looming over the entire moon, the dominant presence of Clarke III. A light gust of snow blew across the landscape, hiding the tracks the shuttle had left when it had come down hard. Five of the troopers hastily hid the shuttle below camo netting, ensuring that no one overhead would see her if they bothered to peer down at the surface. The others - and Percy - moved the supplies away from the shuttle and concealed them under the snow, waiting for the moment they started the march to the colony. When he looked back, the remains of the shuttle were almost impossible to see.

Lewis caught his attention. "We move in twenty minutes," he said, using hand signals. It was too dangerous to risk radio transmissions, not with the Indians holding the high orbitals. "Are you ready?"

"Yes, sir," Percy signalled back.

The troopers hastily sorted out the supplies, then started the long march to the colony. Percy found it oddly relaxing; he'd been on forced marches on Vesy and, despite being trapped in a spacesuit, he had to admit that marching on Clarke III was considerably easier. It wasn't so hot or awkward; the only real danger was being spotted from orbit and the suits were camouflaged to make it hard for the Indians to notice them. Drake set a hard pace, but seemed willing not to push the limits too far. They might have to fight when they reached their destination.

I hope not, Percy thought. Seventeen men couldn't hope to overwhelm the Indian defenders, not when the Indians were supported by orbiting starships. He was sure the troopers would give a good account of themselves, but the outcome would be inevitable. *We need to dig in and find a way to scout out the Indian positions.*

It was nearly five hours before they started to cross through terrain that looked familiar, terrain Percy recalled from the exercises they'd held on Clarke before they'd been summoned to Cromwell and Vesy. The troopers paused for a brief conference, then altered course slightly so they would be climbing up the rear of the mountain between them and the colony in hopes of avoiding detection. Percy was silently grateful for the mountaineering course he'd taken during training - and then the climbing he'd been encouraged to do on his first leave - as he followed Lewis up the treacherous slope. The troopers, it seemed, had no difficulty whatsoever handling the climb.

They are the best of the best, Percy reminded himself, as they reached a suitable vantage point. *And they've fought all over the world.*

He leaned forward and sucked in his breath as the colony came into view. The briefings had told him that it had been expanded radically from the smaller installations he remembered, yet the Indians had clearly been working to expand it themselves. A number of prefabricated buildings were as he remembered - the original plan had been to expand underground, rather than expand the surface facilities - but the Indians had added a number of others to suit themselves. One looked rather like a barracks he'd seen on Mars complete with large airlock for suited soldiers; the others looked like warehouses, crammed with goodies from the orbiting starships. Dozens of men and machines were working on the landscape beyond the colony, carving out a far larger spaceport and a number of installations. One of them looked alarmingly like a ground-based mass driver.

They could hit anything in orbit, he thought. Mass drivers had been set up all over Earth, after the start of the war. They'd helped save the planet from the Tadpoles. *And they could probably hit something much further away, if they got lucky.*

Drake slipped up next to him as a shuttle flew overhead and landed on the makeshift landing pad. Percy watched a long line of suited men - or women - emerging from the craft and making their way into the nearest prefabricated building. Assuming the underground facilities hadn't expanded much further, he told himself, the Indians could have landed over four thousand people on the moon. Supporting them wouldn't be a problem, provided they had sufficient living space. The life support unit the original colonists had landed was massively over-engineered. It could have provided enough air and basic foodstuffs to supply over fifty *thousand* people, if pushed to the limits.

"We need to set up a camp," Drake signalled. "Move back."

The troopers had done it before, Percy noted; they'd probably practiced ever since it had become clear that war was the only realistic option. A site was chosen, on the rear of the mountain; a set of tents was established, then camouflaged under netting and handfuls of gathered snow. Percy was sure it was only a matter of time until it snowed again, providing additional cover. The troopers would be undetectable unless someone stumbled over them and *that* was unlikely. He doubted the Indians would be keen on letting their men go climbing when there was a war on.

Unless they conclude it would be the perfect vantage point, he thought. The Indians didn't seem to have detected the shuttle, but they might be simply playing a very long game. *They might want to run sweeps through the mountains anyway, just to be sure there's nothing here.*

He shook his head as he stumbled through the makeshift airlock and into the tent. The Indians would have to be mad to *let* an SAS team just wander around the landscape at will, even if they *thought* they had the situation under control. No, the smart thing for them to have done would have been to blow *Sneaky Bastard* out of space as soon as they detected her - or, if they waited for the shuttle to enter the atmosphere, claim it was an accident if they still wanted to avoid a shooting war. Given the planet's atmosphere and the shuttle's design, it wouldn't have been an unbelievable claim.

"Keep your suit on at all times," Lewis reminded him. "We might have to run in a hurry."

If the Indians stumble across us, Percy thought. *We'd be pretty close to dead the moment they set eyes on our positions.*

He took a ration bar and chewed it, thankfully. It tasted better than anything he'd eaten in the marines. The SAS, it seemed, got a better class of rations. But then, even on Vesy during the first mission, he hadn't been anything like as exposed. Lewis rattled through a box of supplies, passing out tiny sensors and monitoring devices that would have to be emplaced near the colony. Given time, they could parse out the enemy patterns and decide what to do next.

"Link into the stealthed platforms," Drake ordered. He glanced at Cook. "Send a message to *Warspite*. Tell them we're on the ground."

"Aye, sir," Cook said. He sounded doubtful. "That storm is coming in fast, sir. We may not be able to maintain a laser link indefinitely."

And now we're trapped, Percy thought, darkly. *Sneaky Bastard* could no longer fly. They were stuck until the moon was liberated or the war came to a negotiated end. It was vaguely possible they could steal an Indian shuttle, he knew, but he doubted they could get very far before the craft was blown out of space. The Indians would have to be asleep at the switch to miss them leaving in a stolen shuttle. *But at least they don't know we're here.*

"The storm will provide us with some cover, so we'll start probing once *Warspite* has left the system," Drake continued. "I want Ed, Martin and James on watch. Dale; you and your troopers set up the rest of the gear. Percy, you're on overlook with me."

"Yes, sir," Percy said. Drake wouldn't want to risk the cruiser, if something went badly wrong and the SAS were caught. "There may be other vantage points further around the mountain range."

Drake nodded. "I want to know what's changed too," he added. His voice turned thoughtful. "And which buildings can be attacked without risking the civilians."

"Yes, sir," Percy said, again.

CHAPTER SIXTEEN

HMS Warspite, Pegasus System

"The insertion team has made it down," Lieutenant Gillian Forbes reported. "They're in position now."

John allowed himself a moment of relief. The plan had seemed good on paper - and the SAS had been confident they could handle it - but he'd been far too aware of just how many things could go wrong. Landing on Clarke was hard enough without having to hide from watchful enemy eyes. But it looked as though he'd been wrong. The SAS had made it down and had marched overland to a vantage point near the colony.

He took a breath. It went against the grain to abandon anyone, even though it had been part of the plan from the start. The brushfire wars of the Age of Unrest had been marred by countless atrocities committed against British personnel who'd been captured by the enemy; these days, the mere *prospect* of someone falling into enemy hands demanded a full-scale response. He'd been raised in the tradition of leaving no man behind - or, if it was already too late, recovering the body. But now...

"Helm," he ordered. "Pull us back to open space."

"Aye, sir," Armstrong said.

John watched, grimly, as *Warspite* slowly moved away from Clarke. He sometimes wondered just how many people had been left behind on Vesy, just how many humans had been unaccounted for in the chaos. It was quite possible that a number had been captured and *not* handed over to the Indians. The Vesy had good reason to be angry at the human race. If they had captives, would they milk those captives for all they could get...or would they sacrifice them to the gods? Either answer was possible.

Particularly as building a technological civilisation is beyond any one man, he thought, darkly. *No matter who they captured, they couldn't jump from basic gunpowder to plasma cannons and orbital bombardment overnight.*

The Indian starfighters had returned to their carrier, he noted with some relief. He'd spent some time studying their formations, but it was impossible to say anything for certain. It didn't *look* as though the Indians expected attack, yet that was meaningless. They'd know the task force was on its way; they'd have plenty of time to prepare for battle before Admiral Fitzwilliam steered his ships through the tramlines and into Pegasus. John wondered, idly, if there *was* a way to sneak the fleet through, but he rather doubted it. The fleet train, at least, had no stealth mode.

"Captain," Armstrong said. "We are in clear space."

John nodded, studying the display. One Indian destroyer was making a beeline back to the carrier; another, more sedately, was heading towards the tramline to Vesy. The carrier herself was still holding position, surrounded by her flock of attendants. If they knew that *Warspite* was in the system, they were doing a very good job of playing dumb. They *could* be waiting for *Warspite* to leave before they altered their dispositions...

He sighed. It had been so much simpler fighting an alien foe.

"Take us directly to the tramline, as planned," he ordered. The SAS would be on their own, but that had been true since the moment they'd left. "Stealth mode is to be maintained."

"Aye, sir," Armstrong said. "Seven hours until we make transit."

John resisted the temptation to rub his eyes. He'd been on duty for far too long, but he didn't want to leave the bridge until they were well clear of the gas giant. There was no reason to believe they'd run into an Indian starship between their current position and the tramline, but he wanted to be sure. He shook his head, mentally; Howard would be perfectly capable of handling it, if they did. They'd already agreed to avoid contact if possible...

And if there's no way out, he told himself, *we can engage the enemy without waiting for them to fire first.*

"Local space is clear, sir," Tara said, as they glided further away from the planet. "There's no evidence they saw us."

"Understood," John said. It was frustrating; he would have preferred a straight-up battle to sneaking around, definitely. But there *would* be a battle soon, unless the Indians backed down and withdrew. He didn't expect it to happen. "Mr. Howard, you have the bridge."

"Aye, sir," Howard said.

"Inform me when we're nearing the tramline," John ordered. "Or if the Indians show any marked change in their posture."

"Aye, sir," Howard said, again.

John nodded and strode through the hatch, feeling tired and worn. The lack of shore leave - the chance to put the burden of command down for a few days - was taking its toll. A few nights in a hotel room in Sin City, a handsome young man to share his bed...what more could he want? The thought of meeting someone who would take Colin's place was tempting, but he didn't have the time. Even if he did, would he meet someone who liked him for himself or someone who merely wanted to be close to fame?

He shook his head as he stepped into the cabin, the hatch hissing closed behind him. It wouldn't take longer than a day to survey Vesy, then another couple of days to reach Cromwell and do the same there before heading through the tramlines to Hannibal, where they were supposed to link up with the task force. The Admiral would be glad to hear from them, he was sure; John would just be glad to have a chance to return to Pegasus and attack the Indian positions...

We'll have to sneak in again, he thought darkly, as he climbed into his bunk without bothering to undress. *Someone will have to link into the stealthed platforms and take the report from the people on the ground.*

The odd thing about the Vesy System, Penny had decided long ago, was just how *normal* it was. There wasn't anything odd in the system, save for a gas giant that was unusable for a reason she didn't pretend to understand; there didn't seem to be anything that could account for the presence of an intelligent race. But then, there wasn't anything uncommon about Earth either, as far as she knew. The only odd world to produce an intelligent form of life was Tadpole Prime.

But then, she told herself, *we don't really have enough samples to judge.*

"That's very definitely a second supercarrier hanging between the tramlines," Lieutenant-Commander Tara Rosenberg said. They stood together in the tactical compartment, watching the holographic display. "They probably wanted to compromise on location."

Penny frowned. "Why aren't they orbiting Vesy itself?"

"There's nothing on the planet worth protecting," Tara explained. "If they needed to respond to trouble from the natives, they'd only really need a destroyer and a few units of armoured soldiers to turn the balance in their favour. Keeping the supercarrier in open space allows them to respond to a crisis in either Pegasus or Gandhi."

She shrugged. "They'd probably be happier with a *third* carrier, so they could have one permanently posted to Gandhi and one kept in reserve here, but they don't have a third carrier," she added, after a moment. "They have to make do with what they have."

"They might get caught out of position," Penny speculated. She wasn't a military expert, but she *had* read a lot of books and watched dozens of tactical simulations. "By the time they respond to an alarm call it may already be too late."

"They have to make do with what they have," Tara repeated. She shrugged. "It is a gamble, I admit, but they don't have any choice. Putting the second carrier in Vesy lets them respond to a crisis without fatally compromising their ability to hold one of their core systems. I imagine there won't be anything more than an escort carrier, at best, within Cromwell."

Penny considered it. "So we might manage to defeat one carrier and then the other?"

"We'd certainly prefer to handle them one carrier at a time," Tara agreed. She tapped a switch, deactivating the display. "Did you find it informative?"

"It's not something I can report," Penny said. There was no way she'd be allowed to report on *Warspite's* mission until the end of the war. "But it was very useful background material."

"No one ever looks at background material," Tara said. She gave Penny a thin smile. "If someone wants to bury an embarrassing fact, they put it in the files of background material, safe in the knowledge no one else will ever find it."

"I'll have to spend time reading it," Penny said, dryly. "There isn't much else to do on the ship."

Tara gave her an odd look. "There's *always* something to do onboard ship," she said. "I made the mistake of complaining about being bored when I was a midshipwoman and the lieutenant promptly found me a few million tasks that needed doing."

Penny blinked. "A few *million* tasks?"

"They do tend to add up," Tara pointed out. "There are thousands of components throughout the ship that need to be checked regularly, then the decks need to be washed on a regular basis, the tubes need to be cleaned and the life support system needs to be monitored. And then there's the constant need to exercise regularly..."

"Not for me," Penny said. "There's nothing to do beyond writing reports that won't get past the censors."

"If you think that's true," Tara said, "why are you even here?"

"I can write a proper report after the war," Penny said, after the moment. "But it wasn't quite what I was promised. Anything that will get past the censors won't interest people back home."

Tara looked doubtful. "What *does* interest people on Earth?"

Penny sighed. "Sex, violence, royalty, baby animals...my editor used to say that the perfect headline included at least three of them. One of the reporters managed to sell a story entitled 'Duke of Something shoots down mating birds on hunting trip.' It was a hit."

"Some people have too much time on their hands," Tara said. "I suppose we could get the sex and violence part, if we tried. Or would that come under the heading of bringing the navy into disrepute."

Penny gave her a sharp look. "Sex and violence?"

"There was a right Casanova on my last ship," Tara said. "I honestly don't know how he managed to bonk two separate girls at the same time. It shouldn't have been possible, not when everyone knows everything that's going on. But he actually made it last for over three months before they found out and...well, they had to be dragged off him. That was after he made the crack about wanting to have a catfight, of course."

"I don't think I'd be allowed to report *that* story," Penny said. There were quite a few books written by spacers after they left the navy, but she couldn't recall actually reading about anything like Tara's story. "The censors would probably complain I wasn't focusing on the meat of the matter."

"I'm going to write it down myself," Tara said. "Do you think I can get a whole book out of it?"

"I don't know," Penny said. She suspected her editor would run it, after the war, but filling a whole book would require a few hundred more stories. "Does it have a happy ending?"

Tara smirked. "For whom?"

"Good question," Penny agreed.

Tara cleared her throat. "You have to put in the effort before you can be anything," she said, dryly. "Your time here might seem boring now, but you'd have the experience you needed to write a kick-ass report after the war is over. The censors wouldn't be so censorious once the shooting has stopped.

"I have the same problem, of course. I want to be a commanding officer, one day, but I can't walk out of the Academy and straight into a command chair. No, I have to work my way up the ranks; ideally, I should be promoted to commander in a year or two and win a chance to be an XO."

Penny smiled. "Should?"

"There are fewer ships than there are ambitious officers," Tara said. "If I get to commander and there isn't a chance to serve as an XO, I might lose my opportunity to become a captain and take command of my own ship. The Admiralty would eventually note that I hadn't moved up in rank again and ship me sideways into a desk job. At that point...I might well bend over and kiss any further advancement goodbye."

She shrugged. "Actual experience in fighting a war would be helpful," she admitted. "But even then I would have to be lucky. There're always at least five or six officers competing for any given post."

"Ouch," Penny said. "Is there nothing you can do to improve your chances?"

"Work extremely hard," Tara said. "Having political connections helps, sometimes, but I don't have any. That said, if I *do* get to become a commander, the odds of getting my own command become a great deal better. Experience as an XO is vitally important."

Penny frowned. "Wouldn't you still have command experience?"

"It's not the same," Tara said. "The XO does a great deal of the work, true, but the XO isn't the one *responsible* for the ship. That's the commanding officer's job."

"Like the editor is responsible for the news," Penny mused. "You can fire a reporter if necessary, but that doesn't keep the editor from getting the blame."

"Pretty much," Tara said. She glanced at her wristcom. "I'm due on the bridge in thirty minutes. Do you want to grab a cup of coffee before I go?"

"Sure," Penny said. She paused. "What do you do when you're *not* on the bridge?"

"I should make you wait to read my book," Tara said. "I spend a third of my time on the bridge, as tactical officer; a third of my time supervising the tactical department and a third of my time in bed. I'm supposed to stuff meals, exercise and studying for the promotion board exams into there somehow, but I'm damned if I know how. That's one good thing about long cruises, I suppose. You can take the time to do your duty *and* look to your future prospects."

She led the way to the hatch. "Coming?"

"Of course," Penny said. "I thought I wasn't supposed to stay here without an escort."

"You're not," Tara said, deadpan. "You might push the wrong button and blow up the ship."

Penny was sure - as sure as she could be - that Tara was joking. But, as she walked out of the compartment, she was careful not to touch anything anyway, just in case.

"We could take her, you know."

John nodded, slowly. Cromwell - an Earth-type world that had been settled scant months before the First Interstellar War - hadn't been occupied, as far as they could tell. The only Indian presence in the system was a single destroyer, holding position in geostationary orbit and maintaining a direct line of sight to Cromwell City. Given that there were only a few thousand colonists on the surface, without any way of reaching orbit, the ship was very definitely overkill.

Although they might be shipping in countless settlers soon, he thought. *Who knows what will happen when the colonists become a minority on their own world?*

"Captain," Howard urged. "We might not have a chance to take her out again."

"I know," John said. A single Indian destroyer, isolated from the rest of the Indian fleet... *Warspite* could take her out easily, assuming she got in the first blow. And *that* wouldn't be hard. The Indians weren't even sweeping space with active sensors. "But that would remove all hope of a diplomatic solution."

The words tasted like ashes in his mouth. He was *sure* there was no realistic hope of a peaceful solution, of anything other than a brief and violent conflict between Britain and India. Taking out the destroyer now might save lives in the long run. But the Rules of Engagement were inflexible. They were not to switch to an aggressive posture until the task force entered Pegasus.

He looked at the display. "Is there any trace of Indian activity on the surface?"

"No, sir," Tara said. "The colonists may not even be aware they've been conquered."

John's lips twitched at the thought. It wasn't as absurd as it sounded. Cromwell was a farming colony; it had almost nothing else, beyond a tiny spaceport. The Indians might not have bothered to announce their presence...and if they hadn't, the locals might not even know the destroyer was there. It would just be another light in the sky.

"Take us to the tramline," he ordered. It would be a week before they reached Hannibal, but once they were there they could stop sneaking around. "We'll be back."

"Aye, sir," Armstrong said.

Howard looked disappointed. John didn't blame him. Royal Navy officers were taught to be offensive and the opportunity looked too good to miss. But it would remove all hope of a diplomatic solution...

"Once we're through the tramline, I'll want your report," John said. It would be better for Howard to have something to do, rather than brood on missed opportunities. "We'll need to discuss options with the Admiral."

"Aye, sir," Howard said. "The ships could move, of course."

John nodded. The Indians could move their second carrier - INS *Vikramaditya*, if her IFF was accurate - into Pegasus, given a few hours. MI6 believed that the Indian carriers didn't carry as many starfighters as the latest British designs, but collectively they would tip the balance against *Theodore Smith...*

Unless we come up with a way to surprise them, he thought. He'd already had a couple of ideas, but the Admiral would need to approve them. *And that might be difficult.*

CHAPTER SEVENTEEN

Clarke III, Pegasus System

"Here comes the transport, boss," Lewis said.

"Good," Drake said. "Percy, you're with me."

"Yes, sir," Percy said. He'd expected to remain at the rear, but he had a feeling he was more expendable than any of the troopers. "I'm with you."

The transport slowly came into view. Percy had half-expected a normal lorry, but the vehicle cruising slowly towards him looked like a cross between a railway locomotive that had been forced to travel on normal ground and an army transport. It was massive too, easily twice the size of a shuttle. If he hadn't been forced to learn to drive transports when he'd joined the marines, he would have wondered if they were wrong and there was an entire crew on the vehicle, rather than just one driver. But only one person was visible through the viewport at the front.

Which means nothing, he reminded himself. The marines preferred to have at least two people in the cab at all times, although there were sometimes moments when only one person could be spared to drive. *There could be someone asleep in the rear.*

"Get ready," Drake ordered. "We'll only get one chance to scramble onboard."

"Aye, sir," Percy said. He watched the transport growing closer, marking out the ladder up to the hatch. "I'm ready."

"Go," Drake ordered.

Lillian would not willingly have credited the Indians with anything, but she had to concede they were efficient. The more supplies they brought down to the surface, the more work they found for the colony's original settlers...which made it harder and harder to avoid outright collaboration. Lillian did as little as she felt she could get away with, but others were less capable of passive resistance. A number of colonists had even thrown their lot in completely with the Indians, as far as she could tell. It helped that the Indians were paying wages well above the average for even the simplest task.

Bastards, she thought, as she drove the all-terrain transport over the icy ground. *They could at least refuse to volunteer for anything.*

She shook her head in dismay. The Indians were setting up military installations all over the moon, putting her and the other engineers to work shipping supplies from the colony to the satellite outposts. Lillian had welcomed it at first, despite having to sleep in the vehicle's cab, but now it was just a nuisance. The pleasure of being away from the colony paled when compared to the irritation of having to assist the Indians at the far end. She was tempted to call in sick, but the Indians had made it clear that there were limits to how much passive resistance they would tolerate. By the time the colony was liberated, if indeed it was *ever* liberated, sorting out who resisted passively from those who collaborated openly would be a nightmare.

A dull thump echoed through the transport. Lillian cursed under her breath and glanced out of the cab, looking to see what - if anything - she'd hit. The transport was rated for environments a great deal harsher than Clarke, but the icy ground was far from stable. *She* would have preferred to take a different route each time; the Indians, however, preferred her to follow the same path. They didn't seem to realise that there weren't any solid roads on Clarke, merely paths through the ice.

And one of them goes far too close to the ocean, she thought. She had no illusions about what would happen if she accidentally drove onto the ice and fell through. The transport was airtight - it had been designed for operations in a poisonous atmosphere - but recovering her would be incredibly difficult, even if the Indians helped. *I could die out here and they'd only moan about losing the supplies.*

She tensed suddenly as she heard the sound of a hatch opening. It was impossible; she *had* to be imagining it. There was no one else on the transport; she'd hoped to share the transport duties with someone else, but there weren't enough qualified drivers on the colony to give her a partner. And yet...the transport *did* produce odd sounds from time to time... could she be imagining it? Or...she jumped and spun around as she heard the hatch behind her opening, her mouth dropping open in shock as she saw two black-clad men emerging from the sleeping compartment. They couldn't be real...

"Please don't sound an alarm," the leader said. "We're friendly."

Lillian found her voice. "Who...who are you?"

"SAS," the leader said. "And you?"

"Lillian Turner," Lillian stammered. SAS? Who *else* would be picked to sneak onto the colony? And yet she had no way of knowing if they were telling the truth. Their English was perfect, but the Indians spoke perfect English too. It could be a trap to get her to do something stupid. She'd never laid eyed on an SAS officer before. "How...how did you get onboard?"

"Jumped on while you were driving past, opened the airlock and made our way forward," the leader said. "We need to talk to you."

Lillian stared at him, trying to think. Were they genuine? The black suits they wore were completely unmarked, although that proved nothing. She could have worn a soldier's uniform herself without being a soldier. The accents were understandable and...

The second trooper removed his helmet. Lillian blinked in surprise as she recognised him, vaguely. He'd been a Royal Marine, one of the complement assigned to *Warspite*; he'd been her guard during her brief imprisonment on the starship. He didn't seem too pleased to see her - it was hard to blame him, as he'd know how stupid she'd been - but at least it proved their *bona fides*. She just wished she could remember his *name*!

"Percy," the trooper said. "It's been quite some time."

"Yeah, yeah it has," Lillian said. She sagged back into the driver's seat. "What can I do for you?"

"Start with the obvious," the leader said. "How long do you have until you need to check in?"

Lillian glanced at her radio. "I'm meant to call in every two hours," she said, shortly. "And once more before I park up for the night."

"I see," the leader said. "And do you believe you're being watched?"

"I don't think so," Lillian said. She hesitated. The Indians could produce bugs so tiny they couldn't be seen with the naked eye. As far as she knew, there hadn't been any counter-surveillance technology on the colony before the invasion. *She* certainly didn't have access to any of it. "But I don't know."

The troopers exchanged glances, then started to sweep the cab with a handful of sensor devices. Lillian watched, feeling her body starting to shake. The Indians *might* have hidden a few bugs in the cab and, if they had, she was dead. They'd know the SAS had landed and that the Royal Navy wouldn't be far behind. The Royal Marine - Percy, she reminded herself - winked at her. He wasn't exactly ugly, she decided; indeed, he was remarkably handsome in many ways.

And you're being an idiot, she told herself. *Letting yourself get distracted when you should be driving.*

"Clear," the leader announced, finally. "You're not being watched."

"That means you can do what you like in the sleeping compartment," Percy jibed. He sounded as relieved as Lillian felt. "It's bigger than *our* sleeping compartments."

"No doubt," Lillian said. The Indians would probably notice if she stopped the transport, but otherwise...they were safe. "What can I do for you?"

"We need answers," the leader said. He squatted down, facing her. "Percy, take the wheel."

"Yes, sir," Percy said.

"Keep her on a steady course," Lillian advised, as she surrendered the driver's seat to him. "There shouldn't be anything to run into here, but keep a sharp eye out anyway."

The leader removed his helmet and frowned. "Indian patrols?"

"They don't bother to patrol the landscape away from the colony, as far as we know," Lillian said. She cursed under her breath as she remembered the most important piece of information. "They're installing mass drivers, sir."

"We know," Percy said, without taking his eyes off the landscape. "How many of them?"

"They're setting up at least a dozen outposts," Lillian supplied. "If each of them houses a mass driver..."

"They could hit anything within a light minute of Clarke before it knew it was under attack," the leader said. He didn't sound angry, merely curious. "I have a long string of questions for you."

He wasn't lying, Lillian discovered. The interrogation was so intensive that her head started to pound halfway through, even though she knew she was innocent this time. How many Indians were on the moon? How many occupied the colony? How many colonists were collaborating and how many were resisting passively? What had the Indians told the colonists and why? What had happened when the Indians invaded? What had happened to the POWs taken during the landing? By the time he was finished, Lillian wanted nothing more than a strong painkiller, a glass of water and a chance to get some sleep.

"I think she's had enough for the moment, sir," Percy said, glancing round. "You're very intense."

"*You* didn't collapse under my questions," the leader observed.

"I knew what I was getting into," Percy countered. "And I *volunteered* for the job."

"Thank you," Lillian said. If she could have kissed him, she would have. "We've been trying to collect information, but the Indians have the datanet and control systems thoroughly sewn up."

"So you don't know how many soldiers there are on the planet," the leader mused. He looked her in the eye. "You have no idea at all?"

Lillian hesitated. "We set up nine prefabricated barracks for them," she said. She didn't miss the sudden flicker of alarm in the leader's eyes. "Assuming that those barracks are only used for soldiers, sir, they have at least ten thousand on the moon."

"Seems a bit of a heavy investment," Percy said, lightly. "Are they really *that* determined to hold Clarke?"

"The Governor was fond of saying that the next few decades would bring massive changes," Lillian said. "Just controlling the tramlines alone would make the system wealthy. Being able to settle Wells and mine space junk would only enhance our position. Those of us who got in at the ground floor, he said, would wind up very wealthy."

Percy blinked. "Really?"

"Yeah," Lillian said. She wasn't sure if it applied to *her*, but it might. "The settlement corporation offered vast incentives to anyone willing to come to Clarke, rather than Britannia or Nova Scotia. Everyone who came to Clarke has non-voting shares in the corporation and is thus guaranteed a share in the profits. The Indians have good reason to want to hang on to the system."

"I see," Percy said. He shrugged. "When are you expected at your destination?"

Lillian glanced at the GPS. "Four days," she said. The only advantage, as far as she could tell, was being away from the Indians for ten days. "These transports aren't very fast."

She hesitated and started to shake. Were they going to kill her? She had no illusions about how long she'd be able to hold out if the Indians used truth drugs...or merely pulled out her teeth, one by one, until she talked. The SAS troopers needed to maintain their secrecy, whatever happened, or the Indians would start tracking them down. Their safest course of action was to kill her.

"We're not going to hurt you," the leader said, as if he'd read her mind. "We just need you to keep quiet about our presence."

"I will," Lillian said, quietly. "I won't even mention it to anyone else who might be interested in resisting."

She swallowed hard. It must be a common problem for the troopers. If they were spotted, did they kill the spotter or risk being betrayed? She knew she couldn't stop them, if she'd been armed. If they wanted to break her neck and fake an accident, perhaps by triggering an explosion in the fuel tank, it would be easy.

"Good," the leader said. "Now...what are you expected to do at the far end?"

Lillian nodded towards the rear of the giant transport. "Get their boxes unloaded and head back to the colony," she said. "They don't normally insist on riding with us, but Pat did have to take a couple of Indian soldiers back with him. I've never had to do that, at least not yet. I think they may prefer to use shuttles for themselves."

The leader frowned. "Or they're worried about putting their soldiers in with defenceless females," he mused. Lillian shuddered at the thought. "But you'd think they'd put the best of their men on Clarke."

"Unless they don't think the moon can be held," Percy offered. "If something were to happen to that carrier, sir, the Indians would be in a very bad position."

"And so they might have rated the soldiers as expendable," the leader said. "I've seen that happen, Percy, but only on Earth. I don't think anyone would waste the training necessary to prepare men for Clarke so casually."

Lillian looked from one to the other. "How can you be so calm?"

"Panic wouldn't actually help," the leader pointed out. "Do you know what they're shipping?"

"We're not allowed to open the boxes," Lillian said. "They told us that we'd be shot if there were any signs of tampering. It could be anything from mass driver projectiles to ration bars and reading matter."

"Maybe they should just keep eating our ration bars," Percy said. "A few weeks of chewing and farting loudly and their men will desert."

"Indeed," the leader said. He smiled, suddenly. "Most of *our* men deserted after eating them."

Lillian smiled too, even though she knew they were trying to make her feel better. "Are you going to try to open the boxes?"

"I'll take a look at them," the leader said. "Percy will stay and keep you company."

And make sure I don't call the Indians while you're gone, Lillian added, mentally.

"It's been a while," Percy said, once they were alone. "How were you coping down here?"

"It was better, I think," Lillian said, slowly. She wasn't sure why she wanted to open up to him. They *had* been on the same ship, but they'd barely known one another. Hell, he'd practically been her arresting officer. "They were suspicious of me at first, yet I slowly earned their trust."

"And then the Indians arrived," Percy said. He seemed inclined to repeat some of his superior's questions. "How many people are collaborating?"

Lillian sighed. "There are around fourteen people who seem to have gone over completely," she said, "but there're over a hundred other colonists who are being pushed into assisting the bastards. People like me, Percy; people who don't want to find out what happens if we say no. The line between outright collaboration and doing the bare minimum is getting thinner every day."

"And they have you supplying military installations," Percy mused. "They're certainly pushing the limits of the surrender agreement."

"I know," Lillian said. "They took the governor after they occupied the colony. I don't know what happened to him after that. Was he returned to Earth?"

"Not as far as I know," Percy said. "He may have been moved to the carrier and held there."

Lillian blinked. "The carrier?"

"The Indians have a supercarrier in the system," Percy said. "Didn't they tell you?"

The hatch opened, again, before Lillian could answer. "The boxes are completely sealed," the leader said. "Breaking in would be easy, but sealing them up again to remove all evidence of tampering would be impossible. I think we'll just have to leave the mystery unsolved for the moment."

Lillian breathed a sigh of relief. "I'm sorry," she said. "It's...I don't know what to do."

"Here," the leader said. He produced a small pen from his suit and passed it to her. "This emits a very low-level radio signal. To make it work, push the top down hard for thirty seconds; to deactivate the signal, click the top up again. The next time you're on one of these transports, alone, use the pen to signal us. Do *not* use it within a kilometre of the colony or any Indian outpost."

"James Bond would be proud," Lillian said. She examined the device thoughtfully. "Can it serve as a real pen?"

"Of course," the leader said. "Just keep it in your pocket like you would with an engineering pen. Even if the Indians confiscate it, they'd have to take the device apart to prove it wasn't anything other than a normal pen. Just make sure you don't try to use it anywhere near the Indians. They may detect the signal and track it down."

"I understand," Lillian said. She tucked the pen into her shirt and looked at them. "I'm normally out again within the week. Do you have anything in particular you want me to do?"

"Just keep your eyes open," the leader said. "And...see if you can work out just how much freedom of movement we'd have if we slipped into the colony. We need that sort of information."

"I'll do my best," Lillian promised. "And thank you."

"Don't tell *anyone* about us," the leader warned. "No one."

"I won't," Lillian said.

"Good luck," Percy said.

He waved cheerfully as he rose and headed for the hatch, followed by his superior. Lillian took the driver's seat again and smiled to herself as she heard the hatch opening and closing behind her. The SAS wouldn't have any problems if they jumped down, she was sure. It wasn't as if the transport was moving particularly fast.

Good luck, she thought, feeling better than she had for weeks. *I'll see you again soon.*

CHAPTER EIGHTEEN

HMS Theodore Smith, Hannibal System

"Welcome onboard, Captain," Commander Sally Acorn said. "The Admiral is waiting for you in the briefing compartment."

"Thank you," John said. He would have liked a tour of the giant carrier - he hadn't had a chance to visit a *Theodore Smith*-class carrier - but he had a feeling there was no time. The task force had been delayed long enough, giving the Indians far too much time to dig into the Pegasus System and ready their defences. "Please show me to him."

He looked around with interest as the commander led him through a maze of corridors. It had been years since he'd served on *any* carrier and he had to admit that many of the lessons learned during the war had been integrated into *Theodore Smith*. Her hull was armoured, her interior was designed to seal compartments and make life difficult for boarders and *everything* was massively over-engineered. He had never met Admiral Smith, but if what he'd heard was true, the old man would probably have approved. His namesake was definitely a direct descendent of *Ark Royal*.

The CIC was massive, crammed with consoles and holographic displays. He took a moment to study the one showing the task force, then followed the commander through a hatch and into a small briefing room. It was still large, certainly by *Warspite's* standards; he couldn't help wondering if a small army of officers were expected to attend the briefing. The compartment was just *too* large for two officers.

"Captain," Admiral Fitzwilliam said. He rose and held out a hand. "Congratulations on your successful cruise."

"Thank you, sir," John said. He shook the Admiral's hand and sat as the Admiral indicated a chair. "I'll pass your kind words on to my crew."

"The tactical staff are already analysing your sensor records," the Admiral said. "I concur, however, that the Indians are trying to muddy the issue of who owns the facilities within the system as a fallback measure. However, from a tactical point of view, we can probably either claim everything we seize as the spoils of war or compensate the Indians for it afterwards."

"That will cause political problems, sir," John said. "There could be another Terra Nova incident."

"We're not Terra Nova," the Admiral said, curtly. "And it's pretty damn cheeky for the Indians to be investing in *our* system without *our* permission. I don't think the other powers will be particularly interested in setting a very dangerous precedent. What's to stop the Chinese from setting up a mining facility in New Washington if the Indians get away with doing it to us?"

"Nothing legal," John said.

"The Chinese have every interest in keeping the Indians from creating such a precedent too," the Admiral added. He shrugged. "All this will be moot, of course, if we fail to evict the Indians."

He keyed a switch, activating the holographic display. "You noted thirty-seven starships in the system, including one fleet carrier and twenty-two warships," he added. "That gives them a slight advantage in numbers and perhaps technology, although we do have more experience. They may also have brought in reinforcements from Vesy."

"Yes, sir," John said. "They have a second carrier battle group lurking there."

"Which can be in Pegasus within two hours of deployment," the Admiral mused. "And if we let them unite the two fleets, we may be in some trouble."

"That *would* let us snap up their settled worlds," John pointed out. "We'd have bargaining chips for the moment the war stalemated."

"They wouldn't be particularly useful," the Admiral pointed out. "Ideally, we need to deal with the carriers separately."

"Yes, sir," John said.

He had his doubts. The Indians presumably knew that they faced only one British carrier - and that her destruction would be enough to end the war. In their place, he would have brought the second carrier into the Pegasus System and forced an engagement on favourable terms, relying on superior numbers to triumph over experience. It would cost the Indians badly, but if they won the engagement they'd win the war. Unless, of course, they lost both of their carriers in the fight...

"And we also need more data from the surface," the Admiral added slowly. "I assume the recon platforms were placed correctly?"

"Yes, sir," John said. "There was no sign they were detected."

"Then you'll be returning to the system soon," the Admiral said. "You'll be needed to collect data from the platforms - and the ground. We need to know what we're likely to encounter when we enter the system."

He took a breath. "This is pretty much the last chance the Indians have to avoid hostilities, Captain. Either they pull back and concede the systems or they prepare to resist attack."

"They won't pull back, sir," John said. "They've already made a sizable investment in the system."

"I know," the Admiral said. He studied the display for a long moment, allowing his anger to show. "Such a fucking waste."

"Sir?"

"If we win," the Admiral said, "we will probably have destroyed at least one Indian fleet carrier - one *human* fleet carrier. If *they* win, *Theodore Smith* will probably have been destroyed or - at least - severely damaged. She's built to take punishment, but the Indians can dish out a hell of a lot. And *that*, Captain, weakens the entire human race against alien threats. How can we unite against a new threat if we've wasted our strength in civil wars?"

John frowned. "Is there a new threat?"

"Six years ago, the thought of aliens would have been laughable," the Admiral commented, slowly. "The highest form of life we'd encountered, away from Earth, were the neo-dogs of New Washington, creatures so easy to domesticate that they became popular pets for American children. They certainly didn't possess any real intelligence. We told ourselves that we were alone in the universe. There were even cults that believed we were destined to spread through the galaxies, spreading intelligence far and wide.

"Now, Captain, there are two known intelligent races," he added. "One of them believed it had good reason to wage war against us, one of them was so primitive that contact with us proved disastrous to their society. How do we know that the next race we encounter won't be as far above us as we are above the Vesy? Or that the next race we encounter will be so alien that direct communication is impossible? That nothing short of total war will be enough to answer the threat they pose?"

John considered it for a long moment. The Tadpoles were hard to understand, certainly when it came to talking about anything beyond hard science and numbers. Their outlook on the universe was very...*alien*. The Vesy, by contrast, were understandable, perhaps *too* understandable. They fitted into the same ecological niches as humanity...indeed, in many ways, they were alarmingly close to humans. Their resentment at looking up at the stars and knowing they were *taken* was easy to understand. And they had good reason to want human technology for themselves.

"We don't," he said, finally. "There's no way to know what's on the other side of the next tramline."

"Exactly," the Admiral said. "I've actually tried to convince the Admiralty to put a freeze on further exploration until we rebuild our fighting power. The Admiralty understood my point, I think, but it was impossible to convince the rest of humanity. India...among others...objected to a freeze that would leave them permanently disadvantaged."

John scowled. "That probably didn't help their attitude toward us."

"No," the Admiral agreed, regretfully. "It probably didn't."

He shrugged. "Grab yourself a cup of coffee, Captain," he added. "We'll start the main briefing in thirty minutes."

The briefing compartment on *Theodore Smith* was designed to hold, if necessary, the commanding officer of every ship in the task force. James, in order to keep the meeting under some kind of control, had ruled that commanding officers were to attend via hologram, rather than in person. It was a breach of etiquette, at least as it applied on Earth, but he preferred to be efficient rather than polite. Besides, there *was* a very real danger of the Indians launching a pre-emptive strike and, if they did, he needed his commanding officers on their ships. The only officers who were attending in person were himself, his tactical staff and Captain Naiser. Even *Susan* was attending via hologram.

"You have all seen the tactical situation," he said, once the final holograms had blinked into existence. Looking at them made his eyes hurt, but he ignored the slight discomfort. "The Indians have occupied the system *thoroughly* and show no sign of being willing to withdraw peacefully. Assuming the timetable holds true, they will be receiving the final ultimatum today, on Earth. Ten days from now, the war will begin in earnest."

He kept his expression blank with an effort. The politicians hadn't *quite* realised that attempting to synchronise military and political operations across interstellar space was impossible. There was no way to *guarantee* that the task force had reached its destination on time, no matter how much delay one built into the system. By the time the Indians on Pegasus received their orders, they would have had plenty of time to prepare themselves for the inevitable attack. He rather doubted they would do anything but fight.

But we do have to give them the chance, he reminded himself, sternly. *It was so much easier when we were fighting the Tadpoles.*

"We will assume, of course, that they are aware of our position," he said. Given the number of foreign ships that had followed the task force, much to his annoyance, it was pretty much inevitable. "Accordingly, we will move up the tramline to J-35 and establish ourselves there after this meeting. That will cut down on the warning time before we advance into Pegasus itself."

There was a long pause. "*Warspite* will travel ahead of us and make contact with the recon platforms, allowing us to obtain up-to-date information," he added. "Should the Indians not back down, we will commence offensive operations without further ado. Smaller flotillas will raid the outskirts of their system, allowing us to gauge their strength and determination to fight. We will also work to cut the Indians off from their supply lines. I imagine the Indians will feel the urge to take the offensive sooner rather than later."

He gritted his teeth in annoyance. Every instinct told him to take the task force directly into the system and challenge the Indians to open battle, carrier against carrier. *Theodore Smith* carried more starfighters, he was sure, and his pilots were more experienced. But there were strong reasons *against* such a step, reasons he could not afford to discard. Let the Indians be tested first, let their technological advancements - if they had any - be parsed out before he took the offensive.

And besides, he thought darkly, *we do have strong reason to keep the Indian fleet intact, if we could just stop them trying to take our worlds.*

"When they do," he added, "we will be ready to meet them.

"This will, of course, require us to keep our distance from our foreign friends," he warned. "Once we enter J-35, we will go into stealth mode and conceal as much as possible; we'll issue warnings to the observers, ordering them not to approach within one light minute of the task force. Legally, we do have authority to drive anyone away if they get too close, but for political reasons we would prefer to avoid it. Are there any questions?"

"Yes, sir," Captain Morrison said. "What do we do if we discover proof the Turks *are* spying for the Indians?"

James scowled. "Legally, again, we can drive their ships away or arrest them," he said. "It may not be practical, however. We may just have to endure their presence."

It wasn't a pleasant thought. The Indians would already know far too much about the task force, no matter what precautions he'd taken. Given up-to-date information, they could plot ambushes or simply avoid his probes until his crews were run ragged. And being unable to do anything about the spies would be immensely frustrating. But he understood the problem facing the politicians. An incident that led to the death of foreign nationals, even ones spying on British ships, could lead to calls for peace based on the *status quo*. The Indians would win by default.

He cleared his throat. "If the Indians refuse to accept the bait, even though we are weakening their position," he added, "we will move the task force into the system and advance towards Clarke, forcing them into an engagement on our terms. They will almost certainly call for the second carrier, allowing us a chance to destroy *both* carriers...assuming, of course, we can deal with one before the other arrives. We will be simulating the engagement extensively over the next couple of days."

There was a long pause. "Any other questions?"

"Yes, sir," Commodore Blake said. "What happens if they *do* manage to concentrate their forces against us?"

"We avoid engagement," James said, simply. He actually had a couple of ideas for dealing with the carriers, but he would prefer to avoid facing both of them at once. "If worst comes to worst, we simply fall back down the tramlines and wait for a second carrier of our own."

He looked from face to face. "We leave in two hours, gentlemen," he said. "Good luck to us all."

One by one, the holograms blinked out. James rubbed his forehead as the tactical staff - and Captain Naiser - took their leave, leaving him alone. Getting the task force to Hannibal had been a masterwork of logistics, but they were already seeing problems. Many of the support ships in the RFA had been destroyed during the war and never replaced, a mistake that might cost the Royal Navy dearly. And yet, what choice had they had? There was no value in beans without bullets, coffee without fuel. They'd thought they'd needed to rebuild the warship squadrons as quickly as possible and they'd been right.

He tapped the console, bringing up the near-space display. A handful of yellow icons hung in space, keeping their distance from the task force. Foreign observers, media representatives...it was a given that some of them were spying, directly or indirectly, for the Indians. James had no doubt of it. The Turks were the prime suspects, but they weren't the only ones. *He* was one of the few people alive who knew why the Russians had become international pariahs...and just how far the Russians would go to recover their former position.

They'd ally with the Indians if they thought it would get them back to where they were, he thought, coldly. The truth couldn't be allowed out, not when it might restart the First Interstellar War. It wouldn't be long before the Russians decided that Britain - and every other Great Power - had as strong an incentive to keep the secret as themselves. *And the Indians would probably pay through the nose for their support.*

He sighed. He'd contemplated suggesting trying to bring the Russians back into the fold, but he'd known it was a political non-starter. Too much had been at risk for *anyone* to feel comfortable with the proposal, even though nothing had ever been written down. He felt a stab of guilt and shame for Percy and Penny, the former trapped on Clarke until liberation or death; they would never know how their father had died. The secret had to remain secret.

"Admiral," Susan's voice said. He looked up to see her standing at the hatch. "*Warspite* did well, didn't she?"

"Yes, she did," James agreed. He knew better than to assume the Indians would continue to hold the same dispositions - they'd probably concentrate their forces as soon as they knew the task force was in J-35 - but it was a start. Getting the SAS down to the moon would give them something they lacked, too: solid information on just what the Indians were doing. "I think Admiral Soskice scored one, there."

"It would look that way," Susan agreed. She closed the hatch and took a seat facing him. "Is that good news?"

James shrugged. "I spent the last five years battling Admiral Soskice's theoretical concepts of new ways of war," he said. "And *Warspite* may have proved that at least some of them are solid."

Susan smiled. "Is that a bad thing?"

"I wish I knew," James admitted. "If one idea works, does that mean the next idea is certain to work too?"

"No," Susan said. "But an idea failing doesn't mean you should dismiss them all."

James nodded, tiredly. Susan had never hesitated to tell him when she thought he was wrong, even though he outranked her. It was one of the reasons he'd worked to keep her with him as they'd both climbed up the rank ladder. Hell, Uncle Winchester wanted him to marry someone; perhaps, just perhaps, he should consider asking her. It wouldn't be a love match, but they worked well together.

Maybe after the war, he told himself firmly.

"The Indians aren't likely to back down," he said. He understood the reasoning, but it ran the risk of compromising military victory. And yet, thanks to their unwanted escorts, it would be very hard to surprise the Indians. "Politicians."

"Probably not," Susan agreed. "They'd save their ships, they'd save their men, but they'd lose their prestige."

"Funny," James observed. "That's how we feel too."

He sighed, inwardly. It had been *so* much easier, he reflected once again, when they'd been fighting the Tadpoles. At least they hadn't had to worry about being knifed in the back...

Until the Russians proved us wrong, he reminded himself. *Humanity is more than capable of fighting itself as well as an alien foe.*

CHAPTER NINETEEN

New Delhi, India

"Are you sure you're up to this?"

Ambassador Joelle Richardson nodded impatiently. She'd been injured on Vesy, when the uprising had begun, but she'd had plenty of time to recuperate. It had been a surprise when she'd been told she would be carrying the message to the Indians, yet it made a certain amount of sense. The Indians would get her message, true, but they'd also understand that her *presence* was a message, a warning that the uprising on Vesy was neither forgiven nor forgotten. One way or the other, the Indians would pay a price for the deaths...

And, of course, for the damage they'd done to the Vesy, she thought. *They were on the verge of all-out war when we left.*

She pushed the thought out of her mind as the car came to a halt outside the Prime Minister's residence, New Delhi. It was an impressive building, she had to admit; the original building had been destroyed by a suicide bomber during the Age of Unrest and the Indians had rebuilt it bigger and better than ever. They'd also added layer upon layer of additional protection, MI6 had informed her; the building was designed to survive a nuke at close range. The handful of shootings, bombings and one attempted missile attack hadn't done more than scratch the paint.

"I'm fine," she said. "It won't take very long."

"Good luck," her driver said, as they were waved into a parking slot. "I'll be here."

Joelle nodded and checked her appearance in the mirror. Her face looked pale - her brown hair had had to be regrown hastily - yet she looked businesslike. The formal suit she wore, despite the heat, made her look mannish, but there was little choice. Wearing a loose dress would have conveyed entirely the wrong expression. She pasted a dispassionate expression on her face, then keyed a switch. The door opened, allowing her to step out onto the concrete. It was hotter than she'd expected - sweat started to trickle down her back - but it was surprisingly cool compared to Vesy.

"Ambassador," a female voice said. She looked up to see a young dark-skinned woman wearing a long sari. "The Prime Minister is waiting for you."

"Thank you," Joelle said. "Lead on, please."

She followed the young woman - barely out of her teens, at a guess - through a handful of security scanners and up a long flight of stairs. The air conditioning was welcome; she breathed a sigh of relief as the air suddenly became a great deal cooler. It was impossible, she was sure, for anyone to work in the heat. The paperwork would probably melt, if nothing else. Her lips twitched at the thought; she fought to keep them under control, knowing that a smile could be disastrous. The guide stopped outside a pair of wooden doors, knocked once and then opened them for her. Joelle nodded her thanks and stepped into the office.

Prime Minister Singh was older than she, Joelle recalled from the file. She'd never actually met him in person before. He was paler than his assistant, a dull reminder that caste and open racism still cast a long shadow over India. Joelle had read, once, that Islam had offered better opportunities to those of the lower castes, accounting for some level of distrust between the upper and lower castes. India still banned the treatments that changed skin colour permanently, she recalled. It wouldn't do for the lower castes to start aping their betters.

And to think they claim to have overcome the sins of the past, she thought, coldly. *But then, the Troubles caused us to regress too.*

She shook the Indian Prime Minister's hand, shortly. It was easy to understand *why* the Indians wanted to be considered a Great Power. The tacit agreement - that the Great Powers were completely independent, free even of criticism, within their own territory - would save them the brunt of moralistic outrage. And the fact that most of that outrage would be largely hypocritical wouldn't make them any more inclined to take it seriously. But their plans had caused an alien uprising and cost thousands of lives. They couldn't be allowed to get away with it.

"Ambassador Richardson," Singh said. "Ambassador Begum spoke highly of you."

"I'm sure she did," Joelle said. Ambassador Rani Begum had stalled on Vesy, delaying any international agreements until the Indians held the whip hand. No doubt Rani had reported that Joelle was a soft touch or something equally unpleasant. "I remember her well."

Singh smiled, coolly. "I assume you weren't sent here to discuss pleasantries or remember old friends," he said. "And, as you're *here*, you're definitely speaking for your superiors."

Joelle kept her annoyance off her face. On Vesy, she'd had a great deal of practical authority; on Earth, she was little more than a puppet, repeating the words of the Prime Minister. There was no way to escape the datanet, or the simple fact that the Prime Minister could change his mind and issue new orders at the drop of a hat. She had a feeling, based on her experience, that the Prime Minister had simply grown too used to the idea of being able to command events at will, but there was nothing she could do about it now.

"I am," she said. She cleared her throat. "You have committed acts of aggression against the possessions and personnel of Great Britain. There is no room to debate your acts. None of the excuses you have offered justify, for a moment, either the conquests of British territories or the deaths of British personnel. We will not - we cannot - surrender any of your ill-gotten gains to you."

Singh's expression darkened, but he said nothing.

"This is our formal response to your ultimatum. Withdraw your ships from Pegasus, Cromwell and Vesy. The first two will be returned to their true owners; the latter will be placed under international supervision until the Vesy are ready to claim authority in their own system. If you choose to do so now, Britain will agree to recognise India as a Great Power."

She'd argued against making any sort of concessions to the Indians, but the Prime Minister - understanding his counterpart better than either of them would have cared to admit - had insisted they had to offer the Indians *something*. Joelle had tried to argue that recognition as a Great Power wasn't *enough*, if they *had* to make a concession, yet there wasn't much else they *could* concede without undermining the whole rationale for the war. It was a tiny fig-leaf to satisfy the doves in Parliament that, she was sure, wouldn't satisfy anyone else.

"If you refuse to abandon your conquests, if you refuse to order your ships to withdraw, there will be no further talks," she continued, after a moment. "Your forces will be unceremoniously evicted from Cromwell and Pegasus, using all necessary force. We will do whatever we have to do to ensure that you no longer pose a threat to us or interplanetary peace."

Singh met her eyes. "Is that everything?"

"That is the formal message," Joelle said. "The Prime Minister, however, asked me to remind you about the dangers of both gambling with the future of India and the future of the entire human race."

"*He* is the one launching the offensive," Singh snapped.

Joelle controlled her temper with an effort. "The issue is not up for debate," she said. She removed a datachip from her handbag and placed it on the desk. "You gambled, Prime Minister; you gambled that we would roll over and allow you to get away with a glorified snatch-and-grab. Your gamble was lost. Now, you have the choice between withdrawing your ships and conceding defeat or war."

"We are not a rogue state," Singh said, "and it has been a *very* long time since India was ruled by the British. You do not get to talk to us in such a manner."

"You're *acting* like a rogue state," Joelle said. It was also a great deal easier to *deal* with a rogue state. If Iran, or Algeria, or Arabia threatened British interests, as they did from time to time, the KEWs would be dropped from high overhead without any warning. India, on the other hand, was too strong to be bullied easily. "There is no room for compromise, Prime Minister. I strongly advise you to withdraw your ships."

Singh met her eyes. "I will discuss the matter with my advisors," he said. "Will you wait for an hour or two?"

"I have orders to wait for no longer than an hour," Joelle said, recognising the power play. If she'd stayed longer, it would have suggested there was room for compromise. "I will assume that you have chosen to reject our demands if you fail to give us an answer by then."

She rose and headed for the door. Singh was angry, but she didn't really fear he would try to hold her prisoner. The entire world would turn on India if an ambassador was harmed, no matter the excuse. Outside, the young aide was already waiting, her face an expressionless mask. Joelle smiled to herself and allowed the younger woman to lead her to a side room.

"I can offer refreshments," the woman said. "Tea? Coffee? Iced Lemon Tea? Juice?"

"Iced Lemon Tea would be fine, thank you," Joelle said. She'd acquired a taste for the drink in Malaysia. "I won't be staying long."

"So they rejected the ultimatum," Bose said.

Prime Minister Mohandas Singh nodded, controlling his fury with an effort. He had known the British were unlikely to accept the Indian demands - no one dispatched a full-sized task force and *then* backed down - but he hadn't managed to steel himself to accept their Ambassador's tone. She'd been injured, according to her file, on Vesy. Sending her was an odd choice, unless one chose to take it as a subtle threat.

"They are telling us to get out or get thumped," he said. He would have been more diplomatic in a meeting of the full cabinet, but he was damned if he was moderating his tone for Bose. The milksop didn't have the stomach for international power politics. "Or thump *them*, of course."

"They *did* send a task force," Bose pointed out, mildly. "That is not a minor commitment."

"Of course not," Mohandas snarled.

He wasn't blind to the dangers of playing with fire. The British Ambassador - as rude and undiplomatic as she'd been - had had a point. They couldn't risk weakening the human race to the point where an alien threat - known or unknown - could tear its way through the human sphere. But the only alternative was backing down. His position would be fatally undermined - his enemies in the government would see an opportunity to weaken him - but so too would India's. He'd presented the British with a situation where the only reasonable step was to back down, yet now they'd presented him with the same problem.

If we back down, he thought, *we look weak. But if we fight and lose, we prove ourselves to be weak.*

It wouldn't matter, he was sure, if the British recognised India as a Great Power, not if India backed down. The rest of the human race wouldn't take it seriously. They certainly wouldn't stand aside to allow India to assert itself. The British offer was nothing more than smoke and mirrors, a tiny concession to allow him to claim the whole exercise had been worthwhile. If it had been offered a month ago, he would have accepted. But now...

"We have the choice," Bose said pedantically, "between fighting and backing down. Correct?"

"Correct," Mohandas said. He'd said as much himself. Surely, Bose would reach a point sometime before the deadline ran out. "Do you have a point?"

"We tried," Bose said. "The British didn't submit. Now we do the smart thing and back down ourselves."

"And make ourselves look weak," Mohandas snapped.

"We would not *be* weak," Bose said. "I do understand that military matters are a little out of my sphere" - Mohandas glared; he'd cut Bose out of those decisions for a reason - "but I *do* understand that building those carriers was a colossal commitment. We spent *billions* of rupees on the ships. I don't want to *think* about just how much money we spent on establishing two out-system colonies and building up our space-based industrial base..."

Mohandas cut him off. "Do you have a *point*?"

Bose showed a flicker of irritation. "My *point*, Prime Minister, is that even a victorious conflict would leave us bankrupt," he said. "I imagine the

British are already preparing to wage financial warfare against us. They may not be able to convince the other Great Powers to get involved directly, but cutting off credit lines or calling in loans would be just as bad."

"If we win the war," Mohandas said, "the credit lines would reopen."

"Assuming we win," Bose said. "The loss of a single carrier, Prime Minister, would be devastating. We spent over *six hundred billion* rupees on each of those ships. The British are simply in a better place to recover from the cost of a war than us. I won't even go into the cost we'll pay when all the other powers start regarding us with suspicion..."

"Enough," Mohandas said. "What will it do to us if we just back down?"

"We will lose nothing," Bose said. "Our military force would remain intact. Our ability to defend our worlds and positions would be undamaged. Anyone carrying out a sober analysis of the balance of power would draw the same conclusions..."

"Except we would look weak," Mohandas said. "The only way to survive is through victory."

"So we win a very limited victory," Bose said. "Do you believe we can defeat the British completely, even if the other Great Powers refuse to get involved?"

"We have the power to prevent them from recovering their worlds," Mohandas hissed.

"But not enough to stop them from rebuilding their forces far faster than ours," Bose countered. "Ten years from now, assuming no problems on either side, they will have fifteen carriers to our five. Twenty years from now, they will have over forty carriers and we will have ten..."

"Assuming they keep building," Mohandas said.

Bose scowled. "Do you think they won't?"

He tapped the table, once. "These estimates are conservative, Prime Minister," he added, sharply. "They have a far sounder financial base than us. They are far more capable of sustaining a long arms race. And they have good reason to know they need the ships."

"Then we need to fight now," Mohandas said.

"No, we don't," Bose said. "The gamble failed. Take what they're offering you and be glad."

"The cabinet voted for war," Mohandas snapped.

"A mistake," Bose countered. "I think you can convince them to back down."

"But I won't," Mohandas said. "We have this window of opportunity. I will not let it go."

"Nor will the British," Bose said. "We may win now - if everything goes our way - but what about the next war? How long did the British bear a grudge over the Falklands?"

"We cannot back down," Mohandas said. "And *that* is what I will tell the Ambassador."

Joelle was privately surprised when the aide returned forty minutes after showing Joelle to the side room and providing her with a large glass of Iced Lemon Tea. Given Singh's attitude, she had expected either a hasty agreement or a flat refusal to back down - or even see her again. She would have left, of course, taking with her the last hope of peace...

But, as she stepped into the office, she knew that the entire mission had been a forlorn hope.

"Prime Minister," she said.

"We have considered the matter," Singh said. "Britain has committed many crimes against us..."

Joelle cut him off. She'd heard too many similar rants from the leaders of rogue states and they never really changed, even though the scripts were different. These were not the days when every world leader could claim to have majored in western hypocrisy or get away with unpleasant behaviour because of political correctness. And hearing it from a major world power was simply annoying.

"This isn't a debate," she said, flatly. "Are you going to withdraw your ships or not?"

"No," Singh said.

"I see," Joelle said. She rose to her feet. "In that case, Prime Minister, we have nothing more to say to one another."

She strode out of the office, not looking back. It was no surprise that the aide was already waiting for her, ready to take Joelle back to the car. Joelle kept her face under tight control as they left the building, then nodded to the aide as she climbed back into the car.

"Take us back to the embassy," she ordered. She had a feeling the Indians would declare her *persona non grata* within the hour. "And get me a secure link to London."

"Of course, Ambassador," the driver said.

Joelle scowled as the car pulled away from the building and passed through the guardpost and onto the road. The lack of any protesters was the only real difference between India and a rogue state, she decided. She wasn't sure if that was a good thing or not.

"He rejected the ultimatum," she said, when the Prime Minister's face appeared in front of her. "There will be war."

"Understood," the Prime Minister said. He looked worried, but determined. Matters were no longer in his hands, now the Indians had rejected the last attempt at a diplomatic solution. "If they'll let you stay at the embassy, do so. If not, catch a flight straight back home."

"I will," Joelle promised. "All we can do now is wait."

CHAPTER TWENTY

Clarke III, Pegasus System

"The British have moved into J-35, General."

"As expected," General Anjeet Patel said. The warning from Earth had been passed up the chain a scant day before the British had arrived. Timing wise, it could have worked out better. "Order our ships to concentrate, as per the deployment plan."

The young man nodded and hurried off. Anjeet snorted and turned his attention to the display. The British had flatly refused to accept anything, but complete withdrawal; they'd come, soon enough, to test themselves against his fleet. And now they were in J-35. They could be on him within hours, if they wished. What would *he* do, in their place? He'd be tempted to try to defeat one carrier before the other could arrive...

He cursed under his breath. If it had been entirely up to him, he would have concentrated both carriers right from the start, but there had been no way to know which way the British would jump. The Prime Minister had made it clear that they couldn't afford an attack on Gandhi...even though all their calculations agreed the British wouldn't be able to hold the world, certainly not for very long. No, the only way to square the circle was to keep one carrier in Vesy, ready to move either way if necessary.

"Dispatch a pair of recon ships to J-35," he ordered. He already had a good idea of just how many ships the British had assigned to their task force, thanks to the foreign media, but it was well to be sure. "I want one of them on standby to jump back the moment the British move towards the tramlines."

"Aye, sir," his aide said.

Anjeet nodded. He couldn't help feeling nervous. Technically, he'd served in the war, but he'd never seen any real action. His experience was limited to punitive strikes against rogue states, while the British Admiral had served in the fires of war. Anjeet had read Admiral Fitzwilliam's file and had to admit he was impressed. Even by the standards of the post-war Royal Navy, Admiral Fitzwilliam was young for his post. Anjeet would have liked to believe it was a sign of political connections rather than actual competence, but he suspected otherwise. Admiral Fitzwilliam had served on - and then commanded - *Ark Royal.*

But we have surprises too, he thought, savagely. He didn't have any real hatred for the British, but they couldn't be allowed to win. *We're ready to give them a black eye.*

"Ships dispatched, General," his aide called. "They're due in J-35 in nine hours."

And then they will have to locate the enemy, Anjeet thought. It wouldn't be hard, not if the British were being shadowed by the media, but they'd have to get dangerously close to the British ships. If *he* was in command of the task force, he would have fired on anything that came suspiciously close to his ships. *But we should get some advance warning of a thrust into our territory.*

He shrugged, then keyed his console to call Colonel Darzi. The forces on the ground would have to be alerted to ready themselves to repel attack. Their mass drivers, if nothing else, might give the British pause before they launched an offensive. Targeting would be a bitch beyond high orbit - the slightest error would send a projectile hundreds of miles off course - but the British would still have to take them into account. If, of course, they knew the mass drivers existed.

And if they don't, he thought coldly, *they're going to be in for one hell of a surprise when they get too close to the moon.*

"The carrier is still in place, sir," Tara reported. "She hasn't moved at all."

"They must not have seen us last time, sir," Howard commented. "They'd have altered their position if they had."

"Probably," John agreed. The display kept updating, revealing that the Indians were sweeping space with active sensors. They didn't seem inclined to try to hide the carrier, something that surprised him. Even a ship the size of interstellar bulk freighter could be hidden with a little effort. There were so many sensor pulses that he was convinced he wasn't looking at a decoy. "Unless that's what they want us to think."

He tapped his console, pulling back the display. The remaining Indian ships were heading back to the carrier, concentrating their forces around her. *That* wasn't too surprising - the Indians couldn't afford to lose their carrier - but it was odd they didn't seem to be planning on taking the offensive. It wasn't as if they could get into more trouble. Maybe they were planning on trying to spin the whole affair as a *British* act of aggression. If the Indians weren't inclined to come out to fight, the Royal Navy would have to go in after them...

Which is insane, he thought, coldly. *They have to know they're not going to get any help.*

He looked at Armstrong. "Helm, take us into laser range of the stealth platform," he ordered, grimly. "Keep us ready to back out if necessary."

"Aye, sir," Armstrong said.

John nodded to himself as *Warspite* inched forward. The Indians *should* have received the ultimatum by now, along with instructions on how to inform Admiral Fitzwilliam that the war had ended without a shot being fired. Admiral Fitzwilliam had been determined to give the Indians as long as possible to come to a decision, but it was clear that neither he nor anyone else believed the Indians intended to simply give up. They certainly hadn't sent a ship to J-35 with a coded message to report the end of the war.

And if they're not going to give up, he thought, *they'll be seeding space with passive sensor platforms of their own.*

He felt the tension rising slowly on the bridge. Crewmen were speaking in hushed voices, even though there was no way the Indians could hear them. The slightest sound made the less experienced officers jump, as if they thought the ship was haunted. John smiled at the thought - there had been stories of haunted starships longer than mankind had been exploring space - and then pushed it aside. As tired as he was of sneaking around, he knew life would get a great deal more exciting when the shooting actually started.

And it will start soon, he told himself. He hadn't been given any details, but it was clear that Admiral Fitzwilliam intended to be aggressive. The tactical data *Warspite* collected would be used to update the attack plans before the task force advanced into Pegasus. *And then we get to see how good we are, compared to them.*

"Captain," Tara said. "They've actually expanded the mining operations. I think they're even pushing an asteroid into orbit around Clarke III."

John blinked. "Show me."

The display zeroed in on an asteroid that was slowly tumbling towards Clarke III. John frowned, hastily running a comparison between the current sensor reports and the ship's records. The asteroid was definitely new. He ran the trajectory back and realised that the Indians had to have knocked it out of its previous orbit a day or so after *Warspite* had left the system. It almost looked as though they were planning to *bombard* the colony they'd occupied.

"That's odd, Captain," Howard said. "They *could* intend to set up another colony."

"But they'd have plenty of space junk to use as raw materials, sir," Tara offered. "And they used nukes to knock the asteroid onto a new trajectory."

John shook his head, puzzled. Modern nukes were barely radioactive, not compared to the dirty bombs that had held the world spellbound for over a century, but using them on an asteroid you intended to turn into a colony was still risky. Hell, the force of the blast might do real damage to the asteroid's structure, making hollowing it out impossible. Logically, the Indians had to want to mine the asteroid, rather than turn it into a colony, but it made no economic sense. There was no way the system could hope to pay off such an investment within the next fifty years.

Unless they think they can overcharge us for the use of the tramlines, he thought. *But that makes no sense too.*

He scowled. Anyone could use a tramline without paying, if they were ready to sneak through the system rather than move openly - and they would, if the price for using the tramline was too high. They were normally set low to *discourage* cheating. The Indians might have less experience in interstellar expansion than the British, but they weren't idiots and they could certainly learn from someone else's experience. Logically, there was something he was missing, but what?

"Keep an eye on the asteroid," he said. It made no sense. The Indians wouldn't be plotting to bombard their own troops, he was sure. His lips quirked in bitter amusement. If they wanted to kill their own men there were easier ways to do it. But unless they wanted to subsidize the entire system for over a decade, perhaps longer, it was hard to see what they gained from moving another asteroid into orbit. "Let me know if anything changes."

"Aye, sir," Tara said. She paused. "We're approaching the stealthed platform now."

John braced himself. If something had gone wrong - if the Indians had discovered the platforms or captured the SAS team or even caught a sniff of *Warspite* as she left the system - they were about to find out the hard way. They could have mined local space, if they wanted to catch a starship, or placed one of their own ships in perfect position for an ambush...

"Open the link," he ordered.

There was a long chilling pause. "Link open, sir," Tara reported. "I've verified the security codes. The data is flowing now."

"Send a signal to the SAS," John ordered. "Let them know we're here."

He took another breath. The data would be shunted directly into a secure core, just in case the Indians had decided to try to be subtle. They could have uploaded a virus into the platform, if they'd managed to subvert the security firewalls; their virus could easily attempt to take over *Warspite's* computers or simply ransack her secure files. John doubted it would succeed - the Royal Navy's computer security was second to none - but it might be enough to disable the drives and take them out of stealth mode, revealing their presence to the Indian ships. By the time everything was switched to manual, it might be too late.

"The data is secure, sir," Tara said. "Do you wish to review it?"

"No," John said. There would be time to study the data once they returned to the carrier. "Is there any response from the surface?"

"No, sir," Tara said. "They may not be near the transmitter."

John nodded. The SAS would have set up a laser transmitter on the surface, but they might not have placed it too close to their camp. They'd want to avoid leading the Indians right to them, if something went badly wrong and the laser beam was detected. He'd read the briefing notes carefully; the transmitters were rigged to explode if someone touched them without the right codes, but their mere presence would be enough to alert the Indians. They'd know that *someone* was watching them...

Tara's console *pinged*. "Contact, sir," she reported. "Data dump coming through now."

———

Percy had been told, back when he'd entered basic training, that military service was long hours of boredom mixed with fleeting seconds of absolute terror. In his own opinion, military service was actually long hours of training and chores in preparation for the moment when everything was put to the test. Standing guard on the transmitter, perched far too high up the mountain for comfort, was hardly his idea of a good time, but it was infinitely preferable to being hunted across hill and dale by determined enemy forces, or being captured and interrogated by terrorists.

But I could be doing something more useful, he thought, crossly. *I could be crawling up to the installations with the others.*

He shook his head. The SAS had divided up and started to probe the Indian defences, slowly putting together a picture of just what they were doing on Clarke III, but he'd been left behind with the transmitter. He had a feeling, in fact, that his expertise was now useless. The SAS knew everything he did and more. And, as he hadn't trained with them, they probably considered him something of a third wheel. Putting him at the transmitter was a good way to get some use out of him without putting themselves at risk.

It was a galling thought. Percy knew, without false modesty, that he'd done well on Cromwell and Vesy. His promotion, he'd thought, was a recognition that he'd done very well; he'd honestly expected to be thanked for his service and told to return to his old rank and duty station. But the SAS were something different. Even the couple who'd been drawn from the Royal Marines - not that they'd admitted so; Percy had had to deduce it from the handful of mannerisms they'd been unable to hide - fitted into the troop perfectly. Their casual, almost jocular manner and their disdain for hierarchy hid a staggering level of competence and experience. He wanted to be one of them and yet he was scared he might not be able to live up to it.

He'd read about SAS Selection, once when he'd completed basic training and again when he'd been seconded to the SAS. It was made as hard as possible - on purpose - and soldiers who were binned were sometimes placed on suicide watch. Percy hadn't believed it at the time, but he thought he did now. To fail the ultimate test of soldiering, when one had the self-confidence to try, would sting. How could one go back to one's original unit as a failure?

But there is no shame in trying and failing, he told himself. *Only in not having the guts to try...*

The transmitter lit up. Percy blinked in surprise and tapped the keyboard. It wasn't easy in his suit, but he'd had a great deal of practice. Drake had uploaded his reports to the transmitter regularly, just waiting for *Warspite* to return to collect them. Now, Percy watched the first set of messages downloading before transmitting Drake's reports in return. He wondered, briefly, if Penny was still onboard the cruiser, before dismissing the thought as absurd. No matter how he felt about it, or the danger of death if the cruiser was detected, Penny wasn't likely to walk away from her scoop. How could she?

There was no message for him in the bundle, he noted. It wasn't really a surprise. He'd been warned, more than once, that the SAS were completely detached from the rest of the world while on covert deployment. There would be no personal messages for any of them; hell, he'd been told he couldn't even keep a personal log! It felt weird not to be jotting down a brief account of the day's events and his personal observations - he'd had to do it as a Royal Marine - but the risks were just too high. The enemy would certainly read his notes with great interest if they were captured.

He watched the transmitter deactivate itself, once the last of the messages were gone, and sighed to himself. There was no point in trying to read the messages. *He* hadn't been given any of the codes to decrypt them. Percy found it more than a little irritating, but he understood the logic. The troopers had been prepared for interrogation on a scale he couldn't hope to match. If *they* were pushed too hard, they'd die rather than give up anything, even something as minor as their wife's bra size. He knew he couldn't say the same for himself.

Good luck, he thought, glancing upwards. The sky was clear, for once; it had been hours since the last poisonous snowfall. *Come back soon.*

"Download complete, sir," Tara reported.

John nodded. "Deactivate the link to the platform," he ordered. "Helm, back us out of here, quietly."

"Aye, sir," Armstrong said.

"Captain," Tara said. "Two Indian starfighters were just launched."

John felt his eyes narrow. "Just two?"

"Yes, sir," Tara said. "They could be a long-range recon patrol..."

"Perhaps," John said. It made sense...unless, of course, the Indians were running more exercises. *He* would have preferred to stick to the simulators if there was a prospect of actually having to *fight*, but the Indians might disagree. "Helm, keep us well away from their projected flight path."

"Aye, sir," Armstrong said.

Howard frowned. "Two starfighters against us?"

John shrugged. Two starfighters weren't much of a threat...but then, the Royal Navy had thought the same about starfighters in general before the Battle of New Russia. *Warspite* was far tougher than either of the British carriers that had been ripped apart in the battle, yet the Indians could easily launch enough starfighters to overwhelm her defences if they wished...

"Better to be careful," he said. He took a long breath. "Besides, we don't want to be detected yet. We need to get our intelligence back to the Admiral."

He glanced at the stream of reports from the SAS. One of them was marked urgent. He hesitated, then keyed in his command code and opened it as *Warspite* picked up speed, angling away from the Indian ships orbiting the gas giant. The message unfolded in front of him, a grim warning that things weren't quite what they seemed.

Mass drivers, he thought. *That* changed everything. All of a sudden, the asteroid made a great deal of sense. *Shit.*

CHAPTER TWENTY ONE

Theodore Smith, J-35

"Bugger," James said, mildly.

He concealed his amusement at Sally's astonishment with an effort. No doubt she'd expected a rather more...*deafening* response. It was frustrating to discover that the Indians had done something that put them one step ahead of him, but at least he'd found out before it was far too late. A projectile slamming into one of his ships would have been disastrous. As it was, he had time to alter his plans to compensate.

"They'll have near-complete coverage of the space around the moon," Lieutenant-Colonel Wilson Boone said. 3 Para's commanding officer - and the overall commander of the groundpounders - leaned forward. "Their accuracy will be shit beyond a certain point, but it will be enough to force us to keep our distance."

James nodded. The SAS - and their contact on the ground - had been able to identify several mass driver installations, while the stealthed satellites had been able to locate the rest. It looked, very much, as though the Indians could hit starships approaching from any angle to the moon, even if they tried to keep the moon's mass between themselves and the colony. In fact, assuming the Indian mass drivers were at least as capable as *British* designs, they could probably throw enough buckshot into space to make approaching the moon thoroughly hazardous. Boone was right - their accuracy would be appallingly bad - but it hardly mattered. He couldn't risk taking a carrier close to the moon.

"Then they will have to be knocked out on the ground," he mused. There were overlapping fields of fire; knocking out one mass driver wouldn't be enough to provide a zone of clear space. The analysts would need to work through it, but at a guess they'd need to take out at least two or three mass drivers to clear the way. It was going to be a major headache, even with the SAS already on the ground. "What level of defences do they have?"

"Back-up plasma cannons and railguns, according to the reports," Boone said. "Their ground-based defences are quite weak."

That's something, at least, James thought. Mass drivers on Earth were heavily protected - but then, there were more crazies on Earth, willing to risk everything to strike a blow for their cause. Clarke III had a tiny population, most of which was firmly under enemy control. The SAS probably couldn't support a resistance movement, if one existed. *We could slip more troops down to the surface, then take out the mass drivers...*

"Start looking at ways to deploy more troops to the surface," he ordered, curtly. They *did* have a second SAS troop - and four more stealth shuttles - but they really needed more troops on the ground. "I wonder... could you get down without a stealth shuttle?"

"Not if you want to remain undetected," Boone told him, bluntly. "The SAS had real problems getting down to the surface, Admiral. A normal shuttle would definitely be detected in transit and blown out of the sky."

"I see," James said.

He shifted his gaze to the system display. The task force had established a perimeter around its location, but the foreign ships were right on the edge...and, beyond them, a pair of Indian warships were holding position on the tramline. He was surprised they weren't trying to hide, but it was quite possible that they were trying to be intimidating. Besides, if he sent ships to intercept them, they'd have plenty of time to jump back down the tramline and vanish.

Or they could be in contact with the foreign ships, he thought, coldly. *That would explain why they're not in stealth mode.*

It was possible, he supposed, that the Indians simply didn't *trust* their stealth systems, but he didn't dare take it for granted. They'd had access to Tadpole technology reports too. James had had his captains drill their crews relentlessly, training them to watch for signs that a stealthed starship was trying to slip into firing range, but it was extremely tricky. A skilled crew might be able to get within a bare kilometre of the target's hull without being detected. He couldn't take the risk of assuming that the Indians weren't at least that good.

He cleared his throat. "See what you can come up with," he said. "Is there anything else I ought to take into account?"

"Pretty much all of the moon's population has been concentrated in the main colony," Boone observed. "Indiscriminate bombardment isn't an option."

"It never was," James pointed out.

"But in this case, the Indians have dug in *around* the main colony," Boone said. "We might have to winkle them out, *without* the heavy weapons we would normally bring to bear on their locations."

James sucked in his breath. "You think they're using the settlers as hostages?"

He was genuinely shocked at the concept. The world was far too used to atrocities committed by rogue states, insurgents and outright terrorists, but the more civilised nations tended to try to avoid such measures. They tended to provoke counter-atrocities. Hell, it had been agreed since the Age of Unrest that retaliation in kind was the only way to keep a lid on atrocities...

"It doesn't matter what they intend to do, sir," Boone said calmly, cutting off his train of thought. "That *is* what they're doing. We cannot bombard their positions from orbit without risking the lives of our people."

James sucked in his breath. A *sane* commander would surrender the moment the high orbitals were taken, knowing his forces were hopelessly exposed to orbital bombardment - and doomed, if they tried to continue the fight. But the Indians, between the mass drivers and their positions, had safeguarded themselves. The British would need to fight it out on the ground.

"Draw up plans for an assault," he ordered, softly. "It will be some time before we're ready to proceed, anyway. We'll just have to take steps to weaken them until we're ready to engage the enemy in a decisive battle."

"Yes, sir," Boone said.

James glanced at Sally. "Sally, organise a conference for one hour," he said. "Every commanding officer is invited to attend via hologram."

"Aye, sir," Sally said.

Boone frowned. "Sir," he said. "There may be no way to avoid massive civilian casualties."

"We could always offer to evacuate the colony first," James said. He had a feeling the Indians would decline, which might not be a bad thing. If they *were* intentionally using the colonists as human shields, the offer to pull them out before the forces started fighting in earnest would expose their conduct to the universe. "It might benefit us to try."

He cursed under his breath. Civilians had died in the First Interstellar War - the Tadpoles had killed more humans than Adolf Hitler - but that had been different. They hadn't precisely *intended* to kill countless humans, although Earth First and other radical groups insisted they had. This time, British civilians were being used as human shields by a government desperate enough to take the risk of harming them...and creating a whole new precedent for trouble.

"It might," Boone said. "But if the Indians have already rejected the offer to withdraw peacefully, sir, they're unlikely to show weakness elsewhere."

James sighed. Back at the Academy, he'd been told that once a military build-up reached a specific level, war was inevitable. Human nature simply didn't allow such forces to go unused, the lecturer had insisted; the war had to be fought to make the gathering of such immense firepower worthwhile. It hadn't made sense to him at the time and, in many ways, it still didn't. The cost of dispatching the task force was immense, true, but replacing the ships and men that were bound to be lost would be a great deal higher. Surely, it would be better for the Indians to back down before the shooting started.

But they've made a colossal investment in the system, he thought, darkly. *To back down would throw all that into jeopardy.*

He thought, briefly, about trying to negotiate, but it would be futile. His orders didn't allow him to offer the Indians anything they could use as a fig leaf to reclaim the system later. The best he could do was offer to compensate the Indians for their investment, but Parliament would be unlikely to approve it. They'd see the Indians as having made an investment at their own risk. There would *certainly* be no agreement that the Indians deserved to be repaid when no deal had been struck.

"I'll speak to you after the conference," he said. "Good luck."

"Thank you, sir," Boone said, dryly. "I'll see what my planning staff can come up with."

John disliked holographic communications, although he had to admit their value. The military-grade transmitters and projectors were so good that it was easy, too easy, to forget that he wasn't actually on the giant carrier in person. People had been known to fall into holographic realities and never emerge, the illusions reinforced by sensory feeds that blurred the line between fiction and reality. He'd even heard stories about people who'd entered fantasy worlds in Sin City and never emerged, right up until the day Sin City had been destroyed by the Tadpoles. He rather doubted that any of the VR addicts had survived.

They probably found reality too hard to handle, he thought, as his hologram took its place among the throng. He'd always found the holographic system a little hard to handle - his mind rebelled at the thought of thirty men crammed into a space intended for ten - but he'd never seen the point of dismissing reality. *But then, my life is better than most.*

It was an odd thought. As a starfighter pilot, he'd been as flirty as the rest of the breed; he'd laughed, he'd joked, he'd been careful to wear his uniform in a manner that would have upset his instructors...he'd known, of course, that the odds of survival were very low. So had their commanding officers; starfighter pilots had to eat, drink and be merry, because they might be dead by the end of the day. But now, as a Captain, he was more driven than he cared to admit, even though he was at the very pinnacle of his career. He had something to live for...

"Ladies and gentlemen, be seated," Admiral Fitzwilliam said. If *he* found being surrounded by holograms a disconcerting experience he didn't show it. "As you can see, the situation has changed" - his lips twisted - "in a manner not entirely to our advantage."

He tapped a switch, allowing the assembled commanding officers to see the report from the surface. The mass drivers - and their fields of fire - were clearly marked. Behind them, intelligence's best guess on their *accurate* range was underlined. It was chillingly clear that taking the fleet to Clarke III without doing something about the mass drivers would result in catastrophe.

"The Indians have made it considerably harder for us to land on Clarke III," Admiral Fitzwilliam said. "Accordingly, I am modifying the plan. We will proceed with Gamma-Sigma instead of Alpha-Beta. The main body of the task force will move into the Pegasus System and hold position here" - he tapped a location on the display - "well out of the effective range of the mass drivers. We will threaten the Indian control of the system without risking our ships to their fire."

And they won't be able to bring the second carrier into the system without being detected, John thought, coldly. *They'll run the risk of us sneaking past them and raiding their possessions beyond Vesy.*

"In the meantime, we will harass the Indian presence with smaller ships," Fitzwilliam continued. "We know they've been running supply convoys into the system. Those convoys will no longer be allowed to travel unmolested. Two flotillas - Bulldog Beta and Bulldog Charlie - will be responsible for destroying or capturing those convoys. Their mining installations will also come under heavy attack."

He paused. "It is quite likely that the Indians intend to use that asteroid as a source of raw material for the mass drivers," he warned. "They could dump it into the atmosphere and mine it on the surface, if they're willing to take the risk."

John had his doubts. Getting the rock to the surface without causing a disaster in a planetary scale would be difficult. Massive chunks of rock had been lowered to the surface before, but never on an inhabited world. The risk was simply too high. But the Indians, if they wished, could probably slice the asteroid up in orbit and drop smaller loads to the mass drivers. It wouldn't be too hard.

Or they could be planning to break it up and scatter more rock into orbit around Clarke III, he thought. *It would make our life harder.*

"We depart in two hours," Admiral Fitzwilliam warned. "The two flotillas will receive separate orders from me."

He held up a hand. "We're already on a war footing, but we have to assume the Indians have rejected the ultimatum," he added. "They will have to dislodge us from Pegasus if they want to win the war. I've already warned our friends" - he jabbed a finger towards the foreign ships - "that anyone who comes too close risks being fired on without warning, and I don't want you to hesitate. The Indians will not hesitate themselves."

There was a long pause. "Captain Naiser, remain behind," he concluded. "Everyone else, dismissed."

The holograms blinked out of existence, leaving John alone. "Admiral?"

"*Warspite* will be the flagship of Bulldog Beta," Admiral Fitzwilliam said. "You'll have command of three other ships, all destroyers."

"Yes, sir," John said. He assumed that Commodore Blake would be in command of Bulldog Charlie, with Fitzwilliam himself in command of Bulldog Alpha. "We know *precisely* where to harass the Indians."

"Of course," Admiral Fitzwilliam said. "However, I have a specific set of orders for you. I do *not* want you to use your main gun against their convoys."

John frowned. "Sir?"

"I do not want you to remind the Indians that it exists," Admiral Fitzwilliam said, flatly. "I can give you the orders in writing, if you wish."

"It won't be necessary, sir," John said.

"You'll have them anyway," Admiral Fitzwilliam said. His lips twitched into a humourless smile. "The armchair admirals who'll dissect the battle piece by piece will not take them into account unless you do. Some damn fool of a historian will say you were a complete moron who managed to forget the colossal gun built into his ship, someone so idiotic it was a minor miracle you didn't manage to hit an asteroid."

"Yes, sir," John said. There was something deeply personal in Admiral Fitzwilliam's comment, but he knew he couldn't ask. God knew there had been hundreds of studies of *Ark Royal* and her missions, some of which had been highly critical. As the senior survivor, Admiral Fitzwilliam had probably gotten more than his fair share. "May I ask why?"

"I have an idea," Admiral Fitzwilliam said. "It depends on just how the Indians react to our moves, Captain, but I'd prefer not to play that card until we know we can use it."

"Yes, sir," John said.

"You'll have detailed orders waiting for you in the datanet," Admiral Fitzwilliam said. "I don't think we can hide the main body of the fleet, but we can probably get your ships away from the Indians and their allies."

"Yes, sir," John said. The Indian convoys had been fairly regular, according to the stealthed platforms. It was difficult to be sure, but it looked as if the Indians had devoted most of their freighters to supporting the war. "We can get to the interception point without anyone being any the wiser."

"I hope so," Admiral Fitzwilliam said. "Commodore Blake will be harassing their fleet while you take out the convoy."

He smiled, coldly. "Your mission was very well done, Captain. Do you have any other observations before you go?"

John hesitated. "We could broadcast a message to the colonists," he said. "The Indians would have had to replace the datanet completely if they wanted to keep us from uploading messages into it."

Admiral Fitzwilliam frowned. "And you believe it would help?"

"If the report is accurate, sir, the colonists are being gently pushed into outright collaboration," he said. "It might be better to remind them, now, that we're on the way. The Indians will know when we enter the system, won't they?"

"Yes," Admiral Fitzwilliam said. He cleared his throat, loudly. "However, you would also run the risk of convincing them to do something stupid. I don't think there are many people on the surface with any genuine military experience. We still don't know what happened to the POWs."

"Yes, sir," John agreed. The potential consequences were horrific. In wartime, the Indians would presumably clamp down as hard as they could. "But the risk might be worth it."

"Might," Admiral Fitzwilliam said. He looked down at the deck. "I'll give it some thought, Captain. Until then...return to your ship and prepare for departure."

"Yes, sir," John said.

He disengaged the hologram. His head spun, as always; he removed the goggles and headband, reminded himself savagely that he'd never left

Warspite and hastily keyed the terminal in front of him. The orders were already there; HMS *London, Cardiff* and *Manchester* had been assigned to his command. He glanced at the files - he knew the captains of two of them personally, which was a relief - and then read the second half of the orders. Disengaging from the task force without being seen would be a challenge, but doable if they were careful. The Indians wouldn't realise that two flotillas had left the main body until it was far too late.

"Two hours," he mused. "And then we can engage the Indians at will."

CHAPTER TWENTY TWO

J-35/Pegasus System

"All ships have checked in, Admiral," Sally said. "They're ready to deploy."

"Prepare to start ECM on my mark," James ordered. There was *some* room for error, but not much. "Are our guests still watching?"

"Yes, sir," Sally said. "They're right on the line."

Spies, James thought, crossly. He couldn't imagine being bombarded with requests for interviews during Operation Nelson, or the desperate flight to Alien Prime. The media ships would definitely not have dared to come so close to an alien ship. *We should open fire and blow them all into dust.*

He pushed the thought aside, savagely. "Activate ECM," he ordered. "Inform Beta and Charlie that they may depart as planned."

"Aye, sir," Sally said. She watched her console for a long moment. "ECM field is active, Admiral. Drones are in place and ready to activate. Beta and Charlie are signalling that they're ready to slip into stealth mode."

"Activate the drones," James ordered. He sucked in his breath. Anyone watching with passive sensors would see the entire task force suddenly wrapped in a blaze of ECM. It would be impossible, assuming the boffins were correct, to pick out individual starships among the throng. "And order the fleet to advance."

"Aye, sir," Sally said.

James settled back in his command chair. If everything went according to plan, neither the Indians nor the other foreigners would be aware that the task force had dispatched two flotillas on separate vectors. They'd assume he was keeping the fleet as a united body, which wouldn't actually be a bad idea...if, of course, one knew nothing about the mass drivers and the threat they posed. As it was, he'd have to abandon the pretence a long time before they slipped towards Pegasus.

"Admiral," Sally reported. "One of the Indian ships has jumped out."

"Off to warn its commander," James noted. He'd considered attempting to jump the Indian ships, but they'd been lurking right on the tramline. The attack would have had to succeed in the first few seconds or fail utterly. "The other?"

"Still watching us, sir," Sally said.

"We'll take her out with starfighters if she's still there when we get into engagement range," James said. He would be surprised if she was - the Indians wouldn't throw a ship away for nothing - but he had to prepare for it anyway. "Keep a sharp eye on her."

"Aye, sir," Sally said. She paused as the display updated. "Admiral, our shadows are following us."

We won't be able to do anything secretly while they're here, James through, grimly. But he couldn't do anything about it, not now. *They'll just have to keep their distance.*

"Keep the task force on course," he ordered. They'd be nice and predictable, exactly what the Indians were expecting to see. "And take us through the tramline as soon as we enter jump radius."

"Aye, sir," Sally said.

"We've broken free, sir," Tara said. "There's no sign they've detected us."

John nodded. If they were lucky, the watchers were still convinced that Bulldog Beta and Bulldog Charlie were still with the task force. The Indian ship on the tramline wouldn't have a clue that his tiny flotilla was bypassing her and sneaking into the Pegasus System. Unless, of course, the Indians were just *playing* dumb.

"Helm, take us to the tramline," he ordered. It was quite possible the Indians had a stealthed ship watching the tramline, but it would have some problems detecting the British flotilla unless they risked using active sensors. "And jump us through as soon as we arrive."

"Aye, sir," Armstrong said.

John smiled coldly, feeling his heart starting to race in his chest. This was it; they'd sneaked into the enemy system twice now, but this time they intended to launch the first strike against the Indian Navy. Part of him regretted it; the rest of him relished the challenge, relished the chance to prove he was better than his Indian counterparts. He pushed that feeling into the back of his mind - he didn't want to make himself overconfident - and watched as *Warspite* advanced towards the invisible tramline. The single red icon representing the Indian ship didn't move.

They must be mesmerised by the advancing task force, he thought. Had the Indians assumed Britain would back down without a fight? It might have been the only thing that had convinced them to invade the systems in the first place. *Are they now regretting their choice*?

He shook his head, slowly. The Indians could withdraw at any moment - or even signal their willingness to withdraw - and the Royal Navy would let them go. He'd read the Admiral's briefings; there was no hope, whatever happened, of a complete victory. The Solar Treaty would see to that, unfortunately. All they could do was drive the Indians out of British territory and declare victory. If the Indians wanted to run, they could. No one would try to stop them.

"Captain," Armstrong said. "We are entering the tramline."

"Jump us through," John ordered.

The display flickered and rebooted itself, hastily. John had braced himself for everything from an immediate attack to an Indian battle fleet holding position where the task force was likely to appear, but the display was empty. The Indians were either holding position near the planet - which made a certain kind of sense - or hidden under stealth.

"Link into the remote platforms," he ordered. "We need to locate that carrier."

He sucked in a breath as the carrier appeared, still in position near the gas giant. But the gas giant was several light hours away...he shook his head as the display updated again, showing the carrier's possible locations. No starship, certainly not one as large as a supercarrier, could have travelled over five light hours in less than a day.

"She hasn't moved, sir," Tara said.

"That's about to change," John muttered. The Indian CO would probably know the task force was on the way...he'd probably already started putting his contingency plans into operation. "Keep a very sharp eye on her."

"Aye, sir," Tara said.

At least we know the Indians haven't cracked the secret of FTL communications, John thought wryly, as *Warspite* continued to slip further into the system. *They'd have reacted by now if they had.*

The display changed, again. "Captain," Tara said. "The task force is transiting into the system now."

"Understood," John said. If the Indians *were* planning an ambush, it would be sprung now...if, of course, they'd had time to get an ambush into position. "Inform me the moment anything changes."

General Anjeet Patel jerked awake as alarms began ringing through the giant ship, calling her crew to battlestations. He grabbed his trousers as he rolled out of bed, pulled them on as quickly as possible and ran out of the cabin while buttoning his jacket. The alarms were still sounding as he entered the CIC, just in time to see the first set of red icons appearing near the tramlines. A line of text at the bottom warned that the data was five hours out of date - the British task force had had plenty of time to alter course before the Indians received their first warning. Anjeet would have been surprised if they'd stayed near the tramline.

"Report," he ordered.

His aide looked up. "General, we received a warning from the picket ships, just before the British started to jump through the tramline," he said. "The full task force has entered the system."

"Understood," Anjeet said. He cursed the alarms under his breath. Even if the British made a beeline for his fleet, and it didn't look as though they had, it would still take several hours before the two fleets were in engagement range. "Order the fleet to stand down to yellow alert."

The young man frowned. "Sir?"

"There's no point in tensing ourselves up now," Anjeet said, sharply. He disliked having to explain the rationale behind his orders, but it was a reasonable request. "They're not going to be on us in seconds, are they?"

"No, sir," the aide said.

"Of course not," Anjeet said. If the British *had* managed to find a way to move at FTL speeds without the tramlines the war was already lost. "It will take them at least ten to fifteen hours to close with us, if that's what they want to do. So we will prepare to meet them, as calmly as you please, without overstressing the crews."

"Yes, sir," the aide said.

"Cancel those alarms," Anjeet ordered. He took a moment to study the display, silently breathing a sigh of relief when the alarms were silenced. The noise was bad enough to give him a pounding headache. "Deploy an additional line of pickets to surround the fleet - inform the captains that I am authorising the deployment of the laser net. Dispatch two destroyers to watch the British ships from a safe distance. Make it clear to their commanders that I want intelligence, not heroics. If they get jumped by the British, they'd better hope they go down with their ships or I'll kill them personally."

"Yes, sir," his aide said.

Anjeet nodded at the younger man, then sat down in his command chair and forced himself to relax. What would the British do? If they came right for his fleet, he intended to pull back and see if they could be induced to come into range of the mass drivers on Clarke III. If not...well, he could wait and see what happened before committing himself. He had a whole string of useful options he could use.

"Inform all ships committed to Operation Sitka to prepare for deployment," he added, after a moment. It still didn't look as though the British intended to challenge his fleet directly, but he couldn't allow the British to hold position indefinitely. "And send a signal to *Vikramaditya*. I want her to hold herself at readiness to advance into Pegasus if necessary."

"Yes, sir," his aide said.

Anjeet smiled, coldly. One way or another, he told himself firmly, there was a nasty surprise in store for the British.

———

"The Indians are still holding position near the gas giant," Sally reported. "They're dispatching at least two ships towards us, but no other notable reaction."

"Understood," James said. He cursed the speed of light delay under his breath, but consoled himself with the thought the Indians would be having the same problem. On the other hand, they also had a horde of spies following the British ships. "And the detached units?"

"They're in stealth mode, sir," Sally said. "I am currently unable to track them."

James nodded, shortly. Commodore Blake was an old friend - they'd been at the Academy together - while he'd come to respect Captain Naiser. The man might have started life as a starfighter pilot, which wasn't the best of pedigrees, but he'd matured into a capable commanding officer. But it still felt wrong to remain in the rear, to issue the orders and watch junior officers carry them out. He should be in danger too.

I am in danger, he reminded himself. The Indians couldn't leave the task force in place for long, not without risking their control over the system. *And when they come, this ship will be the main target.*

"Captain Pole is deploying the CSP," Sally informed him. "One squadron of starfighters on CSP; the remainder held in readiness for immediate launch."

"Understood," James said. He frowned as he turned his gaze back to the display. "Launch a spread of probes to monitor local space and to hell with the beancounters. I want to know the moment one of their ships tries to sneak up to us."

"Aye, sir," Sally said.

———

It was impossible, John knew from bitter experience, to coordinate an operation across interstellar distances. Hell, it was hard enough coordinating one over interplanetary distances. The Indians would have real problems bringing their second carrier into the Pegasus System if they intended to launch a joint attack. They'd also - if the analysts were correct - have problems telling their convoys to abort course and return to Earth.

Unless they did manage to get a message off in time, he thought, as the small flotilla approached Tramline D. It still annoyed him that they hadn't discovered it led to Vesy until after they'd gone the long way around, although if they had *Warspite* might have been jumped by the Russian deserters and destroyed. *But even if they did, they'd start running out of supplies pretty quickly.*

He looked down at the analyst's report and scowled, inwardly. There were just too many question marks - he silently gave them points for admitting as much - but certain things couldn't be avoided. The Indians would have no trouble using British components...if, of course, they'd managed to capture any. Clarke III might have been intended as a fleet base, eventually, but none of the installations had been established, not even a standard supply dump for Royal Navy starships on long-range patrols. The moment the Indians were cut off from their supply lines, the analysts had concluded, their fighting power would start to decay.

That's true of us too, of course, he thought wryly. *The Indians will probably already be preparing deep-strike missions into J-35. All of our supplies have to come through that system.*

The display changed, sharply. "Captain," Tara snapped. "Six ships have just jumped through the tramline. Two long-range frigates, sir, and four freighters."

John shared a dark look with Howard. "Right on time," he said. "Helm, move us into interception range."

He worked through the vectors in his head. Assuming the Indians knew *precisely* when the convoy was going to arrive, they could have sent a warning message...or, more likely, ordered one of their ships to wait for the convoy and pass on a warning at once. But the timing would be *very* complex. Given the arrival of the task force, on the other side of the system, it wasn't too likely the Indians would manage to get a warning off in time...

"We're in position, sir," Armstrong reported. "Enemy ships moving into missile range."

"Enemy warships targeted, sir," Tara added. They'd picked the interception point with malice aforethought; the chances of the enemy being warned were minimised, while the incoming ships would have no time to jump back into Vesy. "Missiles online, ready to fire; defence grid active, ready to fire."

John braced himself. He was about to fire the first shot of the war. He knew shots had been exchanged on Clarke III - the SAS report had been very detailed - but that had been a minor skirmish. Now...there wouldn't be any hope of a peaceful solution left, once the convoy was smashed.

But then, there wasn't much hope of a peaceful solution anyway, he thought, grimly. *They know they had ample opportunity to withdraw, once we showed ourselves ready to fight.*

"Fire," he ordered.

Warspite shook as she unleashed the first salvo, a dozen missiles plunging towards their targets. The destroyers fired a moment later, overwhelming the Indian defences through a combination of ECM and sheer weight of fire. John watched, dispassionately, as the Indians struggled to bring their defence online, but simply ran out of fire. The destroyers weren't modern either, part of his mind noted. Bomb-pumped lasers were more than enough to rip them apart, slaughtering the crews before they had a chance to escape.

"Targets destroyed," Tara said. Her voice was very calm. "I say again, targets destroyed."

John sucked in his breath. "Hail the freighters," he said. The ships were trying to alter course, but they were too underpowered to hope to escape. He doubted the Indians had bothered to cram weapons into their hulls... and, even if they had, it would make no difference to the final outcome. "Order them to surrender or be destroyed."

"Aye, sir," Gillian said. "Message sent."

There was a long pause. John cursed under his breath as the silence lengthened, wondering just what he should do if the Indians refused to surrender. His orders were clear - the freighters were to be captured or destroyed - but he didn't want to fire into helpless ships. It would look very bad in a war where public and international opinion was actually important.

And I may not be able to capture the ships and get them home, he thought, grimly. *They will have screamed for help the moment we attacked.*

"Hail them again," he ordered. "This time, order them to surrender or take to the lifepods."

"Aye, sir," Gillian said.

A new red icon appeared on the display. "Captain," Tara said. "We have a cruiser on intercept vector. Firing range in seven minutes."

John swallowed an oath. "Communications, inform the freighters that they will be destroyed in five minutes," he said. He briefly considered fighting - *Warspite* and her consorts should have the advantage - but he didn't want to fight a more equal opponent without his main gun. "I want you to repeat the message until the countdown reaches zero."

"Aye, Captain," Gillian said.

"They're launching lifeboats, sir," Tara reported. New icons flickered into life on the display. "I estimate they'll have crammed the entire crew into them."

"Wait until the timer runs out," John ordered. He kept a sharp eye on the approaching cruiser. "Weapons locked?"

"Weapons locked," Tara confirmed. "Ready to fire."

"Fire," John ordered. He didn't wait to see the results. The Indian cruiser was closing in rapidly. "Helm, swing the ship around and take us away from the tramline."

"Aye, sir," Armstrong said.

Six-nil, our favour, John thought, as the freighters died in fire. The cruiser was slowing, clearly ready to recover the lifepods. There was no reason to interfere, not when the Indians had already taken a black eye. *And what will the next score be*?

CHAPTER TWENTY THREE

Pegasus System

"General," the aide said. "We just received an urgent message from *Delhi*. The incoming convoy was attacked and destroyed."

Anjeet cursed, savagely. The British had tricked him. They'd distracted him with their task force, while the *true* threat was moving into position. A glance at the report told him that the freighter crews had been allowed to take to the lifepods before their ships were destroyed, but it hardly made up for the loss of the ships. Starships took far longer to replace than trained crewmen. He'd have *real* problems keeping his garrisons supplied if the British ruthlessly targeted his convoys.

But we moved plenty of war material into the system before the shooting actually started, he thought, coldly. *And we can supply the troops from Clarke, if necessary*.

"Inform *Delhi* that she is to return to Vesy and warn the following convoys," Anjeet ordered, slowly. The cruiser would already have recovered the lifepods. There was no point in punishing the freighter crews, not when they'd had little choice. Their ships had been sitting ducks. "They are *not* to enter the system without a powerful escort."

He mentally saluted the British commander as the aide hurried off to carry out Anjeet's orders. Losing the escorts was annoying - and, if he wanted to ship more supplies into the system, he would have to divert more warships to protect the convoys. And *that* would weaken his position near Clarke. He could find himself too weak at *both* points when the

British finally stopped playing around and came in for the kill. The mass drivers would be a nasty surprise, but the British would definitely smell a rat if he took his remaining ships closer to Clarke III. They'd assume he was baiting a trap.

Which I would be, he acknowledged wryly.

He frowned inwardly as Yahya Khan - the Public Relations officer - entered the compartment and hurried over to Anjeet's chair. It wasn't that he disliked the man, although he had a slimy attitude that annoyed Anjeet more than he cared to admit; it was that he had a rank and a position of power even though he'd never seen combat until now. The nasty part of Anjeet's mind was mildly surprised that Khan hadn't remained in his cabin, cowering in fear. A flight of incoming missiles wouldn't give a damn about good press, or anything other than killing their targets.

"General," the PR officer said. "We could use this."

Anjeet lifted an eyebrow. "How?"

"The British had no time to inspect our freighters," Khan pointed out. "We could claim they were carrying thousands of harmless workers..."

"And then accuse the British of perpetrating a massacre," Anjeet snapped.

"But sir..."

"The British would not care," Anjeet said. "These aren't the days when people cried crocodile tears over dead enemy soldiers. More to the point, it would be very hard to prove that the British *knew* they were firing on defenceless workers..."

He shook his head. "No," he added, flatly. "We will not attempt to lie to them or the rest of the human sphere."

Khan looked astonished. "It could shorten the war, General."

"It might also put us completely beyond the pale, if we got caught at it," Anjeet snapped, coldly. "How many people believed the exaggerated death tolls during the Age of Unrest?"

"Too many," Khan said. "I..."

"Dismissed," Anjeet said. "Go back to your cabin and work on a press release about the engagement, but clear it with me before you show it to *anyone* else."

He glared at Khan until he got the message and scuttled out of the Flag Bridge, looking as though he wanted to crawl out on his hands and knees. The Crazy Years, the Americans had called them; the years when an entire country could claim to have been depopulated several times over and be *believed*. But then, the terrorists who had plagued the world had been fond of using human shields. A high-value target might turn a school into a base, safe in the knowledge that his enemies would consider it off-limits for fear of harming the children.

And if they did harm the children, or even take out the school when it was unoccupied, they'd still be blamed for killing children, he thought, savagely. He understood the sickening practicalities, but it was still a dishonourable way to fight a war. Besides, India was no terrorist state. *We can win the war without resorting to such measures.*

He fought down the urge to go for a shower - it was funny how he always had that urge after meeting Khan - and turned his attention back to the main display. The British flotilla that had attacked the convoy was already off the screen, although an ever-expanding sphere on the display showed its potential vectors. Anjeet was fairly sure it would still be lurking along the tramline, in hopes of snatching up another target, or making its way back to join the task force. Either way, there was nothing he could do about it. Instead, he studied the task force itself. The live feed from the shadowing ships revealed that it was still wrapped in a blaze of ECM, making it hard to be sure just how many ships surrounded the giant carrier. If the British were feeling *very* daring, they might have cut loose all but a tiny handful of their ships to raid his positions.

No, he thought, dismissing the idea. *They wouldn't risk uncovering the carrier.*

"Not that it matters," he mused, out loud. "We'd have to drive them out of the system anyway."

It was annoying, but the longer the British kept their task force in place, the weaker his forces - and his country's position - would become. The report from Earth had made it very clear that he needed to seek a decisive battle as soon as possible, even though allowing the British to come into range of the mass drivers on Clarke would have evened the odds. As it was, he had a slight advantage in numbers, which might well be balanced by greater experience and resources.

"General," his aide said, returning to stand next to him. "The messages have been sent."

"Good," Anjeet said. He keyed a switch, bringing up one of the contingency plans he'd worked out when he'd first heard the British were sending a task force to Pegasus. "Inform the tactical staff that I want Plan Kali reviewed and updated to match what we're facing."

"Yes, sir," the aide said.

"Once it's ready, we'll earmark forces for deployment," Anjeet continued. Plan Kali was risky - they'd be revealing all of their surprises in one engagement - but it was his best shot at crippling the British before they advanced on Clarke. "And then prepare to engage..."

He broke off as new red icons flashed to life in the display. "Report!"

"Enemy starfighters are diving into the junk field, sir," a tactical officer called. "They're going after the miners."

Anjeet blinked. The miners were well outside starfighter range. Had the British developed their own variant of the deep-space fuelling system? Or...

Another set of icons appeared, far too close to Clarke for comfort. "I'm picking up five ships, sir," the tactical officer added. "One of them is almost certainly an escort carrier; the others are a single cruiser and three destroyers."

"Launch a strike package," Anjeet ordered, smoothly. "Take them out."

"Aye, sir," his aide said.

Anjeet silently thanked all the gods that they were light years from Earth. It was easy, all too easy, to see what the British were trying to do. By raiding the outer edge of his formations, it would create an impression of weakness, an impression the Prime Minister would order him to rebut as soon as possible by attacking the British at once. There was no way to prevent the *media* from reporting the attacks, of course, but by the time the reports reached Earth and the Prime Minister's response reached *Clarke* the whole matter would be immaterial anyway. Or so he hoped.

Quite why the British didn't drive the reporters away I'll never know, he thought. If nothing else, it was easier to lie without nosy foreign observers poking their noses into everything. It wasn't as if local space was *safe. But at least we'll both be inconvenienced by the bastards...*

"General," his aide said. "The strike package is away."

"Understood," Anjeet said. "Inform the analysts that I need the revised Plan Kali as soon as possible."

He watched the younger man hurry off, then looked back at the display. The British warships were already withdrawing, the escort carrier slipping away while the smaller ships moved to cover its departure. Their starfighters would have plenty of time to catch up with the carrier, unless they were delayed...he contemplated several ways to slow them down, before deciding none of them were likely to work. The British had definitely won the first engagement.

But only the first, he told himself, firmly. *They won't be expecting Plan Kali.*

Flying Officer Harriet Monsey gritted her teeth as the starfighter plunged deeper into the layers of space junk surrounding the immense gas giant. She'd seen countless simulations where she'd had to pick her way though unrealistic asteroid fields - and fly down a trench to launch a missile into an air vent - but this was the first time she'd ever seen anything like it in real life. Sensible pilots didn't try to fly into gas giant rings. The mining craft, however, gave her no choice. They were making their slow way through the rings, hunting for metallic asteroids they could turn into raw materials...

"Remember, Harriet, use the force," Flying Officer Danny Pearson called.

Harriet rolled her eyes. "Fuck off, Danny," she said. "You just keep an eye on our rear."

"They're launching starfighters themselves," Pearson snapped. "At least two full squadrons."

It must be bad, Harriet thought, wryly. She'd given him the perfect opening for a piece of sexual innuendo and he'd missed it. *Or maybe he's ill.*

She resisted the temptation to needle him about it as the enemy miner came into view. It looked like a giant spider, surrounded by a handful of automated platforms that moved through the smaller pieces of rock, poking and prodding for the next target. She couldn't help feeling a flicker of nostalgia - she'd grown up on a similar platform before applying to join the Royal Navy - but she knew she couldn't let her feelings get in her way. Tapping the console, she sent the pre-recorded message to the mining platform. The Indians had two minutes to jump into their lifeboat and cast off before their platform was blown to pieces.

They should have time to get out, she thought. *But not enough time to get into mischief.*

She hoped - prayed - that the Indians were either government-sponsored or had insurance. Her father had told her, often enough, just how deeply they'd gone into debt to purchase their mining platform - and how much they'd risked if they'd been unable to make a living. They might have had - and he'd always shuddered theatrically at this point - to go work for the government. The Indian government presumably offered similar terms to its asteroid miners as the British Government; they'd take a share of the ore in exchange for *very* favourable loan terms. But they'd have sacrificed their independence in exchange for security.

"Enemy starfighters are entering the debris field," Pearson warned. "They'll be on us in a minute."

Harriet nodded. "They're launching the lifeboat now," she said. The lifeboat on *her* miner had always been more of a tip of the hat to Earthers who'd worried more about safety than practicality, but there was no shortage of Indian ships who could recover the miners. "I'm killing the platform in three...two...one..."

She fired her plasma cannons, directly into the miner's hull. It was no less fragile than a pre-war fleet carrier; the plasma pulses burned through the hull, ripping the structure apart. One of the pulses must have hit something explosive - an oxygen tank, perhaps - and the remainder of the miner shattered. Harriet pushed aside the sense of guilt as best as she could, then yanked her starfighter around and blazed towards the edge of the space junk field. Her wingman followed her, keeping up a running commentary on the Indian starfighters. Two more were apparently skirting the edge of the asteroid field, watching for the British craft.

"Here we go," she said.

"Right behind you," Pearson said.

The Indian pilots opened fire, sending streaks of plasma fire towards the starfighters. Harriet threw herself into a random evasive pattern, blasting past the Indians and heading upwards to the carrier. The Indians swooped around and gave chase, pushing their drives to the limit. They didn't seem to have *quite* the polish of the British fighters, but they *were* enthusiastic...and very, very determined. Harriet found herself dancing backwards and forwards as they tried to close the range, then sighed in relief as the Indians backed off. She had no doubt they could have taken them, but the Indians had reinforcements on the way.

And we might have wound up stranded, she thought, as they made their way towards the retreating carrier. An escort carrier had no business being in the line of battle and everyone knew it. *The CO couldn't stay in range to recover us with the Indians breathing down his neck.*

"Well, you can paint a mining spider on your hull," Pearson mocked. "Good shooting, by the way."

"Asshole," Harriet said, without heat. The hell of it was that the flight deck staff would probably do just that. "That wasn't a moving target. Hitting one of their starfighters would have been far harder and you know it."

"Yeah," Pearson agreed. "I kept missing the bastards."

"You're a lousy shot," Harriet countered. It *wasn't* easy to hit another starfighter when the pilot knew to keep moving, but she had no intention of taking *that* into account. "Anyway, first blood to us."

"Yep," Pearson said.

She was still smiling at the thought, twenty minutes later, when they returned to the carrier, which was retreating from Clarke. The Indian pilots were good, but the Royal Navy pilots were better. *She* hadn't served in the war - a fact that had been pointed out to her, time and time again, by the old hands - yet she'd acquitted herself well. And so had the rest of her year mates.

We can fight, she thought. *And now we have experience of our own.*

"Bulldog Beta is retreating from Clarke, sir," Sally reported. "Targets One through Seven were hit; Commodore Blake judged Targets Eight and Nine to be too dangerous to approach without risking the flotilla."

"Understood," James said. The time delay was turning into a right headache, but at least the enemy would be having the same problem. "And Charlie?"

"Returning to the task force, as per orders," Sally said. "The enemy did not attempt to give chase."

"Probably for the best," James said.

He allowed himself a cold smile as he studied the display. The Indians had been hit, twice; losing the freighters had to hurt, but losing the miners had to be *humiliating*. British ships had raided their positions and escaped without losses; hell, they'd even broadcast warnings to the miners before wiping the mining craft from existence. The Indians would look like fools when the news reports reached home...

But it doesn't weaken them enough, he thought. *We have to keep wearing them down, while tempting them into a major fleet engagement. And if we can weaken them before that engagement, the easier it will be to win.*

"Order Beta and Charlie to ready themselves for more raids," he ordered. He doubted the Indians would send a convoy into the system again, not without a heavy escort; it would tie up ships and men that would be better used elsewhere. "And earmark a couple of frigates for a brief raid on Cromwell. I want the orbiting ship taken out."

"Yes, sir," Sally said.

She hesitated, noticeably. James smiled, inwardly.

"Spit it out," he said. *Susan* would not have hesitated to comment on his plans. Sally was too junior to be willing to contradict her commanding officer. "What do you want to say?"

"We could raid Gandhi," Sally said. She seemed to find it hard to meet his eyes. "Even a brief missile attack on their installations would be alarming."

"We could," James agreed. It was certainly a *tempting* thought. At the very least, the Indians would have to face the prospect of losing *all* of their extra-solar investment. "But they would probably keep their cool and write off the damage."

"Yes, sir," Sally said.

James nodded in dismissal, then turned back to his thoughts. Blood had been drawn now and his forces had performed well. The Indians hadn't *quite* lived up to their claims, although it was only a matter of time before they garnered a considerable amount of experience of their own. James's tactical analysts had already deduced that the Indians hadn't even indulged in live-fire exercises until recently, perhaps attempting to conserve their strength. The prospect of a lethal accident, even during an exercise, could not be discounted.

Or maybe they're just trying to lure us in, he thought. The mass drivers on Clarke couldn't be underestimated - or knocked out, not at *very* long range. *They want us to get closer before they start hurling rocks at us.*

He shrugged and keyed his console. "Prime Minister," he said. There was no point in trying to delay matters. The damned reporters would already be sending messages back home. If the Prime Minister didn't receive a proper report, questions would be asked in Parliament and the government's position might be undermined. "We have engaged the enemy for the first time. Tactical reports indicate..."

CHAPTER TWENTY FOUR

Clarke III, Pegasus System

"They're here," Sharon said.

Lillian stared at her, shocked. For a moment, she thought Sharon meant the SAS, even though Lillian hadn't mentioned their presence to anyone on the colony. Had the Indians stumbled across them? Or had the troopers somehow sneaked into the underground chambers and made contact with Sharon? And then it struck her that Sharon meant the Royal Navy.

David Majors leaned forward. "I've heard nothing," he said. "Are you *sure*?"

"A couple of the Indian soldiers were talking about it when they brought their friend into the infirmary," Sharon said. "They've been here for a couple of days, apparently. There have been some brief engagements, but no major battle."

"They don't know about the mass drivers," Majors said. "Shit."

Yes, they do, Lillian thought. The SAS would have passed on the warning. *But how do I tell him that without betraying them*?

She agonised over it for long seconds. She trusted Majors. There was certainly no reason to assume he'd betray the underground resistance, such as it was. But she'd been warned, in no uncertain terms, not to reveal the SAS's presence to anyone. She didn't dare breathe a word to Majors about them.

"They will have inched stealthed drones and platforms close to Clarke," she said, instead. "I think they'll have seen the mass drivers on the ground."

Majors swung round to look at her. "Are you sure?"

"They couldn't be anything else," Lillian pointed out, calmly. What *else* could the mass drivers be? "Who would imagine the Indians would cover the surface with *telescopes*?"

"We can't take the chance," Majors said. He seemed to tense to realise he was being teased lightly. "We have to get a warning out, somehow."

Sharon cleared her throat. "How?"

Majors glowered. Lillian sighed, inwardly. She understood his frustration. The Indians controlled *everything*. At worst, they could simply turn off the life support or destroy the colony from orbit. Resistance was futile. And yet, they had to do *something*. She didn't dare tell him anything that might betray the SAS...

"There is one possibility," Majors said, slowly. "Lillian; you're still taking supplies out to their bases, aren't you? You could take a jury-rigged transmitter and make a broadcast..."

"They'd detect the signal," Lillian pointed out. She had no doubt Majors could put together a transmitter from cannibalised spare parts - he was a *very* capable engineer - but the Indian satellites would pick up the radio signal. "And then we'd be exposed."

"You could keep your mouth shut," Majors snarled.

"She couldn't," Sharon said. "An injection of a standard truth drug and she'd be spilling everything she knows."

"Maybe we could feed the Indians something nasty," Majors suggested glumly. "Do you have anything that would drive them mad? Or make them do whatever we want?"

"No," Sharon said. "We never imagined we might have to poison an occupation force."

"Clearly, an oversight in our imagination," Majors said. "If we'd been armed..."

"We would have ripped the colony apart while we were trying to hold the Indians off," Lillian said, bluntly. She wondered, absently, if Majors had been drinking and then decided it was unlikely. The Indians had banned alcohol and confiscated the two illicit stills they'd found. "There was no way to prevent them from occupying the colony short of blowing ourselves up."

She held up her hand. "If you can put together a directional transmitter, I should be able to send a signal to the navy, once I'm well away from the colony," she said. "We would, of course, have to *locate* the navy ships first...and make sure we sent the signal to the *right* navy. Sending it to the wrong one would probably give the Indians a laugh right before they arrested us."

Majors smiled. "Maybe they'd be too busy laughing to arrest us properly."

Sharon gave Lillian an odd look. "Are you sure you can *find* the right set of ships?"

"Of course," Lillian lied. "I was a crewwoman, after all."

She kept her face under tight control. Majors would be easy to fool - he wanted to find a way to hit back at the Indians so desperately that he'd overlook any little flaws in the plan - but Sharon would be tougher. She might well realise that Lillian was lying about *something*, even if she wasn't sure *what*. And that meant...Sharon might assume the worst, that Lillian intended to betray them. God knew she had the least motivation to return to Great Britain.

And she's more than just a doctor, Lillian thought. *She's a psychologist as well.*

"It won't take more than a day or two," Majors assured her. "Assuming the Indians don't find anything else for me to do..."

"You'll be fine," Sharon said, bluntly. "Good luck."

Majors nodded to them both - looking happier than he'd been in weeks - and hurried out of the compartment. Sharon hesitated, as if she wanted to have a private chat with Lillian, and then followed him. Lillian allowed herself a sigh of relief as she slumped back into her chair, feeling as if she'd just passed a test of some kind. There was no reason to use the transmitter, not when she could make contact with the SAS once she left the colony, but there was no harm in letting Majors believe she'd passed on his message. Hell, it *was* a way to strike back at the Indians. It was just...a little more useless than he imagined.

Unless Sharon decides to do something stupid, she thought. Sharon could be a dangerous enemy, if crossed; a doctor was simply too perceptive to be ignored. *Maybe I should try to seduce Majors instead...*

She pushed the thought aside, angrily. She'd already dismissed the idea of trying to seduce one of the Indians, even though she could see advantages to sharing Colonel Darzi's bed. If nothing else, she could knife him as soon as the Royal Navy began its attack. But it probably wouldn't have worked, even if she *had* been a seductress. The Indians kept their distance from the British colonists.

All I can do is hope, she told herself. *And...*

She looked up as a chime echoed through the air. "All personnel are to report to the main hall," a voice said. "I say again, all personnel are to report to the main hall."

Lillian hesitated, then rose to her feet and hurried out the hatch. The main hall was large enough to hold most of the colonists, if they didn't mind standing room only. She'd only ever been there once since the Indians had landed, when they'd spoken briefly to the colonists to lay down the law. Now...she joined the throng of colonists as they headed into the hall, somehow unsurprised to see that the tables and chairs had been pushed to the rear. The Indian Governor, Colonel Darzi, was standing at the front of the room, surrounded by four men in powered combat armour.

Coward, Lillian thought, coldly. There was literally nothing on the colony that could burn through combat armour, certainly not now the Indians had stripped the colonists of anything that could reasonably be used as a weapon. *You don't need to wear armour to make a point.*

She leaned against the stone wall and waited for the rest of the colonists to enter the compartment. A number had clearly been sleeping and looked less than happy to be awoken, others looked relieved. There was no way the Indians could blame them for avoiding work when they'd been summoned by Darzi himself. Lillian hoped, savagely, that the delays would wind up causing problems for the Indians, although she had a feeling that any such problems would be minor. The Indians wouldn't have summoned essential personnel from their tasks.

But they didn't say so, she recalled, as the hatches were closed. *They called everyone.*

"Thank you for coming," Darzi said, smoothly. "I'm afraid there have been developments."

He paused for a long second before continuing. "As some of you may already have heard, your nation has dispatched a task force into the Pegasus System and skirmished with our outlying defenders. Honours so far have been around even. They have yet to push against our main defence line."

Lillian winced, inwardly. It might have been better if the Indians had tried to keep the arrival of the Royal Navy secret. Now, some hothead might just try something stupid, something she couldn't head off in time. Majors couldn't be the only one planning overt resistance to the Indians, could he?

"The situation has not changed, however," Darzi added. "We still control the colony and the orbital space surrounding it. There is no point in trying to resist - or to impede our plans to defend this colony. Should any of you try, you will be shot out of hand. This is the one warning you will get."

Which matches the one you offered us earlier, Lillian thought, wryly. It sounded as though the Indians were more worried than they wanted to admit. *Do you have reason to believe your positions are not invincible*?

"Some of you will be drafted to assist with the defence preparations," Darzi warned. "For those of you...yes?"

A middle-aged man had stuck up a hand. "You cannot legally ask us to assist in preparing defences..."

"You have a choice between working and starving," Darzi said, curtly. Lillian was surprised he hadn't ordered the man dragged out of the room and shot. "Yes, we *can* make you work for us. For what it's worth, you probably won't be counted as willing collaborators."

Probably, Lillian thought. She'd tried to look up the regulations, but they were terrifyingly imprecise. Like far too many war criminals, the collaborator would only be told he'd crossed the line *after* the war. It would depend, she suspected, on public reaction to their crimes. *But you can't promise us anything, can you*?

"In the event of your navy gaining control of the system," Darzi concluded, "we will surrender without further ado. Until then...*behave*."

And that, Lillian was sure, as Darzi turned and strutted out of the compartment, was a flat-out lie. Control of the system was one thing, but control of the gas giant's moons was quite another. The Indians would have ample opportunity to lure the Royal Navy in close and then open fire with their mass drivers, even if their fleet was beaten in open combat. And the Indians had poured men and material into Clarke. They wouldn't surrender while they could still bleed the Royal Navy white.

She was still mulling over the issue when she checked her terminal and found a blunt order to report to one of the work gangs, after lunchtime. Cursing under her breath, she hurried to the nearest diner, ate a meal that tasted like ashes and then joined some of the other colonists in the vehicle bay. The Indians had gathered forty colonists, it seemed; they were all men and women who had no constantly useful purpose.

"Get your suits on," an Indian ordered, striding into the bay. "Check and recheck your radios; set to CLARKE frequency only."

Of course, Lillian thought, coldly. Given the presence of the gas giant, a low-power radio signal would probably be undetectable except at very close range. *You wouldn't want us trying to signal the fleet, would you*?

She donned her suit, checked her neighbour's while he checked hers, then picked up her shovel and followed the Indian guards out onto the surface. It looked clear, for once, but she could see clouds in the distance, shrouding the further mountains. She wondered if the SAS team were lurking there, watching from a safe distance, then put it out of her mind. There was no way to know.

And hope I do get sent to take the next lot of supplies, she thought. She *was* on the rota, but that had been before the Royal Navy arrived. *They may think I should be kept here instead.*

"You'll be digging trenches around the colony," the guard ordered. Someone had been busy; they'd placed tiny flags in position to illustrate where the workers were supposed to dig. The Indians would probably emplace weapons later, Lillian thought. They wouldn't trust the British colonists with heavy weapons. "Get to work."

Lillian sighed and did as she was told.

"They're digging a network of trenches, sir," Percy observed.

He peered through the binoculars as the workers started to do their job. It *looked* as though they weren't being given a choice, although he was mildly surprised the Indians hadn't brought out the heavy digging equipment. A single bulldozer, adapted for local conditions, could dig a trench within minutes, while a military-grade handling machine could do the rest of the work in a day. Putting the colonists to work was just pointless.

"Interesting," Lewis said. He sounded rather amused. "They must want to keep the colonists busy."

"Looks that way," Drake agreed. "Is there any sign of our friend?"

"None," Lewis said. He glanced at Percy, sharply. He'd been doubtful about making any sort of contact with the colonists. Even if they were loyal, they might not be trustworthy and accidentally betray the SAS. "The last two transports we saw weren't broadcasting the signal."

Percy frowned, inwardly. Had they signed Lillian's death warrant by giving her the transmitter? It was certainly possible...but then, if she had been caught, surely the Indians would have used it to bait a trap. They did seem to be running random patrols around the colony, yet as far as he could tell they *were* just random. There certainly didn't seem to be a proper search effort underway.

Long hours ticked by, slowly. The Indians brought out heavy weapons emplacements, then ordered the workers back inside as they slowly fitted their equipment into the trenches. It wouldn't have lasted long against orbital bombardment, Percy knew, but the combination of ground-based plasma cannons, railguns and human shields would be enough to keep the Royal Navy from simply flattening the colony from orbit. They'd have to launch an assault on the ground and *that* would be tricky.

But we could do it, he thought, as the Indians kept expanding their lines. He'd been taught a great deal about defences, back on Earth, and one of the things he'd been taught was that defences were only as strong as the soldiers manning them. The Indians didn't have enough soldiers to man them *all. As long as we could get the marines down to the surface, we could overwhelm the defenders before they could react.*

"We'll have to forward this back through the link," Drake said. "Boone will need to know about it as soon as possible."

"Yes, sir," Lewis said.

Percy kept his amusement to himself. The Royal Marines had picked fights with the Paras - and vice versa - on Vesy, but the SAS didn't seem to care that they were *reporting* to a Para Lieutenant-Colonel. On the other hand, the SAS *knew* they were the best; they didn't *need* to engage in the rivalry that dominated interactions between the Royal Marines and the Paras. *And* they had freedom to carry out their orders as they saw fit...

"Percy, take the recordings to the transmitter," Drake ordered. "We may have to pull back if they keep establishing spotter outposts."

"Aye, sir," Percy said.

He took the datachips, placed them within his suit and headed off. Drake was right; if the Indians were genuinely preparing for an offensive on the ground, it wouldn't be long before they started putting spotters on the nearby hills. The SAS were past masters at sneaking around observers, but it would be harder to fool the Indians than terrorists on Earth. They might have to take down the tents and head somewhere further into the wilderness before re-establishing themselves.

And if that happens, he thought, *it won't be so easy to keep an eye on them.*

By the time she was allowed to re-enter the colony, Lillian was tired, sweaty, cross and sick of the endless grumbling about the pointless task. The colony had plenty of digging equipment, designed to make it easier to emplace the prefabricated buildings in the frozen ground; there was no *need* to make them dig the trenches manually. She couldn't decide if it was a deliberate attempt to keep them from thinking about the Royal Navy or simple sadism, but either way it was unpleasant, frustrating and largely useless. The Indians ignored her as she made her way back to her tiny compartment, closed and locked the door behind her and fell on the bed. She was aching everywhere.

And you'll probably have to do it again tomorrow, she thought, as she forced herself to sit up and start undressing. Her pale skin was bruised badly; she wondered absently if one of the Indians had beaten her so hard she'd forgotten it, before remembering similar bruises from basic training. The unaccustomed hard work had made her sore. *Unless they decide to put someone else to work.*

She wrapped a dressing grown around herself, then keyed her terminal. A message popped up in front of her eyes, reminding her that she would still be driving the transport to one of the mass drivers in two days. Until then, she was still on trench-digging duty. The Indians, it seemed, intended to keep the colonists busy. By the time the Royal Navy attacked, the colony would be at the centre of an impossibly-large network of defences.

At least I'll be outside the colony for a while, she told herself. She wanted a shower, but she was really too tired. *And I can meet them.*

She touched the pen in her pocket, then smiled to herself as she lay back on the bed. Majors could have his transmitter, if he had time; she'd pass his words on to the SAS before destroying it. And they *would* go to the Royal Navy...

And then they can come get us, she thought. *We'll be safe at last.*

CHAPTER TWENTY FIVE

Clarke III, Pegasus System

"You understand how to make it work?"

"I *was* a starship crewwoman," Lillian said, gently. "I'm not a complete dunce when it comes to modern technology."

"You point this part at the stars," Majors said, ignoring her. "Once you lock into the target, you push this button to trigger the pre-recorded message. It repeats ten times, then the system automatically wipes itself. You throw the transmitter out of the vehicle and try to crush it beneath the treads."

"Understood," Lillian said. It might be better to throw it into the ocean, but she'd prefer not to take the risk. Falling through the ice would be bad enough even with the Indians willing and able to help rescue her. "I'll see that it gets destroyed."

"Good luck," Majors said. He gave her a brief hug. "If they do catch you, tell them it was my fault and you didn't have the slightest idea what I was asking you to do."

Lillian snorted. There was no shortage of war movies from the Age of Unrest where women - regarded as little better than animals by the bad guys - ran rings around the terrorists, just because the terrorists didn't take them seriously. One of the spies had been blindingly obvious to anyone who hadn't been blinded themselves by their own preconceptions. The movies had always struck her as funny - she particularly liked the one where a topless spy had hypnotised the enemy merely by waving her breasts in their faces - but the Indians weren't anything like that stupid. *They* wouldn't dismiss her simply because she happened to be born without a penis.

"I think they'll shoot us both," she said. Some of the *other* war movies had lingered too much on precisely what kind of fates certain spies had endured for her comfort, but at least the Indians weren't *that* unpleasant. "Are you sure you want me to do this?"

"Yes," Majors said, flatly. "Go."

Lillian nodded, then took the transmitter, stuffed it into her bag and headed up the corridor towards the vehicle bay. Sweat trickled down her back as she approached the two guards on duty - the Indians hadn't bothered to search her bag before, but they might change their minds now the Royal Navy was actually investing the system - and then breathed a sigh of relief as they waved her past. Neither of the young men looked particularly nasty, she noted; they seemed more inclined to worry about the conflict than her presence. She walked up to the vehicle, slipped through the hatch and carefully hid the transmitter in the engineering compartment. Someone would have to search the transport *thoroughly* to find it, if they wanted...

Pity it wasn't small enough to be hidden under my clothes, she thought, as she walked back into the cab and checked the rota. She would be driving to Outpost Seven, it seemed; a six-day round trip. It wasn't as long as she could have preferred, but still...six days away from the colony and digging trenches was something to be enjoyed. *I could have forced them to strip search me if they'd wanted to make sure I wasn't carrying anything dangerous.*

The engine hummed to life as she checked in with the control room; the entire vehicle shuddered slightly as the hatch opened, allowing her to drive out of the colony and past the growing network of trenches. Someone had noticed - unfortunately too soon for the Indians to trap themselves - that they needed to leave an open path for the transports; the Indians had cut a gap through the defences for the vehicles and then expanding the surrounding fortifications. She silently bade the colony goodbye as she drove onwards, silently grateful for the modified caterpillar tracks. There was no such thing as a *road* on Clarke.

"Good thing too," she told herself, as she kept a wary eye on the timer. "The transport would probably wreck it within hours."

She smiled at the thought. She'd been told that tanks and other heavy military vehicles weren't allowed to travel on motorways, unless it was genuinely urgent. They were simply too heavy and smashed up the roads when they drove down them. The transport, if anything, was heavier. She checked the timer again, decided she was far enough from the colony and carefully removed the pen from her pocket. She'd looked at it before, time and time again, but as far as she could tell it was a perfectly normal pen. It even *wrote* normally.

Let's just hope you're listening, she thought, as she clicked on the transmitter. *Because if you're not, I may be in some trouble.*

It was an hour before the sound of the hatch opening made her jump. She braced herself, careful to remain quiet, as the door behind her opened; she turned, slowly, and smiled as she saw Percy Schneider. He tapped his lips as he produced a bug detector from his pocket and swept the compartment, then the rest of the vehicle. Lillian almost didn't dare to breathe until he returned, smiling openly. This time, she noted, he was alone.

"It should be safe to talk," he said. "How are you?"

"They know about the fleet," Lillian said. "They've been making us dig trenches for them."

"Wankers," Percy said. He sat down facing her. "I've got quite a few questions, I'm afraid."

"So do I," Lillian said. She went on before he could say a word. "A friend of mine built a transmitter to send a signal to the navy. I said I'd take it and transmit..."

Percy cut her off. "You'd never be able to send the signal without being caught," he said. "Is he mad?"

"Desperate," Lillian said. "He wants to do something."

"And then leave you with the transmitter," Percy pointed out. "Did you intend to destroy it?"

"I planned to give it to you," Lillian said. "If you take the message, you can forward it to the fleet, can't you?"

"Probably," Percy said. "Unless this is an elaborate trap for us."

He shrugged. "I'll take a look at the transmitter in a moment," he said. "Now...*my* questions."

Lillian sighed and braced herself for another interrogation.

Percy had to admit, when he finally looked at the transmitter, that David Majors was actually a *very* capable technician. The Indians had presumably confiscated any purpose-built transmitters that might have been able to get a signal out, but Majors had strung together a dozen different components to produce the same effect. Percy carefully removed the datachip storing the message itself - Majors hadn't rigged a proper self-destruct system, which was a dangerous oversight - and then broke the transmitter back into its component pieces, which he dumped into his bag. They could be hidden somewhere or dumped under the waves if necessary.

He put the bag out of sight and walked back into the driving compartment. "You're on your way to one of their bases, correct?"

"Correct," Lillian said. "I don't know what I'm carrying, but they consider it important."

"It could be anything," Percy agreed. He took a breath. "I brought a set of tools this time, Lillian. If I tried, I could open the boxes."

He winced at her expression. Taking him onboard and chatting to him was reasonably safe - she was practically unmonitored until she reached the outpost - but opening the boxes, which might reveal signs of tampering, was a whole other matter. If someone took a careful look and discovered what he'd done, *she* would probably get the blame. The Indians would be unlikely to accept her curiosity as an excuse.

She swallowed, hard. "Do it."

Percy frowned. There was something about her that spurred his protective instincts. "Are you sure?"

"Yes," Lillian said. She reminded him, just for a moment, of the same determination Penny showed. "Do it, before I have an attack of brains to the head and realise just how dangerous it is."

"All right," Percy said.

He gave her a reassuring smile - if necessary, they could arrange an accident for the vehicle and smuggle her back to the tents - and walked through the hatch, into the hold. It was suddenly very cold, but the atmosphere was breathable. The Indians, he was amused to note, had largely copied the Royal Navy's standardised transportation containers, although *that* might have been caused by the global push towards standardizing as much as possible. He moved from container to container, looking for one that could be used to fake an accident if necessary and finally chose one near the rear. If the vehicle happened to hit something big enough to make it shake, he decided, it was just possible that the container would be damaged in transit.

"Let's see," he muttered to himself. Burglary skills had been part of his basic training, although he'd never quite understood why until he'd been seconded to the SAS. A burglar needed to think about ways to bypass locks and security protections, as well as developing the nerve to proceed with something that could get him in deep shit if he were caught. "At least they used the standard duct tape."

The thought made him smile - he'd had a sergeant who rhapsodised about the power of duct tape - as he carefully cut his way into the container. It would be simple enough to replace, once he was through. Inside, he found a set of smaller boxes, clearly marked as ration bars and sealed bottles of water. He puzzled over the latter for a long moment - Clarke III wasn't short of water, even though it did need to be purified - and then dismissed the thought. It wouldn't be the first time some bureaucrat back home had decided it would be better to ship supplies to the front rather than let the troops source it for themselves.

At least this time someone else has the barmy bureaucrats, he thought, coldly. *Good to know they learned more than just tactics from us.*

"Now," he mused, pushing the thought to the back of his mind. "How many soldiers are based on the outpost?"

There was no way to be sure, he knew, but it couldn't be more than a few dozen at most. The Indians weren't crazy enough to stick an entire regiment on top of each of the outposts, even if they were going to be defending the mass drivers. There were enough ration bars in the crate he'd opened to feed a company of Royal Marines for several months, at least. If the rest of the containers were *all* crammed with ration bars...

He did the math, slowly. The Indians would need at least a couple of thousand men on the outpost to make the expenditure worthwhile. Either that, or they were establishing a supply dump for later expansion. But with the task force bearing down on them, why bother? They could do it afterwards, if they won the war. He sealed up the container and went looking for a second that could be opened, gingerly. This time, he found a stockpile of railgun pellets.

Shit, he swore. Lillian was transporting *ammunition*. If that wasn't a breach of the laws of war, he wasn't sure what *was*. And she didn't even *know* she was transporting ammunition; hell, food and drink alone was skirting the edge of the rules. *She could wind up being hung for this.*

He sealed up the box, then opened a third. It held more railgun pellets. The Indians, clearly, were anticipating KEW strikes on their positions. It wouldn't be a bad bet, either; the task force would need to clear the mass drivers before they could get into orbit and KEW strikes would work, given half a chance. But the Indians had clearly taken precautions of their own...

But they don't know about us, he thought, as he sealed the box carefully. *If they did, they would have made different choices.*

There didn't seem to be any boxes left that could be opened and still maintain plausible deniability, so he repacked his tools - taking extreme care that none of them were left behind - and walked back into the cab. Outside, the snowfall was growing stronger; Lillian had already slowed the vehicle as visibility had dropped to zero. It would be too dangerous to try to make his way back to the team until it cleared.

"You took your time," Lillian observed. She sounded quieter now, as if she knew the die was cast. "What did you find?"

Percy hesitated, then decided to be honest. "I found railgun pellets and ration bars," he said, bluntly. "You're supporting their war effort."

"I could just crash this vehicle into the mass driver," Lillian said, after a second. "I..."

Her hands were starting to shake. "I...I'm going to be killed, aren't I?"

"Probably not," Percy said. He wasn't sure how to be reassuring. Penny had always thrown a fit when he'd slipped into over-protective mode, even during the floods. "You didn't know what you were shipping, did you?"

"No," Lillian said. "But I do now."

"You're helping us," Percy said. He understood what she was going through, but he honestly didn't know quite what to say. "You will be forgiven, really."

Lillian looked at him. "With *my* record? Can you swear to that?"

Percy hesitated. He understood her concerns far too well. She had blotted her copybook once and anyone who wanted to throw the book at her would have ample excuse, now she'd been duped into assisting the enemy war effort. But, at the same time, she *had* redeemed herself.

"I can contact the fleet and ask the Admiral," he said. He neglected to mention that the Admiral was effectively his adopted father. He'd tried not to use the influence that brought him for himself, but Lillian deserved *some* kind of reassurance. "And I will testify in your favour if you wish."

He peered out of the window. The snowstorm was only growing stronger. Lillian pulled the vehicle to a stop, then tapped her console, sending a quick message to the colony. Given the weather, he knew she could only wait until the snow had stopped falling before resuming her journey. Trying to steer a path when she could no longer see clearly was asking for trouble.

"I'll hold you to that," Lillian said. She was shaking as she spoke. "Percy, I...I really wish I was braver."

"You're doing fine," Percy said. "I'm not sure I would have been able to cope so coolly with enemy occupation."

"You'd probably have chased them off the planet by now," Lillian said.

Percy shook his head. Neither Lillian nor their quiet probing had been able to determine just what had happened to the Governor and the handful of military personnel on the colony. His own theory was that they'd been hurried off-world and probably shipped straight to Gandhi or Vesy - the latter, in particular, presenting a whole set of challenges to any rescuers. But it wouldn't have mattered. Mounting a full-fledged resistance on Clarke - with the Indians firmly in control of the colony's life support systems - was impossible.

"I think I would be in the same boat as you," he said, finally.

"Yeah," Lillian said. She smiled, bitterly. "The *Titanic*."

She glanced at her console as it bleeped. "Weather control says the storm is not going to go away for at least two hours," she warned. Percy read the message over her shoulder and sighed inwardly. "Maybe longer."

"I'll just have to wait here," Percy said. He threw her an embarrassed look. "If that's alright with you."

Lillian smiled wanly and then rose. "It is," she said. She reached for him as he stood and pulled him into a long desperate kiss. He stared at her as their lips parted, feeling shocked; she kissed him again, hard enough to make him lose all sense of propriety. "I...just don't say anything, ok?"

Percy's last thought for quite some time, as their hands struggled to undo their clothes, was that Drake was going to kill him.

Afterwards, with the storm fading away, Lillian watched him go, feeling oddly torn. She'd wanted to feel *human* again, just for a while; she'd wanted to feel as if someone cared. It had been hard to make any sort of *real* connection on the colony - everyone knew she was in exile, even the ones who were prepared to be friendly - and harder still after the Indians had taken over the colony. She was part of the resistance and yet she still needed to keep secrets from her fellows.

She looked down at herself as she started to dress. Percy hadn't mocked her, or taken advantage of her, or treated her as anyone other than someone who needed comfort. It said too much about her life, she reasoned, that she'd allowed too many people to walk all over her because of her desperate need to *belong*. But now...she had no illusions about Percy, yet he hadn't lied to her. And he hadn't promised her anything either.

And he was good in bed, part of her mind noted. She wasn't very experienced, but she'd enjoyed just being able to throw away caution and concern and throw herself headfirst into making love. Somehow, that had made it better. *And...*

She shook her head as she restarted the engine. The Indians would be defeated, sooner or later...and, if Percy spoke for her, maybe there would be a life afterwards. And, if not, at least she would have her revenge. The Indians would rue the day they'd turned her into an ammunition carrier.

Maybe I can spike their guns, next time, she thought. She'd have to be ready to run for it afterwards, but somehow the thought was no longer intimidating. *And give them a nasty surprise when they start to open fire.*

CHAPTER TWENTY SIX

HMS Warspite, Pegasus System

"Thank you for allowing me this interview, Captain," Penny said.

"The Admiral cleared it," Captain Naiser said. She was sure she could detect a hint of irritation in his tone. Did he *know* she'd been effectively adopted by Vice Admiral Fitzwilliam? It was probably in her file. "And you may be feeling as if you're missing out."

Penny nodded as she sat down and crossed her legs. Captain Naiser's profile had made it clear he was homosexual, so there was probably no point in trying to use her wiles to make him say more than he ought. Even if he'd been straight, he was too annoyed at the whole situation to be manipulated easily. Besides, a week of constant skirmishing had taken a toll on everyone. She'd seen officers being sharper than usual, while she'd heard rumours that two crewmen had come to blows and beaten each other bloody. No one had said anything to confirm it, at least not to her.

"The media ships are sending back constant reports," she said. They were *also* broadcasting them over the system, although she wasn't sure who they thought was receiving them. The colonists? The Indians? "They're full of speculation and nearly devoid of facts."

The captain's lips twitched. One report had confidently claimed that the two sides were secretly in alliance and the reason neither one had sought a decisive battle was that they were planning a joint attack on the Americans or the Chinese. It was absurd, given the amount of blood that had already been spilt, and Penny was sure the reporter who'd come up with the theory would be hastily recalled to Earth and promoted into upper management, where he could do less harm. She would have preferred to see him fired, but it was very hard to fire a reporter for anything less than outright lying. Their union was very powerful.

"I don't have much time," the captain said. "What would you like to ask?"

"Several questions," Penny said. She knew the answers wouldn't pass the censors, at least until the end of the war, but she'd use them for her tell-all book afterwards. "Why *aren't* we confronting the Indians directly?"

"The Admiral prefers a policy of gradually weakening the Indian position, rather than a frontal attack," the captain said. It had the air of an answer carefully prepared for the interview. "The longer we cut their supply lines, the weaker they will become; the more ships they have to cut loose to guard their convoys, the harder they will find it to hold onto the system."

Penny nodded. One of the more experienced reporters on *Theodore Smith* had already produced a tactical analysis that largely agreed with the captain. She was surprised the censors had allowed it to slip out, although they might have decided that it actually worked in the Royal Navy's favour. It certainly made it sound as though the whole affair was under control and the Indians were dancing to the British tune. The Indians were probably doing their damndest to keep it from their people, if it had reached Earth yet.

"And they have that second carrier," she mused. "You don't want to encourage the Indians to bring it into play."

"No," the captain agreed. "It would tip the local balance of power in their favour."

Penny nodded, shortly. "I've been given to understand that the Indians have emplaced mass drivers on Clarke III," she said. "Why can't they be simply taken out from long range?"

The captain's eyes narrowed, clearly wondering where she'd learned about the mass drivers. So far, none of the media reports had referred to the weapons; *Penny* had only heard about them through listening carefully to a pair of tactical officers in the mess. She knew the censors would never let her tell the universe they existed, but she could at least ask why they hadn't been smashed from orbit. The answer would be written in her book.

"Accurately targeting the mass drivers from outside the gas giant's gravity well would be tricky," the captain said. "In theory, it would be a simple exercise in orbital mechanics, but in practice it would be incredibly complex. The slightest error could put the projectile thousands of miles off course. We only really deploy KEWs from low orbit because accuracy is paramount. They do not have the ability to adjust course while in flight."

"Because they're just rocks," Penny said.

"Correct," the captain agreed. "However, there is another problem. The Indians have surrounded the mass driver emplacements with railguns and plasma cannons. They would see a projectile coming and open fire, blasting it off course before it could strike the target."

Penny frowned. "I was under the impression that intercepting a KEW strike was impossible."

"It is, if you don't have the right tools," the captain said. "The Indians *do* have the tools. We *could* keep firing projectiles until one finally got through, but it would be immensely costly and give the Indians plenty of time to respond."

"By bringing in the other carrier," Penny guessed.

"Or coming up with something new," the captain offered. "And there would be an unacceptable risk of accidentally harming the colonists."

"Which would be inconvenient," Penny said. "And embarrassing."

She sighed, inwardly. She'd been warned, on Vesy, that hostages might well find themselves on their own. The only way to deal with hostage-takers, humanity had learned during the Age of Unrest, was to make it clear that the mere presence of hostages wouldn't be enough to deter a military assault. Everyone would be pleased if the hostages were recovered alive, but if they weren't the blame would be placed firmly on the terrorists. There would certainly be no attempt to ransom the hostages. Who knew how many others would wind up dead because the terrorists had a sudden cash windfall?

But the Indians aren't terrorists, she thought. *They wouldn't harm the colonists just to make a point.*

"Very embarrassing," the captain said. "Hit the moon hard enough and it would shatter."

Penny had to smile. "I don't want to think of the government's reaction if you went home and told them you accidentally blew up the moon."

"They'd blame it on the French," the captain predicted. He shook his head. "We'd need a *very* big KEW to actually destroy the moon, but it could be done."

"Or a mercury bomb," Penny said. "Were any actually built?"

"It's a simple matter of engineering," the captain said. "But emplacing them would be a major pain if you were trying to do it without being detected."

Penny nodded, thoughtfully. Back in the early days of space exploration, the Belt Alliance - a rough confederation of independent asteroid miners and settlements - had seriously proposed blowing up Mercury to make it easier to mine. They'd talked about emplacing a number of nuclear bombs under the surface, then detonating them in unison, shattering the planet and creating a whole new asteroid belt. The idea hadn't gotten very far - the tramlines had been discovered shortly afterwards, opening up whole new vistas for human exploration - but no one had forgotten. Blowing up an entire planet was now well within humanity's capabilities.

And there are people who believe we will one day abandon planets completely, she thought, dully. *They'd see them as nothing more than sources of raw material.*

"The Indians wouldn't consider threatening to blow up the whole moon themselves, if they were losing the war," she mused. "They'd become pariahs overnight."

"They have to understand that crossing the line would only make it harder for them to return to the family of nations," the captain said. He gave her a long considering look. "I hope you're not planning to mention *that* possibility in your reports."

"I wasn't inclined to suggest it," Penny said. She had a feeling the Indians could have thought of it for themselves, if they'd wanted to. "If I can ask, sir, has there been any news from the ground?"

"From your brother, you mean," the captain said. He gave her a sympathetic look. "I'm afraid all such reports are highly classified. The only thing I can tell you is that they're alive, down on the ground and undetected."

"Thank you, sir," Penny said. She took a breath. "Do you think we're winning the war?"

The captain hesitated. "So far, honours have been about even," he said. "But they're going to have to tip the balance themselves or risk wasting away to irrelevance."

Penny considered it. "How long will that take?" She asked. "Things are built to last these days."

"Some things last longer than others," the captain said. "Yeah, a lot of our technology is built to last for years; there's no longer any such thing as planned obsolescence. But some of the more advanced military systems *cannot* be run at full power indefinitely without causing considerable wear and tear. Cutting the Indians off from their supply lines and forcing them to push their equipment to the limit will wear them down savagely. Keeping their crews on alert will also take its toll."

"But it will take a toll on our crews too," Penny pointed out.

"Yes, it will," the captain agreed. "But we have more crewmen than they do. We also have the option of pulling back into J-35 for a rest, if necessary. They don't have that option."

"Because you've been buzzing their installations with drones," Penny said. "They *have* to take each contact report seriously."

The captain smirked. At a distance, it was very hard to tell the difference between a warship and a drone *playing* at being a warship. The Indians would suspect, perhaps, that some of the ships violating their defence perimeter weren't real, but they wouldn't be able to let the contacts just go past. Instead, they had to respond to each and every contact, placing further wear and tear on their crews.

"They do," he confirmed. "And as long as they're tied to Clarke, they can't pull away and relax."

Penny nodded. "Why don't they just give in?"

"Pride, I imagine," the captain said. "It's like gambling, in a sense. You keep raising the stakes...and at some point, you'll find it hard to back down even though cold logic tells you that you can't possibly win."

"I suppose," Penny said.

She understood, better than she cared to admit. Years ago, when she'd been barely twelve, she'd played a game of Monopoly with Percy and a couple of his friends. One of them had offered to sell Mayfair to whoever made the highest bid and Penny had found herself in a contest with Percy, constantly raising her offer even though they'd both long since passed the point where the purchase would be worthwhile. And she'd kept bidding because she'd wanted to spit in Percy's eye...

And I won the bidding war, she thought, *but I lost the game because I gave away too much ready cash.*

"You'd think a world leader would know better," she commented. "They could gamble so hard they lose everything."

The captain shrugged. "Most world leaders are isolated from the world," he said. "They don't serve on the front lines, nor are they really threatened by terrorists. Government offices are hardened targets, surrounded by security guards and equipped with escape tunnels. The death and suffering of both their soldiers and civilians is alien to their experience. They rarely see the consequences of their decisions until the war is completely lost - and even then, they can go into exile rather than surrender to the enemy."

Like I was playing with Monopoly money, Penny mused. *I might have wound up embarrassed by losing, I might have been teased by my older brother, but I wouldn't have lost anything significant. My life didn't rest on the outcome.*

"That makes sense," she said. A thought struck her. "But wouldn't it be true of the British Government too?"

"On the record, of course not," the captain said. He smiled. "Off the record, the British Government cannot afford to back down. If it does, it conveys an impression of weakness that other enemies will be quick to capitalise upon. The more times the government backs down, the harder it will be to convince the *next* set of aggressors that the government is serious about fighting *this* time. The Indians have basically forced us into a position where we have to fight or surrender - and they gambled we would surrender."

"But we haven't," Penny said.

"That flips the problem into *their* lap," the captain said. "If *they* back down now, *they* look weak; they'd have problems convincing others that they would fight, if pushed. India has more natural enemies we do too; both China and Russia have reason to fear Indian influence in East and Central Asia. They've gambled their way into a position where their only *real* hope is to win the war on the cheap, to do it without losing one or both of their carriers."

"Because the Chinese might stab them in the back, even if they beat us," Penny muttered.

"Of course," the captain agreed. "The Chinese would even be able to claim that they were enforcing the Great Power system."

"And so all we can do is carry on the war," Penny said. She shook her head in amused disbelief. "There's no room for a compromise, is there?"

"There's nothing to compromise *with*," the captain pointed out. "Anything we could reasonably offer them would be seen as a sign of weakness, a sign that being aggressive gets you rewards. Either we win or they win with no middle ground."

"We could offer them Vesy," Penny suggested. "There isn't anything there we *want*."

The captain shook his head. "That's arguable," he said. "The Indians would certainly be able to gain a great deal, simply by controlling access to the natives. They'd also be able to take advantage of their insights into our technology, if the Indians start training them in human methods..."

"They're primitives," Penny snapped. She knew that wasn't entirely fair, but they'd taken her prisoner and would have eaten her, perhaps, if the Indians hadn't ransomed her. It was hard to consider them anything other than barbarians. "They're not going to open the doorway to tramline-free FTL."

"How do you know?" The captain asked. "The Tadpoles introduced us to plasma cannons - we had the theory, we could just never get them to work. Now, we've actually improved on the design; the latest generation of human-built plasma weapons are an order of magnitude more powerful than anything the Tadpoles deployed."

"That you know about," Penny said, tartly. She couldn't imagine the Tadpoles declining to improve their own technology while humanity developed its own. "They will have advanced themselves, won't they?"

"Probably," the captain agreed. "They *did* design their fleet mix to overwhelm ours - or so they thought. New Russia proved they certainly had the advantage against our modern warships. In that case, we inspired them; hell, the concepts the Vesy learned from human contact were already causing innovation amongst their city-states when we had to leave the planet for good. I wouldn't be so quick to dismiss the suggestion that we couldn't learn anything from them."

Penny scowled. "But the Tadpoles...the Tadpoles know that solid matter is composed of atoms," she said, searching for something simple. "They understand the universe around them on a level the Vesy can't match. The Vesy still think that chanting loudly brings the favour of the gods."

"Yet," the captain said. He cleared his throat. "But this is a little off-topic, isn't it?"

"Yeah," Penny agreed. She sighed inwardly. It wasn't easy to admit she was bored, but perhaps she should. Half of her insights into the war would never get past the censors - and if she tried, she'd wind up in the brig. She spent far too long watching movies, reading books and writing long emails to Hamish. "It's quite a way off-topic."

She turned to look at the display. "I meant to ask," she said. It wasn't *precisely* a lie - the issue had been bugging her for weeks. "Why doesn't Clarke III have its own name? Half the public seems convinced we're attacking a planet rather than a moon?"

The captain shrugged. "It's generally the practice for the settlers to name their world, if it wasn't already named by the discoverer," he said. If he was surprised by the question, he didn't show it. "I imagine the settlers will hold a referendum on the question in a year or so, once everything is nicely established. They'll have plenty of time to choose a name."

Penny smiled. "Penny is a lovely name."

"Find your own planet," the captain said, dryly. "You get to name it whatever you please."

"Fat chance," Penny said. "Most exploration missions are run by either governments or large corporations. I couldn't buy an exploration ship for love or money."

"Probably not," the captain agreed. "But you *could* add a name to the list of *suggested* planetary names."

"It sounds a bit pointless," Penny mused. "You can name the world, if you discover it, but you can only choose from a list of pre-approved names."

"It could be worse," the captain pointed out. "The first men to land on Mars, Venus, Titan and Terra Nova all had to say lines that were carefully scripted by PR hacks. After that, it became more acceptable to say 'I claim this world for my country.'"

"True," Penny said. "I..."

She broke off as an alarm buzzed. "Captain?"

The captain held up a hand as he keyed his console. "Report!"

"Captain," Tara said. "We just picked up a warning from the stealthed platforms. A number of Indian starships are leaving orbit."

"Understood," the captain said. "I'm on my way."

He glanced at Penny. "Duty calls, I'm afraid."

"Good luck, captain," Penny said. "And thank you."

CHAPTER TWENTY SEVEN

Pegasus System

"Report," James barked, as he strode into the CIC. "What do we have?"

"Admiral," Sally said. "Two large flotillas of Indian ships have departed Clarke."

James sat and keyed his console, activating the main display. "Where are they going?"

"Unsure," Sally said. "They're not heading towards us or any of the tramlines."

James frowned. The time-delay was a problem - the Indians could have changed course already and he wouldn't know about it for at least ten minutes - but the more he looked at it, the less sense it made. Sally was right; the Indians didn't seem to have *any* real destination in mind. They'd have to alter course before they travelled too far from Clarke to do anything.

Unless they're trying to convince us to attack Clarke, he thought, slowly. *They might not realise we know about the mass drivers.*

"Admiral," Sally warned. "Three more fleets have been detected leaving Clarke. The total *apparent* ship count is over seventy, including three carriers."

James looked down at the display, shaking his head in disbelief. The Indians didn't *have* seventy ships, not in Pegasus. And if they'd had three carriers, they would have pushed for a decisive battle as soon as possible. No, those carriers had to be fakes, drones posing as enemy ships. They'd probably copied the tactic from the raiders he'd sent to keep the Indians on alert.

They'd know we wouldn't be fooled, he thought. They might manage to get away with inflating their ship count, but only if they stuck to smaller ships. A carrier couldn't be faked realistically. There was no way the Indians could believe that *anyone* would be convinced by the fake carriers. And that meant...what? *Do they want us to know the carriers are faked?*

He contemplated it for a long moment. The Indians *had* to want him to know; there was no other possibility that made any kind of sense. Did they truly believe he'd be unable to determine which carrier was the real one? Or were they intent on forcing him to keep an eye on all five dummy fleets? One of them might well be real.

Or they might all have some real ships, he mused. *But if they come into close range, it would be easier to determine which ones are real and which ones are fakes.*

"Admiral," Sally said. "The task force is requesting orders."

James nodded, slowly. "Signal to *Warspite*," he ordered. It would be at least eight minutes before *Warspite* received her orders and sixteen before James knew she was ready to carry them out, but there was no way to avoid it. "She is to probe the edge of the Indian defence zone and attempt to confirm if the carrier remains in orbit."

"Aye, sir," Sally said.

"And order the task force to stand by," James added. Even if the Indians changed course immediately, it would still be hours before they came into engagement range. "Yellow alert; I say again, yellow alert."

"Yes, sir," Sally said.

James forced himself to relax, thinking hard. It was hard to escape the impression the Indians were taunting him; they'd launched five separate fleets they *knew* he'd recognise as fakes, right from the start. And yet, he couldn't afford to completely dismiss them. One of those fleets might be real, protecting a full-sized fleet carrier. Or he might be meant to allow himself to be mesmerised by the sheer weight of firepower drifting through the system. It might be intended to keep him from noticing the *real* threat.

"Order the escort ships to launch an additional shell of sensor drones," he said. "I want to know about it if something comes within a million kilometres of our location, stealthed or not."

"Aye, sir," Sally said.

"And signal the foreign observers," James said. A number of ships were already retreating from the task force, but others were obstinately remaining where they were. "Inform them that local space might be about to get hot."

He sat back in his chair, watching the Indians closely. They didn't seem inclined to alter course, but there was nothing to be gained by powering out of the system. The only scenario that made sense was that they thought they could escape his sensors entirely, then reverse course and strike him in the rear, but he'd already covered his back. Unless the *real* ships were making a beeline for him in stealth mode...

They'll be inclined to gamble, he thought, coldly. There was no easy way to avoid it. *The long-term advantage lies with us.*

"Inform me the moment *Warspite* responds," he ordered. If the *real* carrier was still in orbit around the gas giant, he had some manoeuvring room. "And signal *Hotchpotch.* I want them to confirm the second carrier is still in the Vesy System."

Unless they've replaced that carrier with a drone and slipped it into this system, he thought, darkly. There were too many options if the Indians were prepared to gamble he wouldn't try to attack Gandhi. Putting one carrier into the system without being detected, certainly not at such long range, wouldn't be difficult. *But they'd still need to get into attack range before they launched their fighters.*

He scowled at the display showing the foreign ships. There was no way he could take his own ships into stealth, not when the foreigners would point the Indians right to him. He could order them away from the task force, but not all of them would obey and opening fire on them would be a PR disaster. It had been *far* simpler when they'd been fighting the Tadpoles.

But then we were also fighting to the finish, he reminded himself. *Or so we thought.*

"Captain," Tara said. "I believe the carrier is still in position."

John leaned forward. "How can you be sure?"

"She's launching starfighters," Tara said. "I think they're sweeping local space for drones."

"Looks that way," Howard agreed. "Unless they've managed to find a way to fake starfighters."

John rather doubted it. Unless the Indians had made a breakthrough, drones capable of faking starfighters convincingly would be staggeringly expensive. It would be cheaper to fly starfighters on remote control, even though it would be blindingly obvious that that was what they were doing within minutes. Combat AI simply couldn't cope with the decisions required to fly a starfighter into combat.

But we were always wary about actually creating artificial intelligence, John reminded himself. Countless movies about rogue AIs turning on their creators had left a scar. *The Indians might have decided to violate the taboo.*

"Prepare to pull us back," he ordered. The last thing he wanted was to be detected and overwhelmed by a flight of starfighters. "Communications, raise the Admiral. Inform him that we have confirmed the presence of one fleet carrier in orbit around Clarke."

"Aye, sir," Gillian said.

John nodded as he studied the display. The Indians were playing at something, but what?

"See if you can determine how many of those destroyers are real," he added, after a moment's thought. The Indians had concentrated their forces, following the task force's arrival; they hadn't even diverted ships to serve as convoy escorts. "They may be trying to dupe us into believing the carrier is unescorted."

But surely they wouldn't have deliberately shown us more ships than they have, he thought, as Tara went to work. *They'd know we'd deduce that that were fakes...*

He scowled, inwardly. What if they *weren't* fakes? What if the Indians had secretly managed to build or buy more ships than MI6 had realised? The Russians were desperately short of foreign currency; they could easily have transferred a handful of smaller ships to the Indians in exchange for hard cash. It wasn't as if the Russians would feel obliged to warn anyone, either. Whatever had happened to isolate them from the other Great Powers, it had clearly been bad. They might want a little indirect revenge.

"I think some of the ships are real," Tara said, slowly. "But others are definitely drone-created images."

John frowned. "I see," he said. "Upload the data to the Admiral."

"Aye, sir," Tara said.

"The fleets are on their way, General," his aide said.

Anjeet nodded, curtly. The British didn't realise it, but they had an advantage. His dispersed forces were so far apart that coordinating would be a bitch, while the British were concentrated in one location. They *would* have problems working out which of the starships were actually *real*, but once they figured it out they'd find it easier to react than any of the dispersed Indian formations.

And I can't take command directly, he thought, sourly. *I have to remain with the carrier.*

He gritted his teeth. The Prime Minister had told him to stay with the carrier, pointing out that India could hardly afford to lose one of its most experienced officers. Anjeet had argued that the carrier would draw fire, to which the Prime Minister had countered that it was also the most heavily-defended ship in the fleet. It was galling - he disliked the thought of remaining in safety while his men plunged into danger - but it did have some advantages. He could coordinate the dispersed fleets from the Flag Bridge...

But not command the engagements personally, he told himself. *My orders would be out of date before they were even issued.*

"Order the fleets to execute Kali One on the designated moment," he ordered, finally. The British would see the ships coming, but that was part of the point. "And inform Admiral Joshi that he may deploy the...special units when he sees fit."

"Aye, sir," his aide said.

Anjeet cursed under his breath. The greatest naval battle since Operation Nelson - and the first major space battle between two human navies - and he, the commander of one side, was effectively stuck on the sidelines. His counterpart would be right in the thick of it. If only he hadn't been given orders not to risk the carrier...

But at least the British will get a surprise, he thought. *And if they are disabled, I can finish them off personally.*

"Admiral," Sally reported. "The Indian ships are altering course."

"They must have altered course simultaneously," James commented. The display showed the Indian formations changing course one by one, but in reality they'd probably started their movements at the same time. "They're heading towards us - confirm."

"Yes, sir," Sally said. "Indian One will be within firing range in two hours, seventeen minutes; Indians Two through Five will be within firing range in two hours, thirty minutes."

"Expect Indian One to slow at some point," James said. Given the problems they'd had to face, the Indians had done remarkably well. It *looked* as though his fleet was being attacked from several different angles at once. The reporters were probably even taking the reports of fleet carriers for granted. "Launch a new spread of drones towards each of the oncoming formations."

"Aye, Admiral," Sally said.

James sat back in his chair, thinking hard. *Warspite* had confirmed that one carrier and a number of smaller ships remained in orbit over Clarke, which meant that at least thirty of the ships in the advancing formations had to be fakes. The carriers definitely were, unless the Indians had sneaked the *second* carrier into Pegasus - and if they had, he'd still be reasonably confident about a battle. There would be the danger of the *first* carrier getting involved, but if he smashed one ship he could mousetrap the other.

And if they are trying to sneak up on us while relying on us to be watching the formations, he thought, *they've picked a very odd way to do it.*

He studied the sensor drones for a long moment. The Indians would have real problems sneaking anything larger than a destroyer through the electronic netting and into firing range, no matter what they did. A destroyer *might* do some damage, but it could be swatted before it did anything lethal. It would be embarrassing, yet it would be *just* embarrassing. His task force would survive.

Unless they expect us to prepare for the formations and not to be alert now, he added, mentally. *But such a plan would rely on us doing what they wanted.*

The display looked ominous. Five formations were closing from one side of the task force; the other side looked empty, untouched. And yet... he hadn't dropped his guard. The Indians would have to be fools to assume he *would.* After all, they'd gone out of their way to make it clear that at least half the ships advancing on his position were fakes.

"Bring the task force to red alert when the formations are twenty minutes from missile range," he ordered. "But keep the tactical crews on alert."

"Aye, sir," Sally said. She paused as a new report flashed up on her display. "A couple of the reporters have been apprehended trying to get into the CIC."

James frowned. He hadn't wanted the reporters. Given what had happened on *Ark Royal's* final flight, he'd been reluctant to have *anyone* onboard who wasn't a naval officer. The Prime Minister had overruled him; the only concession he'd managed to get was an agreement that the reporters could be searched carefully before they were allowed to board and told, firmly, that large parts of the supercarrier were definitely off limits to them. Even so...it was far too easy to come up with scenarios where the reporters accidentally or deliberately betrayed the ship.

He pushed the thought aside. "Inform the marines that the reporters are to be dumped in the brig," he ordered, curtly. There was a battle underway, even though neither side had fired a shot. "I'll deal with them later."

"Yes, sir," Sally said. There was a pause. "They're making a fuss, but the marines have them well in hand."

James pushed the reporters out of his mind as he turned back to the display. The Indians were still inching forward - as he'd expected, Indian One slowed slightly to ensure it entered engagement range with its fellows - and local space was clear. It looked as though the Indians *weren't* trying to be clever.

And that makes no sense, he told himself. *What are they trying to do.*

The display updated again as the drones flashed through the enemy formation, but they offered him no answers. A number of Indian ships were marked as *real* when they opened fire on the drones; others, showing nothing beyond a bare signature, were almost certainly fakes. Or they merely *wanted* the British to think they were fakes. James couldn't imagine any scenario where he'd *want* the enemy to get a close look at his hulls, but the Indian CO might have a more active imagination.

"Interesting," Sally said. She sounded surprised - and puzzled. "Indian Three was *much* more aggressive about shooting down the drones."

"Show me," James ordered. Did Indian Three simply have more *real* ships? Or did their CO have something to hide? The more he looked at it, the less sense the Indian tactics made; they were risking defeat in detail, simply by splitting up their ships. Unless they had a surprise up their sleeves. "What are they doing?"

"The long-range passive sensors insist that Indian Three consists of twenty-one destroyers and frigates," Sally said. "By noting the ships that actually opened fire, we know that eleven of them are actually *real*. No other formation showed more than four real starships."

James frowned. "A shell game, then," he mused. The Indians didn't want to fool him - they knew that was impossible, the way they'd set it up - but they wanted to keep him guessing which ships were real. And yet, by opening fire, they'd kindly identified a number of real ships for him. "But why?"

Vice Admiral Joshi was mildly surprised the British hadn't attempted to avoid combat, given the apparent combat superiority of the formations bearing down on them, but he was quite willing to take advantage of it. The planners had assumed the British would - correctly - deduce that two-thirds of the ships heading towards them were nothing more than drones, particularly the carriers. They might even assume that *they* held a decisive advantage and ready themselves to wipe out half the Indian Navy. It would - he hoped - leave them open for the true threat.

"Inform the crews that they may start deploying on my mark," he ordered. The British ships were drawing closer, into missile range. They'd be prepping themselves to open fire on the warships they *knew* to be real. "Prepare to fire."

"The task force is going to red alert," Sally reported. The alarms were automatically dampened in the CIC. "Indians One through Five will be in firing range in twenty minutes."

And nothing - seemingly - ready to stab us in the back, James thought. He took another look at the remorselessly empty display. *Why*?

"Inform all ships that they are cleared to open fire on my command," he ordered. "ROE Prime are now in effect; I say again, ROE Prime are now in effect."

"Aye, sir," Sally said.

And if any reporters get hurt in the crossfire, it's their own stupid fault, James thought, as the Indians drew closer. *Their ships might be mistaken for enemy vessels and blown out of space in passing.*

He cleared his throat. "Inform Captain Pole that she may launch starfighters at will," he ordered. They'd worked out deployment plans while waiting for the Indians to come into range. One third of the starfighters would cover the task force, while the remainder would take the fight to the Indians. "Plan Beta, I think; I say again, Plan Beta..."

"Aye, Admiral," Sally said.

She broke off as the display suddenly spangled with red icons. "Incoming fire! I say again, incoming fire!"

CHAPTER TWENTY EIGHT

Pegasus System

That's impossible, James thought.

It wasn't just missiles, either; missiles fired from a range that would see them burning out long before they reached their targets. The Indians had launched *starfighters*. But they didn't have a carrier...or did they? Had they concealed a makeshift escort carrier or two under ECM? Or simply mounted the starfighters on the hulls of a dozen destroyers? It was certainly technically possible.

"Ready the point defence," he ordered, sharply. If the Indians had fired missiles from outside the normal range, it was quite possible that they'd somehow managed to improve on the standard missile designs. They wouldn't want to waste ammunition on a clear diversion, not when cold logic would *insist* it was a diversion. "Stand by to repel attack."

"Admiral," Sally said. "They're launching a wave of smaller craft. They look like modified shuttles."

James stared at the display. There was something about it that was familiar, too familiar; it was almost as if he'd seen something like it before, during the war. And then it struck him.

"Those are boarding pods," he snapped. The Tadpoles had tried to board *Ark Royal* during Operation Nelson. It had failed, badly, but the Tadpoles had never been particularly adept out of the water. The Indians, on the other hand, had powered combat armour of their own - and, perhaps, deck plans for *Theodore Smith*. "Alert the marines. The Indians are attempting to board the carrier."

Sally blinked. "Us, sir?"

"There's no other target worth the effort," James snapped. The Indian ships were coming into range too. "Order all ships to engage the Indians at will; I say again, engage the Indians at will."

"Aye, sir," Sally said. She paused as new information popped up on her screen. "Sir, the CAG is diverting starfighters to target the boarding pods."

"Order him to ensure that at least two squadrons confront the Indian ships," James said. "We cannot let them shoot at us without retaliation."

He turned his attention to the missiles as they reached the point where they should have burned out their drives and gone ballistic. It wasn't a surprise, not really, to see the missiles split up, each one launching a second stage towards the task force. A two-stage missile had been a theoretical concept for a long time, but reworking the missile tubes to fire a missile over twice the size of standard missiles had kept running into bureaucratic objections. And then the new focus on plasma weapons had restricted development elsewhere.

Looks like they did come up with a new concept, he thought, as the missiles swept towards their targets, followed by the starfighters. *But so did we.*

Theodore Smith's point defence went active, spewing hundreds of plasma bolts into space. The missiles were surrounded by ECM - he was disconcerted to note that several of the missiles seemed to be nothing more than portable ECM generators - but there were so many plasma bolts that hitting *something* was almost inevitable. Other ships added their own fire, hacking hundreds of missiles out of space. Only a handful survived to enter terminal attack range and only one detonated, sending a bomb-pumped laser beam into the hull, before it was too late.

The giant carrier shuddered, violently. "Direct hit, decks nine through twelve," Sally snapped, as alerts flashed up on the display. "I say again, direct hit!"

James had to resist the temptation to snap orders to the damage control parties. It was Susan's job to fight her ship, his to control the overall battle...and yet, it was hard *not* to take command directly. He understood, in a sudden flicker of insight, just how Admiral Smith had felt. And *he'd* had the excuse of serving on *Ark Royal* for years before taking her into combat for the first time.

"Alert the starfighters," he ordered. The boarding pods were closing in, half-hidden behind a sheen of ECM. "They are to press the offensive against the Indian ships."

He watched the display, grimly, as it kept updating. Thankfully, most of the faked ships had already been revealed...although he had to admit it was possible that *some* captains were playing it *very* cool. A couple had flickered and vanished, suggesting that the drones had finally given out under the strain. The remainder of the Indian ships were firing again, hammering his ships with missiles; this time, they seemed to be launching standard missiles rather than their modified designs.

They must have been unable to produce more than a handful, he thought. Even if they *were* willing to gamble, they'd have been unable to afford them - and, of course, avoid the *Superiority* danger. *And they risked them all here.*

"Admiral," Sally said. "*Petunia* is gone."

James nodded. The escort carriers were vital targets, particularly if the Indians couldn't get close to the fleet carrier. They were too large to be agile, too small to be crammed with point defence. The cold part of his mind noted that there would be no problem taking her starfighters on *Theodore Smith*; the rest of him was horrified at such callousness. But then, death had been a part of his life ever since the last war. The delusion that the universe was *safe* had killed far more people than anything else in human history.

"*Dashing* is taking heavy damage," she added. "*Glasgow* has been crippled; her crew are abandoning ship..."

She broke off for a long second. "*Glasgow* has been destroyed, sir," she warned. "*Churchill* is requesting permission to withdraw."

"Denied," James said. It was unlikely that the Indians would let her go - and, when she was away from the fleet, she would be an easy target. "Continue driving them back."

"Aye, sir," Sally said.

The Indian starfighter buzzed up in front of her, shooting madly. Flying Officer Harriet Monsey picked it off with a quick burst of plasma fire and drove onwards, heedless of the man or woman she'd just killed. No one had been expecting a dogfight between rival starfighter forces, but *Teddy's* crew were living up to their training. The Indians, too, were fighting with a skill she rather wished they'd never developed. Right now, a turkey shoot was starting to look like a damn good idea.

"Target destroyed," Pearson snapped. "We've a clear run!"

"Understood," Harriet said. Nine other starfighters were coming up behind them, weapons at the ready. "Let's go."

The Indian cruiser was turning towards them as she led the charge into weapons range. There was nothing wrong with her point defence, Harriet noted; the Indians opened fire the moment she came into effective range, forcing her to corkscrew randomly through the hail of fire to avoid being hit. Their electronic servants would be doing everything they could to predict the starfighter's trajectory and put a plasma bolt in her path; she jinked backwards and forwards, daring the enemy to score a direct hit. A stream of plasma passed so close she saw it with her naked eye as she swooped down on the enemy hull; she bottomed out and opened fire, spraying plasma fire into the enemy ship. Its armour was lighter than *Teddy's*, she saw, but still good enough to ward off plasma bolts...

Good thing it isn't good enough to keep us from wiping out sensor blisters and weapons turrets, she thought. She'd had plenty of experience at snapping off shots at everything that might be a weapon, crippling the ship even if it could still run for its life. *And here come the torpedo-bombers!*

"The enemy are directing starfighters back to deal with us," Pearson reported. "Suggest we turn to engage them."

"Wilco," Harriet said. Flying directly away from the cruiser was a risk, but the enemy crews had too much else to worry about. A handful of plasma bolts chased her as she fled, none coming close enough to scorch her paint. "We'll go right at them."

She smirked as the torpedo-bombers opened fire on the cruiser. Their missiles were smaller than the giant weapons launched by capital ships, but they were designed to punch right through armour and explode inside the hull. And, unlike a fleet carrier, the cruiser wasn't designed to take such an impact. The cruiser staggered and exploded into debris.

"Scratch one cruiser," the torpedo-bomber pilot jeered. "I say again, scratch one cruiser."

"Very good," Harriet said. The Indian starfighters were altering course, moving to protect their other ships. She silently saluted them - their first impulse had probably been to tear into the torpedo-bombers - and gave chase. "Now go kill yourself another one."

She smiled as the Indians ran from her and her fellows, then swooped around and came back firing as they reached a destroyer. The destroyer opened fire; it looked suspiciously as though they'd forgotten how to work their IFF systems. Their fire was so wild that Harriet couldn't help wondering if they were just shooting at random. It was sheer luck they didn't hit one of their own starfighters.

"This one is a little *too* enthusiastic," Pearson said. "He's trying to take me up the butt."

"Evidently he doesn't know anything about your disgusting bathroom habits," Harriet said, as she swooped down on Pearson's opponent. The Indian hesitated too long, then flipped his craft over and tried to open fire on Harriet. It was too late; she blew him apart before he could bring his weapons to bear. "What a moron."

"Good shooting," Pearson said. "I guess I owe you a life debt. Can I be your slave tonight?"

"Well...I *do* need someone to clean the deck, I suppose," Harriet said. It was *her* turn on deck-swabbing duty, although she had a feeling the CAG wouldn't insist on it, not after the battle. "I'm sure everyone else will be happy to watch and jeer as you do it."

"That wasn't what I meant," Pearson protested. He snapped off a shot at an Indian starfighter; the pilot evaded, only to run straight into a second shot. "Got him!"

Harriet rolled her eyes, then watched as the torpedo-bombers closed in on the Indian destroyer. The ship tried to turn away, but it was already too late; three missiles slammed into its hull and detonated inside the ship, blowing her into a colossal fireball. She blasted a starfighter that was trying to escape and then looked around for new targets. The remainder of the Indian fleet was launching yet another spread of missiles towards the task force. They were already travelling too fast for her to intercept them.

"We need to rearm," Flying Officer Mulligan reported. "We buried our last torpedo in that ship."

"Get back to *Teddy* and reload," Harriet ordered. She glanced at her display. One definite advantage of the newer Hurricane starfighters was that they had nearly twice the endurance of the older models. "We'll try and make life easier for you."

"Understood," Mulligan said. "Good luck."

Harriet looked around for another target. An Indian frigate was turning towards the battle, its weapons already tracking the starfighters. They probably wouldn't be able to take the ship out without the torpedo-bombers, but they could strip her of her point defence and sensors, leaving her blind and helpless. She smirked at the thought, then gunned her engine. Pearson and the rest of the squadron followed her as she led the way towards the new target.

"Take this one out alone and the CAG will be your slave," Pearson offered.

"I think he'll have shit duty for you when you get back," Harriet reminded him. "You do realise the press is listening, don't you?"

She had to bite her lip to keep from giggling. People who weren't pilots didn't appreciate pilot humour - or the attitude that every moment should be savoured, if only because death could come at any second. Pearson's wit - or what passed for wit - would probably lead to questions in Parliament. Or another edition of *Starfighter Pilots Gone Wild*.

"Let's go," she said, as the Indian ship opened fire. "Follow me!"

"The enemy took out two destroyers and an escort carrier, Admiral."

Joshi swore, savagely. He'd only had two escort carriers - and makeshift ones at that - assigned to his formation. In hindsight, perhaps it had been a mistake not to convert more freighters into carriers, but the government had been determined to pour resources into fleet carriers. And yet, it had cost them. Two fleet carriers - and a third taking shape in the yards - weren't enough to have a carrier everywhere it might be needed.

And without my carrier, I cannot recover and resupply my starfighters, he thought, numbly. The British might have been surprised, but they were fighting back savagely. Seven of his ships had been blown out of space; five more were so badly damaged, thanks to the enemy starfighters, that they were effectively useless. *I may be able to recover the crews, but the starfighters will have to be written off.*

"Admiral, the second wave of boarding pods is ready for deployment," his aide said. She gave him a sharp look. "They're primed and ready to go."

"Deploy them," Joshi ordered. He'd had his doubts about the whole concept - the British had wiped out the first set of boarding pods before they got close to the target ships - but he saw no alternative. If nothing else, at least they would soak up some plasma fire that might otherwise be aimed at his starfighters. "And prepare to fire missiles to cover them."

He tapped a switch, bringing up the ammunition expenditure chart. Between the rounds he'd fired and the destroyed ships, he didn't have many missiles left. He didn't dare close any further with the British ships either, not when their mass drivers were almost painfully accurate. It was ironic - he knew what weapons had been emplaced on Clarke - but it did have its advantages. At least the theories for intercepting mass driver projectiles had been proved correct.

"Admiral," his aide warned. "We only have enough missiles for one final salvo."

"Better make it count," Joshi said. He keyed a series of commands into his console, plotting out the final strike. General Patel would regret not accompanying the fleet. "And break off the moment we fire the missiles."

"Aye, sir," his aide said.

At least we gave them a battering, Joshi thought. It was something to be proud of, he was sure. The Tadpoles had done worse, but the Tadpoles had keyed their weapons mix to take advantage of human weaknesses. *And if we succeed with the second wave of pods, we may just win outright.*

"And order the starfighters to hold out as long as they can," he added. There was no way they could be recovered, not unless the British kindly allowed the starships to shut down their drives. They couldn't even save the crews. "They're to fight to the last."

"Aye, Admiral," the aide said.

"They're refocusing their attack on us, Admiral," Sally reported.

"Alter course," James ordered. If there was nothing to one side of them, they'd force the enemy to unite their formations. "Continue firing."

The Indians were doing well, he had to admit; their starfighters were a little inexperienced, yet their point defence was good - even against mass drivers - and the long-range missiles had been a nasty surprise. Three of his ships were gone, four more were heavily damaged; he thought five or six Indian vessels had been taken out, but the damned drones made it hard to be sure. The only consolation was that the Indians had to be having similar problems.

"The boarding pods are closing in on us, Admiral," Sally added. "A number are also being diverted to *Lillian*."

"Understood," James said. A wave of starfighters was also closing in on *Theodore Smith*. They'd be unable to punch through the armour, but they'd sure as hell be able to weaken the point defence. The Tadpoles had used a similar trick against *Ark Royal*. "Order two of the frigates to provide additional covering fire."

He braced himself as the Indian starfighters swooped down. It was unlikely he'd feel anything, he told himself, when they opened fire, but memories of the war ran deep. Red icons flashed up on the status board, alerting him to smashed plasma cannons and useless sensors; three Indian starfighters survived to break off as *Theodore Smith's* starfighters counter-attacked. The boarding pods slipped closer, trying to move into the blind spots created by the starfighters. A dozen died, picked off harmlessly, but three survived long enough to latch onto the hull.

They're not large ships, James thought. *They could only carry a dozen marines in combat amour apiece.*

"Marines are already being deployed," Sally said. "I..."

Theodore Smith rang like a bell. For a long moment, the displays blanked out before the emergency power came on and the system rebooted itself. James stared in disbelief at the red icons covering the status board, slowly putting together what must have happened. They'd been tricked. The boarding pods hadn't been crammed with Indian marines, but enemy warheads.

"Only one detonated," Sally reported, checking the live feed from the surrounding starships. "It did considerable damage, though; one of our drive units and two launch tubes are out of commission."

James cursed. It looked very much as though the Indians had started to shoot themselves dry, but they'd already inflicted more than enough damage to make the expenditure worthwhile. Without a shipyard, it would take weeks to repair the damage...and, unless it was fixed in time, the carrier was far too vulnerable.

"Admiral," Sally said. "The remaining Indian ships are breaking off."

"It looks that way," James agreed. He sucked in his breath. The Indians had hammered the task force, but they'd taken a beating themselves. They'd need resupply before they could complete the job. "They're waiting for the carrier to come finish us off."

CHAPTER TWENTY NINE

Pegasus System

"The enemy carrier is badly damaged, sir."

Anjeet hesitated. "*How* badly damaged?"

"Unsure," the aide admitted. "She took at least one of the faked boarding pods - the ones tactical assumed would be overlooked in favour of shooting at the missiles."

"I know the theory," Anjeet snapped. "How badly was the carrier damaged?"

"She took at least one major hit," the aide said. "Tactical analysis suggests she's probably lost one of her drive compartments and a starfighter launch tube. She also lost a considerable number of weapons and sensor blisters before our starfighters were beaten off."

Anjeet frowned. If the British carrier *was* crippled, he had an opportunity to force a decisive victory; the British would hardly wish to continue the war if they lost their proudest carrier to an inferior foe. And yet, the only way to push his advantage now was to take *Viraat* out of orbit and advance on the enemy ship, battering her to uselessness with his mass drivers. The remainder of his fleet needed time to repair and rearm.

He closed his eyes, torn between two equally unpalatable problems. Delay favoured the British; the longer the war lasted, the weaker India's position would become. And yet, if it were a trap, he'd be risking everything on one throw of the dice. But the rewards for victory would be immense. The war would be over, India would have secured her gains and he would have won the first major interstellar conflict between two different human powers. No one would be able to look down on India after she'd beaten Britain in even combat.

"Contact the bridge," he ordered, finally. The opportunity was too good to miss. "We are to advance out of orbit towards the enemy position."

"Aye, sir," the aide said.

"Two frigates are to accompany us," Anjeet added, after a moment. "The remaining ships are to hold position in orbit."

Anjeet nodded as he turned his attention to the main display, mentally calculating possible vectors. It would take at least nine hours to reach engagement range - *Viraat* wasn't anything like as fast as a frigate, let alone a courier boat - but he doubted the British could repair their ship before he could arrive. The smartest thing for them to do would be to fall back to J-35, forcing him to choose between giving chase and letting them go. But if they couldn't escape before he arrived, he'd have an excellent chance to win. One undamaged carrier against one that had already been badly damaged. It wouldn't be a remotely fair contest.

Good, he thought, savagely.

"Order Admiral Joshi to split his remaining fleet," he ordered. "Ships that are still in fighting trim are to reverse course and hold position, twenty minutes from the British task force. The remainder are to head directly to the tramline and jump out to Vesy."

"Aye, sir," the aide said. He paused; Anjeet gave him a sharp look. "The remaining ships have largely shot themselves dry."

"They can still keep a sharp eye on the British ships," Anjeet said. It was quite likely the British had shot themselves dry too - he made a mental note to send raiders into J-35 once the main battle was concluded - and they would need time to rearm too. "And make sure the reporters don't come too close."

"Aye, sir," the aide said, again.

Anjeet smiled, coldly. The reporters were impudent, even the ones he'd had carefully vetted before allowing them to board his flagship. If anything, the ones who had booked their own passage to the system were even worse. His inbox was overflowing with requests for interviews, tours of the carrier and details of his future plans, as if he would be so foolish as to share them. He wondered, absently, if his British counterpart had the same problem. No doubt the British found the reporters as irritating as he did...

Maybe we should have organised the battle so the reporters were trapped between the fleets, he thought, nastily. *And sworn blind it was a terrible accident.*

He pushed the thought aside, regretfully. The reporters might be gadflies, but killing them would lead to more trouble than he cared to endure. It was important, vitally so, to present India's point of view to the rest of humanity and killing reporters would only make that harder. The Prime Minister would be furious if everything India did was painted in the worst possible light, simply because a reporter too stupid to know better had climbed into a missile tube seconds before it was opened to interstellar space. No doubt it would be portrayed as deliberate murder. God knew that countless reporters *had* died during the Age of Unrest.

And they learned nothing useful from it, he thought. *Not even the concept of telling the truth, the whole truth, and nothing but the truth.*

A shudder ran through the giant carrier as her main drives came online. Anjeet watched the status board for a long moment - he'd always been a little nervous about the overpowered drives - and then relaxed as everything showed green. They were on their way to the final battle.

"Course laid in, General," the aide confirmed. "Bridge estimates nine hours, seventeen minutes to engagement range."

Anjeet nodded. It was possible, he supposed, that the British would try to slip around the carrier and attack Clarke III, but they'd run straight into the remaining escort ships and the mass drivers if they tried. The entire moon was ringed with active sensors, ready to detect and track even a starship in stealth mode. And then they could be targeted and destroyed, perhaps without even knowing what had hit them.

And besides, if they try, they won't gain anything, he thought. *They'd need to land troops to evict us unless they're prepared to write off their own settlers.*

It galled him to have to rely, however indirectly, on human shields. The fact that they hadn't handcuffed the settlers to the mass drivers didn't change what they'd done. But there was no alternative. The British couldn't be allowed to secure orbital supremacy and drop KEWs at will or the war would come to a short sharp end. Perhaps it would have been more honourable to send the settlers home, or to Vesy, before the war started in earnest, but honour was only for those who could afford it. India had long since learnt that honour was nothing more than a word.

"Inform me when we are one hour from the enemy," Anjeet ordered. Perhaps the British *would* retreat, if they could. He'd fall back if they did, allowing the spin doctors to spin a tale of how he kindly let the damaged carrier go. "Until then, put the beta crews on duty and have the starfighter pilots get some rest. They're going to be needed."

He studied the final report from Admiral Joshi and noted, carefully, all the questions it left unanswered. *Theodore Smith* had *six* starfighter launching tubes; she'd lost one, according to the analysts, but could she still launch and recover starfighters from the others? If so, she would be far from defenceless. The post-battle analysis had barely begun, but it was already clear that the British torpedo-bombers were *very* effective. Their torpedoes had taken out half a dozen starships during the brief engagement.

But our long-range missiles were a nasty surprise too, he thought. *If only we'd had more of them.*

He shook his head, bitterly. Nations went to war with what they had on hand, not with what they wanted. India had gone into debt to build the navy and a relative handful of special weapons; it was churlish to complain that he didn't have everything he wanted. A wonder weapon that could take out a British carrier from halfway across the system would be very useful...but if he'd had something like it, the British would probably have it too. Both fleets would have been wiped out within seconds.

"And inform Khan that I wish to review his files before they're dispatched to Earth," he warned. "This isn't the time to boast our success."

"Aye, sir," the aide said.

"The carrier is leaving orbit, sir," Tara reported. "She's on a direct-line course for *Theodore Smith*."

"Understood," John said. They hadn't been able to do more than watch the battle, knowing that the whole affair had been resolved long before the first signals reached *Warspite*. The Royal Navy had held its own, but the carrier had been badly damaged. "Helm, move us into intercept position."

"Aye, sir," Armstrong said.

John felt his heartbeat starting to pound as the giant red icon moved closer. Admiral Fitzwilliam had ordered him to refrain from using *Warspite's* main weapon, anticipating her deployment when the two sides stopped skirmishing and went for one another's throats. He hadn't expected the Indians to take the offensive so savagely, but now...now they had the perfect opportunity to take a shot at the Indian carrier. It would mean defying his orders, yet he knew what the Admiral had had in mind. They could hardly hope for a better chance...if, of course, *Warspite* and her main gun lived up to Admiral Soskice's predictions.

"I want to be so deeply buried in stealth mode they can't hear a whisper," he ordered, keying his console. "Engineering; drives are to be placed on standby, ready to be flash-woken."

"Aye, Captain," Johnston said. "I must warn you that this will take a heavy toll on the drives."

"So will Indian weapons tearing us apart," John said, tartly. The bean-counters would probably make a fuss - Johnston was right; *Warspite's* drives would lose at least a couple of years off their expected lifespan if he held them on standby - but success and survival were more important. "We'll only have one shot at this."

"Captain," Armstrong said. "We're in the right position, assuming they don't change course."

They'll want to get to the carrier before she can make her escape to J-35, John told himself, firmly. *Theodore Smith* was badly damaged; her repair crews were already going to work, but it would take at least a week before she was ready to return to the fray. *They'll never have a better chance to win the war outright.*

"Hold us here," he ordered. "Tactical?"

"Main gun is online," Tara said. "We are ready to engage the enemy."

"Hold point defence in readiness too," John ordered. "They'll counter-attack as soon as they realise what we've done."

"Aye, sir," Tara said.

John nodded, then exchanged a look with Howard. No matter how they sliced it, there was a very good chance they were on a suicide mission. The Indians would react badly, the moment they knew they were under attack...

...And they *might* know, if they picked up traces of the plasma gun being readied to fire. It *had* been intensely modified, after the first time it had been used against a live target, but no one had tested the modifications in actual combat. If the Indians detected them before they entered engagement range, they could either engage *Warspite* themselves or merely alter course, forcing her to play catch-up. And if they *did* engage *Warspite*, John had no illusions about how long they'd survive.

But it was what we signed up for, he reminded himself. *And trading Warspite for one of their carriers is a win in anyone's book.*

He studied the Indian carrier as *Warspite's* passive sensors tracked her approach. She was colossal, easily two kilometres long, although it was clear that some of her design had been influenced by America rather than Britain - or the Tadpoles, for that matter. The Americans had built the largest fleet carriers before the war, choosing to deploy vast numbers of starfighters rather than cramming their ships with mass drivers, missile tubes and other long-range weapons. And three American carriers had died in the Battle of New Russia because they lacked heavy armour too...

They may have skimped on the armour, he thought. It didn't *look* as though their drives were any more powerful than comparable British designs, but their carrier definitely had a tighter acceleration curve than anything in the Royal Navy. *Their mass must have been reduced somehow.*

"She'll be in range in forty minutes," Tara reported. "Her two escorts are holding position on either side of her."

"Ignore them," John ordered. It would be a mistake, under normal circumstances, but there was no choice. *Warspite* was expendable compared to the giant carrier. "When I give the order, I want you to throw everything we have at the carrier, including the kitchen sink."

"Aye, sir," Tara said. "I suggest we focus the main gun on her drive section, assuming we can get a clear shot. It would disable the carrier even if it didn't destroy her."

"Make it so," John ordered.

He forced himself to relax. If they did disable the carrier, she would be out of the war permanently even if the Admiral didn't take the opportunity to finish her off. The Indians would still have a second carrier, but they'd be wary about risking her when the tactical situation had changed so completely. They'd certainly want to rethink their options if they lost their first carrier.

"All weapons ready," Tara reported.

"I have an evasive escape course programmed in," Armstrong added. "We can be on the move as soon as the drives come online."

And pray they don't actually fail under the sudden demand, John thought. It hadn't been *that* long ago that a faulty power conduit had crippled the entire ship. The engineers had worked in several bypasses after that, just in case, but he was far too aware that a single mistake at the worst possible time would be disastrous. *This could go horrendously wrong.*

"Thirty minutes to engagement range," Tara said. "Recommend we adjust position slightly, very slightly."

"Send the details to the helm," John ordered. "But be careful we don't do anything that could be detected."

He fought down the urge to grip his command chair, knowing he had to present an appearance of being calm and in control at all times. Centuries ago, a distant ancestor had commanded a submarine during the Second World War, charged with sneaking up and torpedoing an enemy ship. John had read his account of life under the waves as a child and wondered at all the difficulties submariners had faced, difficulties that had seemed so absurd in the modern world. But now, he understood his ancestor perfectly. He'd only ever had one shot at his targets, knowing that even a handful of depth charges would be enough to scuttle his rickety boat.

Come into my parlour, said the spider to the fly, he thought. *I'm ready for you.*

"We're in position," Armstrong said. "I used reaction jets to move us, sir. They shouldn't have been able to detect them."

And the shortage of incoming missiles suggests they haven't detected us, John thought. *Unless, of course, they're trying to lure us into a false sense of complacency...*

"Good," he said, coolly. "Hold our position."

"Aye, sir," Armstrong said.

"Communications, send a tactical download via laser to the Admiral, marked DNR," John ordered. The entire engagement would be over and done with by the time the Admiral received the download, but at least *someone* would know what had happened if *Warspite* never made it home. "And then shut everything down."

"Aye, sir," Gillian said.

John turned his attention back to the display. The Indian carrier was still advancing, showing no sign she knew she was inching towards a trap. Her two escorts were holding position; one of them would be in position to fire on *Warspite*, if they knew she was there. They *would* know the moment *Warspite* opened fire...

And even if we die, John told himself again, *the Indians will have taken one hell of a beating.*

"Twenty minutes to go," Tara said. "Weapons locked on target; I say again, weapons locked on target. I'm even reprioritising the point defence to hammer their hull."

John nodded. He was fairly sure the Indians had skimped on their armour, but it would still be tough enough to shrug off point defence plasma cannons. And yet, if the fire swept the hull, it would smash sensor blisters and missile tubes, just like starfighters had tried to do since the concept had been turned into a viable weapon of war. The Indians would wind up blind as well as crippled. He remembered the nightmarish hours *Warspite* had drifted helplessly in space and smiled, darkly. The Indians deserved no less.

"Ten minutes to optimum firing range." Tara reported.

"Fire as soon as they reach optimum firing range or they detect us, whichever comes first," John ordered. If there hadn't been a war on, the Indians would probably be much more careful, but as there was they'd probably shoot first at any sensor contacts that were alarmingly close to their hull and ask questions later. "Do *not* wait for orders."

"Aye, sir," Tara said. She sounded professional, although there was an undercurrent of excitement in her voice. If nothing else, the anti-carrier mission would go down in the history books. "Nine minutes to optimum firing range."

John braced himself. Admiral Soskice's team of engineers and dreamers had taken the original plasma cannon concept and improved on it, creating a magnetic bottle that held a far stronger plasma charge for longer. It was practically guaranteed to burn through anything short of solid-state armour; the only downside was that it had a relatively short range. John had only fired the weapon in anger once before, against one of the Russian deserter ships during the Battle of Vesy. It had been devastating...

"Five minutes to optimum firing range," Tara said. "We are tracking the targeted location; I say again, we are tracking the targeted location."

And we can hammer them now even if they detect us, John thought. *The closer, the better, but we're already too close...*

An alarm sounded. "*Contact*," Tara snapped, as the display turned red. One of the enemy ships had detected them. Her hands danced over her console, triggering a firing sequence she'd programmed once he'd given the final orders. "Firing...*now*!"

"Flash-wake all systems," John snapped. *Warspite* shook violently as she unleashed a full spread of missiles, right after the plasma shot. There was no time to assess the result of their strike, not with two Indian frigates far too close to his ship. "Get us out of here!"

CHAPTER THIRTY

Pegasus System

"Enemy contact," the sensor officer snapped. "Enemy..."

The entire carrier shuddered. Anjeet was halfway to his feet when the gravity field flickered off, sending him drifting into the air. The main lighting failed a second later, plunging the entire compartment into darkness; half the sensor displays, dependent on main power, went dark immediately afterwards. Shouts of alarm rang through the darkened compartment...

"Quiet," Anjeet bellowed. He could hear the hull groaning and creaking in the distance, even though they were practically at the centre of the giant warship. *Something* hit the ship and it shuddered again. A missile hit? Without sensors, there was no way to know. "What happened?"

"There was a sensor contact," the sensor officer said. He was tapping at one of the few consoles that still worked, but it was hard to pull anything meaningful out of the system. "An enemy warship at point-blank range. And then they fired...*something*...at us."

A new weapon, Anjeet thought. He forced himself to *think. A single bomb-pumped laser couldn't have done this much damage, not unless they somehow managed to supercharge the laser beam...*

He pushed the thought aside. "Get into suits, then activate your radios," he ordered. It was basic survival training, even though none of the carrier's crew had ever expected to *need* it. If power was out, there was a good chance that hatches that should have slammed closed, in the event of a hull breach, hadn't done anything of the sort. "I want two volunteers to head to the bridge. If the ship has lost power completely, we'll need to find out and coordinate an evacuation."

"I'll go, sir," his aide said.

"Radio back to me as soon as you know," he ordered. "And I want two more volunteers to head to the launch tubes. I need to get in touch with the escort ships."

He pulled himself back down to the deck as the lights flickered on again for a long second, then dimmed until they seemed on the very verge of going out. There was no sensation that suggested *gravity* was returning, although that wasn't necessarily a bad thing. If they did have to evacuate the carrier before the British came to finish her off, a lack of gravity would be helpful. Somehow, he managed to pull his suit on and check the radio. Not entirely to his surprise, someone was already trying to call him.

"General," Captain Sharma said. "We have lost main power. Whatever they hit us with took out all four fusion reactors, either directly or indirectly. Successive hits crippled launch tubes one, three and four; we have lost contact with anything outside our hull. I'm working on launching starfighters and rescue craft from launch tube two. The ship is currently being powered from batteries, sir, and they won't last longer than a few hours. There's too much damage to the datanet to cut down usage to essential functions."

He paused. "*Viraat* is doomed, sir," he added. "I strongly advise you to make your way, if possible, to the nearest shuttle docking point."

Anjeet gritted his teeth. "Can you track the bastards who did this to us?"

"Not yet," Sharma admitted. "I'm hoping the escorts have given chase, but we have been unable to make contact to confirm. Right now, sir, we're trying to get some shuttles out so we can start evacuating the crew. We're a sitting duck."

"I see," Anjeet said.

He had to force himself to think straight. All *four* fusion reactors gone? It seemed impossible...but they *were* tied together, in the same compartment. A single hit might have disabled a reactor it hadn't actually managed to destroy. There was no point in worrying about it now. The plain fact of the matter was that the starship was doomed. Either they got the crew off in time or they had to surrender when the British arrived.

"Make contact with the escorts as fast as possible," he said. Once a shuttle was out in space, it *should* be able to raise the starships. "Tell them to prepare to offload as many crewmen as possible."

"Aye, sir," Sharma said.

"Get a link to Admiral Joshi too," Anjeet added. "His ships are to abandon the observation operation and join the evacuation effort. If the damaged ships I sent to Vesy can take more survivors, they are to be recalled too."

He scowled. The largest cruiser in the fleet couldn't hold more than a couple of hundred crewmen - three hundred, perhaps, if they pushed the life support to the limit. *Viraat* had - had had - over three *thousand* crewmen. A great many would be dead, thanks to the British, but he might not have the lifting capability to get all the survivors off. And if that happened...

At least the British will be reasonably civilised about POWs, he thought. *God knows we have enough of their people we could trade for our own men.*

"Aye, sir," Sharma said.

"And get teams working on the datacores," Anjeet concluded. The limited self-destruct system was unlikely to work - and even if it did, he wasn't sure *he* could be sure it had worked. Blowing up the remains of the ship would ensure there would be no chance to repair the carrier at a later date. "I want them all reduced to powder."

"Aye, sir," Sharma said. He paused. "Sir, I just got an update from the shuttle crews. Two shuttles are already heading into space and a squadron of starfighters is ready to follow."

"Order them to hunt down our enemy and kill him," Anjeet snarled. It would be small compensation for the loss of the giant supercarrier - it struck him that his career had just come to a screeching halt - but at least he would have that mild satisfaction. "And then start withdrawing the rest of the crew to evacuation points."

He cursed the British under his breath as the connection broke. Hundreds, perhaps thousands, of trained spacers were dead...but others, perhaps, were trapped in compartments that were behind vacuum, or simply out of contact with the rest of the ship. There would be no way to go through the entire hull, not before any trapped survivors ran out of oxygen or the British arrived. He doubted more than a thousand crewmen could be saved before it was too late.

"This compartment is to be evacuated," he ordered, raising his voice. There was no point in trying to keep the Flag Bridge active. "Make your way through cleared corridors to the nearest airlock."

It was tempting to just stay where he was. Admiral Joshi would have to be informed he was in command of the fleet, of course, but after that... Anjeet could just sit down in his chair, buckle himself in and wait to die. There was no point in going home when he'd almost certainly be blamed for the loss of a carrier that had cost literally *billions* of rupees. It was unlikely the Prime Minister could save him, even if he wanted to *try*. *Viraat* and her sister were the pride of India. The man who'd lost a supercarrier to a sucker punch would be lucky to live long enough to face a court martial.

But he knew his duty. He couldn't abandon it, even if it meant going home and facing the music.

"I'll follow you," he said, quietly. "Now *go*."

"Direct hit, sir," Tara reported. "The enemy ship has lost power."

"Pull us back," John ordered. The carrier had definitely lost power - her point defence had barely started to engage the incoming missiles when it had suddenly stopped firing - but her escorts were already moving to intercept *Warspite*. "Continue firing."

Score one for Admiral Soskice, he thought. The plasma cannon had been *devastatingly* effective, burning right through the Indian armour. Indeed, he had a feeling it would be just as effective against anything weaker than modern ablative armour. *The Indians have lost a carrier and we may get away yet.*

"Enemy ships launching missiles," Tara reported.

"Evasive action," John snapped. Armstrong was already pulling them back, but they needed time to power up the drives completely. "Point defence; switch targeting to incoming missiles and open fire."

"Aye, sir," Tara said.

John braced himself as the missiles entered engagement range. Nine of them were picked off; two survived long enough to detonate, blasting bomb-pumped laser beams into *Warspite's* armour. The ship lurched violently - alarms howled through the vessel - but kept going. John glanced at the status board and sighed in relief as he realised the Indians had hit almost nothing, although they had damaged the hull itself. There was no way the cruiser could carry the armour of a giant supercarrier.

"Captain, the escort ships are breaking off," Tara reported.

John frowned. *Warspite* was heading away from the ambush site, but the Indians still had a fair chance of destroying her before she made her escape. He puzzled over it for a moment, then decided the Indians clearly wanted to evacuate as many of their crewmen as they could from the giant supercarrier before it was too late. No matter how badly she'd been hit, he was reasonably sure they hadn't lost *everyone*. Even the pre-war ships had been prepared for unexpected hull breaches.

But they weren't prepared for weapons that went through their armour like knives through butter, he thought. *I...*

"They're launching starfighters," Tara reported. "One squadron, deployed from launch tube two."

"Understood," John said. The Indians had nothing to gain from launching starfighters, besides - perhaps - the chance for a little revenge. "Prepare to repel attack."

"Aye, sir," Tara said.

John studied the display as the red icons flashed away from the stricken carrier. The Indians were launching a small formation of shuttles too, preparing to evacuate the supercarrier and transfer their crews to a smaller ship, but they weren't a problem. He wouldn't have fired on rescue ships anyway, even if it hadn't been a universally-acknowledged war crime. The carrier was crippled beyond hope of immediate repair, even if the Indians had the best repair crews in the galaxy. And, without their ship, the crewmen were irrelevant.

"Captain," Tara said. "The Vesy-bound ships from their original flotilla are altering course. They're advancing towards our position."

"They must want to recover the crew too," John said. It would be at least an hour before they arrived, by which time the whole issue would be settled, one way or the other. "Ignore them for the moment."

"Aye, sir," Tara said. "Starfighters on approach vector now."

John sucked in his breath. The Indian starfighters were very similar to the British and American designs that dominated interstellar warfare, at least in the years immediately following the First Interstellar War. They'd probably been *given* the original plans, in hopes of ensuring that all starfighter designs were standardised. There were some minor differences, but they were close enough to the designs he knew - the designs he'd flown - for him to be fairly sure they hadn't managed to launch any torpedo-bombers. It was unlikely their plasma cannons could do any real damage...

He swore, mentally. If they managed to fire into the gash in the hull, they'd do *real* damage.

"Open fire as soon as they enter engagement range," he ordered. "Helm; spin the ship, if necessary, to keep them away from the damaged section."

"Aye, sir," Armstrong said.

Howard tossed him a sharp look. John understood all too well. There was no way that *Warspite* could turn fast enough to avoid the starfighters getting into position to fire into the gash, not unless the Indians were particularly slow. The ship was nowhere near as nimble as any starfighter.

"Enemy fighters entering engagement range," Tara reported. "Point defence engaging...*now*."

John watched, grimly, as the Indians plunged defiantly into the teeth of *Warspite's* plasma cannons. They'd learned well, he noted, from the endless skirmishes between the task force's arrival and the battle; they'd mastered the art of random flying and constant evasion. Four starfighters died, but the remainder lived long enough to strafe the hull and fire plasma bolts of their own into the damaged section. Alarms howled through the ship...

"Evacuate that section and the surrounding compartments," John ordered. He cursed himself silently. He should have thought to do that earlier. There *were* lighter layers of armour running through the interior of the starship, but not enough to keep the Indians from inflicting significant damage. “Keep altering course...”

The ship shuddered, slightly. “One enemy target slammed into our hull,” Tara reported. “A piece of armour plating may have been knocked loose.”

It can be replaced, John thought. The fleet train included a couple of freighters crammed with replacement armour, if they managed to get back to the task force in time. *But we need to deal with the threat first.*

“The Indians are regrouping,” Tara reported. “They’re concentrating on the damaged section again...”

“Launch missiles, set to detonate near their position,” John snapped. It was a desperation move - *Warspite* was far too close to the blast radius - but he couldn’t risk allowing them a second shot at the hull. A starfighter ramming into the damaged section would probably cripple the ship. “Fire!”

“Aye, Captain,” Tara said. “Missiles away...enemy starfighters spreading out...”

The missiles detonated. “Enemy starfighters destroyed,” Tara reported. “I say again, enemy starfighters destroyed.”

“Helm, keep us heading away from them,” John ordered. They should be safe now, unless the Indians decided to order their smaller ships to give chase, but he wouldn’t be able to relax until there was considerably more distance between *Warspite* and the Indian ships. “Launch a pair of stealth probes to monitor the Indian deployments; I want to know the moment they prepare to return to the fight.”

“Aye, sir,” Tara said.

John smiled, darkly. *Warspite* could paint an entire fleet carrier on her hull now, even though the carrier hadn’t been completely destroyed. She was certainly crippled, out of the fight for the foreseeable future. Hell, John honestly wasn’t sure if the Indians could get her out of the system before it was too late. They’d probably be better served by putting the carrier on a course into interstellar space and leaving her there until the end of the war. As long as she wasn’t a threat, Admiral Fitzwilliam would probably leave her alone.

And we won the engagement, he thought. Honours had been slightly less than even - the Indians had definitely been ahead on points - but the loss of the Indian carrier had been decisive. *The pathway to Clarke III lies open.*

"General," Captain Misra said, as Anjeet stepped through the airlock. "Welcome onboard."

Anjeet scowled. *Delhi* was a cruiser, rather than a fleet carrier; she wasn't configured to serve as a command ship. Not, he suspected, that it mattered; the Indian Navy needed time to lick its wounds before it could return to the fight. Half the remaining ships were damaged; the other half had largely shot themselves dry or were crammed with evacuees from *Viraat*.

"Thank you, Captain," he said, finally. He knew Misra too well; the man was an ass-kisser, plain and simple. Anjeet wouldn't have promoted him to command rank if the man hadn't been very good at making political allies. "I shall be moving my staff into your secondary bridge and converting it into a flag bridge."

"Of course, General," Misra said. "If there is anything I can do to make the transition easier, please let me know."

"I will," Anjeet said. The suggestions that came to mind were either anatomically impossible or useless. "Until the compartment is ready, Admiral Joshi will hold tactical command. I will need to speak with him as soon as possible."

Misra looked mystified - his mindset didn't allow for anyone giving up command, when one's subordinates might take advantage of the opportunity to prove themselves - but led him straight to the communications compartment. Anjeet took one of the consoles, chased the commanding officer out with a few well-chosen words and started to record a message. It would be at least two hours before Admiral Joshi heard it. There was definitely no hope of a real-time conversation.

"Admiral," he said. It hurt to admit it, but there was no point in trying to do otherwise. "You have tactical command of the fleet. The undamaged ships are to maintain a watch on the tramline; the damaged ships are to pass through the tramline to Vesy, where the survivors are to be offloaded. For the moment, there will be no attempt to continue the engagement with the British ships."

Anjeet paused. “They may take advantage of this to press the offensive against Clarke III,” he added. “In that case, they will have to test themselves against the ground-based weapons.”

He tapped a switch, encrypting the message, then started to work on a more complex signal to Earth. There was no point in trying to hide the lost carrier. The reporters would already have started to send signals back to Earth. He needed to get the bare facts to India before the reporters transformed the defeat - and it had been a defeat - into utter disaster.

“Bastards,” he muttered.

He looked at the display. It was puny, compared to the one he was used to, but it was clear the British had won the engagement. The only consolation was that they would now have to force a landing on Clarke, despite the battering they’d taken. And the moon was heavily defended.

We can still give them a bloody nose, he thought. There was no way to know just how badly the British carrier had been damaged. The long-range sensors insisted it hadn’t moved since the engagement. Were her drives still in working order? *And perhaps win the war on points.*

CHAPTER THIRTY ONE

Pegasus System

"Well," James said, as he entered the conference room. "The only thing costlier than a battle won is a battle lost."

Susan smiled. "That's a misquote, sir," she said. "The Duke of Wellington won the battle."

"But at least he had victory to console himself," James said. He smiled, looking at the display. The remaining Indian ships, save for the wrecked and abandoned carrier, were making their way to the tramline. "Think how *they* must be feeling."

He felt his smile grow wider. The Indians had lost an entire carrier! They'd know they'd been in a war. Even if they somehow drove the task force back out of the system and declared victory, the cost would be staggeringly high. *Theodore Smith* had been damaged, but her repair crews were confident that the ship would be ready to return to the war within three days. The damage hadn't been *that* bad.

And they lost their one chance to really drive the boot in, he thought. *We won the engagement!*

"But we haven't won the war," Susan said. "The question now is how do we capitalise on our victory."

James nodded in agreement as the steward handed him a cup of coffee. Twenty-seven hours had passed since the battle and he really hadn't managed to get enough sleep, between monitoring the repairs and keeping a sharp eye on the Indians. It *looked* as though the enemy navy was in full retreat, but they'd already managed to pull the wool over his eyes once. And besides, he'd have to engage the defences surrounding Clarke. They might be hoping he'd lead his fleet straight into the mass drivers and get slaughtered.

"True," he agreed. He keyed a switch. "It's time for the conference to begin."

There were fewer holograms this time, he noted; seven warships were gone, while others were badly damaged and had had to withdraw to J-35. The Indians might have a chance to harry the wounded ships, if they had time to think of it; he'd taken a calculated risk sending so many ships back with only a handful of protective starships. But there was no choice. He needed everything he had to capitalise on his victory.

"Thank you for coming," he said, once the final hologram was in position. "As you know" - it was unlikely there was a single officer who didn't - "the Indians have effectively conceded control of the system to us. The last reports from the tramline indicate that their sole presence, apart from the garrison on Clarke III, is a handful of starships holding position on the tramline itself. I think they're currently regrouping and considering their next move.

"That gives us an opportunity to take the war to Clarke III and liberate the moon," he continued, when it became clear that no one was going to comment. "Once the garrison is taken out - or captured - the war will be within shouting distance of being won. I don't believe the Indians will attempt to continue once we have chased them out of our territory."

"There's Cromwell," Captain Roebuck said.

"There are two ships on their way to Cromwell to liberate the world," James said. "In any case, Cromwell is simply not as useful as Pegasus. The Indians would be foolish to continue the war."

"Some would say they were foolish even to *start* the war," Commodore Blake said.

"They gambled and they lost," James said, flatly. He held up a hand. "We will, of course, draw up contingency plans to handle their remaining carrier, if they bring her into the system, but for the moment our focus must be on Clarke. We will be as battle-ready as we will ever be in two days - three, to give ourselves some leeway. At that point, we must be ready to liberate Clarke. We will, of course, transmit a demand for surrender beforehand, but we have to assume the Indians will try to hold out.

He paused. "Major Rainer?"

The tactical analyst rose to his feet. "As of the last report from Clarke, the Indians have emplaced fourteen mass drivers on the surface, spread out to allow them to target anything approaching from any angle. Their projectiles, of course, will keep going until they actually *hit* something, but we believe their effective range is around one light minute at most. The nearer we get to the planet, of course, the more their accuracy will improve, while our ability to either intercept or avoid them decreases."

"I'd be surprised if they managed to hit anything beyond a few light seconds," Blake commented. "Their targeting will be shitty and they'll have the time-delay problem too."

"Yes, sir," Major Rainer said. "However, they are *physically* capable of hurling projectiles at targets that far from the moon.

"Each of these mass drivers is surrounded by a handful of railguns and plasma cannons, while they are supported by a network of active sensor platforms and ground-based radar transmitters. Firing KEWs at them from long range is unlikely to work. However, in order to land on the moon, we need to knock out at least two or three of the mass drivers and then approach from the blindspot. This will not be an easy task."

James nodded, clearing his throat for attention. "Forces already on the ground are insufficient to complete the destruction of more than one or two of the installations," he said, "although the mere destruction of the mass driver itself would suffice to render the installation useless. Therefore, we will attempt to slip a second stealth shuttle through the defences. However, as they are now on the alert, the task force will advance and launch ARM missiles to suppress the enemy's defences. We will, of course, launch these missiles from a relatively safe distance."

There were some smiles from the various holograms, although he knew that no one had any illusions. Mass drivers were dangerous weapons; a single hit would be more than enough to cripple even a giant carrier. It *was* possible to intercept a projectile or deflect it, but the slightest mistake could wind up costing the Royal Navy an expensive starship. There was nothing stopping the Indians, either, from firing as many projectiles as they liked towards the task force. Hell, they could just mine Clarke itself for the raw materials.

"Once we have a window, the landing craft will be deployed," he added, smoothly. "The Royal Marines and Paras will link up with the forces on the ground, then advance on the colony and suppress resistance. I believe the Indians will surrender at that point, as there would be nothing stopping us from stripping away the remainder of the defences and flattening the colony from orbit; they'd have to be insane to consider using human shields, now they've lost a carrier."

"They might be insane," Blake offered. "Or desperate."

"We'd have ample excuse to annex both of their worlds," James pointed out. "No one would object in the slightest, even if we couldn't touch India itself."

He kept his face expressionless with an effort. What if the Indians *were* that insane? They weren't a defenceless rogue nation. There were limits to how far India could be punished without triggering off a major war on Earth itself. And *that* would weaken the human race as a whole. Surely, they'd see sense and throw in the towel. They'd fought hard, and well, but they'd lost. There was no point in throwing good money after bad.

Unless they think they still have a chance to win, he thought. *But they're already down a carrier.*

He held up a hand. "In the event of them using human shields, we will seal their positions off and strike out towards Vesy and Gandhi," he said. "Or simply communicate with Earth and invite the Indian Government to consider a truce."

Susan looked doubtful and he knew she wasn't the only one. The Indians had kept raising the stakes until they'd found it impossible to just fold. And if they *did* try to hold out, the colony would have to be stormed, which would almost certainly kill a great many colonists even if the Indians *didn't* use them as human shields.

And if I pass this question to the government, he asked himself, *what will they say*?

"In any case, we will deal with the situation as it arises," he said. "For the moment, tactical deployment plans have been uploaded into your datacores. I expect you to be ready to deploy in three days. Dismissed."

One by one, the holograms winked out. "Admiral," Boone said. He'd chosen to stay. "Do you want to board the Indian carrier?"

James considered it, briefly. It was possible there were still trapped crew onboard, but the Indians hadn't tried to ask for assistance in recovering them. Other than that..."Would it be worth the effort?"

"I don't know, sir," Boone said. "We could put a small team on her with little trouble, but if they've rigged her to blow without the proper access codes..."

"I know the score," James said. He'd already thought about simply finishing off the crippled and abandoned ship as the task force approached the gas giant, only to dismiss the idea as spiteful. They could try to claim the carrier as spoils of war after the shooting stopped. "As long as the hulk is harmless, I see no reason to risk lives."

"As you wish, sir," Boone said. "My forces are ready to deploy once we have a clear window."

"Good," James said. "Inform the SAS that they will have company. And make sure they check to see if they can handle three installations."

"Drake says he has a plan," Boone said. "I trust him."

James nodded, studying the display. If Drake's plan failed, he'd have no choice but to sneak up to the planet and try to clear the way using KEWs. Even with ARM missiles being deployed in vast quantities, it wouldn't be easy to score a hit on the tiny installations from long range. He might wind up bleeding his fleet white...or having to accept something less than outright victory.

"I trust him too," he said, finally. They'd never had to put a recon force on the ground during the First Interstellar War. The Russians had tried, but the Tadpoles had largely kept themselves separate from the Russians on New Russia. "See to your men, Colonel. We'll be deploying in three days."

"Yes, sir," Boone said.

"It could be worse, sir," Johnston said.

John eyed him, sharply. "I suppose it could," he said. "Can we take the ship back into action?"

Johnston pretended to think about it. "Well," he said, drawing out the word, "we *could* refit smaller pieces of armour over the gash in the hull. It would give us a considerable degree of protection against anything smaller than a bomb-pumped laser, although if we get hit by a mass driver projectile we're thoroughly screwed anyway. The only downside is that our point defence network is all fucked up; we can affix spare cannons from the fleet train to the hull, if you don't mind waiting a day, but we wouldn't have perfect control."

"Which we would need, because we'd be moving right into the teeth of enemy fire," John said. After all they'd done, he was damned if *Warspite* was missing the final battle. Nice as it would be to go home and gloat about killing a carrier, he didn't want to leave his fellows in the lurch. "Is there any way to fix it?"

"Not without more time than we have," Johnston said.

He cleared his throat. "The inner framework didn't take such a beating," he said, quickly. "We were lucky they didn't manage to ram a starfighter into the gash. I've started work on strengthening it now, so our structural integrity should remain uncompromised. However, there's still no way we can avoid being blown to bits if we get hit by a projectile."

John eyed him, darkly. He hadn't had more than four hours sleep since the engagement and he was too hyped up on coffee to care. "If you don't start giving me straight answers," he said, "I'm going to keep you on the ship the next time we visit Nelson Base."

"Yes, sir," Johnston said. "In short, we should be good to join the task force for the final battle, but we would probably do better to avoid a missile duel."

"Which should be doable, unless the Indians launch a counterattack," John said. He'd half-expected to see the second carrier within hours. The Indians wouldn't fall for the same trick twice. "If that happens...?"

"We would be well advised to avoid being hit," Johnston said. "There's no way we can bring the ship back to full readiness without either a shipyard or time we don't have."

John nodded. "We'll try and get back to the yards once the battle is over," he said. "Thank you, Mike."

"You're welcome, Captain," Johnston said. He glanced over John's shoulder. "And I think someone wants to see you."

John turned. "Miss Schneider? What are you doing here?"

The reporter looked disgustingly fresh and pretty, he noted, as he motioned for her to precede him out of the compartment. If he'd swung that way, part of his mind suggested, he might even have found her attractive. Blonde hair, long legs, a balcony one could recite sonnets from...it was no wonder that half the crew had been competing to speak with her when she collected interviews for her post-war book. The darker side of his mind wondered if her mixture of hard-hitting questions and touching naivety had led to her assignment to *Warspite*, whose commanding officer could be guaranteed not to fall for her. It wouldn't be the first time the PR department had done something absurd in the desperate quest for good press.

"I was looking for you," she said, guilelessly. She pulled a datapad off her belt and held it out to him. "I wrote the first report on the Battle of Pegasus."

John took the datapad and read through the story, shaking his head in amusement. The bare facts were accurate - someone must have talked her through the entire battle - but she'd made them far more dramatic than he recalled. He didn't *think* he'd stood up and quoted lines from *Moby Dick* before pushing a big red button dramatically...

"It wasn't quite this exciting," he said. *Tara* had pushed the button; he'd just issued the orders to fire. "I would have thought that evading their missiles and then the starfighters would be enough to make any story dramatic."

"It will be by the time the feature film comes out," Penny said. "Would you rather be played by Carlos Rotherham or Danny O'Toole?"

"They don't look anything like me," John protested.

He vaguely recalled watching them in the movies, back when Colin and he had been able to sneak a few hours of shore leave from the Academy. Rotherham was a long-haired galoot who hammed up his lines; O'Toole could at least deliver his lines convincingly, but everything he said was always far too understated, making him more suitable for playing the elder statesman than a starship commander. And neither of them looked remotely like him, unless they went in for intensive plastic surgery.

It seemed a great deal of effort for a crappy movie that would be forgotten within the year.

"Trust me on this," Penny said. She gave him a regretful look that wasn't particularly convincing. "By the time they bring out the movie, you won't know what you actually look like either."

John sighed. It was a good thing, in some ways, that Admiral Smith hadn't survived the First Interstellar War. There were no less than seven movies and four biopics featuring *Ark Royal* and her crew; *none* of the lead actors looked anything like the images in the files. Hell, several of them had even confused *Ark Royal* with a modern fleet carrier and an *American* carrier at that. A few hundred years down the line and everyone would have forgotten which nation Admiral Smith had served.

"I should be able to sue," he muttered.

Penny shook her head. "As a military officer, your life is theirs to sell for PR purposes," she said. "I think they can turn you into a bronzed hulk with naked girls dangling from your legs and you wouldn't be able to complain about it."

"That would probably explain why we had so many recruits after *Starfighter Pilots Gone Wild II* came out," John said. There *had* been an upsurge in new recruits, if he recalled correctly. "I suppose the fact that trying to fit three girls and a pilot in a starfighter cockpit is completely impossible didn't deter the filmmakers from trying. And I don't think I could command the ship if everyone on the bridge was naked."

Penny giggled. "I suppose they're a *little* unrealistic."

"Just a *little*," John confirmed.

He checked the datapad again, thoughtfully. "I'd ask you to make it a *little* less dramatic, as the recordings from the bridge will come out sooner or later, but if you have to have it like that..."

"They'll want to use it as a recruiting tool," Penny said. "It's not easy to recruit trained manpower these days."

John rather thought she was wrong, but he kept that to himself. "I need to catch forty winks," he said, instead. "Send this report to the censors, if you must, and we can try and do a proper interview later."

"Of course, Captain," Penny said. She paused. "Off the record, though... the Indians still have a carrier, don't they? And our carrier is damaged."

"They'd be risking a great deal more, proportionately speaking, if they tried to retake the offensive," John assured her. "They may try to reclaim control of the system, but they'll never keep it. We can hit them where it hurts."

"I hope you're right," Penny said. "Thank you, Captain."

John smiled back. "You're welcome," he said. "Goodnight."

CHAPTER THIRTY TWO

Clarke III, Pegasus System

Colonel Vasanta Darzi was not a happy man.

He hadn't been a happy man, really, since he'd been given his orders, which were so contradictory they just *had* to have been drafted by politicians. On one hand, he was to hold Clarke Colony in an iron grip; on the other, he was to make damn sure that his troops committed no atrocities against the British settlers. He had no particular *inclination* to commit an atrocity, to be fair - it wasn't as if the British were secessionists or jihadists - but keeping them under tight control and ensuring there was as limited contact with his troops as possible was impossible. The only way to square the circle had been to keep the colony's life support systems under control, put the colonists to work and hope the Indian Navy never lost control of the system.

But it had. The tactical briefing he'd been given before the remainder of the fleet scurried off to Vesy had been blunt; the navy had been defeated, the British now held control of the system and they were likely to move on Clarke at any moment. And when they did, he was expected to retain control of the planet despite being cut off from India. No, he was expected to *defeat* the British. And the hell of it was that he knew it probably wasn't possible.

He glared at the display, thinking hard. He had the mass drivers, of course; he could make sure that any British ship foolish enough to venture into range didn't live long enough to regret it. But they wouldn't be enough to keep the British from blockading the colony indefinitely or heading off to Gandhi to wreak havoc there. The only real hope was that the British didn't know about the mass drivers, but he had his doubts. If they could sneak a ship close enough to a carrier to deliver a killing blow, they could sneak a recon satellite or two over Clarke...and the mass drivers weren't particularly concealed. And if they knew about the mass drivers, what would they do?

We do have orbital space under tight control, he told himself. It was true; there were ninety-seven active sensor satellites in orbit, backed up by thirty passive sensor arrays. The British would have real problems getting anything near the planet without being detected, all the more so now as the remaining Indian ships had abandoned the system. *We could let them get in close and then blow their ships to bits.*

He tapped a switch on his console, studying the orders he'd been given by the government before departing Earth. They were masterworks, he had to admit; he had orders to hold out as long as possible, consummate with honour and dignity. But...he was to try to avoid putting the British settlers in danger, another impossible task. If the British bombarded the colony, or somehow managed to land an army on Clarke, the settlers would be caught in the crossfire. The only way to avoid a massacre would be to surrender at once, which would *not* be commensurate with either honour or dignity.

Bastards, he thought, bitterly.

It had seemed a good idea, back on Earth. Give the Great Powers a poke in the eye, secure control over the two most vital systems for future expansion over the next few decades and - if the British put up a fight - give them a bloody nose that would make *anyone* think twice about challenging India. But now the navy had been defeated, he was cut off from his superiors and the British were gathering their strength for the final battle. The grand idea had failed completely.

And all we can do is die bravely, he thought. Governor Brown and his scratch defence force had *tried* to put up a fight, even though the outcome had been inevitable from the start. *He* could do no less...and he was far better equipped to give the British a fight. It wasn't a reassuring thought. *At least we will hurt them before we go down.*

He gritted his teeth as he rose to his feet. The deep-space tracking network insisted that the British were closing in on Clarke, their ships nosing their way into the halo of space junk that orbited the massive gas giant. One way or the other, it would all be over soon.

Gather my officers, plan a defence and keep the colonists under control, he thought, bitterly. *A piece of fucking cake.*

It wouldn't be easy, he knew. The mass drivers would start to run out of ammunition very quickly, forcing him to send them more from the British-built ore processors at the colony. It was an inconvenient position, but the British had probably never expected to have to supply fifteen mass drivers spaced out over the entire moon. He'd even have to press some of the settlers into shifting the projectiles...which was, technically, a war crime, depending on how the British chose to look at it. They'd already carried weapons, but they hadn't known what they'd been carrying. It would be a great deal harder to prevent them from finding out once the fighting actually began.

He strode into the small office and waited for his officers to arrive, tapping the table in irritation. Maybe he should just shoot off his mass driver ammunition and surrender. No one could reasonably claim he could have held out, once the British took the high orbitals, although he knew all too well that some armchair admiral would try to insist that he could still have won the battle. But that still smacked of defeatism to him. Cold logic said one thing; hot emotion said another. He couldn't give in as long as there were cards left to play.

"We can expect to be attacked within hours, at best," he said, once his officers had finally assembled. None of them looked very happy either. "I want all production switched to mass driver projectiles. Draw up a shipment rota and get the settler drivers busy moving them to the outposts."

There was no disagreement. But then, he hadn't expected any.

"Up the patrols around the colony and make sure the defences are manned at all times," he added. Having the settlers dig trenches had led to a great deal of grumbling and even a formal protest - which he'd ignored - but at least it would make it difficult for any attacking force to guess which ones were actually manned. "If they manage to land a force on the surface, I want to give it a bloody nose before it can take the colony."

And even if we can't stop them, at least we can make sure we're not seen as weaklings, he added, silently. Losing the war would embolden others to challenge India on Earth. *By the time we have to give up, we'll have created a new legend.*

"There was a great battle," Majors said, quietly. "The Indians were defeated."

Lillian gave him a sharp look. Majors had been *very* respectful over the past few days, after she'd taken his transmitter out of the colony; indeed, he'd gone so far as to say she was the bravest person he'd met in his entire life. Given that she'd actually taken the transmitter to the SAS, Lillian hadn't been able to avoid being more than a little embarrassed by his constant praise. The only real consolation was that his message *had* been forwarded to the fleet.

Sharon leaned forward. "Are you sure?"

"Yes," Majors said. "I was listening to a couple of their conversations on the radio - I managed to set up a receiver. The Indians lost a carrier and the remainder of their fleet is retreating. It won't be long before we're free!"

"They still have the mass drivers," Lillian pointed out, warningly. She understood his feelings, but she didn't really want him to do something stupid. The Indians were *still* in control of the colony, the settlers were *still* unarmed and the Royal Navy was *still* light minutes - perhaps hours - from the moon. "We may not be liberated in a hurry."

Majors snorted. "They have to surrender now, don't they?"

"They could gamble the Royal Navy wouldn't be willing to bombard the colony," Sharon pointed out. "There's very little they could do if they can't land troops themselves."

Lillian couldn't keep herself from glancing upwards. She'd never had any sympathy for terrorists or rogue states, but she thought she understood now how they must have felt, confronted by drones and KEWs dropped from low orbit. One moment, everything was fine; the next, the KEW had struck and the area was devastated. There wouldn't have been even a second of warning before it was too late. On Clarke, they could be targeted and destroyed...and they wouldn't even know what had hit them. Their own *side* would have fired on the colony.

"We have to do something," Majors insisted. "Really..."

"Like what?" Lillian asked. "Can you think of anything we can do?"

"We could seize the power plant," Majors said, after a moment. "Cut the power to the colony..."

Lillian sighed, loudly. "The Indians have the power plant under heavy guard," she said, tapping off points on her fingers. "Even if we somehow beat a dozen soldiers, *without* weapons, we will have to shut down the fusion plant and render it useless, *before* the Indians launch a counterattack. I don't have the control codes - do you? And even if we succeed, the Indians have generators of their own. We'd be unable to do anything to *them*."

Majors glared. "Then what do you suggest we do?"

"There's nothing we *can* do," Lillian said. She looked at Sharon. "I don't suppose you could infect them with something, could you?"

Sharon scowled, revolted. "I swore an oath to do no harm," she said.

"They're *occupiers*," Majors protested.

"There is no way I can whip up a disease that only targets Indians," Sharon snapped. "And even if I did, the Indians would have no trouble recognising what I'd done and countering it."

"And we couldn't infect all of the Indians," Lillian said.

"We'd be more likely to infect ourselves," Sharon said. Her voice was still angry. "There's no real difference between us and the Indians, certainly not enough of a difference to keep a disease targeted on them from spreading to us. Our basic immunisations probably aren't any different from theirs."

Lillian nodded. Genetically-engineered diseases had caused a considerable number of deaths during the Age of Unrest - and would probably have caused more, if the Great Powers hadn't concentrated their efforts on keeping the diseases from spreading. Sharon had every reason to be horrified at the thought of creating a new disease herself, even if it wouldn't guarantee her immediate execution when the colony was liberated. The genie had been stuffed back in the bottle and no one would thank her for letting it out again.

"So what do we do?" Majors demanded. "Just wait?"

"Yeah," Lillian said. "We wait."

A low chime rang through the air. "All personnel, report to the main hall," a voice said. "I say again, all personnel report to the main hall."

"You go first," Lillian said to Majors. They didn't dare be seen together. "We'll follow in a couple of minutes."

Majors nodded and hurried out of the tiny compartment. Lillian gave Sharon a look and saw she was clenching her fists, trying to get her anger under control. It was hard to blame her, Lillian knew; the risks of creating a disease far outweighed the possible advantages. And Majors would have happily *deployed* such a disease if he'd had one. The hell of it was that she understood them both quite well. Sharon was horrified at the thought of creating such a weapon; Majors was frustrated, helpless and just wanted to hit back at the Indians, no matter who got hurt along the way.

"Don't worry about it," she said, as she reached for the door. "I'm sure we'll be liberated soon enough."

Sharon nodded and followed her through the maze of corridors into the main hall. There were more Indian soldiers this time, wearing powered combat armour. Lillian rather hoped that was a sign of nervousness; the Indians had to know that combat armour was *still* overkill against unarmed and unarmoured settlers. They could charge forward, flailing their arms, and tear the settlers to bloody chunks. The thought made her hesitate; she wanted to back out, but she knew she didn't dare. The Indians would turn on her if she tried to flee.

"There has been a battle," the Indian Governor said, once he'd called for attention. "The situation is still fluid. However, this moon may come under attack..."

"So," Lewis said. "Are you still mooning over your girlfriend?"

Percy ignored the sergeant's sally as he peered through the binoculars towards the Indian patrol. The Indians had been patrolling more and more over the last couple of days, although there was no way to know if they'd detected the SAS troop or if they were just being paranoid, following the naval defeat. It hardly mattered, Percy knew; they'd had to abandon the first camp completely and slip over five kilometres from the colony before they dared set up a second. If this went on, their ability to keep an eye on the Indians would be seriously impaired.

"It's quite understandable," Lewis jibed. "She might have forgotten you."

"I don't think she's my girlfriend," Percy said. He'd made a full confession, of course; Drake had chewed him out in no uncertain terms, then warned him that the whole affair would be added to his post-mission report. "She was just..."

"Desperate," Lewis finished. "I suppose she would have to be, if she made love to you."

Percy felt his cheeks heat. The hell of it was that he knew the sergeant had a point. Everyone - male or female - wanted to forget their troubles and bury themselves into someone else, even if it was just a brief one-night stand. He'd had them himself during his short stay in a refugee camp and his stint on a recovery crew; a brief loveless encounter, only galvanised by the shared desire not to spend the night alone. There was nothing to suggest that Lillian would be interested in him once the colony was liberated.

He kept his attention on the Indians, trying to ignore the steady stream of jibes. Troopers had to keep their tempers at all times, he'd been told; it wasn't uncommon for prospective recruits to be teased and bullied, just to see if they'd lose their temper and deck the tormentor. Some of the troopers had been quite free with their advice, pointing out that he'd be lucky not to see suggestions his sister was a slut or his mother had been a whore. He couldn't quite avoid wondering if SAS training sergeant was among the most dangerous positions in the entire army. A sergeant charged with running the Combat Infantryman Course would be far better trained than any raw recruit, but anyone who tried out for the SAS would already be very well trained, perfectly capable of landing a punch before he was dragged off and binned.

"They're turning back towards the colony," he said. "I think they can see the incoming storm."

"They probably can," Lewis said, shifting effortlessly into businesslike mode. "It's just coming over the mountains."

Percy nodded. "Should we follow them?"

"Probably not, unless we want to go ducking around the observation post," Lewis said. "We're going to have to take that place out, once your friends start to land."

"Understood," Percy said. "We could toss a missile at them."

Lewis snickered. "Where's the fun in that?"

"Safer," Percy pointed out.

"I'll have you know I was once hidden so close to a wanker that his piss splashed down around me," Lewis informed him. Percy shuddered. He hadn't believed *all* of the stories he'd heard, until he'd checked the files. So far, he hadn't caught anyone in a lie. "I dread to imagine what would have happened if he'd taken a shit."

"You'd have beaten the crap out of him," Percy said.

"He wouldn't have had any crap left in him," Lewis said. He glanced up at the darkening sky, then motioned for Percy to follow him. "We'd better get back to the camp."

It was nearly thirty minutes of hard walking before they reached the hidden tents, just as the first flakes of poisonous snow fell from the sky. Drake was waiting inside, reading a datapad; the remainder of the troop was either catching up on their sleep or watching, weapons in hand, for an Indian attack.

"They're not patrolling past a kilometre, so far," Lewis reported, once he'd taken off his helmet. "That may change, of course."

"Of course," Drake agreed. He looked at Percy. "Was there any sign that they'd detected us?"

"None, sir," Percy said, bluntly. He knew Lewis would have said something if he'd been wrong. "They looked to be on a standard patrol."

"They're also randomising their patrol patterns," Lewis added. His face darkened. "Isn't it fun dealing with professionals?"

"Not really," Drake said.

"Even the Vesy know to randomise their patrols," Percy injected. "It's the oldest trick in the book."

Drake snorted, then held out the datapad. "The task force intends to begin sniping the orbiting defences within six hours. Our reinforcements will be landed then, if things go according to plan; we'll be moving out within nine hours to target the outposts. If we're lucky, we can improvise one of the attacks; if not..."

"Percy's girlfriend can be helpful," Lewis said, mischievously.

"We take whoever we can get," Drake said, firmly. "Get some sleep, both of you. I want to be ready to move out thirty minutes before the navy begins the attack."

CHAPTER THIRTY THREE

Clarke III, Pegasus System

"Captain," Tara said. "*Ardent* has uploaded targeting data to the fleet datanet."

"Understood," John said. "Prepare to fire ARMs."

"Aye, sir," Tara said.

"Helm, keep us on our evasive course," John added. "I don't want us to follow a predicable trajectory."

"Aye, sir," Armstrong said. "One round of space-sickness coming up."

"Better space-sickness than a projectile to the belly," Howard observed. "We're coming into effective engagement range now."

John nodded, tightly. Space-sickness wasn't a real problem - the compensators would ensure that the crew wouldn't *feel* any of the erratic manoeuvres - certainly not when compared to taking a direct hit from a mass driver. *Warspite* would be smashed to rubble if she was hit, no matter how much armour the crew bolted to her hull. The only real hope was to avoid being hit in the first place.

But they'll have some real difficulty in targeting us, he thought, savagely. The task force was surrounded by a haze of ECM, while a dozen drones projected false images of starships to draw enemy fire. Some of them would probably be recognisable - the Indians were sweeping space pretty thoroughly - but others would definitely soak up a projectile or two. *And that gives us a chance to take down their defences.*

"Signal from *Ardent*, sir," Gillian reported. "Fire."

John smiled. "Tactical, launch ARMs," he ordered. "I say again, launch ARMs."

He watched, grimly, as the first missile flashed away from *Warspite*, joining countless others on their flight towards the planet. Every spacer knew that lighting up an active sensor would reveal the ship's location and draw fire - it was why starships generally relied on passive sensors in wartime - and ARM missiles were specifically designed to home in on active sensors. The Indians, he suspected, must have intended to keep a handful of ships - or weapons platforms - in orbit at all times. Without them, the active sensor platforms were sitting ducks.

"Incoming fire," Tara reported, grimly. "None inbound on our position."

"Watch them," John ordered. The mass driver projectiles, thankfully, would follow a ballistic course, but they moved so rapidly that their window for interception would be very narrow. "Be ready to snap off a shot at a moment's notice."

He allowed himself a grim smile as the first active sensor platform was hit and vanished from the display. The Indians must not have built them to be very solid, although trying would probably have been a waste of time. One by one, the platforms vanished from the display...

"*Disraeli* is gone, sir," Tara reported. "They scored a direct hit."

John nodded. There would be time to mourn later. "Keep us moving in an evasive pattern," he ordered. This time, at least, he didn't have to worry about deploying a stealth shuttle. The troopers would be launching from *Ardent*. "How many active platforms are left?"

"Four, sir," Tara said. "But our own active sensors are picking up several passive sensor platforms. The flag's updating to compensate."

"There's also the sensor arrays on the ground," Howard pointed out. "We can't get at them so easily."

"True," John said. *That* would be in the hands of the SAS. "We'll do all we can."

The final icon vanished from the display. "All platforms destroyed, sir," Tara reported. "The flag is ordering us to hold formation."

Insofar as it can be called a formation, John thought, wryly. A standard formation would rapidly lead to the destruction of every ship in range. *But as long as we keep moving, we should be reasonably safe.*

"Admiral," Sally said. "The platforms are gone."

"Understood," James said. The time delay was turning into a problem again, but at least he'd been able to bring *Theodore Smith* into position on the other side of Clarke. They might have to send messages through a handful of relay stations, yet the immense bulk of the gas giant would shield the carrier from the mass drivers. "And the shuttle?"

"She's on her way," Sally said. "The enemy is still sweeping space with their ground-based sensors."

And firing off projectiles at a terrifying rate, James thought. It wasn't as if producing mass driver ammunition was difficult, but even so...the Indians had to be burning through their supplies alarmingly quickly. In their place, he suspected he would have done the same. If they thought they could hold out long enough for help to arrive, they really didn't have much choice. *How long will it be until they run out*?

"Keep monitoring their ammunition expenditure," he ordered. It was risky - it was impossible to tell if the Indians were running out without a good idea of just how many projectiles they'd started with - but a reduction in their weight of fire might just indicate that they were feeling the pinch. "Inform me if it slacks significantly."

"Aye, sir," Sally said.

James nodded and returned his attention to the display. There was no need to hurry, even though he knew the politicians would want him to get on with it. He could afford to wait two or three days before landing his forces, or however long it took for the Indians to shoot themselves dry. They'd probably converted the ore processors the original colonists had established to produce more ammunition - it was what *he* would have done - but they'd still have to get the new projectiles to their outposts.

And the SAS will be waiting, he thought. *We might not be able to survive a mass driver strike, but we can make damn sure they run out of ammunition.*

"We're running out of ammunition," the officer reported. "Outposts Four, Five and Seven report that they only have two hundred projectiles left apiece. The remainder are not in a better position."

Colonel Vasanta Darzi gritted his teeth. He'd already ordered his outposts to reduce their rate of fire, but the British kept offering his gunners tempting targets. The analysts believed they'd hit at least three starships, yet it wasn't enough to keep the British from advancing on the planet. And when the outposts ran out of projectiles, the British would be able to enter orbit and start landing troops.

He turned his attention to the production officer. "How many projectiles do we have ready to go?"

The man flinched at his tone. Vasanta felt a stab of guilt - the officer had done an excellent job with the resources available to him - which he pushed aside. They were on the verge of losing their most powerful defences. There was simply no time to be polite.

"Five thousand, sir," the officer reported. "We just need to get them to the mass drivers."

"Get them loaded onto the transports," he ordered. In hindsight, he should have made sure his men knew how to drive the local transports. Now, he had to rely on British settlers to transport ammunition to the outposts. "Put a couple of soldiers in each cab, just to make sure the drivers don't have any heroic thoughts.

"Aye, sir," the officer said.

Vasanta nodded and looked at the display. The British were hovering right at the edge of his effective range, goading the gunners into taking shot after shot. They had to have known about the mass drivers, either through stealthed probes or someone talking out of turn. He was fairly sure his men had rounded up everything that could be used as a tight-beam transmitter on Clarke, but the British were known for being revoltingly inventive. They'd even branded it 'muddling through.'

Not that it matters, he thought, coolly. *We're not done yet.*

Lillian was jerked awake by the sound of someone banging on her door.

For a moment, she believed - honestly believed - that the Indians had worked out what she'd done and come to kill her. She thought frantically, trying to identify something in her tiny quarters that could be used as a weapon, then gave up, clambered out of bed and opened the hatch. The Indian soldier on the far side gave her an appreciative look - her nightgown concealed almost nothing - and then pasted a more businesslike expression on his face.

"You are ordered to report to the transport bay, at once," he said, stiffly. "Grab your clothes and go."

"Yes, sir," Lillian said.

She closed the door - the last thing she wanted was a soldier ogling her as she dressed - tore off her nightgown and pulled her uniform on. On impulse, she pocketed the pen the SAS had given her, grabbed a ration bar to chew on the way and hurried out of the door, down towards the transport bay. A handful of other drivers were heading the same way, their faces tired and worn. It wasn't easy to sleep soundly when their colony was caught in the middle of a war.

"If I could have your attention, please," an Indian said. Lillian knew him, vaguely, but she'd never bothered to learn his name. "You are being charged with transporting various items to the outposts. Those items are already being loaded onto your vehicles. You'll be taking them directly there, without any unnecessary delays."

Ammunition, Lillian guessed. It hadn't been hard to deduce that the ore processors had been converted into ammunition forges. Majors had been looking for a way to sabotage them for the last two days, although he'd found nothing. They were very solid pieces of machinery. It might have been possible to cripple the processors, but the Indians could have replaced them within the hour. *They're wanting us to ship ammunition to the outposts - again.*

"Two soldiers will be accompanying each of you, just to make sure all goes well," the Indian continued. "Please don't cause them any problems."

Lillian said nothing as she was pointed towards her vehicle. The Indians must have liked her, she decided; she was being charged with transporting the ammunition to Outpost Four, rather than one of the outposts that was considerably further away. At least *she* would only have to endure a day with the Indians - perhaps less, if the soldiers stayed at the outpost. It crossed her mind that, with a little luck, she could put the transport in the ocean before the Indians even realised something was wrong, but it would be suicide. Besides, the SAS might be waiting for her.

She scrambled into the cab and glanced around. The Indians were already there, wearing basic environmental suits. They looked composed, but she thought she could detect an undertone of fear. She kept her expression blank as she took the driver's seat, allowing herself a moment of relief. There would be no risk of having to sleep in the same vehicle as two young men. The Indians *seemed* disciplined - and she hadn't heard of any sexual harassment - but that could change.

"We're off," she said. She started the engine, then felt the pen in her pocket. Did she dare turn it on? Perhaps she could fiddle with it, turning the signal on and off, to alert the SAS that she was not alone. "Stay in your seats."

The Indians, thankfully, didn't seem inclined to argue.

"That's your girlfriend," Lewis said, as the vehicle came into view. "But the signal keeps flickering on and off."

"It could be a warning," Percy said. If only there had been time to give Lillian some proper tools and instruction in how to use them. But if she'd been caught, she would probably have been shot out of hand. "She might not be alone."

"Maybe," Lewis said. "She's heading for the outpost, definitely. We need to take that vehicle."

Percy nodded. The second shuttle had made it down, bringing another SAS troop and plenty of supplies. Now, Drake had led the remaining troopers towards one of the enemy outpost, while the newcomers had headed for another. And Percy had been told to handle a third...

"Let's move," he said.

Scrambling up onto the vehicle as it passed was simple enough; if anything, the driver was taking it *very* slowly. It struck him that it could be a form of passive resistance - it wasn't hard to guess what the vehicle was carrying - as he tested the hatch, then keyed it open. Inside, there was no one in the rear compartment; Lewis followed him in, clutching a pistol in one hand, as he opened the hatch to the cab. An Indian soldier spun around, frantically trying to draw a sidearm, too late to keep Percy from rapping him on the head with his pistol. The second soldier managed to get the pistol out of its holster before Lewis shot him in the head.

"Lillian," Percy said, removing his mask. "Are you all right?"

Lillian stared at him, then jumped to her feet and wrapped her arms around him. "I'm fine, now," she said. "What happened?"

A thought clearly struck her. "I can't go back now..."

"You won't have to," Lewis said. He gave Percy an amused look, then unslung his backpack and dropped it on the deck. "What happens when you approach the outpost?"

"They have a checkpoint," Lillian said. She sounded perplexed; she'd gone over it twice when the SAS had first made contact. "They check my ID, they check the codes on the boxes and then they send me in to unload. I stay in the cab while they do the work."

"How gentlemanly of them," Lewis said. "Listen very carefully."

Percy felt a stab of sympathy for Lillian as Lewis kept speaking. "We brought a GDOAB-45 bomb," he said. "It's one of the most powerful conventional explosive weapons in existence - and it is small enough to fit in a backpack."

Lillian looked at the backpack on the deck, then back at him. "And that's it?"

"That's it," Lewis confirmed. "We're going to rig the transport so it keeps going towards the outpost, then jump out. Once it reaches the checkpoint, they'll have to try to stop it; we'll detonate the bomb by remote control."

"Taking out the mass driver," Lillian finished. "And us?"

"We brought a spare camouflage suit for you," Lewis said. "You'll abandon the vehicle with us. We'll take you back to the base until the troops begin to land."

Lillian glanced at Percy. "And that will be the end?"

"For you, the war will be over," Lewis said, gently. He walked past her and examined the controls. "They could have built a more complex processor into the vehicle."

Lillian turned, still holding Percy's hand. "They didn't want something so complex we couldn't repair it," she said. "We were planning to start producing our own tractors and bulldozers within a couple of years."

Percy smiled at her. "But we can still rig it to go, can't we?"

"Of course," Lewis said. He smirked at Percy before returning to his work. "I was hotwiring cars as a lad before I was offered a choice between jail and the army. This is a great deal easier than a commercial car. *They* tend to have security processors you need to bypass to get anywhere. Here...it's just a matter of making sure the system doesn't decide the driver is drunk at the wrong time."

He finished his work and stood. "Percy, help her into her suit," he ordered. "I'll deal with the Indian."

"I'm already wearing a suit," Lillian said. She frowned, doubtfully. "Will yours fit me?"

"They're designed for all sizes," Percy said, leading her into the backroom. He was suddenly nervous to be with her, even though he had a job to do. "And it will change colour to match the background."

Lillian smiled, weakly. "Thank you," she said, as he dug the suit out of his backpack and unfolded it. "What now?"

"Now?" Percy said. He turned his back as she pulled the suit on, even though she wore her civilian clothes underneath. "Now we wait until we're closer to the target."

An hour later, Lewis carried the Indian soldier into the back, wrapped him in a life-support bubble and checked the controls one final time before opening the hatch. Percy could see the outpost in the distance - shooting regular pulses into the sky - as he jumped down to the ground, then caught Lillian and the Indian. Lewis joined them a moment later, holding a detonator in one hand. They hurried to find cover and watched as the vehicle trundled onwards, aimed right at the Indian checkpoint.

Lillian pressed her helmet against his. "They normally expect me to slow down before I reach the checkpoint," she said. "What happens if they open fire?"

"Depends what they start throwing at it," Percy answered. A handful of bullets wouldn't be enough to disable the bomb, but if one of the

Indians opened fire with an antitank weapon the entire mission might fail spectacularly. "We'll see..."

He peered forward as the suited Indian soldiers finally realised that something was wrong and jerked up their rifles. It didn't *look* as though they had anything heavier, although a British checkpoint would have several machine guns or antitank weapons stowed away, just in case of emergency. Maybe they honestly hadn't realised that the SAS team had made it to the surface. They'd know now, he told himself; there could be no other explanation. How could anyone have obtained a GDOAB-45 without access to a military storage dump?

"Get down," he snapped. Lillian wouldn't have any implants to help cope with a sudden flash of blinding light. "And close your eyes..."

The ground shook. He looked up, just in time to see a colossal fireball shatter the giant mass driver, sending pieces of debris flying into the air. The outpost was gone; he felt a moment of sympathy for the Indians before pushing the thought aside. If the other missions had gone as well, the gateway to Clarke was open...

And now, he thought, *the endgame can begin.*

CHAPTER THIRTY FOUR

Clarke III, Pegasus System

"Confirmation from the surface, sir," Sally said. "Three mass drivers are gone. The landing window is open!"

"Signal Colonel Boone," James ordered. "The landing force is to begin deployment; I say again, the landing force is to begin deployment."

He turned his attention back to the display, silently running through the vectors for the final time. There was now a window, a zone of space the Indians could no longer hit; the marine transports would be making their way into that window now, ready to launch landing craft as soon as they entered orbit. And the Indians couldn't do anything to stop them, unless they'd managed to emplace other ground-based defence systems on the surface without being noticed.

They'll be landing at least fifty kilometres from the colony, he thought. *But it will be enough to keep the Indian forces from intervening.*

"Colonel Boone acknowledges," Sally reported. "The marines are on their way."

Link up with the SAS, deploy light armoured forces and start the advance on the colony, James thought. He'd seen the plans, back when they'd been outlining their options. *And then force the Indians to surrender.*

He shivered. *And pray the Indians don't decide to fight to the finish*, he added, inwardly. *We might win, but destroy the colony in the process.*

The operator swallowed. "Sir," he reported. "Outposts Five, Nine and Ten are gone."

Vasanta swore. "Gone? What do you *mean*, gone?"

"They've been destroyed, sir," the operator said. "Outpost Five went off the air ten minutes ago; Outposts Nine and Ten reported that they were coming under attack before we lost contact. They have to have been taken out completely."

They must have slipped a team down to the moon, Vasanta thought. He would have thought it was impossible, but the British had evidently succeeded. There was no way the colonists could have taken out three mass driver outposts simultaneously. *Maybe they managed to get someone down to the moon before their task force arrived.*

He keyed the console, projecting a display showing the mass driver fields of fire. No matter how he looked at it, there was no way to avoid a giant blind spot; the British could funnel their ships through the blind spot and then start landing troops, without running the risk of being picked off by the mass drivers. Hell, they were probably *already* preparing to land troops. *He* wouldn't have given the defenders any time to react if *he'd* been on the opposite side.

"Very well," he said. He might be down, but he wasn't out. "Deploy a MANPAD team - no, *two* teams - into the blind spot. And then start deploying additional patrols around the colony."

"Yes, sir," the operator said.

They have to have the colony under observation, Vasanta thought. *And that means they'd have to be somewhere nearby. We could find them...*

He closed his eyes, in pain. "Order the remaining outposts to tighten their defences," he ordered, finally. The British might have taken advantage of the opportunity to slip inside the defensive lines. "They are to check the transports *carefully* before allowing them to unload."

Lillian couldn't help feeling cold as she slogged along, despite the protection of the environmental suit. Percy held her arm gently; his companion, who seemed inclined to tease him whenever he had a moment, dragged the Indian's survival ball behind him as they hurried northwards. The snow was starting to fall again, drifting down from evil-looking clouds high overhead; she felt nervous as she realised just how exposed they were. If they couldn't make it to the SAS's base camp in time, they were likely to freeze to death and die under the poisonous snow.

It was hard to keep going, despite knowing what was at stake. She honestly wasn't sure how she'd managed to endure for so long. Percy kept smiling at her, as if he thought she could make it; Lillian wasn't sure how she could tell him that she was on the verge of collapse. She just couldn't find the words. They reached the edge of the frozen ocean and turned west, heading along the shoreline; Lillian stared at the ice, wondering if there was anything interesting hidden deep down, where it was warmer. It wasn't so long ago that humanity had discovered primitive life forms under the ice of a dozen different worlds.

And the Tadpoles prefer to stay under the water, she thought, forcing her mind to stay off the walk. She'd been told, long ago, that the key to walking a long distance was not to think about just how far she had to go. *There might be an intelligent form of life under the ice.*

It wasn't a pleasant thought. Some of the settlers had taken to claiming they'd seen living creatures, half-hidden in the snow; no one believed a word of them, but there were moments when they seemed convincing. Lillian herself suspected they were nothing more than wishful thinking - it was easy to delude herself into believing a shape, briefly glimpsed, was a humanoid creature - unless the Indians had been scouting out the colony well before the uprising on Vesy. Maybe they *had* been watching from the very beginning. They certainly hadn't had any trouble establishing their outposts on the surface...

Percy squeezed her arm as the snow began to settle. Darkness was falling over Clarke III, a faint glow over the horizon reminding her of the gas giant's presence. She looked around, half-expecting to see something buried in the ground, but saw nothing. And then she looked up. A dozen shuttles were falling to the ground, landing neatly on the snowy plain. Their hatches opened as soon as they touched down, allowing a stream of armoured soldiers to flow out and take up defensive positions around the craft. They were followed by a handful of armoured vehicles, their weapons swivelling around, searching for targets, as they headed for the edge of the landing field. Percy beckoned her towards the nearest shuttle, his companion following with the Indian in his bubble. The hatch opened, revealing two more armoured men. Lillian swallowed nervously and followed Percy into the vehicle.

"I'm afraid we're going to have to check your ID," one of the armoured men said, once the hatch had closed. "Get your suit off and into the next room."

Lillian nodded and did as she was told.

Percy was privately impressed that Lillian had managed to keep going, even though she was a naval crewwoman who probably hadn't done more exercise than the bare minimum demanded by regulations every week. It would not have been particularly easy for her to keep going, but she'd made it. Watching her nervous face as she removed her suit and walked into the next compartment was more than he could bear, yet he had no choice. All he could do was make his own report and hope that Lillian didn't run into any more trouble.

"She's a keeper," Lewis said, as they hurried through a different hatch. "You could do worse."

"Thank you," Percy said, dryly. He straightened to attention as he saw Colonel Boone. It had been months since they'd last met on Vesy, but he'd come to respect the Para. "Lieutenant Percy Schneider reporting, sir."

"Pleased to see you again, Lieutenant," Boone said. He turned his gaze to Lewis. "And Sergeant Lewis. It's been a long time since Libya."

"Yes, sir," Lewis said.

He cleared his throat. "We took out the mass driver outpost, sir," he reported. "To the best of our knowledge, there were no enemy survivors, but we didn't stick around to check."

"Understood," Boone said. He glanced from one to the other. "I've heard from the other two troops. They were both successful in completing their mission."

Which we knew already, Percy thought, darkly. The landing force wouldn't have been able to make it through if one of the targeted mass drivers had survived. *And you wouldn't have directed us to rendezvous with the shuttles if you hadn't been planning to land.*

"We're currently securing the landing zone and making preparations to advance towards the colony," Boone continued. "I'd recommend that you both got some sleep and then rejoin your unit."

And in my case, I'm not sure which one is *my unit*, Percy thought, numbly. *Do I rejoin the Royal Marines or stick with the SAS*?

"Understood, sir," Lewis said. "I assume we will be bivouacked with the marines?"

"We're setting up tents now, but you might be better off snatching a couple of racks in the command vehicle," Boone said. "Miss Turner will have to answer hundreds of questions from the intelligence staff, then she will probably be shipped back to the carrier until the end of the war. I don't see any further use for her on the surface."

Percy cleared his throat. "She was technically exiled to Clarke, sir," he said. He'd intended to speak to Admiral Fitzwilliam after the war, but the shooting wasn't over yet. "Can you make a note in her file that she didn't leave willingly?"

Boone gave him a sharp look. "I read her file," he said, finally. "She won't be blamed for leaving the planet, at least not for the moment. Afterwards...well, we can settle her precise legal status later."

"Thank you, sir," Percy said.

"Go get some rest," Boone ordered. "I'll see you are both redeployed in the morning."

Lillian hadn't really expected gentle treatment from the newcomers, but she was surprised, despite herself, at just how cautious they were. Her fingerprints were taken, her blood was sampled, her retina patterns were scanned...by the time they ordered her to strip naked and scan every last centimetre of her body, she was starting to feel more than a little exposed, as if she no longer had any secrets worth keeping. Afterwards, clad in a dressing gown, she was led into yet another compartment, where three intelligence officers were waiting for her.

"I'm sorry about your treatment," the first one said. His nametag was blank, as if he intended to keep his identity a secret. Lillian mentally tagged him Alpha. "However, we have to be careful."

"I understand," Lillian said. "The Indians could have bugged me."

"They didn't, as far as we can tell," the second one said. "You were clean."

"And cleaner too, after that examination," Lillian muttered. "What do you want to know?"

"Everything," Alpha said. He took a breath. "I have been ordered to inform you that you are not facing any charges, particularly not as a collaborator. Given the circumstances, you did all you reasonably could to resist and, of course, you played a vital role in the destruction of one of their mass drivers. Indeed, I believe you will be in line for a medal when news reaches home."

"That's good," Lillian said. She wasn't sure she believed him. She'd never had any real contact with counter-intelligence officers, but she'd seen too many movies where they were portrayed as finger-stroking moustache-twirling power brokers, willing to lie, cheat and steal to get *someone* pinned down as the enemy spy. "What would you like me to tell you first?"

"Let's start with the simple question," Beta said. "What happened to Governor Brown and the military personnel on the colony?"

Lillian frowned. "The Governor was taken away two days after the colony was occupied," she said. Majors had gone to some trouble to establish the point. "At least, he was never seen after that date. The military personnel were captured as POWs; I don't think any of them were ever returned to the colony. I don't know what happened to them."

Beta scowled. "Do you think they might have been murdered?"

Lillian hesitated. "I don't *think* so."

"You don't *think* so," Alpha repeated. "Why?"

Lillian took a moment to think, putting her words in order. "The Indians took considerable precautions to prevent atrocities," she said, "or even simple harassment. We - all the women on the colony - were told to report any soldier who tried to grope us, let alone rape us. I think they were serious, because they actually kept a distance from us when we weren't being put to work. We wouldn't have been able to put that transmitter together if they'd watched us constantly."

Alpha met her eyes. "And your point?"

"Murdering surrendered POWs isn't much better than raping civilians," Lillian said. "Why would they take precautions against one while happily committing the other?"

"They may have considered it a disciplinary issue," Beta suggested. "Troops who harass local women might not be very good for hammering the enemy, when the time comes to actually fight."

Lillian cleared her throat. "I've told you all I *know*," she said, tartly. "What other questions do you have?"

"The Indian commander," Alpha said. "What's your impression of him?"

"I've only seen him a few times," Lillian warned. "I always had the impression he didn't like us very much, but he could have been trying to present an aggressive facade."

"Perhaps," Alpha mused. "Do you think he would see sense and surrender?"

"I don't know," Lillian said. Was there actually a point to the question? "I certainly couldn't tell you anything for sure."

It didn't get better as Alpha and Beta - the third man said nothing, merely watched - bounced question after question off her. Sometimes, they repeated themselves; sometimes, they asked the same question in a different way. Lillian suspected the SAS had done a better job of extracting information from her; they, at least, had understood that she wouldn't know everything, even though she'd been living on Clarke for nearly a year. By the time Alpha finally called a halt, her head was pounding savagely.

"You'll be shipped back to the carrier this evening," Alpha informed her. "Your legal status will be sorted out after the war, according to the Colonel, but you won't suffer from being taken off the moon now. It was not your choice, was it?"

"No, sir," Lillian said. She took a breath. "Can I see Percy again, before I go?"

Alpha and Beta exchanged glances. "He's currently sleeping," Alpha said, after a moment. "But if you wish to record a message, you may do so."

Lillian nodded. "Thank you, sir."

"I believe there's nothing to be gained by remaining on the ship," Penny said. "Please could I be attached to the Royal Marines?"

Captain Naiser hesitated, noticeably. "I *am* detaching my marines to join the forces on the surface," he said, "now there's a reasonably secure landing site. *However*, your safety cannot be guaranteed."

"I thought that was always true," Penny said, waspishly. Stevenson had evidently agreed; he'd managed to wrangle a transfer from *Warspite* to *Theodore Smith* once the major confrontation was over and she hadn't heard anything from him since. "I could have been killed in the last engagement."

"You wouldn't be targeted specifically," Captain Naiser said. He looked at her for a long moment. "Have you run this brainstorm past *Major* Hadfield?"

"Yes, sir," Penny said. There was no point in trying to lie. "He told me that I could be attached to his unit, provided I stayed out of the way."

"There's no specific provision for reporters on the surface," the captain warned. "You might find yourself helping to carry weapons and supplies."

Penny nodded. The days when reporters had been neutral observers were long over - if they'd ever truly existed at all. She'd been warned, more than once, that *some* parties considered reporters their natural enemy and targeted them specifically. Terrorists, in particular, loathed reporters for being honest about their atrocities. And, being young and female, her chances of survival if she fell into their hands were minimal.

"I understand, sir," she said. "I'm willing to take the risk."

"Then you may join the marines on their shuttle," the captain said. "Just bear in mind that Major Hadfield *is* in charge. If he says jump, I expect you to be up in the air before asking how high."

"Yes, sir," Penny said. She didn't doubt that the Major was in charge for a moment. "I won't forget."

"So there's no hope of an internal uprising?"

"No, sir," Captain Stryker's hologram said. "The colonists are unarmed. They might get a few blows in, but the Indians are quite solidly established. The colonists would be slaughtered if they tried to rise up."

"I see," James said. He looked at Colonel Boone's hologram. "Are you ready to advance?"

"Yes, sir," Boone said. "We've landed the Royal Marines and 3 Para; our point detachments are already taking up position along the direct route to the colony. The Indians have not, so far, attempted to challenge us."

"So they're conserving their strength?" James asked. "Or planning a counterattack?"

"Unknown," Boone said. "We did trade fire with a handful of patrols - we think they were trying to get eyeballs on us - but they beat feet when we engaged them. I think we will be ready to move our main force within seven hours, perhaps less. Logistics are a pain in the ass" - he shrugged - "but when are they ever anything else?"

"Never," James said. He met the colonel's eyes. "They haven't responded to my message, Colonel. If they were planning to surrender, you'd think they'd do it by now."

"Unless they're planning to make a last stand," Boone said. "They *have* built up quite a network of defences, sir. Breaking through them would be costly in the absence of orbital bombardment."

James nodded. "You have tactical command, Colonel," he said, firmly. There was no point in trying to direct operations himself, not from the giant supercarrier. "You know the objective. Give the bastards hell."

"Yes, sir," Boone said. "They *could* be hoping for reinforcements - or relief."

"I know," James said.

He glanced at the display. The tramline leading to Vesy remained undisturbed, but who knew how long that would last? There was another enemy carrier on the far side, with a handful of undamaged escorts. It wouldn't be too hard for the Indians to bring her into the Pegasus System and try to reverse the verdict of the last engagement.

"Finish it as quickly as you can, commensurate with protecting the lives of the colonists," he said. "We may not have much time."

CHAPTER THIRTY FIVE

Clarke III, Pegasus System

"They're definitely advancing towards our position," the operator warned. "We were unable to get a team close to their landing zone, even in the blizzard."

Vasanta nodded, curtly. The British had definitely planned the operation carefully. They'd already managed to unload at least two thousand soldiers, all prepared for fighting in the inhospitable climate. He still had them outnumbered, but he was pinned down by the need to defend the colony against their attack. Deploying even a smaller force to engage them would make it harder to hold out.

"Let them come into artillery range," he ordered, finally. There was no way to avoid a brutal encounter that would probably end badly, but at least he could bleed them. "And pull back the outer patrols. Let them come right to the edge of the pre-targeted zone."

"Yes, sir," the operator said.

"And make sure the colonists remain under firm control," Vasanta added. They'd already been herded into the main hall and told to stay there, under pain of death. "We don't want any trouble in the rear."

"Welcome back, Percy," Drake said.

Percy nodded. "I was surprised you wanted me," he said. The SAS didn't *need* him any longer, not now they'd been on the moon themselves for two months. "I was expecting to be ordered into the manpower pool."

"We couldn't do that to you," Jimmy said, dryly. "Besides, we still need to clear those observation posts on the mountains. It's all hands on deck."

Drake cleared his throat. "The Donkey Wallopers" - the Royal Artillery - "have been setting up long-range guns behind the perimeter," he said. "We're going to close with the enemy posts and call down fire to obliterate them. Not particularly glamorous, I must admit, but something we can actually do."

Percy smiled in understanding. The SAS troopers *hated* the thought of going to the rear and doing nothing, even though they'd been relieved by 6 Troop. Drake had probably complained to his superior until the team had been given something to do - and, he had to admit, it was something that had to be done. The Indian observation posts were a deadly threat to the advancing force.

"I'm ready," he said. "When do we go?"

"Grab your suit and weapons," Drake ordered. "We're going to be borrowing an ATV for the first part of the journey; they'll let us off near the mountains."

"Hopefully not *too* close," Lewis said. "The Indians will be watching for us."

"True," Drake said. He threw Percy a sharp glance. "What are you waiting for, Percy? Grab your shit and let's go!"

———

Penny wasn't sure what she'd expected from the landing zone. She'd been on three military bases in her time - four, if one counted Fort Knight on Vesy - and they'd all struck her as organised chaos. The landing zone was, if anything, even worse: a handful of vehicles, half-buried in the snow, dozens of shuttles landing, unloading and taking off and hundreds of soldiers in armoured suits being rounded up and moved to the jump-off points. She was so confused, just *looking* at the scene, that it was a relief when one of Colonel Boone's officers met her and led the way to the Colonel's command vehicle. Inside, she could remove her helmet and relax, slightly.

"This isn't quite what I'd prefer," Boone admitted, when he saw her. "If I had a completely free choice, I'd prefer to command the operation from a hole in the ground, but...well, I need the vehicle."

"Thank you," Penny said. She had the nasty feeling the Indians would have thrown a missile at the command vehicle if they'd been able to locate it. It was an unpleasant thought, but there was no way she could go back to *Warspite* now. "I'll just stand against the wall and say nothing."

Boone surprised her by smiling. "I've already issued the orders," he said, as two of his aides hurried out of the compartment. "All I can do now is wait and see what happens."

Penny blinked. "You're not going to command the battle?"

"From here, it would be micromanaging," Boone said. He shrugged. "I can set overall priorities, and the overall engagement plan, but not steer each individual unit."

He pointed to the wall-mounted display. "Do you know how to read a military map?"

"No, sir," Penny said. It wasn't entirely true, but it was better to have him explain it to her in tedious detail rather than miss an important point. Besides, in her experience, men liked explaining things to women. It made them feel useful. "What's happening?"

"My advance forces - a handful of Paras - are probing towards the edge of the Indian defences," Boone said. "They've been digging trenches and emplacing heavy weapons in a dozen locations, each one a potential hazard to my forces. However, we don't know how many of them are actually *manned.* We may not know until our forces come into range and the Indians open fire."

Penny shivered. Inside the command vehicle, where it was warm and dry, it was hard to remember that the soldiers were forced to fight in a poisonous atmosphere. The merest rip or tear in their suits would kill them, if they didn't manage to patch it quickly enough. Merely being outside for a few minutes had been bad enough; she felt a flicker of sympathy for the men who had to march, fight and *sleep* in their suits. She really *didn't* want to think about the plumbing.

"Our follow-up forces will advance slowly towards the colony," Boone added, drawing out a line on the map. "Unfortunately, our approach route is far too predictable; there simply aren't many paths that can handle our vehicles. Once we isolate the manned defensive bunkers and take out the observation posts, we'll secure the high ground and ready ourselves for the final assault on the colony."

"The colony doesn't look very big," Penny observed. "Or am I missing something?"

"Most of it is below the ground," Boone noted. "But you're right. It isn't a very big colony, certainly nowhere near the size of Luna City. It will be a major headache if we have to storm it..."

"The colonists might be killed in the crossfire," Penny realised.

"Correct," Boone said. His voice was flat, but Penny was sure she could hear a note of horror buried within his tone. "I'm hoping the Indians will see sense and surrender before it gets to that point. They're not terrorists; they'll be treated as POWs and returned to their people, once the war is over."

"And they're trapped," Penny said. "Aren't they?"

"Unless they have something completely new buried under the ice, yes they're trapped," Boone said. He jabbed a finger at the map. "*That*... is the very definition of an untenable position. They can't withdraw, they can't hold out long enough to be relieved and if we have to storm the complex hundreds of innocent civilians will be hurt or killed."

Penny eyed him. "If you were in that position," she said, "what would *you* do?"

Boone hesitated. "Surrender, probably," he said, finally. "Maybe, if there was something to be gained by holding out, I'd resist, but here there's literally *nothing*. India's reputation will take a beating - another beating - if the settlers get killed. Their best bet would be to concede defeat and throw in the towel."

"And if they don't?"

"Then we have to beat them," Boone said, briskly. He glanced at a console as a red icon popped into existence. "And now they're starting to fire back."

The Indian observation post didn't look like *much*, but Percy had the uncomfortable feeling he would have missed it if he'd come to the mountains blind. It was nothing more than a small tent, half-buried in the snow; the camouflage netting concealed the handful of Indians inside from orbital surveillance. But it was too far up the mountain for the SAS to approach without being detected.

"Get target lock," Drake ordered.

Percy pointed the laser at a spot just behind the observation post, careful not to let the laser beam rest on the observation post itself. The laser beam was invisible to the naked eye, but the Indians might have rigged their netting to react if someone shone a laser beam at their position. He took a long moment to make sure it was firmly in place, then nodded to Drake.

"Target locked, sir," he said. He'd been told that the SAS microburst transmitters were almost undetectable - and there were a handful of EW satellites in orbit broadcasting random signals to make it harder for the Indians to track the British troops - but it was still better to keep their transmissions to a bare minimum. "Ready."

Drake sent the signal. Percy gritted his teeth and kept a sharp eye on the laser, knowing that the long-range guns had already fired a salvo of shells towards their location. The Indians *might* have a set of guns of their own ready to fire a counterbattery, but it was already too late to save their outpost. Moments later, the first shell splashed down on top of the laser pointer and exploded, destroying the observation point. The remaining four were nothing more than overkill.

"Target destroyed," Drake sent. "No survivors; I say again, no survivors."

The team hurried forward, slipping up the mountain and watching carefully for other Indian positions. Shellfire flared out in the distance; the Indians, it seemed, were trying to shell the British positions, while the British were hastily returning the favour. Percy tried to keep track of the battle through the brief snippets he heard over the command network, even as they clambered into a place where they could call down more fire on Indian positions. It *sounded* as though the Indians were being driven back...

"They have to be mad," he muttered to himself. The latest report informed him that the light tanks were making their way through the pass. They'd be at the colony itself within hours if the Indians didn't manage to stop them. "They can't win."

"They may intend to claw us thoroughly as they go down," Drake muttered back. Another round of shells screeched overhead, coming down amidst the Indian position. "Or they're simply reluctant to surrender as long as they have something to fight with."

Percy shuddered, watching the remains of another Indian outpost. A soldier was lying on the ground, his suit torn open, his body twitching frantically. There was nothing they could do for him, even if they'd been close enough to intervene. He'd already breathed far too much of the poisonous atmosphere. A handful of his comrades, who had clearly been on patrol before the shells slammed down, were making their escape, heading back to the colony. They probably knew as well as he did, Percy reasoned, that there was no real hope of holding out, but where else could they go? It wasn't as if they were on Earth.

They'll run out of air sooner rather than later, he thought, savagely. The SAS had had problems extracting a breathable atmospheric mix and *they'd* prepared specifically for Clarke. *If they run off into the wild, we might stumble across the bodies a hundred years from now.*

"They're trying to make a stand at the pass," Boone observed. Penny had slipped to the rear of the vehicle as his aides returned, but he kept tossing comments her way. She had a private feeling that they actually helped to gather *his* thoughts, yet it was hard to care. All of her observations would be going into her post-war book. "We're going to need to clear the way before we can proceed."

He glanced at one of his aides. "Inform the Royal Marines I expect them to move up to support the Paras, then start planning a heavy bombardment of the Indian trenches," he ordered. His tone admitted of no doubts about the outcome. "I want them smashed flat before we advance."

"Aye, sir," the aide said.

Penny nodded to herself. The Indian outer defence line was already being weakened; now, they'd break through and ram their way towards the colony itself. And then...she'd never been particularly religious, not after the floods that had battered her country, killed her mother and forced her to flee to a refugee camp, but now she found herself praying that the Indians would see sense and surrender. They couldn't hold out for long.

And thousands of people might be killed, she thought, numbly. These days, it was always the hostage-takers who were blamed when the hostages were killed in a botched rescue mission, not the would-be rescuers. India's reputation would be lost forever. *Their name will be mud for a hundred years.*

"They're calling in the bombardment now," Lance Corporal Fisher said. He sounded pleased, too pleased. The Royal Marine tankers hadn't had a chance to test themselves against a real enemy in years. "We're going in immediately afterwards."

"Aye, sir," Driver Bob Pankhurst said. He checked his console as the Marlborough light tank readied itself for combat. "All systems go."

He smiled darkly as he rested his hands on the wheel. The Marlborough had been designed for quick deployment to trouble spots, on or off Earth, including places where the enemy might deploy everything from poison gas to biological weapons. Scaling up the seals until the tank was practically a spacecraft in its own right hadn't been hard, particularly when there had been a very real risk of deployment to an alien world. Clarke might not have been the intended destination, but so far the tanks had performed splendidly.

The ground shook, violently, as HE shells slammed down among the Indian positions. Giant fireballs rose into the air, fading slowly; another volley of shells landed, hoping to cut down the Indians who might be popping their heads back up after the first salvo. Bob didn't hate the Indians, not like he hated the terrorist scum who should all be strangled at birth, but he would sooner see them dead than his comrades. Besides, unlike most terrorists, the Indians might well be armed with weapons that could burn through the tank's armour and explode inside. They'd be dead before knowing what had hit them if that was the case.

"Go," Fisher ordered.

Bob gunned the engine and the tank roared forward, followed by the rest of the troop. Andy Perham, the gunner, hunted for targets as they charged right into the remains of the Indian position; thankfully, it looked as though the heavy weapons had been smashed by the long-range shell-fire before the tanks entered range. A handful of Indians threw down their weapons as the tankers approached them, but there was no time to take prisoners. Bob heard Fisher calling in the enemy location to the following infantry, warning them that the Indians might take up their weapons again and try to engage the Paras. They'd get roughly handled if they did, Bob was sure - the Paras were *almost* as tough as the Royal Marines - and the British would become more reluctant to take prisoners. He hoped the Indians would be smart; these days, a single fake surrender could lead to a massacre.

A flash of light shot over the tank and vanished somewhere in the dark mountains. Bob cursed and evaded rapidly as the hidden plasma cannon came into view. The Indians let rip again; Bob evaded the blast, but one of the following tanks wasn't so lucky and exploded into a colossal fireball. There was no way any of the crew could have escaped in time. Perham fired a long burst from the machine gun into the enemy position; there was a brilliant flash of white light, followed by a colossal fireball as the magnetic containment field shattered, releasing a burst of superheated plasma. An Indian, his suit blazing with white fire, staggered into view, waving his hands desperately. There was nothing anyone could do for him.

"Cut him down," Fisher ordered, quietly.

"Aye, sir," Parham said. He fired a single burst from the machine guns. The Indian disintegrated. "He's dead, sir."

Bob felt a flicker of sympathy for the Indian, then turned his attention back to the path through the mountains. An Indian tank charged at them, firing madly; he yanked the tank to one side as Parham fired back, slamming two armour-piercing shells into the Indian vehicle. It skidded to a halt, two crewmen bailing out before the vehicle exploded; he wondered, absently, why it hadn't gone up immediately as they engaged two more tanks. The Indians seemed surprised by the encounter, which puzzled him; they had to have known the British tanks were on their way.

Maybe their superiors weren't telling them anything, he thought, as the tanks punched through the final part of the defence line and paused to wait for the infantry. The command net was buzzing with news of surrendering Indians; he allowed himself, just for a moment, to hope that the war was coming to an end before a hail of missiles lanced overhead. *Some* Indians, it was clear, were still holding out. *They must not realise that they've run out of time.*

"The Paras have taken seventy prisoners," Fisher commented. "I think we banged them up a little."

"Definitely, sir," Bob said. The Royal Artillery might have softened up the Indian position, but it had been the tanks that had crushed the defenders. At least the Indian POWs - the lucky bastards - would be out of the fighting and well-treated. They'd probably see India before Bob saw Britain. "What now?"

Fisher hesitated, checking the updates. "We're going to ready ourselves for the final push," he said. "Once the reserves catch up, we should be able to strike hard at the Indians and end the war in a single blow."

CHAPTER THIRTY SIX

Clarke III, Pegasus System

"We've taken seventy-nine prisoners," an aide reported. "The reserves are taking them into custody now."

Penny leaned forward as images started to appear on the display. A handful of suited men, holding their hands in the air, watched at gunpoint by more suited men. It was hard to tell the difference between British and Indian soldiers; she hoped, watching the display, that the soldiers themselves could tell the difference. Standardising everything made a great deal of sense, Percy had assured her, but there were times when it was a menace.

"Move them back to the POW camp," Boone ordered. "Keep them well away from the landing zone, just in case."

"Aye, sir," the aide said.

Boone cleared his throat. "Move the remaining tanks through the gap, then prepare to advance to the colony," he added. "Try and raise the Indians again. Repeat the standard surrender broadcast."

"Aye, sir," the aide said.

Penny blinked in surprise as Boone glanced at her. "The Indians have a number of other outposts, but they're immaterial now," he explained. "Once the colony falls, those outposts can either surrender or be left to starve. Either one would suit us."

"Yes, sir," Penny said. "Why aren't they surrendering?"

"I wish I knew," Boone said. "But all we can do at the moment is press the offensive."

He turned his attention back to the map display; Penny followed his gaze. The Indians had dug hundreds of trenches around the colony, but they couldn't hope to hold out when he could rain shells on their heads before sending in the groundpounders. Honour, she was sure, had been more than satisfied. No one in their right mind would expect the Indians to do more, now the British had landed troops and cut the garrison off from all hope of rescue. But the Indians were *still* not surrendering...

"Bombarding the trenches will almost certainly do considerable damage to the colony itself," Boone mused. "They may be hoping we'd refrain from hammering their positions before advancing to the attack."

Penny eyed him. "And are you going to refrain?"

"I can't," Boone said. "We *cannot* set a precedent of allowing human shields to impact on our operations. We'd only see far too many more hostage situations."

"That's a little harsh on the hostages," Penny observed, sharply.

Boone shrugged. "Once you pay the *Danegeld*, you never get rid of the Dane," he countered, sharply. "I don't like it any more than you do, but the Indians cannot be allowed to set such a precedent."

"Even if it means killing our own people," Penny said.

"Yes," Boone said. "Even if it means killing our own people."

Percy couldn't help feeling as though he'd come home as the troop scrambled up the mountain, finally returning to the original observation point they'd chosen when they'd first reached the moon. The Indians, it seemed, were scrambling to defend the colony; troops and armoured vehicles were streaming into the trenches from all directions, while a handful of light aircraft - specially adapted to fly in the poisonous atmosphere - were buzzing overhead.

"They don't look as though they're preparing to surrender," he said.

"No, they don't," Drake agreed. He cleared his throat. "Snipers, start your work; everyone else, cover them."

"Aye, sir," Lewis said.

Percy nodded to himself as he peered down at the colony. *All* of the SAS men were excellent shots, but their snipers were practically inhuman.

They were three kilometres from the colony, yet they were able to pick off officers and men with ease. The Indians would probably guess where the snipers were, eventually, but taking them out would prove a major challenge. By now, it was unlikely they had any patrols close enough to intervene.

And sniping at them has to ruin their morale, he thought. *But how long can they hold out?*

Governor Brown had been a very simple man, Vasanta considered. His office had been very simple, decorated only with a picture of the man's grown up kids and a portrait of the British Royal Family. Vasanta privately approved - he preferred the Spartan design himself - but right now he suspected he could have used a distraction. No matter what he did, there was no way to prevent the British from attacking the colony at will.

He stared down at the map, silently calculating how quickly the British could advance into the vacuum. By his most optimistic assessment, it would only be a few hours before they were in position to attack directly - and he couldn't hope to hold them off. Morale, already low, had collapsed completely when the British had started sniping at his men; a number of officers were already dead, further weakening his grip on events. If he hadn't expended most of his ammunition earlier...

There's no time to worry about what might have been, he thought, sharply. The whole concept of the war had clearly been fatally flawed - never mind that it would have been classed as a brilliant scheme if it had actually succeeded - and India had lost. He was in command, he was expected to fight to the last...

And it will only get my men killed, along with a number of British civilians, he reminded himself. There was no point in trying to avoid the truth. *If we hold out, the British will kill us all. And it will be for nothing.*

He cursed under his breath. He'd been told about the political rationale for the war and he agreed with it, but the war was lost. Any hope of being acknowledged as a Great Power, let alone as the sole owners of Pegasus and Vesy, had been lost with the war. To continue to fight would merely lead to a disaster, all the more so as the British would be unable to overlook the death of so many of their people. They might not be able to attack India itself, but they'd damn well take India's extra-solar possessions and bring immense pressure to bear against the Indian economy. No, the war was lost - and the sooner it came to an end, the better.

And that only left pride. He didn't want to surrender. It was a point of pride in the Indian military that no officer had surrendered since the final Indo-Pakistan War and he had no wish to be the one who broke that streak. But what was pride when measured against the loss of his men and the terrible punishment the outside world would heap on India? Who gave a damn about a loser? They could have gotten away with it, he told himself, if they'd actually won. Losing, on the other hand...

He tasted bile in his mouth. The government would start looking for a scapegoat - he'd met the Prime Minister once and he had a fairly good idea of the man's character - and *he* would almost certainly be their choice. There would be a show trial; he probably wouldn't be executed, not when the military might take exception to someone being blamed completely, but he'd certainly be forced out of the service. His wife and children would be outcasts; his sons would probably be forced to leave the service too. And then...he'd be expected to eat his own gun.

It was tempting, very tempting, just to dig in and force the British to come for him. He'd be dead long before any of the negative consequences struck his country. But that was a selfish attitude, one that revolted him even as it rose up in his mind. The only thing he could do now was surrender and take the blame on himself. Who knew? Perhaps he'd live long enough to be able to write his own account of the war.

He rose and strode into the command centre. "Lieutenant," he ordered. "Raise the British Commander. Inform him that I wish to surrender."

"Aye, sir," his aide said.

Vasanta turned to another officer. "Captain, contact the trenches," he ordered. "They are to fire only in direct self-defence; I say again, they are to fire in direct self-defence. Once we agree on surrender terms, they are to put down their weapons and ready themselves to go into the British camps."

The captain looked pale, but nodded. Vasanta wondered, sardonically, just what *he* had to worry about. There was no way a junior officer would wind up taking the blame for the whole disaster, even though there would be quite enough of it to go around. But he should make sure of it.

"Make a final entry in the occupation log," he ordered. "The decision to surrender was mine and mine alone. I consulted with no one else before issuing the orders."

"Colonel," the Lieutenant said. "I have Colonel Boone on the line for you."

Vasanta took a long breath as the British officer's face appeared on the display. "Colonel," he said. There was no point in wasting time with pleasantries. "Please state your terms for the surrender."

Boone studied him thoughtfully. "Your men are to disarm themselves and wait to be collected," he ordered. "You may destroy your classified files and encryption codes, but everything else is to be left intact - including the remaining mass drivers and industrial equipment. All of that is to be considered spoils of war."

Which will not look good when I get home, Vasanta thought, ruefully. The plan to stake a partial claim to the system had floundered too. *But there's no choice.*

"Very well," he said, finally.

"We will endeavour to return your men to India as quickly as possible," Boone added. "It would be greatly appreciated, however, if you ensured they behaved themselves. Rounding up the shipping to get them home will not be easy."

"I understand," Vasanta said. He wanted to say something else - to congratulate the British officer, perhaps, or to curse him - but the words wouldn't come. "I'll see you when you arrive at the colony."

"We won?"

"It looks that way," Boone confirmed, once the Indian officer's face had vanished from the display. "But accepting so many surrenders isn't going to be easy."

He keyed his console. "Move the Paras forward with orders to accept the surrenders," he said. "They are to ensure the Indians are disarmed and that the colony's vital installations and locations are secured. If necessary, the Indian barracks are to be turned into makeshift POW camps."

"Aye, sir," his aide said.

"And signal Admiral Fitzwilliam," Boone added. "The Indians have surrendered."

Penny breathed a sigh of relief. She'd lived through the war - and so had Percy, unless he'd been killed in the last few minutes. There'd been forty casualties, as far as she knew, but none of them had listed as being SAS. She shuddered as it struck her that Percy might not be *listed* as being SAS...the thought chilled her before she pushed the sensation aside. If Percy had died, she'd hear about it soon enough. God knew they were each the other's next-of-kin.

She looked at Boone. "Doesn't the Indian CO have to surrender to you personally?"

"Not if I can avoid it," Boone said. "I'll be moving into the colony shortly, and I suppose I should meet him in person, but I'm not looking forward to it. I'd be too tempted to punch him in the nose."

Penny blinked in surprise. "Why?"

"Because he risked too many civilian lives," Boone said, simply. "There is no way I can consider that the act of a honourable man."

The remainder of Percy's day, once they'd scrambled down from the mountain, passed in a blur. There were only a few hundred Paras near the colony when the Indians surrendered, so the SAS troopers found themselves attached to 3 Para and assigned to guarding over seven thousand Indian POWs. No one had anticipated taking *quite* so many prisoners so quickly, Percy discovered; the Paras found themselves searching the Indian barracks, then converting them into makeshift POW holding facilities. If the Indians hadn't brought so many ration bars, he had the nasty feeling that *feeding* the prisoners would have been impossible. By the time they were finally allowed to enter the colony itself, it was a very definite relief.

"I would prefer to give my surrender to Colonel Boone," the Indian CO said, stiffly.

"I'm his deputy," a Para officer said, curtly. He cleared his throat. "I am obliged to inform you that your officers may not keep their sidearms, but they will be issued stunners. They will also be held accountable for any unrest, rioting or attempts to break out of the barracks by your soldiers. As there is literally nowhere to go, I assume you will be able to convince them that trying to escape will probably get them killed even if they're not shot."

The Indian CO glared at him, then nodded reluctantly. Percy kept one hand on his rifle as the officers surrendered their sidearms - some of them looked as if they still wanted to fight - and were issued with stunners. *He* would have preferred not to let them have *any* weapons, even the relatively harmless stunners, but it made a certain amount of sense. *They* could get the blame for any brutalising of the POWs.

If the POWs don't blame them for getting them into shit, he thought, as the final officer was issued a stunner. He'd had extensive briefings on POW camps; it wasn't uncommon for soldiers to turn on their officers, particularly if the officers had been staggeringly unpopular, and try to kill them. Some of the officers even had to be put into protective custody for their own safety. *And they may not be the only ones.*

The Indian CO sighed. "There were nineteen British citizens who accepted the offer of Indian citizenship," he said. "They should receive the same level of protection."

Collaborators, Percy thought. He suspected, thanks to Lillian's debrief, that he could put names to them all. *They should be shot.*

"They will be held separately," the Para said, firmly. "Their precise legal status, however, has yet to be determined."

Percy wasn't too surprised when he was assigned to take command of the guard the collaborators, supervising a couple of other soldiers who'd been separated from their units. The collaborators - eleven men, eight women - didn't put up a fuss as they were marched into the brig; they assumed, probably correctly, that they were likely to be torn apart by their fellow citizens, now the war was over. Percy kept a sharp eye on them, carefully matching names to faces; there was no way, he knew, to know what would happen to the genuine collaborators once they were shipped back home. Perhaps they'd simply be sent to India...

He looked up as several men entered the corridor. "We want them," the leader said, gesturing to the brig. "Hand them over."

Percy shook his head, firmly. "They have to be given a fair trial," he said. Lillian had told him that far too many colonists had been forced into limited collaboration; there was no way they could allow a lynching without causing further problems. "And that is what they will receive."

"I didn't risk my life to get a message out just so they could live," the man snapped. Percy frowned. Majors? The man who'd built the transmitter? "They need to die!"

"We got your message," Percy said. The man's eyes opened wide. "You did well.

"*Lillian* did well," the man said. "She...did they kill her?"

"She's fine," Percy said. Was Majors in love with her? He hoped not. "We took her to one of the ships. The appropriate legal authorities will decide what happens to her afterwards."

"That's good," Majors said. "But we still need to kill them..."

Percy hefted his rifle. "I understand the impulse," he said. "But right now, you cannot kill them. Let them have a fair trial."

"I'll be writing to my MP about this," Majors snapped.

"You should, sir," Percy said. "But for the moment, you need to leave."

He watched Majors go, feeling oddly sorry for the man. He'd gone to considerable lengths to get a message out, even though it hadn't gone the way he thought. Majors had found a way to resist despite the near-total control the Indians had held over the colony. To him, the collaborators had to be worse than dirt. They needed to die!

"Percy," Penny called.

For a moment, Percy was sure he was hearing things. Penny had been on *Warspite*, hadn't she? And then he turned round and saw her standing at the door, looking...older, somehow.

"Penny," he said, shaking his head. "What are you doing here?"

"Reporting," Penny said. She looked past him. "Are these the collaborators?"

"I don't think you're allowed to interview them," Percy said. "But at least it's safer down here now."

Penny stuck out her tongue. "I think I saw Hamish somewhere around," she said. "I'll go look him up in an hour."

"Just remember he may be on duty," Percy warned. "And I'd wait for a few days before you try to interview anyone else."

"In total," Sally reported, "we have rounded up eight thousand prisoners, mainly soldiers."

"Ouch," James said. Looking after them all would be a headache, shipping them to Cromwell - let alone back to India - would be a logistics nightmare. Maybe the Indians could be induced to supply the shipping, once the war was formally over. "Can we support them for the moment?"

"Yes, sir," Sally said. "They'll be strictly on ration bars, but they'll survive."

Cruel and unusual punishment, James thought. *He* would have hated a steady diet of ration bars, even if they were cheap, easy to produce and capable of supporting human life. *But they don't have a choice.*

"Very well," he said. "I..."

He broke off as an alarm sounded. "Report!"

"Admiral, we picked up a FLASH signal," an operator reported. "The second carrier just jumped through the tramline. She's advancing on our position."

CHAPTER THIRTY SEVEN

Pegasus System

"General," Captain Ajit said. "The garrison has fallen."

Anjeet scowled. "Are you sure?"

He cursed under his breath. Three days of frantic repair work, three days of shuffling trained and experienced crewmen from the damaged ships to the warships he hoped could be taken back into the Pegasus System; three days...it clearly hadn't been enough to save the garrison before the British landed. And if Clarke III had fallen, along with the soldiers, the war itself was effectively lost.

"Yes, General," Ajit said. He didn't sound very pleased to be questioned on his own bridge, but Anjeet found it hard to care. "The garrison's current status has been confirmed by stealthed recon platforms. It surrendered seven hours ago."

"I see," Anjeet said, finally. "Continue on our current course."

Ajit's face darkened, but he did as he was told. Anjeet watched him for a moment, then turned his attention back to the display. One damaged carrier - the British engineers might be wonder-workers, but there were limits - and twelve smaller warships, presumably including the cruiser that had targeted *Viraat*. This time, *nothing* would be able to sneak up on his carrier; this time, he'd have the firepower advantage and crush the enemy carrier like a bug.

"We will engage the British as soon as we enter firing range," he ordered. "Prepare your crews for deployment."

"Yes, sir," Ajit said. "And then what?"

Anjeet blinked. "Captain?"

"We might be able to beat the British ships," Ajit pointed out, smoothly. "And then...what?"

"We recover Clarke III," Anjeet snapped.

"We have no landing force," Ajit said. "We'd have to arm crewmen and dump them on the planet, sending them right into the teeth of a tough and professional force that has already hammered us once. And even if we did succeed in retaking the world, we'd still effectively have lost the war. The British have *five* more carriers. We have no other."

Anjeet turned his gaze towards the display. The remains of his former carrier were still drifting, inching their way slowly out of the system. He was mildly surprised the British hadn't put a prize crew on the hulk, but they'd probably reasoned she was worthless at the moment. Even if he recovered *Viraat*, it would take longer to repair her than it would take to build a whole new fleet carrier.

"The honour of India is at stake, Captain," he said, finally. "We must not be seen to lose."

"Very well," Ajit said. He frowned. "It will be at least six hours before we enter engagement range, General. Might I suggest you get some sleep?"

Get the hell off my bridge, Anjeet translated, mentally. It was hard to blame the Captain; Anjeet had broken military protocol quite badly. *And I do need to rest.*

"Wake me the moment the situation changes," he ordered, turning towards the hatch. "We must not lose this battle, Captain."

"I have no intention of losing, General," Ajit said.

"It's the second carrier, sir," Sally said. "She'll be within engagement range in six hours."

James cursed under his breath. The Indians - deliberately or otherwise - had created one hell of a moral dilemma. He could fall back and wait for reinforcements, preserving *Theodore Smith* and the remaining ships of the task force, if he was prepared to sacrifice everyone on Clarke

III. There were two thousand Paras and Royal Marines on the surface, along with a thousand civilians and eight thousand Indian POWs. The Indians, of course, would take up weapons again...he'd need to refight his way into the system a second time, if the war continued.

But if I stand and fight, I may lose, he thought.

"Order *Warspite* to prepare a second ambush," he ordered, although - judging by the reports from the ship watching the tramline - it was unlikely the Indians would fall for the same trick twice. They might be practically shouting their exact location to the entire system, but they were pumping out so many radar pulses that a stealthed ship would probably be detected before it got into firing range. "And prime our ships for an engagement."

He shook his head, bitterly. There was no choice; he had to stop the Indians, even at the cost of his entire force. Admiral Smith had rammed an alien superdreadnaught; James had watched, helpless to intervene, as two massive starships had died in fire. Now, ramming *Theodore Smith* into the Indian carrier would constitute a victory, of sorts. Britain had more carriers; the Indians had none. But he didn't want it to end that way.

"And warn Colonel Boone that his men may have to prepare to defend the colony," he added, bitterly. They'd done such a good job of clearing the mass drivers that the Indians could simply land in the same blindspot themselves. "If he thinks it possible, he and his men are to go to ground."

"Yes, sir," Sally said. "What about the POWs?"

James refused to even *begin* to consider ordering a massacre. "They can be held as long as possible," he said. There was no time to organise a parole agreement, even if the Indians were inclined to cooperate. "And then...I suppose they'll go back to their former masters."

He gritted his teeth in frustration. It was *pointless*. The Indians had to know they'd lost the war. Even if they managed to win the coming engagement, it would be so costly that they had no hope of rebuilding their navy before the next carrier arrived. Hell, China or even Russia might take advantage of their weakness to stick a knife in their backs. India would win a victory that might as well be a defeat.

"Record a message," he ordered. He took a long moment to organise his thoughts. "General Patel" - they'd learned the name of their opponent on Clarke III - "this is Admiral Fitzwilliam, commander of Task Force Bulldog. I will not permit you to recover this system without a fight. Our forces are evenly matched; *victory* may go to the side that has only one or two ships left. You may win this fight, General, but you will lose the war."

He took a breath. "We're both military men, General. I don't know what orders your superiors have given you" - the captured officers on Clarke had refused to discuss any contingency plans with their captors - "but you have to know that this battle is going to be disastrous for India, whoever wins. Please, for the sake of your men and country, withdraw from the system. We won't give chase, General; our objectives are merely to regain control of the territories you occupied. Leave now and bring this war to an end before you lose everything."

"Message recorded, sir," Sally said. "Do you think he'll listen?"

"I don't know," James said. "Send it."

He settled back in his chair and forced himself to wait. The Tadpoles had chosen to end the war, only to have a rogue faction launch a final strike at Earth. Would the Indians be so foolish? Cold logic told him they'd back down, but cold logic would have failed to predict so many wars in human history. And who knew just who was in charge on Earth? It wouldn't be the first time a powerful politician or a radical faction had pushed an entire nation to the brink of defeat.

No tricks any longer, he thought. *No way for us to offset their power; no way for them to do it to us. Just a brutal slogging match that will cost them everything, even if they win. And they have to know it.*

Anjeet jerked awake as the communicator buzzed. "Report!"

"General, we received a message addressed to you personally," his aide said. "Do you want me to send it to your console?"

"Yes," Anjeet growled. "Now."

He listened to the message, torn between two separate feelings. The urge to just hammer the British senseless, in response to the loss of a whole carrier, was almost overwhelming. And yet, the British Admiral was correct. Anjeet might win the battle - he might lose his life, given that the carrier would attract fire from the British ships - but it would cost him the war.

Which is what Ajit said, he thought. *The British would only have to rush another fleet carrier into the war zone and then they could snap up Pegasus, Vesy and Gandhi at marginal cost.*

It was a galling thought. His orders admitted of no ambiguity; he was to defeat the British, whatever the cost. And yet, he knew that the cost would be staggeringly high. Losing two carriers would mean losing *everything*. The British would have every incentive to continue the war - victory would fall into their hands - but other powers would have a good reason to jump in. Who knew what Russia could do if she seized the Indian colonies? Or captured Pegasus and then returned the system to Britain as a goodwill gesture.

The Prime Minister would be furious, he knew. There was no way to avoid it. They'd been friends for a long time, as well as allies; the Prime Minister would see any surrender as a betrayal. But this wasn't one of the innumerable wars of the Age of Unrest, where there was no room for surrender, where it was kill or be killed. India could survive, and even prosper, without winning the war. Hell, if they backed down now, they might even manage to avoid further losses. The British wouldn't want to attack the colonies and make themselves the aggressor.

"Record," he ordered. His career was at an end. Even the Prime Minister wouldn't be able to save him. Parliament would want a scapegoat and he was the only one on hand. "Admiral Fitzwilliam. I assume you have been given authority to negotiate. Accordingly, I am prepared to withdraw from the system - and concede your authority over both Pegasus and Cromwell - in exchange for an agreement that Gandhi and our other colonies are to remain untouched and there will be no demand for reparations. If these terms are acceptable to you, I will reverse course at once.

"As a gesture of goodwill," he added, "I will slow my approach until you respond."

He keyed a switch. "Send the message," he ordered. "And then halve our speed."

"Aye, sir," his aide said.

James listened to the message carefully, torn between relief and worry. He *was* effectively an ambassador, at least until the Foreign Office sent a genuine diplomatic representative to Pegasus, but he wasn't an experienced diplomat. It was quite possible that he'd accidentally give something away that would cause problems on Earth, even though he had a feeling the Prime Minister could overrule him if necessary. But, for the moment, he had no choice; he had to do what he could.

"General," he said, carefully. "The United Kingdom has no claim on Gandhi or any colony world settled directly by India. Therefore, I have no hesitation in agreeing that those worlds should remain untouched. However, Vesy is another matter. Your agents deliberately triggered off an alien uprising that killed hundreds of civilians and military personnel from a dozen different countries. I believe you will have to withdraw from Vesy, leaving it open for either a multi-national contact service or a policy of no further intervention, but that is a matter for true diplomats. So too is the issue of reparations for the war."

He smiled, thinly. If his calculations were accurate, the Indians had shipped a remarkable amount of industrial material to Pegasus. Colonel Boone had already claimed it as the spoils of war. He had a feeling that the Indians might wind up losing money anyway, if they lost any remaining claim to that material. They certainly wouldn't be allowed to keep it.

"For the moment, I propose you withdraw your fleet to Vesy and await orders from your government," he concluded. "We will continue to hold position here. Once you receive orders, we can decide what to do with Vesy."

He sent the message, then settled back to wait again.

Anjeet considered the second message carefully. He wasn't blind to the implications of a long delay; he'd get orders from Earth, all right, but the

British would have time to hurry a second carrier to Pegasus. If the war restarted, they'd be in a far stronger position...

But they'd be in a strong position regardless, he thought, bitterly. *Who wants to be the last to die in a pointless war?*

"Record," he ordered. "Admiral. For the moment, I accept your terms; my fleet will return to Vesy and hold position there. However, in return, I must insist that you do not reinforce your position in Pegasus. My government will demand it as a precursor to open diplomatic talks. In return, we will agree not to reinforce Vesy."

It was a useless demand, he knew; the British could easily move a second carrier into J-35 and wait to see what happened without compromising their position. But the politicians probably wouldn't realise it, not at first. They'd have an opportunity to save face without actually forcing the British to concede a point or trading something significant in exchange, as long as the British admiral played along. If he didn't...

And we don't have anything we can send to reinforce Vesy, certainly not anything that will tip the balance, he thought. *The British lose nothing and gain much by stalling.*

He shook his head, slowly. "I will agree that the issue of reparations, both for the war itself and the...events on Vesy should be settled through diplomatic discussions," he continued. "I will be happy, too, to allow you to send a message through our communications chain in the hopes of bringing this war to an end without further casualties."

Except me, he reminded himself as he sent the message. *They'll want my scalp.*

"They don't have the right to demand that, sir," Sally protested. "*Really*!"

James smirked. "There's nothing stopping us from building up a superior force in J-35 and holding position, waiting to see what happens," he said, drolly. "We'd pretty much be doing what they did, only in reverse."

He needs to take something from the talks, he thought. Driving one's enemy into a corner wasn't a good idea, unless one was bent on total victory and sure it could be achieved at acceptable cost. *This costs us nothing and gains us much.*

"Record," he ordered. "General. Your terms are acceptable. I will not alter the number of ships in Pegasus on the condition that you do the same in Vesy. The future disposition of Vesy itself will be settled by the diplomats."

And the Vesy themselves won't get a look in, he thought. Centuries ago, European explorers had decided the fate of the Native Americans without bothering to consult them; he couldn't help wondering if humanity had learned nothing in all that time. But then, no one actually *needed* Vesy. The world could be left alone to develop at its own pace. *If we can't help the natives, we can at least make sure that no one exploits them.*

"I will forward an encrypted message to you," he continued, "and arrange for messages from the prisoners of war to be sent to Vesy. We will continue to hold position until the diplomats put an end to the war."

He sighed. "Send."

"Message sent," Sally said.

James nodded. Would the Indian concede defeat and withdraw, now he'd been given a fig leaf to conceal his collapse on genuinely important issues? Or would he decide to throw good money after bad by pressing the offensive?

We're about to find out, he told himself. *Stand ready.*

Anjeet tapped his console. "Captain?"

"Yes, General?"

"You are to reverse course and take us back through the tramline," Anjeet ordered. "There is to be a total blackout on signals leaving the fleet. I don't want *any* messages reaching Earth until I've sent my report."

"Aye, sir," Ajit said.

Pointless, Anjeet thought. Word of the battle, thanks to the reporters, was probably already halfway to Earth. He'd locked them out of the Indian communication chain, but the British would have thrown *theirs* open, just so they could gloat over their victory. *We might have avoided losing the other carrier, yet we still lost the war.*

He thought, briefly, of the pistol in his desk drawer. Maybe, just maybe...

No, he told himself, firmly. Suicide would be the easy way out. *Someone has to explain this back home.*

"They're leaving, sir," Tara reported. "The carrier just jumped out."

John allowed himself a moment of relief. *Warspite* had been sneaking into position to launch an attack before the Indians turned and reversed course, but he'd doubted they'd get close enough to launch missiles, let alone add a second carrier to their kill list. This time, the Indians had been ready.

"It seems a little anticlimactic," Howard observed. "They just turned and left."

"Perhaps we should be grateful," John said. He'd fought in the first war, when the only thing that mattered had been fighting to the bitter end. "We're alive, we survived, the colony is back in our hands and a human carrier - two human carriers - have been saved."

"And we won," Howard agreed. "And we proved the *Warspite* concept beyond all doubt."

John nodded. The analysts would be tearing the data apart, trying to figure out what had happened, but there was no way to avoid the conclusion that the universe had changed once again. If a carrier could be crippled by a cruiser that cost only a tenth of the carrier itself...

But it doesn't matter right now, he told himself, firmly. He had no doubt he'd be spending weeks, perhaps months justifying his actions on Nelson Base. *All that matters is that we won the war.*

CHAPTER THIRTY EIGHT

New Delhi, India

How could it have gone so wrong?

The first message had arrived down the communications chain, a bland report that a carrier had been lost and the British were advancing on Clarke. Two days later, as Prime Minister Mohandas Singh was considering how best to break the news to his government and his people, a second report arrived. Clarke had fallen, the Royal Navy was firmly in control of the Pegasus System and General Patel had backed down when challenged. And then, as Mohandas struggled to come up with a way to present it to his nation, the independent reports had reached Earth.

He glared out of the window, down towards the crowds gathered outside the building. They were angry, angry enough to defy the ban on public protests. Hundreds of thousands of Indian civilians, led by the family and friends of the spacers who'd died in the war, marched up and down, shouting their rage. A line of armed soldiers were standing by the gates, ready to repel a charge, but he'd already heard mutterings from some of his bodyguards that suggested they weren't so enthusiastic about putting their lives at risk for him. He would have withdrawn to the bunker, or a secure military base, if he hadn't had to remain in the city, trying to find the words to keep the country from lynching him. And doing so risked everything.

Goddamn reporters, he thought, angrily. *Is this how they thank me? By spreading enemy propaganda? By lying to my people?*

It was a bitter thought. He'd gone to bat for them, he'd convinced the sceptical military to let dozens of reporters embed themselves with the troops and *this* was his reward? He'd hastily ordered a ban on foreign transmissions, but it was already too late; the global datanet was effectively censorship-proof and anyone with a little ingenuity could pull transmissions and messages from all over the world into India. Word was spreading, no matter what his people did; word of mouth alone was drawing thousands of people to the government's offices, demanding an end to the war. The gods alone knew how many elected officials would be fearing for their prospects of re-election, if the impending riot didn't lead to civil war.

Cowards, Mohandas told himself. *We should have risen up against the British. Perhaps then we would have found our nerve.*

He looked up, sharply, as the door opened. He'd issued strict orders that no one was to enter and placed two armed guards on the far side, just to keep out interruptions. But Chaudhuri Bose was walking into the room, carrying a handful of pieces of paper under one arm. The Foreign Secretary looked grim, but determined. Mohandas rose to his feet, clenching his fists, as the older man sat down without being invited. There was no respect whatsoever in his gaze.

"I told them to keep everyone out," Mohandas snarled. "What are *you* doing here?"

"I've come from parliament," Bose said, shortly. "They held a straw vote of no-confidence, Mohandas. You're no longer considered suitable to lead our nation."

Mohandas had to fight, hard, to keep himself from slamming his fist into the other man's face. It was clear, all too clear, that Bose was enjoying himself. He'd never liked Mohandas and had opposed him, wherever possible. And now his doubts and fears had infected parliament...a straw vote wasn't fatal, it wasn't real, but it was a very good indicator of just how parliament felt about any given issue.

"I have the right to speak in my own defence," he hissed, finally. He also had the right to twist arms to force some of the politicians to change their stance. "The *real* vote may be different."

"You only wound up with ten percent of the vote," Bose said. He held out a sheet of paper for Mohandas to inspect. "As you can see, only a handful of MPs voted to uphold your position."

"Craven cowards," Mohandas sneered. "How many did you stampede into voting me down?"

"None," Bose said. "The loss of an entire carrier - and a number of smaller ships - and thousands of spacers was quite enough to convince them that you had guided India onto a disastrous course. But then, I suppose the economic rumblings didn't help either. Did you know the British had managed to talk the Americans and French into an embargo on buying our goods? Or that they will probably succeed in talking them into barring all future sales to us too?"

"We will survive," Mohandas snapped.

"But not with you," Bose said. He held out another sheet of paper. "Take it."

Mohandas glared at him. "What's this?"

Bose met his eyes. "Your resignation."

"I will *not* sign," Mohandas flared.

"Yes. Yes, you will," Bose said. "You will sign this document, then you will hold a press conference where you will take full responsibility for the war and, as your policy has proved a failure, you will be standing down from office to tend to your family affairs, etc, etc. Parliament will graciously, in response, confirm your immunity from prosecution - an immunity you would not have, Mohandas, if they passed a *real* vote of no-confidence."

Mohandas stared at him. When had Bose grown a backbone? But then, ninety percent of the vote in parliament supported him. Hardly anyone had tried to abstain. That was enough to grant even the most spineless of men the determination to stand up for themselves.

"Your policy has proved a failure," Bose said. "The best we can hope for, right now, is to avoid the economic embargos that will crush our ability to rebuild after the peace treaty is signed. Your resignation will permit us to move on from this sordid affair without further ado."

"And I take the blame for the war," Mohandas said.

"And why not?" Bose asked. "It *was* your idea."

He placed the paper on the desk. "Sign," he said. "You can quietly give up your seat in parliament and retire to the country, where you can write your autobiography and claim you were the victim of circumstances beyond your control. Or you can refuse to sign, lose a vote of no confidence and probably wind up in jail. The choice is yours."

Mohandas gritted his teeth. He could fight, he knew; he wasn't dead yet. But if ninety percent of parliament had said, in a straw vote, that they'd cast their ballot against him...it was unlikely he could win. He'd neglected too many of his political allies; now, he'd have to make promises he couldn't hope to keep if he wanted to woo them back. And Bose had clearly managed to rally the moderates and align them with the opposition...

"I suppose you'll be the next Prime Minister," he snarled, as he picked up the sheet of paper and read it carefully. It didn't commit him to anything beyond resigning his position and returning to the backbenches. "Would you like thirty pieces of silver to celebrate your inauguration?"

Bose ignored the jibe. "I will head up a caretaker government until new elections can be held," he said, calmly. "I do not believe our party has a hope in hell of winning the next elections."

"We will see," Mohandas said. He signed the paper with savage intensity. "Betraying one's party leader won't look very good."

"We will see," Bose echoed. He took the sheet of paper. "Given the... disturbed...situation outside, I would advise you to move your possessions to the guest rooms and take up residence there. We can have you transferred out of the city once the hubbub has died down."

And make sure I have no opportunity to rally resistance, Mohandas thought. Bose hadn't just developed a backbone, he'd developed a brain! Unless, of course, someone was pulling the strings. *They're closing off all my angles of counterattack.*

He pasted a composed expression on his face. "I would like to wish you the very best of luck," he said. Bose wouldn't miss the true message. "And, as always, I will submit myself to the judgement of history."

"I imagine it will judge poorly," Bose said. "Starting a war and winning is one thing; starting a war and losing is quite another."

Mohandas shrugged, rose to his feet and headed for the door. He'd need to speak with his wife, then move her and their belongings into a guestroom. And then...

He shook his head as he stepped through the door. Two officers, both wearing Parliamentary Security uniforms, were waiting for him. They'd make sure he didn't do anything awkward, at least until the dust had settled. How had he managed to misjudge Bose so badly? The man had practically pulled off a legal coup.

But I'm still immune to prosecution, he thought. Bose wouldn't break his word, if only because someone else might do it to him if he set such a precedent. *And I can fight my corner if necessary.*

Joelle was relieved to discover that the Indians had sent a helicopter to collect her from the embassy compound, rather than force her to drive through the crowded streets to the government offices. The roads were crammed with protesters: some cheering the resignation of Mohandas Singh, others demanding political reform, the recall of parliament or a host of more radical notions. Thankfully, she'd managed to get the British civilians in the city out before the news from Pegasus arrived. A Frenchman had apparently been beaten to death only two hours ago, after being mistaken for an Englishman. She would have expected the Indians to know the difference.

They didn't play any games, either, once the helicopter had landed. She was escorted down a long flight of stairs into the Prime Minister's office. Singh was nowhere to be seen, of course; his seat was occupied by Chaudhuri Bose, the Foreign Minister. Joelle shook his hand politely, then sat down facing him. She could wait to hear what he had to say before the negotiations began in earnest.

"Ambassador," Bose said. She'd met him a couple of times, but not enough to form a real impression of the man. MI6 had argued that he was a non-entity, yet she doubted he could have taken power if he'd been truly unimpressive. It was well to be careful. Either he was smarter than he seemed or he was the front man for someone else. "Thank you for coming."

"It is my pleasure," Joelle said. It was, too. The news from Pegasus practically guaranteed the end of the war on British terms. "Congratulations on your accession."

Bose looked embarrassed. "It was not how I wished to attain the office," he said. "Would you care for a drink? Tea? Or something stronger?"

"Tea would be fine," Joelle said.

She waited patiently for a young woman in a green sari to serve the tea, then leaned forward to meet his eyes. "I assume there was a reason you called me," she said. "Please can we get to the meat of the matter?"

"Yes," Bose said. "My government would like to see a formal end to the war as soon as possible. Accordingly, we are prepared to rubber-stamp the agreement between General Patel and Admiral Fitzwilliam."

"My government has its own opinion of the affair," Joelle said. If the Indians thought they were getting away with it that easily...well, they had another think coming. "I have been told to put their terms before you."

Bose looked pained, but unsurprised. "Please outline those terms."

Joelle took a sip of her tea. "First, you will formally acknowledge our possession of both Pegasus and Cromwell," she said. "The industrial and military equipment you moved into the system is to be transferred to us, free of charge. In exchange for this, we will not demand any reparations for the cost of fighting the war."

Bose nodded, slowly.

"Second," Joelle continued, "you will abandon all claim to Vesy. Your installations on the planet's surface will be placed into lockdown, prior to being handed over to either us or a multinational contact team. Furthermore, you will provide us with a complete account of just what happened on the planet between the arrival of your forces and the uprising."

She held up a hand before he could say a word. "Other governments may demand compensation for the deaths of their nationals," she added. "The British Government insists on receiving the same level of compensation, once you come to an agreement with the other claimants."

"We may agree to forget the whole affair," Bose pointed out, smoothly.

"And if you do, more power to you," Joelle said. *Everyone* would be pressing claims, now the Indians had been badly weakened. It would keep them busy for years. "We will not intervene further in the matter.

"Third, you will not be permitted to move warships into Vesy, Cromwell or Pegasus without special permission from the British representatives. Choosing to do so will be considered an act of war and treated accordingly. Furthermore, you will not be permitted to establish naval bases or fortifications in any of the systems adjacent to those three stars."

Bose scowled. Joelle understood his feelings. If Britain had wanted to resume the war at a later date, or if the Indians wound up fighting someone else, India would find itself at a significant disadvantage. And it was insulting. Given the nature of the tramlines, it was generally agreed that warships and courier boats could pass through without hindrance, as long as they stayed well away from settled worlds. Even the Chinese allowed American warships to pass through their tramlines without objection and vice versa. It suggested, very strongly, that India was simply not trusted. But he said nothing.

He should have seen the original draft, Joelle thought. Some hotheads in the Foreign Office had wanted to crush India, even to the point of demanding the right to import goods into India and Indian-settled worlds without tariffs. But that would almost certainly have guaranteed another war in the future. *Parliament may believe we're letting them off lightly.*

"The British Government does not, as I said, intend to claim any further reparations from your country," Joelle said. "However, for our final demand, we want you to acknowledge, formally, that your country made the cold-blooded decision to launch an unprovoked war of conquest against the United Kingdom. We do not intend to charge your leaders - your former leaders - with war crimes, but there is to be no question, now or ever, over just who was responsible for the war."

She cleared her throat. "These terms are not negotiable," she concluded. "You have one week from today to accept them. Once you do, we will begin working out the details of returning the POWs and ending the war. If you choose to reject our terms, we will continue the war until your ability to threaten galactic peace is removed, permanently."

Bose nodded, slowly. "Do you intend to return the POWs without delay?"

"We would need to round up the ships to transport them to Gandhi," Joelle said. "But we do not intend to keep them, unless evidence surfaces that some of the POWs were involved in as-yet undiscovered war crimes."

"No charges have been filed," Bose said, stiffly.

"No war crimes have been reported," Joelle said. Whatever else could be said about the Indian soldiers, they'd comported themselves in a remarkably civilised manner. "However, if that changes, we reserve the right to punish those responsible."

She removed a datachip from her pocket and placed it on the desk. "You have our terms, Prime Minister," she added, as she rose to her feet. "Please inform us within the week if you intend to accept them or not."

"I will consult with Parliament," Bose said. "And then I will call you personally."

Somewhat to Joelle's surprise, it was only three hours before Bose called her.

"My government has decided to accept your terms," he said. "I am currently preparing orders for General Patel to withdraw the remainder of his ships to Gandhi, then supply you with transports to collect the former POWs. I trust this is acceptable?"

"It will be, as soon as you sign the peace treaty," Joelle said. She'd expected a long argument - or even a decision to continue the war. An entire nation's pride was at stake. "And I thank you, Prime Minister."

Bose nodded. "You'll have the signed treaty tomorrow," he said. "We'll discuss the transport issue afterwards."

His face vanished from the display. Joelle let out a sigh of relief, then keyed her console and tapped in a brief message for the Prime Minister. He'd be relieved too, she knew; he'd had to argue savagely to get the Indians light terms, despite the risk of continuing the war. Now, there would be MPs arguing that they really should have put the boot in as hard as possible, kicking the Indians while they were down. It wouldn't be a pleasant session in Parliament...

She was still working on her message when her aide knocked on her door. "Yes, Frieda?"

The young woman looked worried. "Ambassador, we picked up a message on a secure government channel," she said. "Prime Minister Singh - the *former* Prime Minister - has just committed suicide."

Joelle felt her eyes narrow. "Did he actually commit suicide or did he accidentally brutally cut his own head off while shaving?"

"I don't know, as yet," the aide said. "There aren't many details. But the Indians are advising their security forces to brace for riots."

"I see," Joelle said. She sighed, heavily. No one would actually *miss* Singh, but the Indians might have needed a scapegoat for the whole affair. "Order Captain Nolen to put the security guards on alert, just in case."

"Yes, Ambassador," Frieda said.

"And see what else you can pick up," Joelle added. A real suicide? Or had someone killed him to avoid having to put the former Prime Minister on trial? "If there are more details, let me know."

CHAPTER THIRTY NINE

Nelson Base, Earth Orbit

"So Singh is dead," James mused. "Was it really suicide?"

"MI6 isn't sure," Uncle Winchester said. "Apparently, Singh put a gun to his head and pulled the trigger. If he actually was murdered...well, the Indians aren't talking. But it looks as though no one is mourning his death. Bose managed to shift all the blame onto Singh once he was no longer around to defend himself."

"Whatever floats their boat," James said. "I suppose he didn't manage to shoot himself in the back a dozen times?"

"There's no way to know," Uncle Winchester said. "From what we've been told, the body was identified, then cremated and the ashes handed over to his family. The evidence, if there was any evidence there to find, is gone."

"I see," James said.

He couldn't really blame the Indians, he knew. The British task force had taken heavy losses, but it had emerged victorious; the Indians, unfortunately for them, didn't have that consolation. Putting all the blame on Singh was one way to absolve their caretaker government of any responsibility for the debacle. Four weeks after the formal end of the war, India was still in turmoil. It was unlikely the caretaker government would win the next election.

"We won't be following up, in any case," Uncle Winchester added. "The death of Prime Minister Singh allows us to bring this affair to an end without further delay."

James nodded. The Indians had signed the treaty, then supplied ships to transport the POWs from Clarke III to Gandhi, where they were swapped for Governor Brown and the other long-term British POWs. He'd heard the Indian POWs weren't going any further - their government didn't want to add to the unrest by letting them return home to tell their stories - but that wasn't Britain's concern. As long as the war didn't restart, whatever happened in India was India's problem.

"We won," he said. "I trust that the government was pleased?"

Uncle Winchester beamed. "I dare say we should have no trouble getting the next budget through the house," he said. "It's a shame we can't extort more from the Indians, but it probably doesn't matter. Replacing the lost ships and building the next generation of warships should be funded without too much quibbling in Parliament."

"Polling figures looking good, then," James teased. "And to think that some people doubted our victory."

"It could have gone the other way, if things had been different," Uncle Winchester reminded him. "You'll be confronting the Next Generation Warships Oversight Board on Tuesday, James. Given what happened to the Indian carrier..."

"We need to move ahead with other projects," James finished. He glanced at his watch. "I do have an appointment, Uncle..."

"More important than the Minister of Defence?" Uncle Winchester asked, dryly. He held up a hand before James could say anything. "Percy and Penny, I assume?"

"Remind me to have whoever gave you access to my appointment book shot," James said, crossly. "But yeah, I do need to speak with them before Penny goes off on her book tour and Percy boards ship for Vesy."

"And takes his new girlfriend with him," Uncle Winchester said. "Given her service, James, I dare say we can officially forgive her earlier conduct. Still...perhaps it's for the best she's going to Vesy."

He rose. "I'll be in touch before the board meeting," he warned. "It's important we present a united front."

"I know, Uncle," James said.

"And I shall expect to hear about your engagement soon," Uncle Winchester added. "You are running out of excuses, young man."

James rolled his eyes as Uncle Winchester stepped through the hatch, then glanced at his appointments log. Percy and Penny were due in twenty minutes, just long enough for him to snatch a cup of tea and read the latest set of reports from Earth. And then...

He shook his head. If the topic for the coming discussion was what he expected, it wasn't going to be a pleasant conversation.

Percy - his new rank insignia glittering on his sleeve - couldn't help feeling nervous as the aide showed Penny and him into Admiral Fitzwilliam's office. The man was his commanding officer as well as his semi-adopted father; it was never easy for him to know how to treat the older man. Indeed, he was mildly surprised he'd been allowed to serve under Admiral Fitzwilliam, although there had been quite some distance between them. It wasn't as if the Admiral had been issuing orders to him directly.

"Percy, Penny, please take a seat," Admiral Fitzwilliam said. He'd organised a small table, three comfortable chairs and a pot of tea at one end of the palatial office. "For the moment, I think we can do without rank altogether."

"Thank you, sir," Percy said. Old habits were hard to put aside, particularly ones that had been drummed into his head by a succession of training sergeants. "Thank you for seeing us."

"And congratulations on your promotion," Admiral Fitzwilliam said. "*Captain* at such a young age. I believe General Boone is looking forward to having you under his command on Vesy."

Percy nodded. He'd been promoted, then offered a choice between being sent back to Portsmouth for further training or assignment to Vesy. Given that Lillian was *also* going to Vesy as part of the uplift team, it hadn't been a difficult choice. He had no idea where they were going, but he wanted to find out. Besides, he *was* one of the few officers who had experience on Vesy.

And I can try out for Selection in a couple of years, if things don't work out, he told himself. *Drake's already written me a recommendation.*

He pushed the thought aside. "It should be an interesting deployment, sir," he said. "At least things should be more organised now."

"I would hope so," Admiral Fitzwilliam said. "And Penny! Congratulations on the book deal."

"Thank you," Penny said, flushing slightly. "All I have to do now is write it."

"You've already written a handful of articles that were very well received," Admiral Fitzwilliam pointed out. "Couldn't you just string them together into a book?"

"It's a little more complex than that, sir," Penny said. "I need to provide a great deal more context for my history of the war."

"Just make sure you present your brother as a hero," Admiral Fitzwilliam said. He poured tea for the three of them. "Now, as much as I enjoy spending time with you, I do have quite a few other matters demanding my attention. Might I ask why you requested this meeting?"

Percy swallowed, reminded himself he was a Royal Marine and took the plunge. "We wanted to ask you what happened to our father."

The Admiral's face went very still. "He died on the Old Lady's final deployment," he said, carefully. "His death was not wasted..."

"There are too many things that don't add up," Penny said. Percy would never have dared to interrupt. "Everyone else who died on *Ark Royal* has a note in the naval records stating where and when they died, but our father's file is completely sealed. I've even been...discouraged from asking more questions."

"With reason," Admiral Fitzwilliam said. He studied Percy for a long moment before moving his gaze to Penny. "Do you know how our government classifies information?"

Penny blinked in surprise. "I know the basics, sir."

"Information is classified on a scale from *official* to *top secret*," Admiral Fitzwilliam said, coolly. "There are, of course, sliding scales of classification within each level; Percy, as a marine officer, may have access to some materials classified as *secret* without having guaranteed unquestioned access to everything at the same level. Even *I* could not hope to lay my hands on *top secret* material outside my bailiwick without answering some pretty hard questions."

He paused. "There is another level of security classification," he added. "*Most secret*. It is rarely used, Penny; as far as most people are aware, *most secret* went out of fashion after the Second World War. *Most secret* refers to material that could spark off a war or bring down a foreign government."

Percy frowned. "A *foreign* government?"

"Losing a British Government would be awkward," Admiral Fitzwilliam said. "It would be very embarrassing if the government released papers that forced it to resign. But if we were implicated, accidentally or otherwise, in bringing down a foreign government, it would have unpleasant consequences. What happened to your father is considered *most* secret. To the best of my knowledge, only five or six people know the truth. If it had entered wider circulation...well, we might see a war."

"Another war," Penny said, quietly.

"Yes," Admiral Fitzwilliam agreed.

Percy took a breath. "We can keep secrets."

"I don't doubt it," Admiral Fitzwilliam said. He met Percy's eyes. "I can tell you, if you wish, because I believe the evidence is sufficiently buried or destroyed to make it impossible" - his gaze slipped to Penny - "for even the most intrepid girl reporter to prove what actually happened. Should you decide to go public, you will sound like a pair of cranks. I don't think I need to tell you what that will do to your careers."

"No, sir," Percy said.

"But you won't be able to forget it, either," Admiral Fitzwilliam added. "Knowing something classified as *most secret* is one thing, but there are... personal matters involved and you may not look at your father in the same light ever again. Now...you may feel you're better off not knowing."

He rose. "I have to write a pair of messages," he said. "You have that long to decide if you really want to know."

Percy watched him walk over to the desk, then looked at Penny and raised his eyebrows. She nodded, unhesitatingly. She'd always been braver than him about confronting unpleasant facts, even if they cost her. She wouldn't be pleased, he knew, not to be able to share what she knew, but she did understand the value of keeping secrets. And besides, if the

Admiral was right - if the secret really *could* spark off a war - they'd have to keep it to themselves.

Admiral Fitzwilliam returned and sat down. "Well?"

"We want to know, sir," Percy said.

"We do," Penny echoed.

Admiral Fitzwilliam took a long breath. "Your father, as you know, was recalled to the colours when the First Interstellar War broke out," he said. "He was assigned to *Ark Royal* as CAG - Commander Air Group - but, as we were short of actual fliers, he was also expected to fly a starfighter while commanding the squadrons. It was not an ideal arrangement.

"He...eventually started an affair with one of his pilots, Wing Commander Rose Labara, even though it was in direct defiance of regulations. In their defence, they had good reason to believe they would never return to Earth. If they'd broken it off then, they might well have gotten away with it. However, they saw fit to continue the affair even after they were both assigned to the Academy. They were still lovers during Operation Nelson."

Percy stared. "My father was having an affair?"

"I met Rose," Penny said, quietly. "She was very close to our father."

"Eventually, they were discovered - but not by us," Admiral Fitzwilliam said. "A secret agent working for a foreign power obtained evidence of their affair and used it to blackmail them. They went to Admiral Smith, their ultimate superior, and confessed. This eventually led to a tussle with foreign intelligence officers on *Ark Royal*. Your father gave his life to stop them. Rose Labara died during the final battle. I...honoured a promise and adopted the pair of you."

"The Russians," Penny said, softly. "It was them, wasn't it?"

Percy gave her an odd look. "Why...?"

"The Russians are pariahs," Penny said. "Why? Simply blackmailing a pair of starfighter pilots isn't enough to get themselves permanently blacklisted."

"You would have made a good intelligence officer," Admiral Fitzwilliam said. "The Russians unilaterally intended to deploy a biological weapon against the Tadpoles. It would, at best, have caused huge casualties, but spurred them to launch a final attack against us. And, given how badly the various human militaries had been weakened by the war, we would almost certainly have been exterminated. Your father gave his life to stop it."

"Shit," Percy said.

He wasn't sure how to handle it. His father had had an affair...it wasn't something he really wanted to consider. Why had he cheated on their mother? Percy had overheard some of their arguments when his father had been home on leave, but surely they didn't justify cheating...

Sometimes a relationship just breaks down, he thought, recalling something he'd been taught in school. Humans were living longer and it was proving harder to keep a monogamous relationship going, when one could expect to spend over a hundred years with a single partner. *And sometimes two people discover they're no longer compatible.*

"I don't know what happened between your mother and father," Admiral Fitzwilliam said, as if he'd read Percy's mind. "What I do know, however, is that your father died a hero."

Penny winced. "The Tadpoles don't know how close they came, do they?"

"No," Admiral Fitzwilliam said. "The evidence was destroyed by your father. After that...the Russians have an interest in keeping the matter secret too. They concealed everything themselves. If it got out..."

Percy could imagine. Biological weapons were the one great taboo. Riots in the streets, demands for war against Russia, a renewed war with the Tadpoles...it would not be good.

"There are people who will say I shouldn't have told you," Admiral Fitzwilliam said. "I wouldn't have told you, if the evidence hadn't already been buried. There are thousands upon thousands of crackpot theories on the datanet, some more accurate than others. If you go public with this, if you choose to ignore my warnings, it is highly unlikely you will be believed."

"We won't," Penny said. "It needs to remain buried."

"They'll kick you out of the reporter's club if they ever found out you sat on it," Percy said, amused. "But they probably wouldn't believe it, if you told them."

"One would hope not," Admiral Fitzwilliam agreed. "Officially, the Russians are having considerable economic trouble after the war. There's no *formal* agreement to penalise the Russians, just...an unofficial understanding that we won't lift a finger to help them out of their current mess."

"Which might have pushed them into India's arms," Penny observed.

"Probably," Admiral Fitzwilliam said. "That policy may have to be revised."

He looked at Percy. "For what it's worth," he said, "I don't think your father could be prouder of you two than I am. And, whatever his flaws, he died a hero. That's something to remember."

———

Penny had suspected that both her parents had been having affairs, if not before the war than certainly afterwards. She'd definitely known that her father and Rose were close, far too close, during the brief meeting she'd had with the older woman. But to have it confirmed so bluntly - and then to be told just what had killed their father - was shocking. She knew she would need time to process it all...

"Is there any way," she asked, "that some of these details can be made public?"

"Maybe in a few hundred years, when the world is very different," Admiral Fitzwilliam said, calmly. "But for the moment...the truth will remain buried in the files. Better to conceal a secret than risk a renewed war."

"Dad's a listed hero," Percy said. "That's all we can ask for, isn't it?"

"Yes," Admiral Fitzwilliam said. "And, like I said, I believe he would be proud of you."

He glanced at his watch. "I will probably not have a chance to see you again, Percy, before you take ship for Vesy," he added. "So please let me wish you the very best of luck, both with your new role and your girlfriend."

Penny smiled, weakly. She rather liked Lillian; indeed, she'd interviewed the young crewwoman during the flight back to Earth, if only to ensure that Lillian's heroism wasn't overshadowed by the mistakes of the past. It hadn't been necessary, she'd discovered when they'd returned to Earth. Lillian's case had been reviewed by a naval board, the charges against her had been dropped and she'd been given a medal for her services during the war.

"And I hope to read the advance copy of your book soon," Admiral Fitzwilliam added, looking at Penny. "I'm sure it will make fascinating reading."

"It will," Penny promised. She rose and curtseyed. "Thank you for your time, Admiral."

Percy saluted, then followed Penny out of the compartment. They didn't say a word until they were in one of the mess rooms and seated in a corner.

"Shit," Percy said. "I..."

"It's probably better not to think about it," Penny advised. They'd wanted to know, hadn't they? That might have been a mistake. "Just... enjoy the rest of your life."

"I'll try," Percy said. "And you?"

Penny smiled, impishly. "I have a date with Hamish tomorrow," she said. "He's taking me to see the sights in London."

"Oh," Percy said. He sighed, dramatically. "Just be careful, all right?"

"I wasn't planning on taking him to bed," Penny said, just to watch him splutter. "I want to take it slowly."

"Maybe I should come too," Percy said. He ducked as she picked up her mug and pretended to throw it at him. "I kid, I kid!"

"I'll be careful," Penny said. "And you never know. You might see me on Vesy."

"I might," Percy agreed. "But I have a feeling that contact is going to be limited. It's going to be hard enough for them to learn how to use technology - and the scientific mindset - without reporters bumbling around."

Penny smiled and stuck out her tongue.

CHAPTER FORTY

Nelson Base, Earth Orbit

"I'm afraid we won't be giving you *all* of the prize money for the carrier," the First Space Lord said, once John had been shown into the compartment. "The politicians have insisted that *some* of the prize fund be diverted to pay for repairs to the colony."

John nodded, unsurprised. An Indian salvage team had inspected the damaged carrier carefully, after the treaty had been signed, but concluded that attempting to repair the damage was probably futile. They'd eventually abandoned the hulk, allowing John and his crew to try to claim the prize money. A month of haggling later had eventually led to a settlement, once the Indians had insisted - as part of the agreement - that the carrier never be returned to Earth.

"But you'll have around half the value of the hulk to share out," Admiral Fitzwilliam added, from where he was sitting beside Admiral Soskice. "I don't think that's anything to sniff at."

"No, sir," John said. "The greenest midshipman would still be looking at somewhere around fifty thousand pounds, probably more."

The First Space Lord cleared his throat. "There are certain issues that need to be discussed," he said. "One of them is the future fleet mix. Do you feel that the day of the carrier is over?"

John took a moment to gather his thoughts. "I feel that the universe has changed," he said, finally. "On one hand, we fired on the Indian ship from practically point-blank range; I don't think they - or anyone else - would let us get close enough to do it again. There were too many observers in the system for us to cover up what happened. But, on the other hand, the technicians are already talking about extending the plasma cannon's range."

He took a breath. "More to the point, the improvements in point defence threaten to make it a great deal harder to get either starfighters or missiles into engagement range," he added. "We did deploy improved ECM - and the Indians deployed long-range missiles - but in both cases equally improved point defence proved up to the challenge. The Indians only landed a major hit on *Theodore Smith* because the boarding pods were considered secondary targets, compared to a swarm of incoming missiles.

"On the other hand, we may be able to improve our starfighters and their onboard missiles..."

The First Space Lord held up a hand. "Can you give me a direct answer?"

"No, sir," John said, honestly. "We killed a carrier under ideal conditions. Had we been detected a great deal sooner, the results would have been very different. However, I think the current thread of development is going to push carriers to one side."

"And replace them with gunnery cruisers," Admiral Soskice said. "The war proved that our old fleet mix is on the verge of becoming obsolete."

Admiral Fitzwilliam frowned. "There are some points that definitely need improving," he said. "Our starfighter mix will need to be upgraded; there will still be a use for starfighters, I believe, but their role may be very different."

John looked from one to the other. "It would be unsafe to rely on *one* theory of warfare, sir," he warned. "We may make a new breakthrough tomorrow.

"That is indeed the problem," the First Space Lord said. "Do we push resources into building new carriers or start exploring new ways to make war?"

"With all due respect, sir," Admiral Soskice said. "One new way to make war has proven itself very effective. Trading *Warspite* for an Indian carrier that cost ten times as much wouldn't have been a poor bargain."

"At the same time," Admiral Fitzwilliam commented, "*Warspite* could easily have been blown apart if they'd seen her too early."

He sighed. "However, it does look as though we will need to move towards a combination of heavy armour and energy weapons," he added. "The Indians *did* manage to kill a number of our smaller lightly armoured ships. If nothing else, they will all have to be refitted with the latest composite armour."

John suspected he was right. He'd served in both starfighters and capital ships and he understood the strengths and weaknesses of both. Advances in point defence would seriously limit the role of starfighters in war, perhaps even restrict them to nothing more than scouting duties. But everyone who was emotionally invested in fleet carriers and starfighters would resist such a conclusion. They wouldn't want to believe it.

The First Space Lord leaned forward. "You're talking about the *Vanguard* project."

"Yes, sir," Admiral Fitzwilliam said.

Admiral Soskice looked, briefly, like the cat that had eaten the canary. "Are you saying you now want to proceed with it?"

"I may have been wrong," Admiral Fitzwilliam admitted. "Unless we make a whole series of new breakthroughs, Admiral, the starfighter is eventually doomed. However, as *Warspite* demonstrated, getting close enough to *use* the heavy plasma cannon isn't actually easy. If we mount the cannon - or several cannons - on a much larger ship, we'd improve survivability."

"And a *Vanguard* would be far tougher than any carrier," Admiral Soskice noted. "The absence of any starfighter launch tubes would cut down on the number of vulnerable points on the hull."

John hesitated, then asked. "A *Vanguard*?"

The First Space Lord tapped a control, activating a holographic display. A giant starship, every bit as large as a fleet carrier, appeared over his desk. John drank in the details greedily, even though it looked too sleek to be anything other than an artist's impression. She was as blocky as *Ark Royal*, studded with missile tubes, point defence weapons and sensor blisters...and, on her prow, were two plasma cannons. They looked larger than the weapon built into *Warspite*.

"HMS *Vanguard*, as the designers see her," the First Space Lord said. "Our first true battleship since the days we were messing about in boats."

He nodded to Admiral Soskice, who leaned forward eagerly. "She is heavily armoured, capable of shrugging off a bomb-pumped laser or a direct hit with a nuclear warhead," he stated. "Her weapons are actually placed in an outer shell that makes it harder for the enemy to inflict damage on the interior of the vessel, although we have wrapped plates of solid armour through the interior as well, just in case. The drives - the latest designs - are capable of generating a realspace velocity to match *Warspite*, at least over long distances."

John nodded. Unless someone had made a *real* breakthrough, it was unlikely a battleship or fleet carrier could hope to match a cruiser's acceleration curve.

"She does not, of course, carry starfighters," Admiral Soskice continued. "Her point defence, however, is an order of magnitude more effective than anything currently in existence."

"In theory," Admiral Fitzwilliam commented.

"In theory," Admiral Soskice agreed. "She is also heavily automated; we believe she can be operated safely with a crew of one hundred, although our current estimates suggest that we should aim for a crewing figure of two thousand. There is, of course, no need to include a cadre of starfighter pilots and support staff. She will carry up to a full regiment of marines, along with a number of assault shuttles; they will be geared for everything from covert insertion to boarding missions."

"In short, she's our answer to the Tadpole Dreadnaught," Admiral Fitzwilliam said. He looked at John. "What do you make of her?"

"She looks remarkable, in theory," John said. "However, I would be concerned about the lack of starfighter cover."

"There's no reason she couldn't be escorted by a carrier," Admiral Soskice pointed out.

"But that would defeat the purpose of building *Vanguard*," John argued. "If she needs a carrier, we might as well *build* a carrier instead of her."

"The blunt truth is that our fleet carriers - starting with *Ark Royal* - were expected to either serve as crosses between battleships and carriers or merely platforms for long-range starfighter strikes," Admiral Fitzwilliam said. "In those terms, *Theodore Smith* is a throwback; we may need to advance towards a concept of battleships and carriers rather than vessels that do neither task particularly well."

John nodded. *Theodore Smith* had been heavily armoured and she'd still been badly damaged in the war. The Indian carrier had been crippled so badly the ship had been abandoned. Having more layers of armour around him seemed a good thing.

"We will not, of course, put all our eggs in one basket," the First Space Lord said. "Parliament has voted to support the current military budget, which includes funds for four more fleet carriers as well as seventy smaller ships and a handful of classified research programs. However, we will need to start work on *Vanguard* soon if we intend to have her ready to join the navy."

John considered it. "We'd be looking at around five years of construction time," he said. It might well be optimistic. First-time construction projects always overran. "Might I ask why you wanted me to see this?"

"We'd like you to head the project," the First Space Lord said.

He held up a hand before John could say a word. "You have a considerable level of experience in active service," he said. "No one would question your military record. Your experience is also varied; you've served as a starfighter pilot, tactical officer, executive officer and finally a captain. And you've commanded *Warspite*, which was conceived as the precursor to *Vanguard*."

"Or, in other words, you actually have a good grasp of military realities," Admiral Fitzwilliam added. "You wouldn't waste time trying to produce something impractical."

"You'd be an acting Commodore for the duration of your work," the First Space Lord said. "If you want a ship, once the *Vanguard* Project is completed or passed to other hands, you would be added to the top of the Naval Register."

And guaranteed a command, John finished, silently.

He wasn't blind to the true reason for the discussion, although he had to admit - as much as he hated the thought - he did have the experience to make *Vanguard* work. His service during the war should guarantee him promotion, but his unusual career path would make it harder for him to be promoted into flag rank. And he lacked the ability to kiss enough asses to make up for such a deficiency. Spending several years riding herd on designers and construction workers who had never seen the elephant was a small price to pay for a future command.

And it would be a challenge. He'd always liked a challenge.

"It would be my honour," he said, finally. "I will need some time to settle my affairs on *Warspite*, however."

"You are entitled to a month of leave in any case," the First Space Lord said. "As your ship requires some intensive repairs, we believe it would be best to reassign most of your crew to other ships. *Warspite* will receive a new crew once she leaves the shipyards. I suggest you see her into the yard, then take your leave. Everything should be arranged for you to take command of the project once you return."

"Understood, sir," John said, reluctantly.

"You have good reason to be proud of her," the First Space Lord added. "If her name wasn't already on the naval rolls, John, she would have been added after the war."

John nodded, proudly. A ship that performed with honour would be guaranteed a namesake for almost as long as the Royal Navy existed. *Warspite* had had predecessors, of course, but she deserved no less. Her successor would carry her name with pride.

"And you too will go down in history," the First Space Lord added. "The one-shot killer of a carrier."

"It might have been a mistake to give that interview," John conceded, reluctantly.

"I doubt it," the First Space Lord said. "My office will get in touch, Captain. And, once again, congratulations."

John rose, saluted and left the compartment.

"You haven't given him an easy job, sir," James observed.

"No," the First Space Lord agreed. "He's caught between you and Yeager. On the other hand, he *does* have the experience to tell you both to go pound sand if necessary."

James smiled. *He'd* never dared tell a superior officer to go pound sand and *he* had powerful connections to protect him. But he understood the unspoken warning. There was no longer any time for theoretical debates. The Royal Navy needed to get *Vanguard* into service as soon as possible, before the next war...

...Because, if there was one thing James had learned during his years in the navy, it was that trouble could blow up at terrifying speed.

And we have to be ready, he told himself. There were at least two other known intelligent races out there - and one of them had pushed humanity to the wall. It was almost certain there would be others - and some of them might be even less friendly than the Tadpoles - or simply so alien that communication was impossible. *Who knows what's waiting at the end of the next tramline?*

The End

The *Ark Royal* Universe Will Return In *Vanguard*
Coming Soon!

AFTERWORD

Let me run a scenario past you.

Harry - nine years old - earns money by doing chores for various people in the neighbourhood. Each Sunday, he gets around £50. He puts most of that money in the bank, but keeps a small amount to buy sweets and crisps for the next week at school. That Monday, he buys a packet of crisps and takes them to school...where they are snatched by ten year old Dudley.

"Let's compromise," smirks Dudley. "I'll have *half* your crisps."

If that isn't outrageous enough, consider this small change.

A teacher hurries over to where the two boys are glaring at each other. "Compromise," she says. She has neither the time nor the inclination to establish what's actually happening beyond the basics. "Share the crisps out fairly. Half each."

There's nothing *fair* about either scenario, is there? Harry earned his money, Harry earned the right to buy his crisps...why exactly is Dudley entitled to *half* of them? Anyone with half a brain would argue, of course, that Dudley isn't entitled to *any* of the crisps. There is literally no room for compromise because there are no *grounds* for compromise. One might as well assert that a successful burglar is allowed to keep half of what he hauls off from the house he robs.

It is, of course, obvious what's really happening. In the first example, Dudley is relishing in the belief that his superior might makes right. His offer to return half the crisps is a declaration that he, not Harry, has the right to determine what happens to them. But in the second example, the voice of authority - a timid authority, unwilling to uphold the rule of law - supports him. The idea that Dudley is in the wrong - that there is no way to escape the simple fact that Dudley is in the wrong - is not something she can express. Either she believes that children should share or she's unwilling to confront Dudley directly. And it pretty much sucks to be Harry.

That is a playground example. However, such events happen far too often in the sphere of international politics. An aggressive group - or nation - believes it can pick on a weaker nation. When it does, the target is faced with the task of either accepting the bullying or doing something about it.

The Falklands War is one such event. Despite the islands being a British possession since 1840 (Britain's interest in the islands began much earlier, but they became a Crown Colony in 1840), despite the clearly expressed wish of the islanders to remain Britain, Argentina launched an invasion of the islands in 1982. (To be fair to the Argentineans, the British Foreign Office had been sending very mixed messages on the subject for years.) There was very little room for compromise; the only possible outcomes were Britain recovering the islands or the Argentineans getting to keep them. It took a small war for Britain to dislodge the enemy from their ill-gotten gains.

In hindsight, it was a very close run thing. If Britain had lost a carrier (or Argentina had waited for six months, whereupon one of the UK's carriers would have been sold), continuing the war would have been impossible. Or, if Argentina had planned better, the counter-offensive might never have got further than a bloody failure on the beaches. Or, if Argentina had done a better job of rallying Third World support and successfully muddied the issue, it might have become politically difficult for the UK to continue the war. And, for that matter, if the UK Government had been a little less resolute, it might have been impossible to win.

But the war had to be fought. There was never any real room for compromise, not when the question was who ended up with the islands. Either Britain kept them or Argentina took them. Once the ships were on their way, there was no middle ground...

...And, even if Argentina had tried to push for joint control (also against the wishes of the islanders themselves) it wouldn't have made them any better, morally speaking, than Dudley offering to *let* Harry keep half his crisps.

I'm not entirely sure, to be honest, that the UK Government - even Thatcher - truly understood the problem. Politicians are always looking for common ground and compromise. The long debate over using British submarines to sink enemy capital ships - and then the attempt to lie over just what *General Belgrano* was doing before she was sunk - suggests, very strongly, that they didn't. There was no hope of a peaceful solution because there was no hope either finding a workable compromise or convincing the Junta, which had staked its power on the war, to withdraw without a fight. Their hesitation over taking the offensive - by trying to sink the enemy aircraft carrier as well as *General Belgrano* - does not speak well of them.

I've heard it argued that the decision to *not* sink the ships - at least at first - was taken in hopes of making it easier for the Junta to back down (by not giving them a bloody flag to wave.) Such an argument is simply unworkable; the enemy Junta *could not* back down without risking their power and position. On the other hand, the loss of several capital ships might have convinced the Junta that it was time to fold *before* British troops made their way to Port Stanley. At the very least, it would have both removed a major threat and served as a demonstration of Britain's power, resolution and reach.

We - Britain - won the Falklands War. Or, rather, I should say we won the *first* Falklands War. Like all limited and localised wars (the Gulf War of 1991 being another example) the Falklands War failed to secure a decisive result. Argentina continues to maintain her claim to the Falklands, she continues to harass the islanders and it is not unlikely that, one day, her government will make another try at seizing the islands by force. The next time, we may face an enemy who has learned from the past.

As far as the Falklands are concerned, Argentina is the local bully. And the only way to stop a bully is to make it damn clear that bullying will only result in punishment.

The ongoing Falklands Dispute - and countless other political struggles around the world - only underline another problem that had surfaced over the past thirty years. Conflicts - ranging from localised disputes to all-out war - have drawn in other powers, not as actual fighters, but as 'observers,' 'peace monitors,' and 'honest brokers.' Such missions may be well-intentioned (that is hotly debated) yet they tend to share certain characteristics. Chief amongst them is a touching (and completely misplaced) faith in compromise, that - with enough help from the outsiders - the locals can find a way to get along.

This isn't too surprising, really. Distance lends rather more than *just* enchantment; distance lends *detachment* and *ignorance*. The outsiders - like the school teacher I mentioned above - may outline a high-minded concept of 'fairness' that has nothing to do with *real* fairness. They are rarely capable of grasping the subtleties of any given conflict zone; instead, they tend to buy into a simplified narrative that rarely bears any resemblance to reality. It is for this reason that many states involved in wars positively *hate* outsiders who expect to be humoured, but rarely understand what is going on. In conflicts as wide-ranging as the ongoing Israel-Palestinian conflict and the Sri Lankan Civil War, outsiders have often prolonged the conflict rather than bringing it to an end.

The former, sadly, is practically the poster child. One solution put forward by outsiders is the 'two-state' solution, a division of land into Israel and Palestine. It sounds reasonable, on the surface, but it faces a number of serious problems. For Israel, the solution would require the removal of a number of settlements within Palestinian territories (which would cause major political problems for any Israeli Government that dared to accept the solution) while giving their enemies time to regroup and prepare for a resumption of the war. For Palestine, the solution would probably lead to civil war, the growth of a theocratic state and an eventual resumption of the war.

I would not trust an outside nation to pass judgement on British affairs. How could they truly understand the realities on the ground? But even if I did, there is no outside power with both the ability and the will to impose a solution. In the end, outside meddling tends to merely prolong conflict - and, with it, unimaginable levels of human suffering.

But that's enough of complex international politics and skulduggery.

The first three books in this series were intended to follow the titular starship, *Ark Royal*, performing the first task of the Royal Navy; defending Britain and carrying the war into enemy territory. By contrast, the *Warspite* series was supposed to follow the tasks performed by the Royal Navy in peacetime; surveying new star systems for settlement, providing disaster relief services, chasing down pirates, evacuating British citizens from danger zones and fighting a limited war to uphold British interests. The setting may be science-fictional, but the present-day Royal Navy does all of those and more.

I hope to write a *third* trilogy set within the same universe, following the adventures of HMS *Vanguard* when the Second Interstellar War breaks out, and a stand-alone book covering the Battle of Earth. My current plan is to write either *Vanguard I* or *The Longest Day* in early December, although we will see.

If you enjoyed this book, please feel free to leave a review on Amazon, post on my Facebook page or join the conversations on my discussion forum. (Links on my site: www.chrishanger.net) All comments, reviews, suggestions, spelling mistakes and suchlike are gratefully received.

Thank you.

Christopher G. Nuttall
Edinburgh, United Kingdom, 2015

APPENDIX
GLOSSARY OF UK TERMS AND SLANG

[Author's Note: I've tried to define every incident of specifically UK slang in this glossary, but I can't promise to have spotted everything. If you spot something I've missed, please let me know and it will be included.]

Beasting/Beasted - military slang for anything from a chewing out by one's commander to outright corporal punishment or hazing. The latter two are now officially banned.

Binned - SAS slang for a prospective recruit being kicked from the course, then returned to unit (RTU).

Bootnecks - slang for Royal Marines. Loosely comparable to 'Jarhead.'

Donkey Wallopers - slang for the Royal Horse Artillery.

Fortnight - two weeks. (Hence the terrible pun, courtesy of the *Goon Show*, that Fort Knight cannot possibly last three weeks.)

'Get stuck into' - 'start fighting.'

'I should coco' - 'you're damned right.'

Levies - native troops. The Ghurkhas are the last remnants of native troops from British India.

Lorries - trucks.

MOD - Ministry of Defence. (The UK's Pentagon.)

Panda Cola - Coke as supplied by the British Army to the troops.

RFA - Royal Fleet Auxiliary

Rumbled - discovered/spotted.

SAS - Special Air Service.

SBS - Special Boat Service

Squaddies - slang for British soldiers.

Stag - guard duty.

TAB (tab/tabbing) - Tactical Advance to Battle.

Walt - Poser, i.e. someone who claims to have served in the military and/or a very famous regiment. There's a joke about 22 SAS being the largest regiment in the British Army - it must be, because of all the people who claim to have served in it.

Wanker - Masturbator (jerk-off). Commonly used as an insult.

Wanking - Masturbating.

Yank/Yankee - Americans

Printed in Great Britain
by Amazon

59160160R00220